The Man on the Train

The Man on the Train

Wanda Rhodes

iUniverse, Inc.
Bloomington

THE MAN ON THE TRAIN

Copyright © 2013 by Wanda Rhodes.

All rights reserved. No part of this book may be used or reproduced by any means, graphic, electronic, or mechanical, including photocopying, recording, taping or by any information storage retrieval system without the written permission of the publisher except in the case of brief quotations embodied in critical articles and reviews.

This is a work of fiction. All of the characters, names, incidents, organizations, and dialogue in this novel are either the products of the author's imagination or are used fictitiously.

iUniverse books may be ordered through booksellers or by contacting:

iUniverse
1663 Liberty Drive
Bloomington, IN 47403
www.iuniverse.com
1-800-Authors (1-800-288-4677)

Because of the dynamic nature of the Internet, any web addresses or links contained in this book may have changed since publication and may no longer be valid. The views expressed in this work are solely those of the author and do not necessarily reflect the views of the publisher, and the publisher hereby disclaims any responsibility for them.

Any people depicted in stock imagery provided by Thinkstock are models, and such images are being used for illustrative purposes only.
Certain stock imagery © Thinkstock.

ISBN: 978-1-4759-6681-7 (sc)
ISBN: 978-1-4759-6682-4 (ebk)

Printed in the United States of America

iUniverse rev. date: 05/01/2013

Acknowledgements

I would like to thank my husband John Rhodes for all of his patience and understanding. I would also like to thank my children Scoopy, Deneen, and Jody Rhodes for their love

My cousin (Shirley Shelton for letting me write in her home

Darlene Brown gave me encouragement

Dee Ann King kept me in her prayers.

A Special thanks to my niece RaKeia McNeill for helping me with my book.

Thank to Carlyon Craig for standing by me

Author's Note

This book is fiction it was inspired by my imagination. The characters portrayed in this book are not real the characters were made up in my mind. If some characters seems like it's about your life, it's not this book is fiction.

In 1939, I was born in Derry Oklahoma to John and Mary Chester. We lived in a little shack outside of town, my father worked on a rail road train going from town to town, state to state. Sometimes he would be gone for weeks, and weeks before he came back home. My mama, Mary had me at home, a lady name Bessie Brown help bring me into this world at 1:15PM. They said my daddy was gone, my grandfather live with us. His name was James Leroy Chester, he told my mama to name me after him, and she did. I never had a brother or sister. When I got older the people in my town would tell me about my grandfather. They said he was a very mean man, they would tell me how he would fight all the time and get drunk and rape women.

He would laugh about it because they were shame. And the police didn't always come out; they didn't care that much about colored women or men. Sometimes they would only come out when they would kill someone. I remember my grandfather he died when I was eight years old. My mama would tell me how much he loved me and how proud he was of me. He would take me around to his friends to show me off to them. They would say," James what a fine boy you got there" look just like you, you sure that ain't your boy? James would laugh and say, "Hell yes he's my son, my grandson". James didn't care what he said to people. He didn't care who he hurt, lots of people were scare of him. He would tell my daddy, "Boy you a sorry son of a bitch, I'm going to teach my grandson to kick your ass when he grows up. Because I want him to be kicking nigger ass like me.

One night James went to a joint in the three hundred blocks on Holly Street. The name of it was called Brick's Place. It was full of people they were dancing, drinking, and having fun. Over in the corner they were shooting dice, James got in the game and the next thing he and a guy name Andy Brown started to fight. Andy was scared of no one, he always carried a gun and James always carried a knife. He would sleep with it under his pillow every night, he opened it up it looked like a small sword he was real proud of it. James said, "Andy was cheating" Andy pulled out his gun, and shot at James. He missed and James ran out the door, every one started to laugh at James because he ran like a pussy ass bitch.

They started Laughing, and laughing. But, James waited outside and when Andy come outside James caught him by the neck. Before Andy could pull out his gun James cut his throat from ear to ear; Andy fell to the ground, bleeding so badly he died. Everyone started running they didn't want to be there when the police came. James got on his horse, rode home, he told John what happened. He told him that he needed to get out of town fast. John told him to get back on the horse and ride down by the train track from where we live, and when the train comes by he would help him get on the train. John packs a bag for James and left to go to the train station where he work a few miles to town. John picked James up. The police come to the house, looking for him but he was gone my mother told them she didn't know where he was. They looked around the house, and left.

The people around town said they heard James was in Texas, and was found dead with a gunshot in the heart. No one ever found out who did it. They think it was one of Andy's sons that lived in Texas, but they never could prove it.

John was still working on the train when I was 12 years old in the 1951. The people in Derry was still talking about my granddaddy, "saying I was his child" because John was always gone on the train. He only came home some times, James lived with my mama. They said, "That boy is James Chester he looks just like him." As I got older, I later found out that James was my real daddy.

They would always call me Little Leroy.

As the years passed, my mama and I live alone, because John knew he wasn't my daddy. He didn't came back home, he would send money sometimes, and then one day the money stopped coming. We didn't hear from him anymore, my mama started to work at Bricks Place. She would come home drunk at night, she miss John so much. She would cry and cry at night calling his name saying I love you, John please come back to me.

My mama kept drinking and drinking, she was so sad all of the time. When I reached the age of 18 in 1957, I started to look for John Chester, to see if he would come back to my mama. I thought things would be better for her. I wanted my mama to be happy again. I love my mama she was all that I had in this whole world. I never knew my mama's family because they didn't want her to marry in the Chester family because of James. They did not like him, he never made them welcome in John home, John was scared of him so he didn't say anything. My mama loved John so much, she stopped seeing her family. Mama told me her family lived in Wichita Kansas. She never wanted to talk about her family, she married John in 1938. She said her family never cared about her.

I got on the train, trying to find him. I looked for him for weeks and weeks, going from train to train, town to town. I worked in different towns to get money to catch another train. I would tell people that I was looking for John to take him home to my mama.

No one knew what train he was on. One day, two men said they knew him but hadn't seen him in a long time. I was gone for three months I thought, I better go home to check on my mama. I walked in the door calling out her name. "Mama, Mama "where are you? I'm home. I went out to the barn looking for her and I saw a new car. A 1955 ford, she wasn't home I waited and waited for her. I went to the bar, where she worked no one had seen her in a few days, they said she met a man and she was with him" They said his name was Al Jenkins and he lived on the south side of town. I went back home, I was thinking she maybe home. She didn't come home that night, it was real cold I fixed a fire to have the house warm when she decided to come home, but she didn't. I went looking for Al Jenkins I found out where he lived, he lived on 11th and Boundary. He had a nice place he worked at a car lot, he made a little money. I told him who I was and asked him if my mama was there? Or did he know where she was?

He started crying saying how much he loved her, how nice he was to her, the other night he went to joint and saw her with another man.

He said, they had a few words and he left, and haven't seen her since. That was two days ago. In my heart I knew he was lying so I decided to go back home. all of her clothes were there. I found five hundred dollars in her purse. I got up the next morning, and went out in the back she had a few chickens. I said, "I would feed them and go back on the south side to see if anyone saw her. I got the chicken feed and started to feed them. I went behind the chicken house and there lay my mama she was not moving. Mama! Mama! I said, "Why are you laying on the ground?

She did not move I bent down to pick her up she was dead. I looked at her face the chickens had picked one side of her face. I screamed so hard and loud I couldn't hear my voice. My mama was the only woman in my life I loved her so much. She is dead and someone had left her there and never tried to help her.

Oh my God! I couldn't believe this! Not my mama! God not my mama! I ran for help. The police came out it seemed like it took them an hour. They said, she had been dead for two days, the police said they would find out who killed her. They took her away.

I made arrangements for the funeral. I sat there so hurt, why didn't I stay home with her? So many things ran in the back of my mind. When I was a kid thinking about James killing a man, I also thought about John never coming back to my mama. I thought about me leaving her and she found another man in her life Al Jenkins and he left her.

Oh God! I cried. Why my mama she never hurt anyone? She was always the one who was hurt by some man. While I sit there I made a promise that I would find that bastard that killed her, if it took me the rest of my life. After the funeral, I went home people came over bringing food and drinks. They were telling me how sorry they were and could they do anything for me? Can we help you Little Leroy?

I looked at them and said," yes you can do something for me bring her Back. All you motherfuckers get the hell out of here. How come none of you came to see my mama when she needed you? How come, none of you bastard don't know who killed her? But one of you motherfuckers, know who killed her. All of you are going to pay, do you hear me you're going to pay. Get the fuck out of here, and take your damn food and ass out of here. Get the hell out of here all of you.

They started leaving, and I ran in the kitchen and took the food and started throwing the food out the door at them. They started running to their cars, driving off. I heard someone say that damn fool done went crazy. I slammed the door in their faces. I saw where someone had left three bottles of whisky on the table. And for the first time in my life I got drunk and it felt good. I slept all night and

The Man on the Train

half of the next day. I woke up and got more to drink for three days I drank, no one said they knew who killed my mama.

I went back to Al Jenkins house to talk to him to see if he knew the man he saw her with. When I got there he was gone, the lady next door said he had packed up and left. I asked her if she knew where he was and she said he caught the train out of town for a few days, and would she keep an eye on his place until he got back She said, "She think he went to Texas," I knew then he was the son of a bitch who killed my mama.

You have a good day Ma'am. You too son (she said). I just walked around town for a while to try to think what to do. I went back home got me another drink and started thinking how can I find this Al Jenkins?

Al Jenkins was a slim tall man about 5'9, he had real good hair, he was light skinned, and a fast talker. He dressed real nice he had a nice car in the yard, and lived in a fair neighborhood. He was the kind of man some women like. I sat and all I could think of was how I would find old Al Jenkins. The more I thought about him the more I hated him. I could hear my mama crying out, "Please don't hurt me please stop beating me". I could feel the pain my mama was in. I started seeing Al Jenkins beating her and calling her names. As she cried out he kept beating her, what did my mama do that he would beat her to death? This is the only woman I ever loved in my life and then to have someone take her away from me. After a few weeks, I couldn't take it anymore I got a job working at the train station. I wanted to see every man that got off the train that look like Al Jenkins to see if he would ever come back to Derry. I could be all over the station seeing who was coming and going.

For day, and weeks I looked at the men on the train. After a few months I saw Al Jenkins getting off the train. My heart stop, I couldn't move I looked at him and in my mind I said. "You dirty son of bitch you came back." I promised myself, I would kill your ass. Motherfucker your ass is mine, he didn't see me he was looking like he just got off a magazine cover, dressed to kill.

I waited until I got off of work went home started drinking trying to think how I was going to kill his no good ass. I couldn't stand it anymore. I had been waiting so long to see this bastard and now I got a chance. I'm not going to let his ass leave Oklahoma again. I waited until 3: am in the morning I knew everyone in Derry would be sleep. I went to the south side of town to his house. I was dressed in all black so no one would see me. I wore black gloves so I didn't leave finger prints. I got to his house, I ring the door bell, he came to the door and said," Who the hell is it at this time of night?

I said nothing I kept ringing the door bell until he opened the door. I pushed him back I had a big knife in my hand and I said, motherfucker I came to get you. I knew one day you would come after me. I told him to tell me what happened to my mama? And why he beat her to death? (He said), he really loved her he went in the joint saw her with another man.

I couldn't take it we had a few words I had given her five hundred, dollars and I bought her a car. I thought she loved me I couldn't believe she would do me like that I loved her so much. She got in the car with the man and they drove away. I went back in the joint and started drinking.

I thought I would go talk to her to see why she did me like that. When I got to her house she wasn't home. I pulled my car around the back of the house and waited for her I got out went in her house. I only wanted to talk, I sat in the house with the lights out I heard the car drive up. I could see her and the man kissing I wanted to go out there and beat his ass, they sat there for a few minutes. She got out and he waited until she got in the house and he drove off. When she turned on the lights and saw me she ran outside.

I went after her, she ran around behind the chicken house to hide from me. I followed her, I tried to talk to her and she told me that she didn't love me and to leave her alone. I picked up a piece of firewood and hit her. She started crying and begging me to leave her alone but I kept beating her. Then she stop crying and fell to the ground, I told her I was sorry. I told to her to get up but she didn't move I knew she was dead. I got scared and ran when I got in the car I still had the piece of wood in my hand.

When I got away for the house I threw it in a field.

I went home changed clothes and threw my bloody clothes in the fireplace and burn them. I went back to Bricks Place and stayed there all night so if the police asked anyone about me they would say that I was there all night. I'm sorry man, I didn't mean to kill her, please forgive me I loved her please forgive me. I just wanted to scare her so she would only be with me.

I looked at his sorry ass sitting there with his head down crying and before I knew it I walked behind him. I grabbed him by his hair, pulled his head back and cut his throat he fell to the floor. I kicked his ass like he did my mother. I saw all the blood on me and I didn't want to put it in my mama's car I pulled off my clothes and shoes and put them in a bag.

I ran out of there with all my clothes and gloves off. I went home to the chicken house dug a hole in there and buried the clothes, gloves, shoes, and knife covered the hole up and put hay over it. We kept hay in the chicken house for the, chicken. I took the water hose and washed myself outside. I fixed me a drink and thought what in the hell had I done. Oh my God what have I done!

I woke up four hours later went outside to see if I could see blood or anything that the police could see to think I was at Al Jenkins house. I put the chicken feed everywhere, I had washed myself outside so they could walk all over and peck whatever they could. I washed out the car and cleaned it as good as I could. I put it back in the barn and covered it up. So it was still clean and they would think it was never moved. I got up and walked down the track to work I didn't want to drive. I tried so hard to be my normal self. I didn't talk that much to anyone. I didn't want to say anything that would get me into trouble.

After work, I went home and tried to think what to do. I waited for the police to come and get me, they didn't come. I got up the next day and went back to work. After I was at work for about four hours I heard someone standing around the station talking.

Did you hear about Old Al Jenkins? He was found dead by the lady that lived next door to him.

He was kick to death and this throat was cut, they don't know who did it. They think whoever killed Mary Chester a few months ago may have killed him we ain't safe until they find whoever it is. I'm keeping my gun on me until I find out who did it.

Well you know these cops round here will take their time. All they say is another nigger killing another, someone need to kill all these black bastards around here. I started back cleaning the station. Four weeks have gone by they still had no clue. They came around in the black neighborhood asking if they knew anything or heard anything, nobody knew anything.

I lived outside of town so I didn't get many visitors. They thought, I went crazy after my mama died.

A year has gone by and they still haven't charged anyone with Al Jenkins death. Another year has gone by and I worked my way up at the train station to work in the office. I could catch the train and go where ever I wanted for free. I got on the train one day to go to Dallas Texas.

While on the train, I saw John and he couldn't run from me I asked him if he was John Chester. Yes, he turned around and looked me in the eyes he stood there for a second looking at me. You Leroy my daddy son by my wife when I came home I found out that he had raped her. I wanted to kill him but I couldn't. I stop through Derry to see all of you. I wanted to forgive him because I was gone a lot. When I came back it was the night he killed Andy Brown, I never wanted to come back. When I come through Derry I wouldn't get off the train I stayed in the back because I saw you at the train station, they told me you work there.

Your daddy was right he called me a pussy. I'm a good man I have a family, a wife and a son. I never told them about you fools I don't want them to ever know you.

Did you know that my mother died still loving you? She would cry at night calling out your name to come back to her because she missed you. She started to drink a lot begging for you to come back to her. Why John didn't you just stop and tell her that you didn't want her anymore? All you had to do was tell her how you felt? Why didn't you come back to be with me, you bastard tell me? When my mother died I was along, I had no one to be with me, tell me damn you!

"Because I don't love you, I don't want no part of you or Oklahoma I will never come back to live there. I have nothing there to come back for. I looked at this man and all I could see was hate for him.

Yes, I know that James Chester is my daddy and not my grandfather. He was scared of nothing, like me he always did or said what he wanted to. John Chester turned and walked away from me never looking back at me. My heart was so full of pain and hurt that he didn't give a damn about me or my mama.

The Man on the Train

When we got to Dallas, I got off the train, rented a car. I was driving off and I saw him pull off, I followed him he went to this nice white house with a big porch there were lots of flowers in the yard. It was a very well kept yard. He got out of the car and went inside I waited a few minutes and I got out of the car and went and looked through the window. I saw him kissing this woman they looked so happy together.

He gave this woman everything he should have to my mama. All he gave her was a damn shack outside of town and a few damn chickens that picked her face. He never came back to her, I drove off and found me a bar started to drink and then think about how he did my mama. The more I drank the more I got mad at his ass.

I went back to his house and parked across the street looked at the house and got madder and madder. I fell asleep. Around five am I heard a door slam I got up looked out the window it was him getting ready to leave. I followed him again to see where he was going. He went back to the train station it was five am 1961. He drove in the parking lot and I pulled up beside him. I jumped out of the car and got in the car with him. I made him drive, I held a knife on him; I always carried a knife like my daddy. John was so scared. What the fuck are you doing? Have you lost your damn mind Leroy? My train is leaving in thirty minutes. I have to go to work! Just drive I want to talk to you John, I told you I don't want nothing to do with you so leave me the hell alone.

I'm going back to work. Stop the car! John stop the car damn you.

Talk so I can go! I sat there for a second and made him get out of the car. I slid over to get out the same side as he did. I made him walk away from the car. John, I just want you in my life I have no one I just want to be a part of your family. I just need someone to love me John. I'm scared I need you to listen to me. I need to tell you what I did to the man that killed my mother.

Please John, listen to me! I don't want to know what you did I told you I don't give a damn. All I want you to do is to leave me the hell alone! You stay away from me and my family! I have a good family not a bunch of damn fools!

You sorry son of a bitch, before I knew it I cut his throat. He fell to the ground. I stood there looking at him and he never said another word. I ran back to his car, I was so hurt and scared. What in the hell have I done? What in the world is wrong with me? I got ready to get in the car and drive away, when I looked back in the seat. I saw his suitcase I pulled my clothes off and put his clothes on that he had in the suitcase, so I wouldn't have blood in his car.

I took my clothes and put them in his case I looked around to make sure I didn't leave anything. I knew I had to hurry to get away from there before someone came by and saw me. I drove back to town I got out at the train station, I looked in the renter car and got my bag and went into the train station. As I walking to the restroom a man said hello John. I remembered I had on John's clothes, I said hello and kept walking. When I got in the restroom I pulled his clothes off and put my other clothes on. I took my bag and John's suitcase and got back on the train to Derry.

When I got off the train I saw a man looking at me real strange.

Hello Leroy, he said, I'm Peter Marshall do you remember me? I use to come visit your mother when you were a little boy. Oh yes, how you doing? Where are you coming from? It's nice seeing you again Mr Marshall, I kept walking, I got John suitcase and my bag and started walking home. When Dan Turner came driving by, Leroy do you need a ride home get in, where you coming from? Oh, I been in Guthrie for a few days I just needed to get away. Yes, I know how it is son, they still haven't found out who killed your mama? No! They! haven't. Do you think they will? The police said they still looking. Well, here we go Leroy, thank you Dan, Okay son. Dan drove away and I took Johns clothes and my clothes and buried it in the same hole that I put Al Jenkins things. I covered them back up and burn the suit case. For days I couldn't sleep, I had to try to keep myself calm so no one would think I was trying to hide something. For weeks nothing happened. When I went to work my boss called me in the office said, he need to talk to me. He was a big man about 5'7 and 240 pounds. He had black hair, medium skin he said he was a white man but he looked more like an Indian. His name was Billy Joe Sheets. Leroy Yes, Mr. Sheets. Leroy I need you to go to Arkansas to work in the office to replace Albert Stone

You need to leave in a week if you want the job, there will be a pay raise. Yes, Mr. Sheets I'll go, I can make a change in my life. I packed my things I left. I left all my other things at home. It was not anything that I couldn't live without. I plan to come back and get my mama car later.

1964, I moved to Little Rock, Arkansas I found a place to live at a rooming house. Hello, I'm looking for a room? I see you have one for rent. My name is Leroy Chester I'm from Oklahoma. Hello, my name is Johnnie Mae, Yes, I still have a room I'll take you to see it, I went in the house with her. This is a nice place you have here, very clean and nice. How much do you want for the room? I want fifty dollars a week.

I'll take it can I move in now? Yes, she said.

I want my money on time you can use the bathroom up stairs, you can use my kitchen and clean up after yourself. I don't want you to go in my room or using my bathroom down stairs. She is a nice lady I thought. She said she had this big house and stay by herself. She said, her husband died two years ago. She was a brown skin woman, weight about 126 pounds she had no kids and worked at the hospital. We talked for a while and I told her I was tired and I needed to go to work the next day on my new job at the train station.

I got up the next morning and walked to work, the station was only a few blocks from Johnnie Mae house. I put on one of James Chester suites, I looked real nice.

When I walked in the office I could see all the white men looking at me wondering where is this nigger going? Who the hell is he? May I help you, (said) this old gray head lady behind the desk. Hello, my name is Leroy Chester, I'm the new man sent here to replace Albert Stone. I'm from Oklahoma, station her mouth flew open. Why you're a colored man. Yes, I am.

Oh, oh I'm sorry we were looking for someone else, why here in Arkansas we don't work with colored. I'm sorry you feel that way. I'm Sally Cross, I'm sorry I didn't mean to offend you. This is your office Mr Chester. They sure didn't like me at that desk. They wanted to quit their jobs, but they had been there so long some of them were ready to retire. They, was mad as hell they had a black man to run their train station.

I knew my job wouldn't be easy. Sally tried to be nice I could tell she didn't want to work with me. What would her friends think? As the day pass Sally said, you seem like a nice young man, and she began to feel better. I left work walking home I saw a bar on State

Street. I went in sat down at a table and ordered me a drink. When I wanted another one a young man came over. Hello, my name is Jerry Johnson, everyone call me JJ. I'm Leroy, I just moved here from Oklahoma I work at the train station. I knew you were not one of my regulars.

Well JJ, I maybe one when I looked in his eyes I began to feel so unhappy. I really need a friend someone I could talk to and someone I could trust. My heart began to feel so heavy and sad. I left and went back to Johnnie Mae house. I wanted to just get to my room and relax. When I walk to her house she had a baseball bat in her hand and cussing at this man. You black motherfucker I'll beat your ass, you get the hell away from me she said. I told you that I would kill your black ass. You damn drunken ass bastard.

The man was crying saying Johnnie I love you baby please let me come back home I don't have nowhere to go baby. I don't give a damn take you black ass away from here. I stood there wondering what was going on. Johnnie Mae what's going on? Oh Leroy, I can take care of this go on in the house.

Who in the hell is this man Johnnie? (he said) you got yourself another man? Are you her new boyfriend? I kept walking to the house you hear me nigger! I turn and look back at him, and said to myself fool you don't know me. I'll cut your fucking throat and leave your ass to bleed to death.

The man stared at me and the next thing I knew Johnnie Mae was beating his ass with that bat. "She said," leave you bastard. He started running, I'll be back and I'm going to beat your ass you damn hoe. You ain't seen the last of me, hear me bitch, you ain't seen the last of me. After we went in the house, I asked her what was that all about. She said he was her ex boyfriend his name is Jimmy Adams, they dated after her husband died. He would get drunk all the time he had a drinking problem, when I come home from work I was so tired my house was dirty and he had his friends over eating up my food.

They all over my house passed out, I told them to get their ass out of my house. He would get up and started hitting on me, asking me how come I was so late coming home? He told me to get my ass in the kitchen and cook him and his friends something to eat. He would say you out there fucking some man because you sure not doing it to me. I told him no I don't want his drunk, ass on me cause it's a waste of time and his little dick. He always passed out before he got his little dick up it's not big as my big toe, then he started beating on me again.

I picked up on of his whisky bottles and hit him on the side of his face. His ass ran out of here screaming like his ass was on fire. I haven't see him in two months I put a five inch scar on the side of his face and he have the nerve to want to come back here asking me can he come home. I told him to leave and he started to talk bull shit saying baby take me back. I kept telling him to leave so I got my bat he was telling me how much he loved me. (Baby please let me stay) I told him to take his black ass out of my face.

Leroy, I'm so sorry you had to see all this the first day you here. How was your first day at work? Oh not too bad I know I'm going to have some trouble with some of them red necks, but I can take it. I looked at this nice looking woman and for the first time in my life I looked at a woman like I did. I saw a lot of women but, I never look at them the way I looking at her. My mama was the only woman in my life and I loved her more than anything in this world. I never cared about any woman.

Johnnie Mae asked me if I was hungry she fixed a real nice dinner.

My mama was a real good cook, she would always call out to me Leroy come and eat. We spent a lot of time together because no one would come out that much because of my father. After he died they still didn't come. I was sitting here thinking about my mama's food.

I ate the food Johnnie Mae cooked I looked up and I could see her looking at me, she wasn't saying anything to me while I was eating. After I finished, she said, well what do you think? How was the food? Was the food good? Oh yes, you a real good cook. May I help you clean up for my meal? No you look like you had a tiring day you go on to bed. Thank you again, I really appreciate it I am real tired I will see you tomorrow. I could tell she wanted to talk she wanted to know more about me. I went to my room laid across the bed and starting thinking about my life. I couldn't tell anyone about my life and what I had done. It is so hard keeping all the things I had done inside of me. Some nights I can't sleep, I couldn't tell anyone what I had done to Al Jenkins and my brother John. My brother John didn't deserve to die he didn't do nothing to me. I don't know why I got so mad at him because he didn't want me in his life. Now I understand why he never wanted to come back to Derry. Everyone knew his wife had a baby by his father, and he was shame of it. My eyes filled up with water and I asked God what have, I done. What can I do? Who can I talk to? I need to tell some one what I had done. God I was wrong, help me God I cried out. I was wrong for all the things I had done in my young life. I wanted to put it all behind me but how can I?

I woke up the next morning and I could smell coffee and breakfast cooking my head felt like Johnnie Mae had hit me with that bat. I took a shower got dressed and went down stairs Johnnie Mae looked up at me said you want some breakfast? Yes, thank you. Did you have a good night sleep? Yes. I'm very sorry Leroy about what happen yesterday. You may think the worse of me I'm tired of men mistreating me. Even as a young girl my father mistreated me and my mother. My own father was a dirty bastard. I hated his black ass. I left home as soon as I got big I never wanted to see his sorry ass again. Punk bastard, it wasn't long after I left and his ass died I went back home to be with my mother and I went to his funeral. I got up there in front of his ass and I just danced and danced everyone thought I had gone crazy I was glad his ass was gone he wouldn't be mean to nobody else.

I told her my mama, was also treated bad by men in her life before she died. How did your mother, die? She was beaten to death by a man.

I'm so sorry to hear that, I sure hope they put his ass away for life, did they? No, he was found dead a few months later with his throat cut and his ass kicked. Well good he should have kept his hands to himself. Don't feel sorry for his ass any man that beats a woman need they ass kicked. Leroy tell, me about yourself? I want to know about your father, brothers and sisters are they living in Oklahoma? No, I don't have anyone my father died when I was a young boy. I have no brothers or sisters I have no one. There's not much to tell about me I grew up in a small town in Oklahoma.

Well thank you for the breakfast it was real good you're a good cook. I have to go to work see you later. I walked out and walked to work. I walked in and Sally said "Good morning Mr. Chester. Good Morning Sally. Mr. Chester, my husband don't want me to call you mister and he don't want me to work for you. We got in a fight last night but, I told him I need this job it's the only extra income we have coming in. He fell off a tractor and broke his back and he has a problem with walking sometimes, at times he is in a lot of pain. He sure can raise a lot of hell he wants me to call you Leroy, and makes sure you call me Mrs. Cross. I don't have a problem with that Mrs. Cross, thank you Leroy.

Damn red necks make my ass sick I can't wait to leave for the day. I need to go to the bar on State Street, after work I walked to the bar. I walked in and ordered me a drink. Hi JJ. Hey Leroy! I knew you would be back need another drink. Yes, give me a double. I talk to JJ for a while the next thing I looked up and I had been there for over two hours. I'll see you later JJ. Okay man.

I walked home and on the way I started thinking Oh my God, Johnnie Mae see me as a drunk and will beat me with that damn baseball bat. When got home she wasn't there I went to my room and locked the door pulled off my clothes because it was so hot. I opened the window, laid across the bed, and fell asleep. When I woke up, I was surprised I had been sleep for three hours. I put my clothes back on and went down stairs to get me something to eat. I knew Johnnie Mae was going to ask me where I had been. I had only been here for two days but it seemed like I had been here for weeks. I looked in the ice box to find something to eat I hoped Johnnie Mae didn't say anything. I had planned to go to the store and buy me some food, as soon as I got paid. I looked on the table and I saw a note, Leroy I left some food in the oven, I'll be back in a few days. I had to leave to go out of town in a hurry, you watch the house and I don't want no damn nigger in my house. I started to eat the food she left, the phone started to ring, Hello (I said). Hello Leroy, this is Johnnie Mae I had to go see about my mother they called and said she didn't have long to live. I just jumped in the car and drove all day to South Carolina will you be alright?

I put a key to my house on the table make sure my house is locked everyday when you leave. I don't want to come home and find all my stuff gone. I got to go I don't know when I'll be back home talk to you later (she hung up). She didn't give me a chance to say nothing she must be crazy. I sit there at the table and looked around in the big house it didn't look nothing like the shack I grew up in outside of town. I felt real strange in there by myself I walked outside and sat on the porch. I sat down and started to look at the people walking down the street. Some of them would speak, others kept walking. There were kids playing in the street. Boy I said to myself this is the good life. I saw this man coming across the street with a drink in his hand. Hello my name is Sam Hicks saw you sitting out here are you kin to Johnnie Mae? No, I'm just renting a room from her.

Are you from here? No, just moved here from Oklahoma, I never been here before. I got a job at the train station, Oh I work down the street at old man Gibson's grocery store. I been, working there ever since he opened up ten years ago. I started cleaning up and stocking up I still do that sometimes and I deliver grocery and just help out all over the store. Old man Gibson he a good old white man to work for I been here in Little Rock all my life. I got a wife and four kids we been together ever since we were in high school. Are you married and do you have kids? No, I haven't found the right woman. Oh you will here in Little Rock woman have you going (Ha, Ha) he laughed. You will be married before you know what happened to you boy.

Oh Johnnie Mae, she don't, take shit of no men no more since that last man she had.

You welcome to come over and, holler at me sometimes. Maybe we can get to know each other, my wife has a cook out every week and we have a few of our friends over. So come over and meet some of our friend's maybe you can get to know some of them. Sure I'll do that.

Well nice meeting you Leroy. You too man. I watched Sam walk back across the street I sat there for a few more minutes looking at the kids playing games in the street. When I went to school I didn't have a lot of friends, everyone knew I was James's son.

I went back in the house listened to the radio and fell asleep. When I woke up I didn't smell coffee or breakfast the house was so quiet there was no Johnnie Mae. I got dressed and it was so hot outside I put on slacks pants and just a shirt. Hello Sally oh I mean Mrs. Cross (she smile) Mrs. Cross did you finish the papers I need? Yes Leroy, I put them on your desk. I went into my office and shut the door. I sat down and then I heard noise and some loud voices, I went out to see what was going on. It was Mrs. Cross husband cursing her for still working for me. I heard him say Sally damn you, I don't want you working for no colored man. Get your shit right now come on with me do you hear me? No wife of mines is going to work here no more.

George Cross you know I have to work and I like my job. Leroy is a good man, he won't, hurt nobody. She looked and saw me standing there. Leroy this is my husband. Hello Mr. Cross.

I need Mrs. Cross to help me out I'm new here there is so much work I need to learn. He stood there looking at me. Sally I'll see you when you get home. Mrs. Cross, I don't want any trouble if you need to leave you can. Oh no Leroy, don't worry I'll take care of George he won't be back. Well I don't want him to hurt you, Oh he ain't nothing but talk. Well if you say so. Leroy you are a nice man and I like you. Thank you Mrs. Cross, I went back to my office sat behind the desk and thought about Old George Cross. He better not cross me I'll kill his old ass and never care if they find his ass or not.

After work I stopped by the bar, JJ wasn't there he didn't show up for work they said he would be back tomorrow. Johnnie Mae was gone for a week I heard a car horn blowing outside, I looked out the window and there was Johnnie Mae getting out of the car. I opened the door and walked out on the porch hello Johnnie.

Hello Leroy come help me get my things out of the car.

I helped her with her things. After we got inside I asked her how her mama was.

She said she tried to get her mama to come back with her but she didn't want to and she needed special care day and night, so she put her into a nursing home. She took her mama's car and left her car because her mama car was bigger to bring back a lot of her mama things, she also left a lot of things with her cousin. She said she plan to go back there to live with her mama after she retire in a few months. She put a lot of her mama good stuff in her garage for storage until she go back. Well Leroy, I'm tired. I drove all the way by myself I'll talk to you tomorrow. I heard a knock at the door it was Sam Hicks, hello Leroy, we having a cookout tomorrow you and Johnnie Mae can come over.

Sure Sam. I like that. After Sam left my head started to hurt real bad I went to my room and started wondering what's wrong with me. I laid across the bed, and started to think here I am in Arkansas, and I was thinking about what I did in Oklahoma and Texas. I got up and went to the bar to get me a drink. I sat in the back I didn't want to talk to no one. I didn't want to go back to Johnnie Mae house because I knew she would want to talk. JJ was working he came back to me. Hey Leroy what's up man?

Is something wrong? I'm just scared and unhappy tonight I just need someone to talk to. I don't want to go back home.

Man, I live alone come and go with me. I'm getting off in a few minutes. I started to cry oh God why did I come to Little Rock? I don't know these people here why God did I come here, JJ give me another drink. I'm getting off now come on and go home with me we can have a few drinks at my house let's go. JJ drove to his house, we talked and he gave me another drink, and I don't remember anything until the next morning. Where in the hell am I? I couldn't move my head was worse than the day before. Hey Leroy, man what time do you have to be at work? Oh JJ I can't move. No wonder you had a lot of drinks last night man. Here I made some coffee have some. Thank, you. I didn't want to go back to Johnnie Mae house right now drunk. I don't want her to see me like this.

Johnnie Mae your girlfriend or something, you told me you weren't married.

Oh my God what did I tell him, oh God I don't remember what we talked about last night. I hope I didn't bore you last night. Oh, no you didn't talk much I did all the talking. What did we talk about? I started to tell you about myself and before I knew it you had passed out, I put you to bed.

Man I'm so sorry I moved here to work and it don't look like it will be easy for me. I think I should have stayed home. Well maybe things will get better. I need to call my job may I use your telephone? Yes here. Santa Fe Train Station may I help you. Mrs. Cross this is Leroy I won't be in today I'm not feeling well. Okay Leroy, I'll get Frank to help me today he will know what to do.

Hope you feel better. Thank you Mrs. Cross.

Leroy, why don't you hang out with me today I have some things I need to do would you like that? Maybe you can get your mind off of a few things. I would like that, I like JJ he is a real cool guy. We got in his car and started, driving around he took me to some places I had not been while I was here. He told me places where blacks were not allowed, he took me to a place to eat and the food was so good. We talked about a lot of things but I still didn't talk about my past I

The Man on the Train

wanted to make sure I could trust him. Man I got to go by my sister's house for a few minutes and then I have to go to work then I will take you home. We drove up in front of this nice house JJ opened the door and walked in. Terry! Terry you home? I stood there looking around at this neat house and pretty things all around it was beautiful compared to the shack I lived in Oklahoma.

Leroy lets go outback sometimes she is outback. I walked through the house with J J.

Terry didn't I tell you to keep your door lock anybody can walk in. Terry this is my friend Leroy. When she look at me my heart stop she was beautiful. She was planting flowers she had on a big hat and dirt was on her face. She stood up and said well hello Leroy how come I haven't seen you before. JJ where you been keeping him?

Leroy just moved here a few weeks ago. Leroy this is my sister Terry. It's nice to meet you Terry. I think its going to be nice to meet you too. All I could do was smile. Terry I left my jacket here the other day and I stopped by here to get it, Look in the hall closet. We walked inside and I could feel her eyes all over me. Terry where is David? Over his friends' house David is her son. Leroy, do you like Little Rock? How long you going to be here? Did you bring your wife and kids?

No, I'm not married and I don't have any kids I haven't found the right woman. Well have you been looking? Terry stop asking so many question, come on Leroy lets go,. Hope to see you again Leroy. Yes, hope to see you too. Man Terry say, whatever comes to her mind; don't pay her any attention to her. Oh she seemed cool. Yes, my sister is cool I love her so much.

JJ dropped me off at home, I got out and walked in Johnnie Mae was sitting at the table getting ready to eat. Well are you okay? (she said) Yes I'm fine. You didn't come home last night I didn't know if you was okay or not. I guess you done found you a woman. No do I have to report to you everywhere I go or been? I only rent from you I didn't know you wanted to be all up in my business.

Now listen nigger, I ain't in your business I just wonder where you were since you didn't come home last night. Sorry for asking you next time you can kiss my ass.

She got up and went in the other room I went to my room turned on the music and laid across the bed and tried to go to asleep

I couldn't because I was wondering what did I say to JJ while I was drunk. I have to stop drinking so much I have to be careful what I say. I don't want no, one here to know about my life in Oklahoma. I closed my eyes and started to think about Terry I never been with a woman.

I'm 23 and never been with a woman I was thinking about her small beautiful body, that long black hair and those sweet looking lips. I sure would like to know her. What would I say to her? What would I do for her I never talked to a woman that, way I started to think how do I make love to a woman like her? Oh God what's wrong with me? No woman will ever love me, my mother was the only woman that ever loved me and now she was gone.

Knock, knock, Leroy may I talk to you. Yes, come on in. I'm sorry about what I said to you, you right it's none of my business it won't happen again. I was just worried about you I didn't know if you had gotten lost or if something happened to you. I'm sorry to Johnnie Mae, I been under a lot of stress with my job trying to learn things fast. I just need to work out some thing. Well if you need to talk I'm a good listener. I looked at her as she stood there in this short blue gown smiling at me. If you need anything I'm here would you have a drink with me please? Yes sure I will, well just wait here and I'll get the drinks. I looked at this nice looking woman, but she look nothing like Terry. She came back with a bottle of whisky and two glasses; she poured me a drink and her one as well and gave it to me. She sat on the side of the bed, smiling at me. We kept drinking and drinking after a few drinks I could feel no pain. I couldn't think of my past all I thought about was this woman in front of me and I didn't know what to do. She knew what she was doing; she got up and fixed me another drink bent down to give it to me and one of her breast fell out of her gown my eyes popped out of my head. My heart stop beating and all I could do was just lay there looking at her.

Oh (she said) I'm sorry you never seen a woman's breast.

No, not like this she took my hand put it on her breast and put it in my hand to let me feel it. It was so soft then she told me to put it in my mouth and I did. She put her nipple in my mouth and said suck it like you would a sucker. I didn't know what to do she said go ahead, I started to suck so hard, she screamed fool! Not that hard you, never been with a woman have you?

I felt like a fool, and my mind was lost somewhere, I like what she was teaching me. She said you just lean back and let me teach you what to do to me. She took her hand and put it on my penis and it got so hard. She started to kiss me and putting her body on me and my mind started going crazy. I put my arms around her, and she showed me what to do with my penis and she said all you have to do is start pumping in and out. Oh my God that was the best night I ever had in my life, this woman made love to me. When I woke up the next morning beside her I looked at her and I wanted more I started to kiss her and put my hands all over her body and she wanted more she let me make more love to her. It felt so good it was better than drinking I didn't think I would ever need another drink to make me feel good. I need this woman's body I wanted more, I didn't want to go to work I wanted to stay home with her the rest of the day in bed. No, she said I have a job I have to go I have to be at work in fifty five minutes. We can do this again (she smiled) I have some more to teach you. You need more practice; you have a lot to learn about women.

She kissed me got out of bed and asked me to take a shower with her we both had to be at work. I looked at her naked body and thought I had died and went to heaven.

Hello Leroy, you feel better? Yes, Mrs. Cross I feel wonderful, well you look better than you have since you been working here. Only way a man look like you today is if he found him a woman. She must have been mighty good to you. Oh Mrs. Cross why would you say that?

I been in this world a long time and I know how to put that smile on a man's face.

And you got that smile. I went to my office and look at old lady Cross and wonder what she was like in her younger days because she looked like shit now. Boy my day went so good I didn't even let them get to me. I didn't even feel like going to the bar I just wanted to get home to Johnnie Mae. I went straight home when I got there she was not home

I started to wonder where were she. I'll fix dinner for her to show her how much I appreciate last night. Hours pass and she was not home where the hell is she? Is she out fucking another man?

Then I heard her car driving up be careful don't let her know she got your ass going crazy. She walked in. Hi Leroy. Johnnie you look tired? Yes, I am I had to work in the emergency and you never get off on time. Oh you can cook? Thank you baby, sure smell good I didn't know you can cook. There's a lot about me that you don't know. Yes, I found out one last night. Are you trying to be funny or you making fun of me?

No baby, I like you and I want to teach you more.

I couldn't wait to go to bed with her but I didn't want her to think I couldn't wait so I had to act cool. After dinner, I helped clean the kitchen so she could hurry and get in bed. Well Leroy, I'll see you in the morning I'm real tired. She went to her room and left me standing there. I couldn't believe this, this bitch she got me worked up teaching me something new in my life and go to her room and shut the door. I wanted to kick that damn door open and jump all over that black ass. I was mad as hell, I cooked her food and she took her black ass in her room. I was so mad I just went out on the porch and tried to calm down. Here come Sam Hicks (Where the hell he going?) Hi Leroy, just came over to see why you didn't come over to my cookout? I came over and Johnnie Mae said you were not at home. I'm sorry Sam I forgot I got tied up with business. I promise I'll come over next time man I'm sorry.

My wife wanted to meet you we always have a lot of single women there. I sure will come next time.

Well I better get back my wife get mad when she, cook and I are not on time. Would you like to come over with me and have dinner? Thank you man but I need to go to bed early tonight. We'll get together soon, Sam left and I went back inside, I looked at Johnnie Mae door and it was still closed. I went up the stairs to my room and got in bed I started thinking about the night I had with Johnnie Mae. I went on to sleep I didn't even have a drink. Later in the night before day I felt someone get in the bed with me. Johnnie Mae was back in bed with me she started kissing me getting on top of me pressing her body on me and then she just started wigging her body on me. I just wanted to please her in any way she wanted. Man I like this, she make love to me and it was better than the first time. Every day I came home I didn't go to the bar for weeks I drink at home with Johnnie Mae. We got real close, Johnnie Mae told me to move in her room with her she wanted to wake up every morning with me beside her. I moved in with her and we made love over and over whenever we wanted to, I loved sleeping with her. I really began to like her, she told me she was in love with me. We started to go out together and we were happy.

My day at work was good because I didn't let anyone upset me I didn't care what they thought of me anymore. I felt so good I wasn't sad anymore I didn't think about my life in Oklahoma. Life was going so well I even liked going to work every morning. Johnnie Mae got a call from her cousin in South Carolina that her mother had died. She said she had to go back to South Carolina to take care of her mother. She wanted me to go with her, but I couldn't because some of the people on my job were on vacation and we were short of help. She said you stay and take care of my house. Because I have a lot of nice things. Leroy I like to be along tonight because I need to get my things together. Can I help you?

No, I can do it. I went to my room and took a bottle of rum with me. I began to cry I know how it feels to lose a mother. I took a drink and sat there thinking about my mother wondering why Al Jenkins killed her. He didn't have to take her life. I had to kill him. I got up and went outside to get me some air. I like sitting on the porch, it felt good just sitting there watching the people in their yard talking to each other.

Hello Leroy. Hello Sam, Sam was carrying groceries. I'm looking for you tomorrow around 4:00 don't miss this one. Yes, I'll come over since its Saturday I have no plans. I sat there for a while longer then went to bed.

Leroy, Leroy, get up and take me to the Train Station I don't want to miss my train I don't want to drive back to South Carolina by myself. I got up put on my clothes went down stairs and Johnnie said you got time for a cup of coffee with me before I leave. Now, I'm leaving you my car and you take good care of my car and I don't want a bunch of damn nigger in my house do you hear me? Yes, Mae I here you.

Okay let's go. I helped her put her things in the car and we left to go I dropped her off at the train station. Do you want me to stay with you till you leave?

Yes, the train will be here in a few minutes everyone at the train station was looking at me and Johnnie Mae. I could see old man Cross just talking he was always hanging around the station. He was friends with most of the people that worked there. I wonder what the hell he was doing there so early. Mrs. Cross was off on Saturday, he walked over to me boy you got a woman? Johnnie Mae looked at me and I pretend that I didn't hear him. Johnnie checked her bags in and we stood outside to wait.

Here comes my train I'll talk to you later Leroy. As I was getting ready to leave Johnnie Mae said wait Leroy. She gave me a big kiss and hug. They was all looking she said I will give them something to talk about. Girl you are something else what am I going to do with you?

She laughed and said when I come back home I'll show you what you can do for me. I smiled at Johnnie Mae and walked away. Old man Cross, face turned red and he walked away shaking his head.

I got in the car and decided to just drive around town. Oh God! There's Terry's house I stopped in front of it but, drove off because I didn't know her that well to get out.

I went back home, I decided to put on some different clothes to go over to Sam's house. I saw people going to his house for his cookout; I walked across the street and knocked on his door. A fat black woman opened the door with the biggest smile on her face hello, she said. Hello my name is Leroy is Sam here? Yes, come on in Sam told me he invited you to come. I'm Hattie Sam's wife. Everyone is out back just follow me I followed her through the kitchen and food was everywhere.

I walked outside and Sam came over to me, I see you met Hattie. Yes, well let me introduce you to everybody he started telling me who everyone was but I couldn't remember their names. I was looking at all those beautiful women, I looked over and I saw the most beautiful woman there. Sam took me over to her and said this is Terry Johnson. Hello Leroy, Hello Terry. Do you two know each other? (She said) yes we met. One woman walked up to me and said Terry who is this fine ass man? Leroy, this is my friend Lucille Cook.

Yes, I'm Lucille. I'm the one they sing about. I laugh she was funny to me. Oh Leroy don't pay that Lucille, any attention she tell everyone that when she had too much to drink. Well Leroy if you get to know me I'll have your fine ass singing out my name Lucille. I know you will ha, ha.

The Man on the Train

I talked to Terry she wanted to know why JJ haven't brought me back to her house. Well I haven't seen JJ lately I been real busy working, and I just go straight home after work. I couldn't tell her that I couldn't wait to get home to Johnnie Mae to make love to her. I started to talk to the men. I didn't want them to think that I was stuck up. They started to ask me some questions about myself and I didn't like that. I wanted to tell them none of your damn business but I knew I had to keep my cool. I'm from a small town up north just a plain oh country boy.

How many brothers and sisters you have? I don't have a family, my family is dead. Oh we sorry to hear that. Sam said I'm an only child to I just have Hattie and my kids. I didn't want to tell them about my screwed up life. I knew it was time for me to go, Sam thank you for inviting me to your home I had a nice time. Terry I hope I get to see you again real soon. Oh you will here is my number call me.

As I was leaving I felt some one touch me on my shoulder I turned around and it was Lucille. Handsome here's my number call me and let me rock your world. She was drunk I can't stand a drunk, ass woman. Sure Lucille good to meet you. I left and went back home I sat there for a minute and got bored, the house was so quiet since Johnnie Mae was gone. I decided to go to the bar on State Street I was there for a few minutes. JJ saw me and came over. Where have you been I haven't seen you in weeks Leroy? I been working late and going straight home. I made up my mind I ain't go let them people on my job get on my nerves any more. I'll tell them to kiss my ass. Good for you, want another drink?

Yes, just one I'm driving a friend's car. Oh my God I looked up and here walk in Terry she walked over to JJ and I saw him pointing to me. She walked over to me and said well, well, we have to stop running into each other like this. Maybe this is a beginning what you think? Well maybe. May I sit down? Sure I said JJ brought us our drinks. Why did you leave Sam's house so early? I thought you were tired. Well I don't like being around a lot of people asking me questions about my life. Oh do you have something to hide? Everyone, have something to hide even you, (I said.) Do you have something to hide Terry? Sure I do. We both smile at each other. JJ started calling out time to close. Are you ready to go home Leroy? Do you have something in mind? Yes, I do come go home with me and

25

I'll cook you breakfast. Will that be all? Oh Leroy I hope you're not thinking what I'm thinking. One step at a time, I followed her home she cooked and we ate and talked. It was day break well I guess I will go home I sure hope we can do this again. I like to see more of you. I like to see you again Leroy, do you think you can drive home? Why don't you stay here for a few hours, my son is spending the weekend with his dad. Think his dad may catch me over here what would he think?

I don't care what he thinks we been divorce for over three years.

He married the bitch that he was cheating on while he was with me. When I found out I gave him to her. He was so damn dumb I got me a lawyer and took everything he had and his ass still paying me money and will pay long after David is grown.

Oh well, I will lay here on your couch for a few hours okay she said.

I was waiting for her to tell me to go to bed with her. She came back with a pillow and a blanket good night Leroy. And she took her black ass in her room. I laid there and started to think about Johnnie Mae I knew she would let me get in the bed with her all night. I can't believe Terry, I need her tonight. I fell asleep, and Terry never came out that room. I woke up a few hours later and left her a note telling her thanks for the couch hope to see you again. I left and went to Johnnie Mae's house.

As soon as I walked in the door ring, ring, ring, hello I said. Where in the hell you been? I been calling you all night and don't you lie to me.

Well hello to you Johnnie Mae how is everything going?

Don't change the subject motherfucker I don't want people in my house or car. No one is in your house or car woman. Are you on your way home? I call to tell you what I want you to know, I don't want to come home and beat your ass. Oh women stop acting crazy. Well I have to stay a few more days I'll call you tomorrow here is my number good bye. She hung up the phone. Boy that damn woman is crazy.

What have I got myself in to? I stayed home all day and listened to the ball game and laid around the house most of the day.

I wanted to go back to Terry's house I kept thinking about her.

She is so different from Johnnie Mae, Terry acts like a real lady I really want to get to know her. I want her in my life and I like JJ for some reason, I feel like I've known him all my life. My heart feels good when I'm around him he is the first real friend I made since I have been here. I couldn't stay in the house I started hearing noises, so I got in Johnnie Mae's car and started to drive around. I began to see a familiar place I knew where I was, Oh shit, I said to myself my heart stopped and my body begin to shake. I looked in the ditch and I saw my brother dead in the ditch this is where I killed my brother. Oh shit I had to get away fast as I could I got so scared, all of a sudden I heard sirens oh no the police was behind me. I wanted to keep driving but I pulled over. The police got out come to the car. Where you going so fast boy? Let me see your license, I didn't have a license. I started to drive off but I knew he would follow me and call for back up. All of a sudden the officer got a call, said it was emergency call he ran back to the car and I started crying.

Wondering what to say to him all I could think of was shit, I started to beat on the dash board the officer drove away. I drove off and said to myself Leroy Chester take your ass home you was lucky today. I hurried back home and parked the car.

I was trying to hurry inside I heard Sam calling my name, I didn't want to talk I needed me a drink. Leroy, Leroy, I kept going. I pretend like I didn't hear him. I got in the house and slam the door sat down and tried to calm myself. I sat there and my legs act like they couldn't move. What the hell wrong with me? John was killed in Texas, what am I scared of boy was I glad that the cop drove off.

That was so close, I got up and fixed me a drink I really needed it.

When I was younger I wasn't scared of no damn body. Now, I don't know what's wrong with me I knew I had to stay out of Johnnie Mae's car until I got a license. I was sitting in the dark I didn't even turn on the lights when I came in. Ring, ring, oh shit I jumped the phone scared the shit out of me. Hello, Well I see you got your ass at home.

Johnnie Mae don't start no shit with me I ain't in no damn mood to listen to that shit I hung up. Ring, ring, I knew it was Johnnie Mae so I didn't answer it. God why did I take this job in Little Rock? What the hell was I thinking when I came to this damn town. I must be losing my damn mind I'm drinking more every day.

The job ain't shit I'm getting tired of looking at old lady Cross and her damn husband I don't trust him. I get to work and there is old man Cross, good morning I said. Are you all right Leroy? You look like you had a bad night. Old man Cross spoke up and said you need to lay off that bottle boy, you can't keep a job drinking all the time. See you at home Sally if you need me I'll be back with my gun to help you.

Leroy don't, mind him. Leroy the white people here in Little Rock don't like it that you got this job I been hearing talk you be careful.

Thank you Mrs. Cross.

I know I need to go home after work but, I had to go by the bar to see JJ and ask him about Terry. I don't want her to come by Johnnie Mae's house. I want to get to know her real good I want her. When I got to the bar JJ was there. Hey Leroy be with you in a minute. I found me a table and JJ came over, Terry told me she let you come home with her last night. Terry is a good girl I don't want you to hurt her, her ex-husband didn't treat her right. I like her I would never hurt her. You know Leroy I like you man. Something about you makes me happy we're friends. I like you to JJ I feel the same way about you. I'll talk to you later man I left and went home. About twenty five minutes later there was a knock on the door, I opened the door and Lord there stood Lucille, what the hell you doing here?

I came to see your fine ass (she said). I wanted to slam the door in her face. She stood there grinning two teeth missing from the front of her mouth. She has short hair weigh about two hundred and fifty four pounds. She had a big ass and her left eye was a little cocked. I didn't want to be mean to her. She was drunk and I knew she wasn't thinking clear, I didn't want to be with her ugly ass. I knew she was Terry's friend and I didn't want Terry to think I was a bastard. I wouldn't let Lucille in the house. She was trying to push herself in. I pushed her back and said let's sit on the porch I didn't want anyone telling that crazy ass Johnnie Mae I had a woman in her house. Sit down Lucille.

Well if you don't want my ass, give me a drink.

Look like you have had too many all ready. Oh shit here come Sam have they fired his ass? Hey Leroy did you hear me calling you? No man, I was trying to get in the house when nature call you ain't got time to talk. Yes, I know all about that, I saw Lucille over here and just wanted to tell you man you got to be careful old Lucille like giving up the ass. Sam you get your ass back across that street with them four ass kids you got. Look like all you do is hump Hattie's ass all night, that's why you got all them damn bad kids. So you damn show can't talk about me I may give my ass up it's mine. I ain't got a lot of bad ass kids running around my house eating up every damn thing in sight.

Anyway, Sam get your black ass across that street with Hattie, I came over here to see Leroy.

You kiss my ass, you no teeth bitch. Leroy you see what kind of woman she is nothing but a damn drunk ass bitch. Lucille jumped up from her chair picked up a flower pot off the porch and tried to hit Sam. She lost her balance and fell flat on her ass, Sam and I had to laugh we laughed and laughed. Fuck both of you bastards she left going down the street cussing, Sam look like you just lost a friend. Oh man we been doing each other like this for years, next week she will be back over to the house for the cookout she is always the first one there, and last one to leave to get one more drink before she leaves. She always want to give up that ass, the only one who took her cross eye ass was Jimmy Adams. Jimmy Adams (I said), Johnnie Mae's ex-boyfriend. Yes, (he said). I laughed and laughed. Did Johnnie Mae know? Yes that is one of the reasons Johnnie put him out both of them was drunk, they woke up in Johnnie's bed and scared each other. Boy I laughed and laughed. Did she come over to give you some?

Oh I can't handle that, Lucille have too much ass for me I like a medium size woman. Well, I like a fat woman, Hattie was small when we got married, and every time she had a baby she got fatter. I still love her she is a good woman. Leroy is the women in Oklahoma like the one's here in Little Rock? Well I don't know I never took the time to meet a lot of women. I know I had a real good mother until her husband left her and he never came back. I still haven't got over my mama's death; I don't think I ever will. Since I have been here I met Johnnie Mae and Terry. I like to see more of her, Oh Terry okay she don't take shit off of nobody either. What you going to do about Johnnie? Hattie said Johnnie said, she going to make you her man. Johnnie Mae can't make me do nothing that I don't want to I'm like my dad. I'm my own man I do what the hell I want to and it will always be that way with me no woman can change me.

My mama told me my daddy always wanted me to be like him scared of nothing or no one.

I didn't want to tell Sam about my daddy, how he rape women and wanted me to think he was my grandfather. I'm not ready to tell anyone in Little Rock about my life.

Sam I been seeing you home a lot this week everything okay?

Yes, I took vacation time I don't have money to go nowhere so I'm just helping Hattie doing things around the house. Well I guess I'd go back across the street, when Johnnie Mae coming back? I don't know she didn't say, what are you doing the rest of the day? Oh I don't know. Maybe we can go down to the bar after awhile.

Okay,(I said), Sam left and went back home. I sat on the porch for a little while and then went in the house and started to think about Terry, if I had my license I'll get in that car and go see her. Ring, ring, I knew that was Johnnie Mae, I don't need her ass checking up on me. Hello, took your ass long enough to pick up the phone. I was just getting ready to hang up, what took you so long? Nigger you got some woman in my house? Yes, (I said).

Lucille. Lucille, that damn cross eye no teeth Lucille. The one they sing about. I started laughing I knew I could get her. You pick me up at the train station tomorrow at 2: pm. I can't believe you got that bitch in my house do you need ass that bad. Pick me up and don't be late. I'm getting my bat and I'm going to beat your ass and Lucille with it.

Crazy ass woman I was begging to wonder if all the women in Oklahoma was like the one's I met here. Terry is the best looking woman I've seen since I been here. I'm sure there are others I haven't been here long enough, I got ready to go to the bar.

I love to drink but, I don't get drunk where I don't know what I'm doing anymore since I spent the night with JJ. He said I fell asleep, I sure hope so I like JJ I don't want to kill his ass. Sam came over and we walked to the bar. Oh Sam can you take me to the train station tomorrow to pick up Johnnie Mae?

What time? 2:00 pm. Sure I will. We got to the bar and it was jumping what is tonight? Friday pay day let's find a table (I said) Oh you go ahead Leroy I like to see who all here. I'll find you later. I found me a table it was in the back, I sat down and watched them dance they was having so much fun.

The Man on the Train

This fine ass girl came over to my table, would you like a drink she said? Gin and make it a double. Be right back (she said). Where is JJ? Is he off tonight?

When she came back I said what's your name? Wilma. Wilma what time you get off tonight? Got a boyfriend? No, I got a husband and he taking me home tonight sorry. (She said) and walked off. I looked around and I could see some of the women looking at me I knew they wanted to come over to me. Before I left home I looked in the mirror and I look good. I'm a very handsome man, I'm 5'9 light brown eyes, light brown skin, 142 pounds, and very good hair. I do look just like James Chester. He had a lot of women in Derry.

I never took a good look at myself until tonight. I know I look good, I looked up and here come a lady. Hello, would you like to dance she said. Oh I don't dance.

Come on I'll teach you it's easy, I got up and she took me by the hand and said follow me. Just listen to the music and let your body move to the music. Put your arm around me stand close to me and close your eyes and move your feet side to side. She put her arms around me I closed my eyes and I started to dance. I open my eyes and I was looking into hers she smiled at me and I got a little closer to her. She felt good in my arms, just as it was feeling good another song came on it was faster. I watched the guys and like the way they danced I started to laugh and was having fun. The young woman started laughing and singing I asked her who was singing that song. She said it's was call baby shake that thing.

Man, I was so happy and I was just doing what everyone else was doing. She said, I caught on real fast I wanted to keep dancing but we walked back to our table and she said I'm Addie. I'm Leroy, thank you Miss Addie for the dance you are the first lady I ever dance with. Oh come on good looking man like you, I bet you have all the women after you. Not me, can I buy you another drink?

Do you come here often I said? No this is my first time here I'm meeting a friend she is a little late. Are you here with anyone? Yes, my friend Sam I don't see him, I wonder where he went to. I'm sure he here somewhere, oh there's my friend. Addie started waving at someone. Oh shit, oh shit here come Terry and Lucille all I could do was sit there I couldn't move. Well hello Leroy, I see you don't waste time. I see you know my friend Addie. We just met I said. You two know each other said Addie. Yes we know each other I found your note and you didn't leave your number. I didn't think you wanted to see me again I said. Well I see you now will you dance with me? I got up and went to the dance floor; I put my arm around her and told her I would like to get to know her better.

Terry I been working late and going straight home to rest. I came in here last week looking for you and JJ said he hadn't seen you in a couple of days. I couldn't tell her I was working late at night making love to Johnnie Mae. Can you go home with me tonight? I came here with Sam. I haven't seen him since we got here. Oh he may be back in the other room, they gamble in there. All of a sudden I heard cussing and someone go down on the floor. Someone was beating the hell out of Sam they said he was cheating I went to help him but Terry pulled me back, don't get in it Leroy.

Sam, have to learn to stop cheating this is not his first time he got his ass beat up. I can't just stand here Terry and do nothing. Yes you can.

Terry held on to me.

The man kicked Sam's ass out the door the people kept dancing, the music was loud they was playing a song call all night long. None of them ran out they kept on having fun, they act like nothing was happening. Terry told me to put Sam in her car and she would take him home. She told Lucille and Addie she was leaving and would they be okay.

Lucille said we can find away home. Take your scared ass home Leroy (Lucille said). Terry we need to take Sam to a doctor or the hospital he looked bad. No, let's take him home Hattie can do it. Sam, are you alright? I'll be okay I'm going back and kill that black bastard. No Sam, we are taking you home. When we got to Sam house I told Terry to go to the door and tell Hattie what happened when I got Sam out of the car. Tell Hattie to make sure her kids are sleep I don't want them kids to see him like this it's too much blood for them to see. Hattie came to the door I can hear Sam is he alright? I took him in the house. Put him in the bedroom Hattie said. Hattie went and got a pan of water and I helped her clean him up. Hattie he need, to go to the doctor. Oh Leroy I'll let him sleep it off.

I'll check on him. Hattie, call me if you need me to come back. Thank you Leroy you too Terry I told him not to take his ass back

The Man on the Train

down to that bar. That's why I have cookouts so his dumb ass can go in there and go to sleep when he get drunk.

Thank you for bring him home. I'll check on Sam tomorrow. Okay Leroy.

Come on Leroy go home with me? No I don't feel like sleeping on a cold couch tonight. For some reason I feel strange when I'm around Terry and JJ lately. I don't understand what it is. I'll just walk home I'm just across the street can I come in with you? No, Terry, I only have one room. Johnnie Mae, don't want women in the house when she not home.

I have to respect her house. If she put me out I don't have any place to go. You're a good man Leroy can I kiss you good night? I started to kiss Terry like the way Johnnie Mae taught me but kissing Terry was nice and sweet. We kept kissing and I had to go home with her tonight. Terry baby I need you please baby take me home with you.

I got back in the car with her and she drove home, after we got inside we went straight to her bedroom we made love she made me feel like I was the only man she ever had and I loved every minute of it. Terry I'm in love with you, I don't want to leave. Leroy I think we need to go a little slow I don't even know your last name you haven't told me about you. What do you want to know?

Everything about you start when you were a little boy. Oh Terry it will take me hours and hours. Right now let's just enjoy tonight together okay (she said) we made more love and fell asleep. Oh man she is sweet I wanted to stay all day when we got up I looked at the clock, and shit it was almost time to pick up Johnnie Mae. Terry can you take me home, I need to pick up Johnnie Mae I told her I would that is why she left me her car. Yes. I got out kissed her and told her I would see her later. I got the keys to Johnnie Mae car and drove to the train station. While I was waiting for her to get off the train I saw this man on the train, I stood there oh shit, oh shit it's Al Jenkins. I kept looking until he got off the train I couldn't move I was scared as shit, I just kept standing there. Leroy, what's the hell wrong with you? You look like you seen a ghost, are you alright?

Johnnie Mae I thought I saw someone I knew but it was someone else. Damn I sure would like to know who it was your ass look so scared as if you was a nigger going to be hung(she said), Oh shit get in

33

the car. Are you glad to see me? Yes. Well you don't act like it. Listen Johnnie, I don't want to hear no shit from you.

I'll get your things out of the car she walked into the house. I got all the things out of the car and asked her if she wanted everything in her room? Yes. She start to look at me real strange I didn't feel like trying to explain anything to her so I just walk over to Sam to see how he was doing. I knocked on the door Hattie came to the door.

How is Sam Hattie? He's still in bed come on in you know Leroy, he need to stop getting beat up like this. Next time he may not make it somebody might kill him. Is Sam sleep? Go on in his room. I went to Sam's bed room I walk in he had his back turned to the door. Sam, Sam he turned over. Man you look like you been ran over by a train, you need to go to the doctor.

Leroy thank you again for helping Terry bring me home last night. Terry told me how you wanted to help me but she stop you. Man I don't want you to get hurt because I'm going to get that bastard soon as I get well, he better watch his back, I'm going to get him when he ain't expecting it. Do you need anything Sam?

No thank you Hattie taking good care of me. Sam I can't tell you what to do but you need to stay out of that bar. Man you got kids to take care of you don't, need nothing else happening to you. I'll be alright Leroy thank you. I'll let you get some rest I'll come back tomorrow. Hattie if you need anything let me know. I will Leroy you're a good man. I smiled and walked back to Johnnie Mae's when I got in the house Johnnie was sitting there with her mouth stuck out. What's wrong with you? Leroy I thought you would be glad to see me, did you really have Lucille in my house?

No, she came over here and I sat on the porch with her and Sam. Sam came over and we all talked, Sam made her mad and she left cussing both of us. I was wondering if you wanted Lucille. Hell no! I don't want her ugly ass, I 'm sorry you didn't get the welcome you wanted. I'm not in a good mood today I went to my room and started to think about that man that I saw that look like Al Jenkins.

I thought about John and started to cry, Lord are they coming back to get me? I feel asleep I woke up because I heard a knock on the door I heard someone ask is Leroy Chester here? I went down stairs and there stood the police. Leroy we need you to go down town with

The Man on the Train

us. What for? Come on with us Leroy, get in the car we taking you in. I looked at Johnnie Mae and, her eyes, was as big as a damn owl.

Leroy, what have you done?

Nothing! Yes, you have they wouldn't be taking you to jail for nothing. What did he do officer? We just want to question him. About what (she said). I got in the car and they wouldn't say anything to me. I started to wonder if they had found out I'm the one who killed Al and John. When we got to the police station they took me to a room and told me to wait in there someone will be with me in a minute. I sat there it seem like an hour, so much running through my mind. What was I going to say to them? I was getting so scared oh Lord my life is over. A police detective walked in hello Leroy, I'm detective Wood I understand you were at the State Street Bar last night. "Yes." I understand you came with Sam Hicks. Yea, what is this all about? Sam Hicks died a few hours ago. What! What! What you say?

I just told you Sam Hicks is dead. No you have the wrong man I just talked to Sam a few hours ago. I was over to his house a few hours ago, you have the wrong man. No we have the right man I need you to tell me what happened at the bar last night. Do you know the man who beat Sam to death? I sat there and I looked at the detective like he was crazy. I couldn't believe Sam was dead so fast, Leroy talk to me what do you know about the man you saw everything didn't you? No I was talking to a lady when I saw Sam and a man fighting. Who is the lady? Terry Johnson, we were talking getting ready to leave when Sam and this man came out of a room fighting.

The, man kick Sam out of the bar, Terry and I took Sam home he was in bad shape. His wife told us she would take care of him, I helped clean him up and I left. I went back over there today and he said he would be okay, so I left.

Well he died two hours ago. Oh Lord what in the world Hattie going to do? I don't know a lot of people here I just moved here a few months ago. Yes, I know you're from Oklahoma I understand you maybe a suspect in a murder that happen there. Do you know anything about that? No, I haven't killed nobody. Well, the next time you see a cop coming to your door it will be to pick you up. I looked up at him and I wanted to take off running but I knew I had to keep cool. Do you know the man if you saw him again? No, it was dark in there I was more concerned about Sam.

I couldn't believe it Sam was a nice man. Don't leave town we may need to talk to you again you can go now. I walked out of the room to call Johnnie Mae to pick me up when Terry walked in with the police. Terry what are you doing here? They pick me up and said Sam died. She started to cry they wanted to question me about last night.

I'll wait here for you. Thank, you Leroy. I sat on the bench they had in the hall I was thinking damn they haven't forgot about Al Jenkins I really have to be careful. Damn my life is coming after me I thought if I left Oklahoma. I thought I could leave everything behind me.

I sat there for an hour. Terry came out. Why did you stay so long?

They wanted to know about him to and who he had a fight with. That is why I told you to stay out of it. I can't believe it Terry I just left Sam he said he would be okay. I went home and fell asleep I didn't know I had been sleep so long. The police woke me up knocking on the door they brought me down here for questioning. Terry how are you going home? I called JJ he is on his way he can drop you off at home. I didn't want to go home, Terry will you be alright? No Leroy, I feel so sorry for Sam and Hattie.

Leroy, will you go home with me? Yes. JJ came and took us to Terry's house he had to go back to work. When we were in the house we sat on the couch, I put my arms around Terry and she started to cry again. Baby cry all you want I'm here for you, I started to kiss her and she kiss me back and I told her I loved her. The next thing I knew we were in bed making love. Terry asked me if I would stay all night with her.

What about your son?

What will he think? This is my house I say who stay and who goes. He been, wanting to stay with his dad but I won't let him until he gets older. You can stay in bed if you want to, David will be home soon and I need to get dress. Are you hungry? Yes.

She, made breakfast it felt nice to be with her. This, young man walked in and looked at me and stop. This is my friend Leroy, Leroy this is my son David. Hello David, he gave me a weak hello. Be nice Terry said, Leroy came home with me because Sam died today. Oh he did. Police picked Leroy up for questions. He gave me a look as if I had killed Sam. You know I told you last night Sam got into a fight and Leroy and I was there. Police picked us up to tell them what happened. Food is almost ready you hungry? No, I need to go to my room for a while nice to meet you Leroy you to David he walked out. Terry I better go will you drop me off at work? Thank you for the breakfast hope one day I can get more (I smiled).

David I'll be back in a little bit. Okay mom. Terry drop me off at work.

When I got out of the car I went around to kiss her when will I see you again? Whenever you want to she said and drove off. When I walked in Sally Cross said Leroy what happened? My husband said he saw you in the police car.

A friend of mines died today his name is Sam Hicks. Oh that colored boy that, work at Gibson's grocery store. Yes you know him? Yes I go in the store a lot. I went in my office and closed the door and I thought about how nice Sam was to me when I moved here. I thought about the last time I talked to him about getting the man that beat him up. I thought about my mama when I found her beat to death. God what more going to happen in my life? Will it ever stop?

After work I went home when I walked in Johnnie Mae started in on me.

What lie you going to tell me now? You been gone all day and all night you didn't go to work yesterday because I called there they said you hadn't called in or showed up. I called the police station and they said, you was not locked up. I been worrying sick you didn't come home last night, you could have called me and let me know you were alright. You could have called me to see if I was alright.

You was out with that damn Lucille. I looked at her (and said) I told you before I don't want that damn woman. You are not my wife or my girl friend, I only rent a room from you do you understand that Miss Johnnie Mae? Where I go and who I'm with is none of your damn business do you understand me?

Kiss my ass and if you reach for that bat you're a dead motherfucker she ran out of the room.

I walked out and went over to Hattie's to see if I could do anything for her and the kids. She was trying to make funeral arrangements. Hattie, can I help? No I wish he had stayed home.

She, begin to cry. I put my arms around her and told her everything will be alright Sam was a good man. He loved you and the kids. I know Leroy I'll let you know the day of the funeral. Okay Hattie I left and went back across the street and looked up and saw Johnnie Mae peeping out the window. I didn't want to hear no more shit so I just sat on the porch. Every once in a while I could see Johnnie Mae peeping out the window. I kept sitting there next thing I had fell asleep, when I woke up it was dark I had been out there for over an hour. I could see Johnnie Mae still peeping out her window I got up and went in the house and she didn't say anything to me.

Johnnie I'm sorry the way I been acting I have so much on my mind Sam dying and you coming home all on my case it's to much for me. I went to my room.

A few days later Hattie had Sam's funeral it was nothing like the one I had for my mama. It was a happy funeral the people singing and getting happy the preacher was saying Sam was gone to heaven and he was a good man. God took him to be with him in heaven and he didn't want to come back to this world he found God. Then after the funeral the people started to dance down the street playing music. Sam's body was in a carriage being pulled by horses.

Shit I said to myself people in Little Rock is different from the people in Oklahoma. After everything was over we went to Hattie's house all of her family and friends was there. They had so much food and drinks some of the people were, dancing said they was celebrating Sam's home going.

Terry was there we was standing there talking and in walk.

Johnnie Mae, and of course Lucille was there with her drunk ass. I walk over and started to talk to some of the men there I didn't want trouble out of Johnnie Mae. Things were going fine. People kept talking and dancing, eating just having fun. I fixed me a drink and I was enjoying everything.

Lucille came over got in front of me and said dance with me Leroy with your fine ass. Terry said oh go on with her it's a celebration for Sam go ahead. I started to dance with Lucille just having fun I looked over and I could see Johnnie Mae looking. I felt all of a sudden something was going to happen before I could do anything Johnnie Mae had Lucille by her hair. Telling her she didn't want her at her house when she not home. Lucille was trying to get away from her and Johnnie Mae kept holding on to her hair when old drunk ass Lucille got free she grab Johnnie Mae and man she beat the shit out of Johnnie Mae.

No one tried to stop them because they wanted to see who could whoop the other one ass. Lucille was bad with her big ass, Johnnie Mae got her ass whooped by a short cross eye ugly ass woman. When Lucille got through Johnnie took out running like a rocket shot up her ass. I couldn't help it I laughed and laughed and then the people started to laugh, it was funny. Hattie told Lucille to take her ass home and she put Lucille out.

Terry told me to come home with her, Terry told me to get in the car with her we drove off I looked over to Johnnie Mae house and I couldn't see her peeping out the window. When I got to Terry's house I started to think about Johnnie Mae I wondered if she was alright. I thought about Sam dying after he was beat up, Terry I'm sorry I need to go see if Johnnie Mae is alright. Here take this drink you look like you need it. David, I'll be back in a while get your homework. Terry I hope Lucille didn't hurt Johnnie Mae too bad. Then I started to laugh and laugh. What you laughing about Leroy? I'm thinking about that damn no teeth drunk ass Lucille could beat that bat swinging ass Johnnie Mae.

Let Lucille whoop her ass I bet if Johnnie Mae had that bat with her she would have beat the shit out of Lucille. She would have had Lucille ass running like the police was after her for stealing a chicken. Ha, ha, ha I laughed so hard Terry started to laugh too she was laughing hard as I was. Watch it girl you gone have us in that ditch, after Terry put me out I told her I would see her soon. Do you want me to go in with you to see if I can help you? No I'll take care of everything I love you Terry, I love you too I kissed her by. I went in and I went to Johnnie Mae's door, Johnnie Mae are you okay? She didn't say anything. I opened her door and she was crying she turned over and her face and lips were swollen. Damn Johnnie is that damn Lucille a man?

She really fucked you up. I went in the kitchen got a towel and water and cleaned her up. I felt real bad for her let me take you to the doctor. She looked at me with tears in her eyes Leroy, why didn't you come home with me? Why did you let her beat me like this? You stayed over there knowing I was hurt. You don't care about me I been real good to you since you been here living with me.

Johnnie Mae I didn't know you were beat this bad. I'm sorry. When I see her again I'm going to beat her ass she gone wish she never put her hands on me. I'm going to beat her ass with my bat. Johnnie you better leave her alone you see what happened to Sam. I don't think you want to mess with Lucille anymore just leave it alone. Are you sure you won't let me take you to the doctor before I go to bed?

Leroy, will you sleep with me tonight? I think you should rest, you know I told you I found my mother beat to death and I feel so sad for her and you. I'll be glad to take you to the doctor. Fuck you Leroy.

I looked at this woman tears running down her face. I'll sit here with you until you fall asleep. Do you have anything for pain? I'll go over to Hattie to see if she have anything. Hattie gave me something for pain. I sat there with her until she fell asleep I got up and walked down to the bar. I didn't feel like talking to no one not even JJ.

I just wanted to get drunk. I got me a table in the corner so I could see everyone coming in and out. I thought about the last time I was in here with Sam. They was going on about their business drinking and dancing like nothing had happen there a few days ago. I thought Terry would walk through that door I wanted her to take me back home with her, but she never came. I was getting ready to leave and in walk old drunk ass Lucille. She saw me leaving. Leroy. What the hell do you want Lucille? I want to know why the hell Johnnie Mae tried to jump on me.

I ain't done nothing to her is the bitch crazy? Are you fucking her and Terry too? You listen Lucille, I told you to keep your nose out of my business. I told you that you don't know who you fucking with. One day they may find your drunk ass in a ditch somewhere. Fuck you Leroy you make sure Johnnie Mae don't put your ass in one.

She walked off. I went home went to Johnnie Mae's room to see if she was alright. Johnnie, she wouldn't say nothing I knew she was still alive and mad. I close the door and went up to my room thinking since I've been here it's nothing but trouble.

The people in, Oklahoma wasn't always up in your business.

I'm glad I'm saving all my money so I can one day leave here real soon. I don't have any bills all I do is pay rent I just save my money I give Johnnie Mae a little money on food. I spend a little money on my drinks but that's about all. Johnnie Mae stayed home over a week before she went back to work to make sure her face went down. Every chance I got I went to see Terry I didn't want to make love to Johnnie Mae any more. She kept asking me why I won't move in her bedroom with her. I told her I was tired and she needed to get better. She, still think I'm seeing Lucille, I just stop trying to tell her I was not seeing Lucille. I told Johnnie Mae I need to go get me a license I need me a car.

Leroy you can drive my car. I can't ride my friends in your car. I went the next day to get my license JJ let me use his car. Now I need to find me one I'll be able to see Terry whenever I want to. Johnnie Mae said I been acting strange to her every since she came back from South Carolina.

Leroy if I find out you making a fool out of me you going to be sorry. I just don't want Johnnie Mae. She not the kind of woman I want. A few weeks later they found the man the killed Sam. They said, Sam died because of a blood clot to the head because of the beating. I was sitting on the porch I just fixed me a drink and was just watching the kids play. Johnnie Mae came out and sat down there was people going in and out of Hattie's house. She was still having cook outs. Sam had left her insurance money from working at the Gibson Store. Gibson was still helping her because he felt sorry for her kids.

I was looking to see if Terry car was over there but I didn't see it. I saw that damn Lucille, coming out she looked over and saw me and Johnnie Mae, please God let her keep going please Lucille don't come over here with your drunk ass starting nothing.

God let her keep walking I looked at Johnnie Mae and I could see the fear and rage in her eyes. I could see her tighten up Lucille was still in the street. Johnnie Mae said you better tell that bitch to keep on walking. Lucille looked over and said Johnnie Mae you want some more ass whooping Leroy show know how to please a good woman and it show ain't you. She started laughing and laughing going down the street she turned around and said ain't that right Leroy, I got good ass.

She kept laughing and going down the street. Johnnie Mae looked at me and said you lying bastard. Lucille is drunk I told you I ain't slept with that woman. I'm tired of your bullshit I'm going to find me somewhere else to live. I went up to my room closed the door and I heard Johnnie Mae's car drive off. I ran down the stairs and out the door. I couldn't stop her I didn't have a car to follow her I looked around the corner and Johnnie Mae was gone.

Johnnie Mae's bat was gone oh shit, no, Johnnie, Oh God please don't let her hit Lucille with that bat. Please, please I said to myself. I waited and waited and it seemed so long. I was standing at the door when she drove up she got out of the car and blood was all over her. My heart stopped I couldn't move Johnnie was crying. What the hell did you do Johnnie? What the fuck did you do? Stop crying and talk to me. I beat her ass she won't be fucking nobody else man. I asked her if you was her man and she kept saying no. I kept beating her ass and she kept saying no. She said, she was only trying to make me mad. Then I knew she was telling me the truth. Oh Leroy, what have I done? Leroy, I should have listened to you I'm so sorry. Where is she?

I found her still walking down the street I pulled up beside her and she started to run and I got my bat and followed her she ran in the ally and I started to beat that ass with my bat she lost her balance and tried to get up she said I beat your ass once and I'm going to do it again. I knew if she did she would try to take that bat from me and try to whip me with it. So I hit her again and her ass fell down and she didn't get up. I thought about how she whooped me in front of everyone so I beat her ass before she could get up. Johnnie Mae did you kill her?

I don't know I just beat her until she stopped begging me. Did anyone see you? Yes a lot of people heard her screaming and they were standing around. I ran to the car with the bat still in my hand. A man came to me and I hit him with the bat I dropped it and I drove away and came home. Leroy, help me please what can I do? Come on hurry I'll take you to the train station you go back to South Carolina. Come on Johnnie I'll take care of everything for you after you get to South Carolina call me and tell me what to do.

Leroy I don't want to go to jail. Well come on hurry. She grabbed her purse and as we were walking out the door there was knock, we just stood there. Bam, bam Johnnie Mae opened this damn door this is the police open up. I opened the door and let them in. Johnnie Mae was standing there crying. I'm sorry Leroy, please don't let them take me to jail. The police read her rights, and hand cuffed her and took her off to jail. I watched her cry and they drove away I wished now I had stayed in Oklahoma. Lucille died. Oh my God why did you bring me into this world all I can remember is nothing but unhappiness in my life. I can't believe that this is all happening to me.

I know I'm suffering for killing Al and John God please forgive me. Johnnie Mae was charged with first degree murder they told her she will never get out of prison. I went down the next day to see her Leroy she said, I don't have anyone but my cousin in South Carolina will you help me? Yes, I'll do whatever I can. Call my lawyer his name is in the book beside my telephone, I need to talk to him. Okay. Leroy I wish I had listened to you but after you started to treat me like you did not sleeping with me I thought you were sleeping with Lucille.

I never got over catching her in my bed with Jimmy. After I heard what she said to you I just went crazy I never liked her in the first place. And when you told me she was at my house I just couldn't get over it. I was only teasing you. I'm so sorry Johnnie Mae I didn't know thing would turn out this way.

Now I know I didn't believe you. I only wanted hit her so she could feel a little pain, but after she kept trying to talk smack to me about you, that you don't want me you had another woman. I didn't want to hear it from her so I hit her a little harder at the time I just wanted her to shut up. Johnnie Mae all I can say is I'm so sorry I didn't know you would get that mad. Because I was only playing with you I never thought you would ever think I was really sleeping with Lucille. Leroy, will you take care of all my stuff? Everything I have, what do you want me to do with it? I need to talk to my lawyer first maybe he can help me out of this mess. I'll see you tomorrow Johnnie. Okay Leroy. Leroy. Yes. I want to tell you I love you I wanted you to be my man. I thought you would be the man that would always love me.

Now it will never be because of my jealously, I'm sorry Johnnie I have to go I'll see you tomorrow. After I left I went straight to the bar to make since of all this mess. I just wanted to get so drunk that I could put this night mere behind me and try to make some kind of since of it. I couldn't go to work for days I just got drank for days.

When I did go to work Sally Cross said Leroy where have you been? I been trying to cover for you? There is someone in your office for you thank you Mrs. Cross. I walked in and there was Mr. Sheets from Oklahoma office that sent me to Little Rock. Hi, Mr. Sheets what are you doing here? Hi Leroy, I been getting a lot of complaints about you and your work here. The people that work here said you been coming to work drunk you always late. What happened to you son?

You're a good worker that's why I sent you here. They said, they saw you in a police car you was involved in a murder. Leroy you was my best man, I'm not involved in a murder I was questioned because I saw a man get beat up. I'm sorry Mr. Sheets I been going through a lot since I been here. Why didn't you talk to me son?

Who, been telling you all this Mr. Sheets?

I been getting calls from George Cross he had people following you. He never liked me since I been here. I'm sorry Leroy after I came here I been talking to some of the other workers and they say the same things. They don't want you here so I have no choice but to let you go. Here is your check for the days you work and here is your retirement for the time you work for the company. It's my entire fault Mr. Sheets I'm sorry I let you down. When, you come back to Oklahoma call me. Sure I will. I'll clean out my desk and leave. As I was leaving Sally said she was sorry she gave me a big hug. Leroy, I'm going to miss you, George walked in get your damn hands off my wife boy. I told you I was watching you now get the hell out of here.

I looked at that old man and I wanted to cut his damn head off. I walked toward him and it scared the shit out of him. You better stay away from me boy. Leroy, Sally (said) he ain't worth getting hurt over. Good bye Sally. Good luck Leroy, I walked out after I got home I couldn't stay there I had so much on my mind I had to go to the bar. I was glad I didn't have to go back to that damn job. I knew they didn't want me there when I first came here. I'm glad I saved me some money to last me a long while. I had left the five hundred dollars in the bank in Derry that I found in my mama's purse. She had a small Insurance I used to bury her with.

I sat there in the bar and tried to think where I go from here. Poor Lucille, she was a smart mouth and a damn drunk she don't deserve to die either. I need to get out of this damn town I need to go by to see Terry.

I went to her house when I got there she was not at home her son David said she was out of town and he didn't know when she would be back. Tell her I came by (Okay he said) and closed the door. I drove around and I saw a park I stopped got out and sat on one of the benches to think and just relax. A white man walked up to me sir, sir. I looked at him and he said this park is for white only you can't sit here please leave.

I started to get up and kick the shit out of him. Where in hell can you go in this town without saying color can't do this can't sit here, can't work here. I felt like fucking up everybody I got up and left.

I started to wonder where was Terry she don't call me to see why Johnnie Mae killed Lucille. I wonder if she knew and was mad at me. I went back home and when I drove up in the drive way here come Hattie. Leroy what in the world happened to Johnnie Mae and Lucille? What did Lucille do to Johnnie? Did she have to kill her?

Damn Leroy have, everybody going crazy they got the man that killed Sam. Yes I heard. What they gone do to Johnnie Mae?

Hang her or beat her to death. Why did you say that? Well Leroy that's what the people do down here. They don't give a damn about these color folks you didn't say why Johnnie killed Lucille. It was about something that, happen to them a long time ago, Lucille got smart and teasing her something like that. Well that ain't no damn good reason to kill no body that damn Johnnie Mae is crazy anyway that's why I didn't fool with her.

Hattie I'll talk to you later I'm tired, well are you going to Lucille's funeral? I don't know, well when I find out I'll let you know. Okay Hattie. I went in the house and closed the door I haven't had anything to eat all day. I know I need to eat something I opened the ice box and got me a beer. I don't like beer. The phone ring I pick up the phone waiting for Johnnie Mae to say who you got in my house. Hello, Hi Leroy, this is Terry, David said you came by. I need to talk to you did you hear about Lucille? Yes, I do. What happened? I told her what happened we talked for an hour. I told her that I need to be with her come over she said, I was so glad I hurried and went over.

When I got there I told her about me loosening my job and wondering what was going to happen to Johnnie Mae. Lucille was

Terry's friend she didn't care what happened to Johnnie Mae she shouldn't have killed Lucille. She felt whatever they do was too good. What you going to do stay in Johnnie Mae house? I don't have no place to go unless I move back home to Oklahoma. Where have you been all day?

JJ and I was at our lawyer office, oh something wrong? Yes, a few years ago JJ father was killed and he want to find out who did it he been paying his lawyer to keep the case open If it took the rest of his life. He, want to find who ever killed him. JJ father was a real good man everyone who knew him loved him. He was so good to my mom JJ and me. He wasn't my real father but he loved me like I was his I never knew my real father he left my mom and never came back. JJ father married my mom when I was three years old later JJ was born. What did you say happen to your father? Oh let's talk about something else. What are you going to do about finding a new job?

Where can you work or do you know how to do something else? I don't know yet I have money to last me for a while. I'll wait and see what will come along. I need to get up in the morning to talk to Johnnie Mae to see if she, need me to do something for her. And see if she need anything. Do you care about her? Well yes she helped me when I came to town and showed me where to go. I'm sorry she killed Lucille. I was so tired and confused I didn't want to stay with Terry after all. I didn't even want to spend the night much as I loved making love to Terry I didn't want to. I just need to be by myself. Terry I think I'll go I need to be alone tonight. Okay Leroy, I'm not in the mood either I'll talk to you in a few days because there are things I need to take care of. I need to help JJ, I said good bye to her and we kissed and I left. When I got back to Johnnie Mae's house it was dark there was no lights on in the house. When I drove up in the drive way I saw someone run from the house. I didn't know if someone had broke into the house I sat there a few minutes before going in. After I got inside turned on the lights I looked around and nothing was wrong, I guess I scared whoever it was when I drove up. I didn't want to go up to my room tonight I went in the kitchen got me a knife first time I picked up a knife to hurt someone in a while. I fix me a drink and sit on the porch. When I woke up it was twelve p.m. I fixed me something to eat got dressed and went to see Johnnie Mae. Leroy thank you for coming to see me I hate it in here I want to go home. I

The Man on the Train

told them I didn't mean to kill her I'm so sorry to Johnnie. Have you talked to your lawyer? Yes, and he know what to do about everything I have. I know I may get a few years will you stay in my house until I come back? Yes, I'll take care of everything for you. They say if I plead guilty I would get a few years, but it will be up to the judge and the jury. Leroy you don't have to come here anymore I know you don't want to see me here, I hate being in here.

The food in here looks like a bunch of cat shit and it stink. I haven't had a bath since I been in here, I still have on the same clothes when I got in here. They said, they haven't had time to get to me. Will they let me bring you some clothes? No, I have to put on some orange jump suite when they get to me.

My lawyer said, he will see what he could do for me. My lawyer will come by to get me some clothes when I get ready for court. Will you be there for me? Yes, you know I will. I'll tell my lawyer to come by after you get off work. What time do you get off tomorrow? I was fired, I don't have a job. What because of me? No, Johnnie Mae the white people didn't want me working there anymore. What are you going to do? Oh I'll find something. When you go home look in the back of my closet there is a black bag in there with some money in their use it. I won't need it where I'm going. No I can't do that. Yes, you can and will. My mama left me a little money, my lawyer is paid he loved black women and I paid him a long time ago. He owes me a favor and he is taking care of everything. I told him what to do with all my stuff. Leroy, I don't think I'll ever come back; I can't make it in prison. I may die before I even go. Oh Johnnie, don't say that, I hate it here I can't sleep I hear Lucille laughing at me. Telling me, Johnnie Mae them white folks getting ready to fry your ass. Leroy I just can't take it. I don't know what to say Johnnie. I put my arms around her and kissed her. Johnnie if I only knew all this would have happened I would have done things different.

If they let me I'll trade places with you I'm the one that need to be lock up not you. She cried and cried I held on to her until the officer came in and told me I had to leave.

I'll see you tomorrow Johnnie. No Leroy I don't want you to come back I don't like for you coming here seeing me in here. Please don't come back. Leroy you have been kind to me every man I loved always wanted to beat on me. You never did. Thank you. I love you

Leroy please, don't come back because you will never see me again. Johnnie Mae what are you talking about? She started crying so hard I just wanted to take her by the hand and started running with her. Did you hear what I said boy?

You want me to lock your ass up in there with her? I kissed her bye and told her I love her and I hate to leave her. She was still crying. As I was leaving they came in with Jimmy Adams and locked him up in the cell next to Johnnie Mae I heard him say well, well look like your ass ain't going be swinging that bat no more. Where you going them women gone be batting that ass of yours. Ha, ha.

Poor Johnnie Mae she will have to listen to Jimmy until one of them leaves first. I didn't go back to see Johnnie Mae because the next day she was dead. I thought what did Jimmy do to her what happened so fast? I went down to the police station and asked them what happened? They said she had a heart attack. I thought Jimmy got on her nerves so bad she had a heart attack to get away from his drunk ass.

That afternoon I was sitting on the porch when a man drove up in a bright red nineteen sixty one Lincoln. He got out. May I help you?

Leroy Chester. Yes. I 'm Johnnie's lawyer, she wanted me to come by and talk to you and give you these letters. She wanted you to have them she wanted you to open them if something happened to her. Johnnie didn't want to spend the rest of her life in prison. They were talking about giving her eighty years. She couldn't take it she had a heart attack I loved Johnnie we been friends for years. I didn't want her to spend all her life in prison. I loved her too much. I rather see her dead than to spend the rest of her life unhappy rotting behind bars.

He had tears in his eyes, Leroy she loved you and wanted me to make sure I help take care of everything. Read these letters it's all in there! Good luck, Mr. Chester Thank you I said. Oh what about her cousin? Do I need to get in touch with him, so he can take care of her body? No, he can't do anything he can't walk he have to have someone to take care of him. Read the letters. Good day if you need anything if I can help you in anyway let me know. Johnnie told me to help you. My name is Donald Smith my office is on the corner of fourth and Main. Name is on the building.

The Man on the Train

Donald was a nice looking white man, he had dark brown hair brown eyes he was about five seven and weigh about one hundred and forty five pounds. After Donald left I locked the door and sat down to read the letters Johnnie left me. One letter said open after my death and the other one had the name City Nation Bank.

I just sat there wondering what Johnnie Mae had to say. I opened the first letter it said, Leroy

I'm sorry for what I did I asked God to forgive me. I know killing Lucille was wrong, I hope you never have to kill no one you're a good man. My eyes filled up with water.

If you reading the letter you know that I'm dead. I couldn't go to prison for the rest of my life so I asked Donald to help me. Donald and I go way back together we been friends since we were young. When I moved to Little Rock and even when I was married to my husband we had to keep it a secret. The white folks didn't like it because I was colored. His mom and dad didn't like it either but we kept seeing each other. I know they will be happy that my black ass is gone. Leroy, I'm leaving you everything that I owe even my mother's home in South Carolina, but my cousin will live in the house until he die my cousin is very sick.

My home is your do as you please live in it or sell it. It's yours remember when I told you to look in the bag in my closet there is twenty five thousand dollars I sold my mother's business when I was in South Carolina. I want you to take some of it and bury me with I have a red dress in my closet I like to be buried in. Give me a nice cheap funeral I want my body sent back to South Carolina on the train you don't have to go. Donald know what to do he will take care of the rest. I opened to other letter and it said, I Johnnie Mae La Doux being of sound mind leave, my property, all my money, my personal things to Leroy Chester. If anyone have a problem call my lawyer Donald Smith he know everything Johnnie Mae La Doux. I went to the funeral home and made the arrangement for her but Donald took care of every thing. Donald said he was having her body go straight to the cemetery for burying. I took the next letter to the bank to see, what she was talking about. When I walked in I asked for Mr. Newman, may I have your name? Leroy Chester. Follow me Mr. Chester. What can I do for you? I gave him the letter Johnnie Mae left. Oh Mr. Chester I been looking for you. Johnnie Mae's lawyer came in the other day everything is ready, I need you to sign some papers. Now Mr. Chester do you want to move your money to another bank or leave it here. Fifty thousand he said. What did you say? I'll leave it here. she also has an insurance policy worth thirty thousand it's all yours. I can't believe I didn't know Johnnie Mae had that kind of money. I thought she was struggling like everyone else. Johnnie Mae, own half of a restaurant with her mother it was a very successful one in South Carolina. Her mother was sending her money every month and sometime every week. Johnnie Mae just left it in the bank. She work at, the hospital so she didn't need to use her money. She had planned to stop working in a few more years. I'm sorry to hear about her death she must have love you very much. Thank you Mr. Newman I'll be in touch with you, I'll leave my money in your bank nice doing business with you. As I was walking out I could hear them whisper he the one Johnnie left her money to. I left the bank to go tell Terry the good news but I need to stop by my house first to change and to check my house. When I drove up I saw Jimmy coming down the street, he was out of jail. Hey man wait and talk to me he said, I just got out of the car and he said them white folks killed Johnnie Mae. What do you mean?

    I heard talking, I woke up and I saw Johnnie lawyer and cop talking to her. I heard her say that she didn't want to live in prison for the rest of her life. She was so sorry for killing Lucille and she told that lawyer she need him to help her. And he said Johnnie I will help you all I can but you took a bat and it will be hard for me to prove it was self defense. I heard the cop say Johnnie Mae the people is not going to let you go. I heard Johnnie say, "Yes, I know that's why I need you to let me die. Well I laid there pretending I was asleep and I kept quiet so I could hear more and I heard that lawyer tell her what do you want me to do? Then I couldn't hear no more talking, they left and then they came back I saw them give her something. That lawyer of hers hugged her and then he kissed her and said I love you that is why I am helping you. Johnnie Mae told that white man she loved him too, she thanked him for loving her and being her friend for all those years. I didn't know what she meant about that. Jimmy why would you think they killed her? Because after they left I saw her put something in her mouth and I said Johnnie Mae what you doing? I'm going to tell everybody what I heard and saw she turned around and looked at me like she gone take that bat and start to bat me again with it. She said, to me you old drunk ass bastard keep your mouth shut or I'll tell my lawyer to keep your ass in here the rest of your life.

So I told her I didn't care what they do to her old ass. So doing the night I heard her crying. I said Johnnie you all right? She fell on the floor and her body starting to shake so bad it was jumping off the floor. I call to her Johnnie! Johnnie Mae what's wrong?

So I called for help I kept calling somebody for help. Well when they did hear me and when they came Johnnie Mae was dead. I loved Johnnie Mae too. I know I did her wrong but I still loved her, man they gave something to kill her. Jimmy you need to keep your mouth closed. No one will believe you Johnnie Mae is right she may have told her lawyer to take care of you leave things alone.

She ain't told her lawyer, nothing because she died and he never came back. I ain't scared of these white folks and Johnnie Mae is dead and she ain't gone hit me no more with that damn bat. Yes sir, yes sir, her ass is dead and she ain't gone hit me no damn mo.

He turned around and started to walk down the street. Hattie came out the door and I heard Jimmy say Hattie give me a drink? Oh Jimmy, you just got out of jail for being drunk do you want to go back? Oh girl, give me a drink and I'll tell you what they did to Johnnie Mae when she was in jail. Come on in, they went inside. I said to myself Jimmy you need to keep your damn mouth shut you don't know what will happen to you. I went on in the house sat down and started looking around and thinking all this is mine. This is the best thing that has happened to me since I been here, except for Terry. I don't have to worry about getting up for work for a while. I had saved eight thousand dollars on my own with the money Johnnie Mae left me I have eighty three thousand dollars. I thought that God had forgiven me for what I have done wrong in my life. Thank you God, thank God.

Knock, knock, I got up to see who was at the door. Hi Hattie, come in is everything okay? Yes, I just came over here to tell you what Jimmy told me about Johnnie Mae and what he heard while he was in jail. Oh Hattie, you know Jimmy he stay drunk all the time he letting his mind play tricks on him. I wouldn't believe him. Yea you right Leroy. Leroy what's going to happen to all of Johnnie Mae's stuff? I know her mama is dead and she didn't have, no kids. I think she have a cousin in South Carolina do you know if she left everything to him? Slow down. Hattie give me time to answer your question, she gave me everything. She did! Why did she leave everything to you she didn't know you that well. She loved me and she didn't have anyone else. Her cousin couldn't take care of anything. Well what about that white boy she was so in love with? She thought we didn't know but, I use to see him going in her house late at night and coming out early in the morning. I know she knew we knew she just didn't want to talk about it.

Well he have a lot of money, I'm glad she left it to me instead of him. Well if she knew you was cheating on her with Terry she wouldn't have left your ass nothing she would have beat your ass like she did Lucille. She didn't and there is no way I would have let her beat me with nothing I can take care of myself. You know Leroy I sure miss Sam, my oldest son is getting out of control and won't listen to me since Sam died. He, talking about going down there was killing the man that killed his daddy.

Did they call you to come to court to tell what happened to Sam?

No they ain't told me nothing. Well they called Terry and she had to go in they may call you next. I sure don't want to go Hattie, that man killed my Sam and left me to take care of my kids by myself. When you take someone's life Leroy it's wrong, I don't care who it is. Cause one day you have to pay for what you did wrong and how you treat people. You go sometimes for years Leroy but one day you wake up and there is nothing you can do about it.

You know Leroy, when God took my Sam away from me it was my payback. Sam was a good man to me all I had to do was ask him to do for me and he would. I never told him what I did. He went out drinking down there at that bar and met a woman and started going with her. When I found out I was so mad at his ass. But I was so young and already had four kids, so I didn't know what to do but stay with him. When I asked him about it he said, Oh Hattie, girl you know I love you, you and these kids here I ain't go leave you for nobody. Well I believe him so one night he went back down there to that bar and I waited a while. I put the kids to bed and went down to that bar to see for myself. When I got there I saw him kissing on this woman and dancing with her, he was having so much fun. I was so hurt, I just turned around to leave and one of my friends was there

The Man on the Train

and she told me Sam just won nine hundred dollars, and that bitch was trying to get some of it. Girl you need to go over there and take that money from him before she did.

I was so mad I told her Sam can kiss my ass and he can give her that damn money so he can have a place to stay because his ass won't be staying with me no more. I turned around and left, damn him and the woman. I went back home packed me and my kids some clothes, so I waited to see if he was going to come home or is he giving that bitch all his money. I just had to see for myself. I was ready to kill his ass I waited and waited then I heard him come through that door. I was ready for his ass when he walked in before I could say anything to him. He saw me and said, "Hi Hattie and passed out on the floor. I left his ass there looked in his pocket and he had eight hundred dollars. I was surprised no one followed him and took it off of him. Well, I took it. God wanted me and my kid's to have that money so I took my kid's and we caught that train and we didn't know where we was going. I didn't care all I wanted to do was show his ass I didn't need him he could have that damn cow. Well we ended up in Mississippi I didn't know anybody and didn't know where we were going to stay. I sat there at the train station wondering what do, I do next?

I Was I a damn fool for leaving my Sam. The kid's say they was hungry and they was tired and wanted to go to sleep. I got them some pop and potato chips and told them to shut up until I could think. They started crying they want to go home I want to go back. A man that was working at the station come over and said, Lady are you waiting on someone to pick you up"? I busted into tears and told him me and my kids didn't have no where to go. I told him I didn't have any family there and our money ran out and they put me and my kids off the train. Well lady, why don't you come home with me? I live alone I won't bother your kids, you can stay the night and maybe you can find something tomorrow.

Come on these kids's is tired. Well he seemed like a good man so me and my kids went home with him. He was real nice he fixed up some food and he helped me put the kids to bed. He said his name was Ray Small. I told him I was Hattie and theses, was my kids. I didn't want to talk about their daddy, I left him and I was never going back I ran off with my kids. I'm sorry to hear that Hattie, you know kid's need their daddy. He gave me his bed and put me and the girls in it. He slept on the couch the next morning I woke up smelling breakfast the kids got up. Good morning. I bet your kids hungry. They ran to the table like a bunch of fools that had nothing to eat for days. I was so embarrassed to say anything. While the kids was eating Ray told me I could stay for the day until I could find somewhere, he would take us somewhere for help. The kid's asked Ray if they could stay with him; he ain't got no body. Well now that will be up to your mama, Ray I don't know you and you don't know nothing about me. I just appreciate you letting us stay for the night. Come on kid's we have to go. Where we going mama?

Hattie, why don't you stay a few days? I'm gone a lot for work I feel better knowing someone in my house watching my things. Are you sure?" Yes" Well Leroy, I stayed with Ray. I liked him and he was so good to me and my kids. So I said to myself Sam cheated on me so I was going to cheat on him. I knew I wasn't going back to Arkansas. Ray and I started to sleep together and a month later I was pregnant. I was gone a year Ray had went out of town and one day I saw this truck coming down the road so fast I told the kids to come inside the house. When the truck stop I looked up and here come, Sam out of the truck the kids started to holler mama! Mama! Here's daddy. I was glad to see him I did miss him and my house in Little Rock. He walked up to me and gave me the biggest kiss he held on to me like he would never let me go. Hattie, oh Hattie he was crying, and I started crying and the kid's was crying. Daddy did you come to take us home? Yes, yes. He kissed all the kids.

Hattie why you leave me and take my kids? Girl, I been looking for you over a year I been going crazy. When I found out you was down here in Mississippi, I had to come take you back home. Why did you leave me Hattie? What did I do to you? Get your stuff ready you going home with me come on girl, let's go. Sam I don't know. What you mean you don't know. Have you got somebody else I know it's been over a year? (I lied to him) No I ain't got nobody come on in he came and saw the baby he looked at me and all I could say was this is Billy Ray Hicks meet your son. Hattie why didn't you tell me you was having another baby? I left before I could tell you. He picked Billy up and said Hattie he is a fine boy. Thank you for this fine boy

The Man on the Train

I always wanted another boy. Sam I know you tired you rest while I cook.

I want to enjoy my kids they done grown so much. Hattie I got me three girls and two boys. I love you girl. I won some money and Mr. Gibson gave me money to come get you. I can't stay long only a few days so I can help you pack. Well can you just stay here until tomorrow? Yes, Hattie I ain't leaving here till you come with me. Sam what am I going to do with my stuff? We can take as much and ship the rest on the train. Sam how are you going to put me and five kids in that truck?

Don't worry baby, I ain't leaving none of you. After we had supper I put the kids to bed, he asked me again why I leaved him.

I told him about me coming to the bar and saw him with that woman and winning all that money and giving it to the woman. He looked so funny. Hattie when I woke up and saw you and my kids were gone I ran down the street trying to find you. I couldn't think where in the world you could go with four kids. No one saw you leave, I went to the police. They said they would help look, they said you were grown and you may have just left me. Mr Gibson told the police to see if they could find you someone said they saw you in Mississippi. It took the police this long to find you. When they told me I jumped in the truck and came on. I'm sorry Sam I was so mad after you told me you loved me but you was still seeing that other woman I just got so mad and I left.

Well when you get back home you and my kids will never leave me again. We talked half of the night we made love and I knew he still loved me. He got up the next morning went trade his truck in for a bigger car, and rented a trailer. We packed only a few things and I left everything that belonged to Ray. I told Sam that stuff belong to the people that own the house. I told him I would leave a note for them. I left Ray a note thanked him for all his kindness I told him my husband came to take me back home. I told him I was so sorry. Now my Sam is gone and I never told him Billy was another man's child. You see it's my pay back God took my Sam away from me. Ray never tried to find me, Hattie started to cry. Hattie things will work out for you I hope so Leroy. One of Hattie's little girls came over and said mama Sam Jr. said what you doing over here so long? You were here over an hour. We ready to eat. Hattie told that little girl you get your little fast ass back across that street and tell Sam Jr. He knows how to cook. Now get back over there now. Damn bad ass kids, Leroy I'll talk to you later. I'm going to see about these damn kids. Okay Hattie I'll talk to you later. I looked at the clock and it was after eight pm Hattie was here over an hour. I picked up the phone to call Terry there was no answer. I wondered where were she, I hope nothing was wrong. I hope I didn't say anything wrong to her. I went to the bar to see if she was there. I asked the waiter where was JJ?

He said JJ and his sister went out of town and he didn't know when he would be back. Did they say where they were going? They went some where in Texas. Why did they go there? I wonder why she didn't tell me they were leaving. My mind started to run wild. What the hell they doing in Texas? (I said to myself) Leroy calm down they don't know you been to Texas. They don't know about your father or brother. They haven't gone down there to find out nothing about you. You are from Oklahoma calm down. I decided to go shopping and spend me some of the money Johnnie Mae left me. I was driving and I saw a man shop I went in and they had nice things. I bought me two suits, shirts, shoes, socks, cologne and couple of hats. My name is Linda Edward I own this shop thank you for coming in. I hope you come back. I was driving by and saw your shop. I 'm glad I did. I'm glad you did to Mr. Mum.

(Leroy I said) Well Mr. Leroy thank you and please come back.

Linda looked fine she was a pretty woman long black hair, one hundred and thirty seven pounds. I sure would like to get to know her I thought. I asked her if she know a nice place to eat here. Yes, a few blocks down the street, the food is very good it's called The Paradise Club. You will love the food and the Club. Leroy I'll see you again. I just smiled and left I went to the Club it looked nice. I never been to a Club, when I walk in I was shocked it was beautiful. Lots of flowers, beautiful lights, the tables had cloths on them had nice glasses, silver ware the waiter was dressed in black and white.

The men were dressed in suites the woman was dressed in nice dresses.

I see why it's called Paradise Club it had a live band the bar was the size of half of the room. There was so much liquid behind the bar it, look like a store, nothing like the bar on State Street. They all look like high class colored people and rich white people. I only had on a nice shirt and slack pants I look like I didn't belong there. The waiter walked up to me and said you have to make your delivers to the back.

No, I was sent here by Linda Edward she told me to come here to eat and have a few drinks. Oh well come in are you a friend of Miss Linda?

Here's your table sir. He pulled the chair back for me to sit. What would you like to drink? I didn't know what to say JJ always bought me Gin. I could see all eyes on me like whom the hell are you?

Oh surprise me. I'll bring you a martini sir he gave me a menu I didn't know what to order the food looked good. When he came back with my drink he asked me if I like to order, or do I need more time. I just told him to bring me a steak, mash potatoes, and vegetables. After he brought my food I got another drink and everything was good. Boy, I think that I was going to like this place and the lifestyle. I sat there looking around and there were big chandeliers, hanging from the ceiling I'm coming back to this place. After I finished dinner Linda walked in, I saw her go behind the counter. Then I saw the waiter go over to her and point to me, she looked at me and smiled. I smiled back and she came over. Are they treating you good?

Yes, I like it here I will be coming back. I sure hope so she said. You know the people who own this club? Yes, sure I do. Do you come here often? Yes, I'm here every evening and night.

Oh you like it here that well? She laughed and said I own this Club. You sure have a nice Club. Thank you, I work really hard to get my shop and Club. I always wanted to make money and be my own boss. I don't like taking orders from no one and I mean no one. Most of my customers and lawyers, doctors, and business men or their family has money. My Club is nice because I don't like bums in here are you a bum Leroy?

No, I'm not I don't own a business I don't have a job I was let go from a desk job at the train station. Some white men don't like to see a colored man behind a desk so they let me go. But I do have a little money; I don't know how long it will last before I find me another job. Linda, someone called for her to come to the back she never came back so I left.

I knew I didn't have that kind of money she had. I got in my little Ford and went home. I said to myself Leroy Chester, you're no match for the people up town go back across town where you belong. I went back to the house Johnnie Mae left me. When I got out of the car with all my bags of things I bought here come Hattie. Leroy where you been all day? I see you been shopping what all you got in them bags? Let me see. Hattie it's only a few things, well I'm not leaving until I see. Ok. Ok. Come on in, I took the things out of the bags. Oh these are nice things you paid money for these things Leroy where you going to wear this fancy stuff? You wear them at the bar they think you trying to show off, no one wear clothes like that in a bar. I'll find somewhere to wear them. You, only wear stuff like that to church you done found you a church to go to?

No, I just wanted to buy me something nice what's wrong with that? Oh I just ask. Is everything with the kids okay? Well, they miss Sam a lot and so do I, I'm so lonely without Sam. It's been a few months now I'm really lonely. Hattie I'm sure you will find someone soon. I don't know I got too many kids. There's always someone Hattie that love, kids. Leroy, have you seen Terry since she been back? I didn't know she was back, yes her and JJ been back a few days. I thought you and Terry was real close. I did too, maybe I'm not for her and she got someone else. Did she say why they went to Texas? She didn't say, she didn't see your car at home when she came over here. Leroy I know you are lonely, no Hattie I'm fine. Hattie I'm tired I think I'll go to bed early I'll see you later. That's a hint for me to leave well I don't need a damn hammer to hit me on the head. Hattie left mad. What, the hell she think I want with her big ass. She better take care of all them damn kids and leave me the hell alone. I wonder why Terry or JJ didn't stop by to let me know what they were up to.

To hell with them too I think I found me a new life style. I'm going to move on with my life. Johnnie Mae, thank you for making me a rich man. I waited a few days before I went back to the Paradise Club. I put on the new clothes I bought changed my hairstyle, walked in the same waiter was at the door and didn't even notice me. I felt good and I looked good. I wanted to get to know the people that came in this place it was on the nice side of town. I looked for Linda they said she hadn't made it yet. I ordered me dinner The food I ordered was food I had, never ate before it was so good the deserts was out of this world. I ordered champagne and I liked it, I waited to see if Linda would come in and she walked in. Hello Linda, hello

Mr. Leroy I see you're back I told you that you would like it here. I'm having a party at my house Saturday, why don't you come here is my address and phone number if you get lost call me. She smiled and walked off, I was so happy I found me some new friends when I got home I saw Terry going to Hattie's house. She looked and saw me drive in the yard, hello Leroy. "Hi Terry" I walked over to her I heard you was out of town is everything okay? No so far we haven't got to do the thing we wanted to do. How come you haven't called me or came by to see me? I did, and your son said you were not home and he didn't know where you were. Well I'm back now and I heard about Johnnie Mae leaving you everything she had. I also heard what happened to her, Jimmy was at the bar telling what he saw and heard is it true? I don't know I wasn't there, Jimmy better be careful he, need to keep his mouth close. Why should he? Well it's up to him I don't care he know the people in Little Rock better than I do.

Where you been? You all dressed up you look real good. I was trying to take care of a little business.

You want to come over with me? You remember you told me Johnnie Mae don't want women in her house. Don't be funny girl come on this is my house now and I can let who ever I want. What will your nosy neighbors think? Damn what they think, Terry followed me home and I could see Hattie looking out the door. Hattie knew everything on the hole block I know I will hear everything tomorrow. Well this how Johnnie Mae lived real nice, I didn't know she had all this nice stuff. She never was very friendly, she always stayed to herself. Which room you and her was in? What do you mean?

You know what I mean. I looked at her and all I could say was you jealous. No, she said do you think that I wanted Johnnie Mae? Well Hattie and Lucille said, Stop! I don't want to hear what they said. They didn't live here they didn't see me do nothing. Come here this is Johnnie's room she looked in and saw only Johnnie's things. Come on with me I took her up stairs and show her my room and I said to her now what do you see? Well all your things. Thank you. I don't like hearing about what other people say, all you have to do is ask me what you need to know. She didn't like women in her house I only had this room. How would you feel if you saw other women coming in your house and up stairs in your bed? Okay, Okay Leroy I get the message. Fine, I said. Would you like to stay? This is my house Johnnie Mae, don't live here no more and I can have anybody in my house anytime I want to. I'll stay for a little while since it's your house she smiled.

Tell me Terry, what you and JJ been up to the past week? You went out of town and didn't let me know where you were. Leroy, I don't want to talk about what we doing or where I been. Come on let's go to the bar JJ working tonight. I would like to go dancing and have some fun to take my mind off things that has happened these pass few months. Come on but change you going to the bar not a Club she said. I looked at her and wondered if she knew I was going to the Club. They will tease you saying you spending Johnnie Mae's money so soon. You know how people are when you make a change.

I don't give a damn what people think of me. Leroy do it for me please I want to have a good time I haven't been there since Sam died.

Okay, I'll go upstairs and change I'll be right back. I'll wait for you outside when I came down Terry and Hattie was in the yard talking. Who you two talking about? Hattie said you guilty of something you ain't telling. Terry I think Leroy got something to hide you better watch him. Oh Hattie go home and take care of them kids and stop being so damn noisy. You need to stop watching my damn house all day and find something else to do. Come on Terry. Leroy you don't have to talk to her like that she lonely she misses Sam. Well she need to find someone or a job, I get tired of her running over here every time I drive up asking me questions wanting to know my business. She's your friend, tell her to stay home or go to someone else's house.

Oh Leroy, come on. Terry let me take you to dinner and shopping before we go to the bar. You know Terry I need a life I need to find me a job all I do is go to the bar or be at home. Leroy, things will work out fine for you don't worry. Let's go eat. Where would you like to go? Well I know a place on the other side of town that has good food. (Oh shit I thought to myself I hope it's not the Paradise Club) I'm not ready for Terry to go there with me. We went to a place called Mama Joe's soul food they had all the food my mama use to cook. The food at Paradise Club is so different they have fancy food. After we ate we went shopping, Terry was so happy she bought a few new dresses and shoes. I had so much fun shopping with her, looking at her, smiling and laughing. After we finished shopping she wanted me to go home with her, after we got to her house she told me to relax.

I want to try my new clothes on for you. She came out in one of the outfits then another one and she looked real nice. Leroy, I want you to close your eyes for the next one your eyes closed? "Yes" she came out and said, opens your eyes. I opened my eyes and I almost had a damn heart attack there she stood smiling at me. This, beautiful light brown skin woman was standing there with, only red pumps and, red panties, and a red bra on. She walked slowly to me still smiling do you like this one? Yes, yes, I like this one. You gone just sit there? "Yes" I just want to look at the beautiful woman I see in front of me.

Turn around slow. She turns around and my penis wanted to get out of my pants by itself. I was just grinning she walked over to me and sat with her legs open on my lap and started to kiss me and I kissed her back like never before. Her soft body was right there for me to do as I pleased she started to help me undress. I wanted to pick her up and take her to the bedroom I couldn't make it we just started making love on the couch.

I never did it from behind. Johnnie Mae didn't get to teach me I never been this far with a woman. It felt good to me and she started to scream and I couldn't stop my penis it had a mind of its own. Next thing I knew we was on the floor she lifted one of her legs on the couch and my damn mind almost flew out of my head, she got on top of me and man she was good to me. We went in the bedroom and she couldn't keep her hands off of me we kissed and kissed until we fell asleep. The next morning we woke up and she said she had to get dressed before her son came home.

We got in the shower together and we started all over again. Man I love this woman; I want her to be my wife. We had to get dressed I wanted to lay down and sleep I was tired. But we got dressed she wanted to cook breakfast but I wasn't hungry for food I wanted more of her. She fixed coffee and rolls and we went out in her back yard and sat at the table. Her yard was beautiful the flowers had grown since she planted them when I first met her. She said, they would come up every year. Your yard is beautiful like you, she smiled and said thank you.

We sat there and talked she told me that she and JJ went to Texas to see if there was anything about his father. His father met her mother in Texas where they use to live before moving to Little Rock. JJ's father married her mother when she was three years old and a year later JJ was born in Texas. She said her mother was from Little Rock and after JJ father died they moved back to Little Rock. Oh shit I wonder if my brother is his father. Oh shit, stay calm.

Terry what happened to his father? I don't want to talk about it anymore right now. Well what JJ's fathers name. It's Jerry Allen Johnson. Leroy is you alright? Yes, yes thank you God, thank you God. Leroy did you know Jerry Allen? No, I don't know anyone in Texas I'm from Oklahoma. You know I don't know all about your life Leroy you don't talk much about yourself very much. Yes, you do my name is James Leroy Chester I'm from Oklahoma I don't have a family. They are all dead she walked over to me and started to kiss me I love you Leroy Chester. I thought about her son and didn't want him to see us kissing I know he don't like me. Terry your son may walk in on us, you don't have to worry David moved in with his father when I went to Texas.

I left him over to his father and when I came back he didn't want to come back. I was getting tire of getting into it with him. Leroy, will you move in with me? Terry I need to see what to do with all of Johnnie Mae's stuff, where can I put all that stuff. When I get all that stuff taking care of I'll see. I love you Leroy. I love you too I know if I move in with her I would have to stay home she will start asking me all kinds of questions. When Johnnie Mae was alive I wanted to move in with Terry not now I want to see how those rich black people live I never been a part of that life.

I been poor all my life now I have a chance to be somebody. Terry I need to think what to do with my house that's Johnnie Mae's house she said. Not anymore it's my house and I can do as I please with it. Well rent it out until you decide what you want to do, you want to have a yard sell if you do I'll help you. We can get started as soon as you want to; I need to go Terry I'll see later. Why do you need to go? You don't have a job or nothing to do, Terry I love the time we spent together I love you I just need to think. I hugged her I want to see how to live I'm not ready to live with her now. I can't get the Paradise Club off my mind I got to go back.

Leroy don't go, okay, I stayed another night with Terry. The next day I told her I needed to go home to see if everything was okay. I left I knew she didn't like it, as soon as I drove up in the drive way I got out of the car I looked around and here come Hattie. Leroy, have you heard? Heard what Hattie! Police pick Jimmy up he was still telling people at the bar what happened to Johnnie. When they let him out the next day he was walking home and nobody seen him in three days.

Well this morning some kids were playing down by Jasper Bridge, and found him flowing in the water. You're kidding Hattie! Jimmy dead. (Yeah she said). Maybe he fell off the bridge you know he was a drunk. No he had just got out of jail! You know them white folks killed him on his way home. Oh Hattie you don't know that well those kids said they saw the police driving down the road after they saw Jimmy in the water. Leroy. I told Jimmy to keep his mouth closed did he have a family? Yes, two brothers and a sister his mama and daddy died years ago when he was young. He took it real hard when his daddy died that's why he drank so much, he was the baby boy and they spoiled him a lot. I sure will miss him walking down the street every day.

I met him when I first moved here I came home and Johnnie Mae was beating his ass with that baseball bat. You know Hattie every since I moved here every year somebody dies. So much has happened since I been here I wonder what's going to happen next. I think I'll sell everything and move back to Oklahoma and buy me a house down there. I can't keep going through all this shit, people in Oklahoma ain't always up in your business. You don't hear about police killing colored people.

Leroy where you been you ain't been home in two days, you been with Terry her car still here. Hattie I told you I don't like being questioned about my damn life, it's none of your damn business. Well sorry I asked good day. As Hattie was leaving she turned around and said, "If I hear anything else about Jimmy I'll tell you. Are you, going to his funeral? I went in the house and closed the door. I need me a drink I just wanted to be by myself tonight and think what I was going to do next. I got up the next morning and went looking for me a new house out of this neighborhood. I found two places I liked and I went to the bank for advice from Mr. Newman about the house. He said he would check them out and get back to me as soon as he could. After I left the bank I went to Paradise Club for lunch they said Linda would not be in for the day. I left and went to her shop she wasn't there the lady that work there said she would not be in for the day. The store start to get busy she couldn't help everyone, some of the people thought I worked there and they came up to me to help them. They said, I looked so nice so I just started to help them. I didn't know about clothes but I just put things together that look good and they loved it. By the time everyone left she said, I had sold nine hundred dollars worth of things. The lady was so happy that I help her she kept thanking me. You really good, the men like the way you help them. I been telling Linda that I need help do you need a job?

Yes, I do let me call Linda. Linda there is a young man here that need a job I was so busy today I look for you to come help me. The people thought he worked here and they had him helping he sure is good. They loved him we sold out of a lot of stuff and I need to stock up. I need to put more things out. Sir will you take the job? What is your name? Tell her Leroy. Leroy she wants to talk to you. Hello. Well hello Mr. Leroy, so you want to work for me. Yes, I would. Well the job is yours if you can stay and help out the rest of the day. I'll pay you I need you to come back in the morning at eight a.m. to help open. I'll be there when you come. Thank you Linda I'll be here. I told the girl she wanted me to come the next day. My name is Lilly and thank you for helping me I think I'm going to like working with you. Nice to meet you Lilly, I think I'm going to like it here too. I'll get to meet a lot of nice people I was getting tired of being around all those drunk and Hattie always nosing around in my business. I'll see you tomorrow Leroy. Okay Lilly, and thanks for helping me get this job I really do need it. I went back home when I drove up in the yard I look to see if Hattie was running out to tell me something but she didn't come out.

I went in the house to find me something to eat and to drink. I was tired but I liked the work at the shop I sat down to relax and just as I sat down I heard a knock at the door. I just sat there Knock, knock I got up and went to the door and there stood JJ hello man. Hi JJ what's wrong. Is Terry okay? Nothing wrong man I just came by I haven't seen you in the bar lately. It's been a few days.

Oh man I, just been hanging around. Terry said you and her been hanging out a lot. Terry, really like you. I like her too. Leroy I feel like I've known you all my life for some reason I feel close to you. I feel the same way about you JJ. The pass three years we have become close almost like brothers. Time sure pass fast you know Leroy I still don't know a lot about your life you don't talk about yourself. Are you hiding something? They said if you got something to hide it will come out. I told you there is not much to tell I grew up in Oklahoma, my family are all dead.

I knew nothing about my father's family and I know nothing about my mama's family they never talked about them. I had a brother he left when I was small and never came back. Well did you ever try to find him? No and I don't care. He didn't give a damn about me so I don't give a damn about him.

My father died when I was young. I been all alone all these years taking care of myself.

I was looking for my father's killer for the past two years. Terry and I haven't had too much luck the police said they still looking for the killer but they got it under cold case. I keep on them so they won't forget about my dad I'm going to school to be a detective. That's why I'm working at the bar I get tips that's extra money. I hope you have good luck JJ thank you man. Leroy, I'll be your brother thank you man when you and Terry get married I'll still be your brother.

Leroy, I really do miss my dad I can still remember him because I won't let myself forget. My mother said, he loved Terry as if she was his daughter Terry never knew her father. She loved my dad and she never cared about finding her real dad. Someone saw a man with my dad at the train station the day he was killed. They said they didn't pay too much attention because my dad acted like he knew the man he was with. They said, the man got in the car with my dad and they drove away the man said when he got off of work he saw my dad's car back outside.

But he didn't see my dad or the man that got in the car with him. A few days later they found my dad dead with his throat cut whoever killed him brought his car back. They couldn't find finger prints in my dad's car. They couldn't find much at the place they found my dad's body because it had rained for two days and the blood had washed away. Whoever it was had washed their finger prints off everything, they said it was someone who knew what they were doing because they think he had killed before. They never found the keys to my dad's car to this day.

Leroy, you okay man! You look so scared are you okay? Am I scaring you? You don't like hearing about stuff like this. I'm sorry, I'm so sorry about your dad thank you Leroy, but you didn't know my dad. He was a good man he never hurt anyone I just wish I could find the bastard before the police because I would make his ass suffer before I kill him. My mother was never the same she loved him so much he was good to her, Terry and me. She still misses him she can't sleep at night sometimes and she still cries a lot when someone mentions his name. She aged a lot after he died. Oh my God (I cried to myself) that sound like my brother, John.

I was in shock I didn't know what to say anymore I wanted JJ to leave so I could think. Oh my God that is why I feel so close to him he is like my brother son. Oh shit, I said to myself calm down Leroy calm down. JJ do you have a picture of your dad? No, Terry has them my mother gave all them to her because she didn't want to see them all over the house it would make her so sad. I miss my dad so much. I'm so sorry to hear about your dad I think about my mother a lot she was killed. I didn't want JJ to see me upset or scared. I tried real hard not to let on that I'm the one that killed his father. I need me a drink would you like to have one? Yes man I'll take one. I went in the kitchen took me a big drink before I went back out. Then I fixed us a drink and took it out to him. I wanted to tell him to hurry and drink up and get out before I break down and say I killed your sorry ass daddy. For leaving my mother crying and couldn't sleep at night because he had his black ass with your mama making her happy.

I wanted to tell him how my mama suffered I loved my mama too. All he did for her was put her in a damn shack outside of town and a few damn chickens while his black ass ran up and down on the train to your mama. I wanted to say he fucking your mama while he was still married to my mama. He would ride his black ass through Oklahoma not stopping to care about her or me.

He didn't give a damn after I was born and he found out I was his brother and not his son. My mama was a good woman she couldn't help that my daddy raped her. She was scared of him like all the other women he raped. If John had kept his sorry ass home my mama would still be alive. JJ its nice talking to you I'm tired I been working all day and I have to be back early in the morning. Okay Leroy, you coming to the bar after you get off work? I don't know if I'm not too tired.

JJ left I locked the door went up to my room I took the bottle with me all I wanted to do was drink everything away. I tried to get so damn drunk my pass is coming after me. I couldn't sleep I kept seeing my mama dead. I saw Al Jenkins and John Chester coming to get me I couldn't think but I knew I had to get myself together. I couldn't let JJ and Terry know who I am. Then I got to thinking John had changed his name and made him a new family my heart started to hurt hard. That bastard didn't want to be a part of my pass so to hell with his black ass. What am I going to say to Terry and JJ, how can I face them knowing that I killed their father. What am I going to do? I got up made me some coffee so I could work on my new job. I tried to block it out of my mind what JJ told me. It was so hard I knew it was time for me to pay for the crime I had done. I fell to my knees and I called out to my mama. Oh mama, I cried if you can hear me help me, I killed both of them for hurting you. What can I do help me I need you please help me I'm scared.

If JJ figured out I'm the one who killed his daddy, how can I look at Terry? How can I make love to her I can't move in with her now I have to stay away from them. I went to work the next day when I walked in Linda and Lilly was already there. Hi, Leroy you okay? You look like shit (I felt like shit) are you sick (she said) I couldn't sleep last night. When a man is up all night it means two things he ain't had no loving or his secret is coming out. You have a secret Leroy? No I said.

Linda asked me to follow her in her office. Are you really alright? Do you need to go home and come back tomorrow?

No I need to work I'll be okay; she opened her desk drawer and gave me a hundred dollars. Thank you. Are you sure you are alright? Yes, I think I need to move I don't think I better stay where I'm staying. Think I would like to sell my house and move to the other side of town. Well if that is all I can help you with that. I tried to work but my mind kept thinking about JJ being John's son. I need to think and I need to stay away from him before I say something wrong. Linda came back before I got off of work and we went looking for a house. We found three and I fell in love with a two bedroom house. I told Linda I would go to the bank and have Mr. Newman check it out for me. I told Linda I didn't want to go back to Johnnie Mae's house.

I didn't feel like being bothered with Hattie today. Linda said, "Come home with me" I have a big house and lots of room just follow me home. I followed her home and she said park on the side of the drive way. When I walked in I couldn't believe black people could live like this. Her house was beautiful like her club I thought Johnnie Mae's house was nice but nothing like Linda's. I said is this all yours? Yes, I work hard for this I went to college to learn business made it and I ain't letting anybody take it away from me. I work too damn hard to get where I am I don't care what I have to do to keep it. I live in this big house by myself I have three bedrooms, two and a half baths, living room, kitchen, den, my office and two care garage. I have big swimming pool in the back patio with tables and chairs I can cook outside I can do whatever I want my yard has a six foot stock aid fence I can swim nude if I want. I like my private, I have a yard man and I have a maid. They sometimes stay in the small one bedroom apartment over the garage. Yes, Leroy all this belongs to me. She told her maid to make sure my room has everything I need in it.

Linda thank you for letting me stay here. Well I'm glad don't make me sorry I let you move in with me. I never met a man I like enough to let move in with me. You, seem so different Leroy.

Leroy it's time for me to go to the club would you like to go we could have dinner and a few drinks? Yes.

When we got to the Club we walked in together and all eyes were on us. We both were dressed real nice we did look good together. Linda started to tell her help who I was and introduced me to her friends and I felt like somebody. I know that I 'm going to love this life I made it big time. Linda took me to the kitchen there was three men in all white she said they were her chefs and they were all cooks, each one cooked different food. It was real nice and clean we went in her office and I was very impressed. Linda how long did it take you to get all of this? She said, ("Years and Years") you don't look old enough to own all of this. Well thank you, I'm older than you think, do you mind if I ask how old are you? I'm thirty nine. I started to want things when I was seventeen. I started to work hard I was determine to be

The Man on the Train

somebody my family was real poor. I was living here picking cotton my hands would be bleeding when I came home and we still didn't have enough food to eat.

I would lie in bed at night and cry because my father worked in the field all day in the hot sun for some white man making him richer and richer. My mother cleaned their homes taking care of their kids.

One day I looked in the window of their home and I saw them all sitting at the big table they had nice dishes and sparkling drinking glasses, nice silver ware, and my mother was serving them. I stood at that window looking for a long time that is when I made up my mind that I want to see how it feels to be like them. I made up my mind that I will someday have people working for me serving me food and waiting on my mother and father. It took me twenty years to get all of this I have had to kiss some ass a long the way but I made it. I wear nice clothes, I have a big house, I have a beautiful Club, and my dress shop.

The only thing I hated was that my father didn't live to see it all. My mother lived long enough to enjoy my shop. I would make sure she was dressed nice she loved it, when she would go to church every Sunday the women would come up to her and tell her how nice she looked.

She would say yes my Linda girl want me to look good, when I see the smile on her face it made me feel proud. She didn't live long enough to see my Club, she would always say Linda girl I feel like I'm in paradise that is why I named my Club Paradise. That is why I tried to make it look like paradise for my mother, tears started to run down her face. I work hard Leroy and nobody will ever take this from me it would kill me if they did. You know Linda I wish I could have made my mother happy, my mother died with nothing but five hundred dollars in her pocket and she didn't even have a chance to buy her a dress or shoes. She was killed when I was eighteen years old, I miss her so much. Leroy, how old are you? You look like you eighteen. I'm twenty four, I been through a lot in the past few years I grew up fast.

You know what Leroy lets go out there and have some fun tonight, let's not think about our past. When we walked in everyone was dancing and I followed them this is one of the happiest times I had since I've been here. I drank and danced. Linda was having fun too we danced and drank most of the night. I just needed to forget all my past. This song came up about Lucille and I thought about Lucille and Johnnie Mae I started laughing and then I started to cry. Linda looked at me like I was a damn fool. What's that about she said? I'll tell you one day. Leroy lets go home. Linda went over to the bar to tell Grady to lock up. I walk to the door and this man at the door said I'm the Ice man. What does that mean?

He said no one hurt Miss Linda and I mean no one she is a good woman you don't hurt her you hear me. He pulled a case out of his pocket with an ice pick in it.

Before I could say anything Linda walked up see you tomorrow Ice man. Yes Miss Linda. Let's go Leroy.

Linda drove home because I was too drunk. I remember getting out of the car, I remember going to the door and I remember how good Linda looked. I felt so bad it was my first night with Linda and I blew it. I couldn't remember nothing when I woke up it was about 12:30 p m, I was in a beautiful bed room with my clothes still on. I saw some new clothes, shoes, socks, and underwear in the big chair in my room. I saw a note on the clothes saying "Leroy when you wake up you can come to work or stay home today".

I felt real bad my first night with her and I blew it how can I face her? I got up and went home I left all the clothes in the chair I couldn't take them. I drove in the drive way looked around and no Hattie I hurried and went into the house sat down and fell asleep. I stayed home all day. The next day I heard a knock on the door I wouldn't move. Knock, knock. Go away Hattie! I got up went to the door and there stood this big black man he looked like he was at least 6'5 weigh about 290 pounds I stood there looking up at him. I stood there looking at him to pull that ice pick out. My hand began to shake he stood there looking at me. And I managed to say what do you want? How did you find me? Miss Linda sent me here to check on you she makes it her business to find out about the people that work for her. She made sure she knows where they live she want to know if you okay. She need you at the shop to help Lilly I'm going to wait and drive you. How could you say no to this big ass man. I got dress and ready to go with him. As we was leaving I saw Hattie standing in the door looking as we was driving away, I got to work and Lilly was busy. Leroy where you been? Hi Lilly, I said and started to help people. Talking to people took things off my mind for a while

The Man on the Train

I liked my job. After we closed I asked Lilly if she would drop me off at home. When we walked out the door Ice Man was driving up. Lilly is taking me home. Get the hell in this car! I got in where are you taking me? I'm taking you home you're taking me the wrong way. You sit back and keep quite. We didn't say anything else.

This is Linda's house get out he said and drove off. I went to the door rung the door bell and the maid came to the door and let me in. Where is Linda? She is out on the patio, I went outside she was sitting at a table. Hello, Leroy what happened to you? Why did you leave? I felt embarrassed I passed out the first night I was with you. I didn't know what you would think of me. I like you Leroy. You're welcome to live here save your money and buy you a home later. You can pay me a little and help with some bills or just give me money. I would like to teach you how to make money and own your own business. You can still work for me and I will still help you, you seem like a very nice young man.

Linda there is so much about me you don't know. You may not think I'm nice. Oh we'll talk about that later are you ready to eat? Yes. The maid brought out the food and we talked. Linda asked me if I would go swimming with her when she pulled off her clothes I thought Terry had a beautiful body but for a 39 year old woman she look great. Come on in Leroy the water feels good. I can't swim I never learned. Come on in I'll teach you. Not today I'll just watch. I watched her and it was getting late and I wanted to go to bed. Linda I think I'll go to bed I'm very tired. Okay I need to go to the Club I'll see you tomorrow she said.

I didn't want to make a move on Linda so I went to my room sat in the big chair and tried to think. I knew I didn't want to move back in the house Johnnie Mae left me. I didn't want to see Hattie or run into Terry over there I can't ever see them again. I love Terry but I can't knowing she is my brother's son sister, I'm their uncle. Lord what am I going to do? I wish I could talk to someone I could trust. Holding everything inside of me is so hard. I thought I would be able to talk to Terry but now I can never see her again. I wish my mama was here I could always talk to her she would tell me what to do. I wish I could just see her and hold her and tell her how much I love her. Why did Al Jenkins have to kill her? He could have left her alone. I need to go back to Oklahoma and check on my land. I know the house has fallen down and grass is so high that I can't see where the house was. I was so tired I fell asleep still in the chair. I heard a knock on my door.

Leroy are you up? Yes. Linda came in. Your bed is still made up I fell asleep in this big chair. Linda I need you to do something for me? What. Will you sell my house? Because I don't know how to pack things, sell or give things away. Do you have time to help me? Yes. I'll take care of everything, I'll send Marie to help you. Thank, you Linda. I'll get dress. After I ate breakfast I thank Marie.

After I got to work it felt nice and Lilly was nice to work with. People started to come in and my mind was all on them, this man came in with his wife and she wanted to know why we don't sell clothes for women? The lady that own, the shop only want to sell to men I will tell her. I thought about it and I thought it will be nice and maybe she could make more money. I talk it over with Linda and she told me to do what ever I wanted she was letting me run her shop for her, she need to spend more time at her Club. Lilly and I ordered women's clothes, shoes, jewelry, gloves scarves and before we knew it sells went higher than it had ever been since Linda owned the shop.

Lilly said they were coming in just for me to wait on them women thought I look good. Some of them wanted to talk to me one lady said she wanted me to be the father of her baby. I started to dress real fine so they would come in and buy for their man. Linda was so happy that Lilly and I was making money for her.

I sold Johnnie Mae's car and bought me a new 1961 Cadillac. I was doing good I sold Johnnie Mae's house and had more money in the bank that I ever had in my life. Linda and I was getting closer and closer, I decided to drive in the neighborhood just to take a look at Johnnie Mae's house and maybe see Hattie looking out the door. I was so happy with my new car I just wanted to show it off.

I saw Hattie outside as I was driving by and I stopped and got out. She was looking so hard. Hello Hattie, Hello she said. She said Leroy is that you? I almost didn't know you, man you look sharp. Where in the world have you been. Did you go back to Oklahoma? I saw people moving out your stuff and then people moving in the house they said they bought it from some woman.

The Man on the Train

I never saw you over there so I knew you had to have moved back to your hometown. I wonder why you never came by to say bye to me. Terry said you didn't even say bye to her or JJ.

What happen to you? Is that your car? Damn Hattie if you slow down I can tell you.

I'm part owner of a dress shop for men and women on the other side of town. You mean you still been here in Little Rock all this time? Yes. Well Terry and I didn't know what happened to you and you had your ass across town all these months.

Well you don't know about Terry. What about her? Is she alright? Yes, she's only eight months pregnant with your baby. What! Hattie stop lying to me I'm not lying she is and it's yours. Why didn't she tell me? How could she when she didn't know where you were. I need to go see her.

Here she comes now. Terry drove up and got out of the car she looked at me and almost didn't know me. Hi Terry, I'm sorry I didn't know Hattie just told me you're going to have my baby.

Where the hell you been you never said good bye? Why you never came to see me? What happened to you? I'm sorry Terry. Leroy after all you mean to me you knew how much I love you.

I tried to take her in my arms to talk to her; she got so mad at me and went in the house. I went in after her and she started cussing at me, next thing I know she had a knife in her hand.

Put the knife down Terry, we can talk I'm here for you now. Please Terry, you don't have to act like this let me explain. She ran to me and stab me I pushed her back from me and I remember seeing her fall. I tried to get to her I fell to the floor I heard Hattie screaming I heard her saying send the ambulance too and I passed out.

The next thing I knew I woke up in the hospital. Leroy how you feeling? Do you know where you are? I looked around and I could see I was in a hospital. Linda was there with me holding my hand. Do you remember what happened? I just looked at her. Some lady named Terry Johnson stabbed you near your heart, in the stomach and on your arm. She was trying to kill you, you really lucky Leroy you didn't bleed to death you been here for two days. They had a hard time trying to stop the bleeding can you hear me?

What happened to Terry is she okay? They said she lost her baby she fell on the knife she had in her hand when she fell. Oh my God!

She's still in the hospital they said she will be okay. Leroy you feel like telling me what happened? No I don't not right now. But I will tell you later. I told you there was a lot you don't know about me or my past I don't want to talk about Terry, I don't want to ever see her again. I'm sorry about her losing her baby. Linda so much has happened to me in my life time so much sadness.

I'm so tired of everything I just need to lay here and die. When I met you I just knew my life would change I was so happy I met you. I love the life style you live I wanted to be a part of it, that in why I sold the house. I didn't want to live in that neighborhood. Why did you go back? I went to see Hattie to show her my new car.

Hattie's husband was nice to me when I first moved here. Hattie always came and talked to me telling me everything that happened in the neighborhood. I met Terry a few months after I moved here we dated and I left her after I met you. I didn't want to be around her anymore I didn't know she was having a baby. I haven't seen her since I met you she is a part of my past.

When you get out of the hospital I'll come pick you up or I'll send Ice Man. I have to go check on things. Thank, you Linda for being here for me. I caught her by the hand I'll tell you everything I believe I can trust you. a week later Ice Man came and picked me up and took me back to Linda's house. He helped me to my room and Marie brought me food. Mr. Chester it's good to have you back home. If I can do anything for you just ring this bell. Thank, you Marie. I was in bed for two more weeks, Linda told Ice Man and Marie to take good care of me. She was helping at the shop and Club every day. She came home late at night, she was always tired.

After a few weeks I was fine, I was ready to go back to work. I later found out Terry was out of the hospital, I drop all the charge on her. I told them she did it in self defense I didn't want to press charges on her. I wanted to go back home to Derry. I told Linda I wanted to leave for a few days to get myself together. How long will you be gone? I don't know I just want to leave Little Rock. I packed my things and told Linda how much I appreciate everything she did for me but I had to leave. Can I leave my car here I don't feel like driving? Yes and you know where to find me when you come back. Can Ice Man take you to the train station?

The Man on the Train

I bought me a one way ticket to Derry Oklahoma. I didn't know why I wanted to go back for but I felt like I needed to. I knew it wouldn't be quite the same I didn't know where I would stay after I was there but, I just wanted to go. When I got off the train in Derry, I saw Peter Marshall he was still working at the train station. Hey Leroy Chester, (he said.) Man you still dress to kill. Don't say that Pete!

Well what you doing back here to get your old job back?. You can have it I was just keeping it for you I knew you would be back someday. He started to laugh. I knew that one day I would see you get off that train. When things happen sometime in people life they come back where they started from.

Where, they have unfinished business. I'm really glad to see you Leroy. I'm getting off in a few minutes wait on me Mr. Sheets is in the office he will be glad to see you. I went in Mr. Sheets office he looked up. May I help you? Hello, Mr. Sheets. Leroy is that you? Did you come for your old job? I need to take off for a long while. No, I just came back for a few days. I'm glad to see you.

You look good. Leroy you ready to go? I'll see you later Mr. Sheets. Okay Leroy. Pete, can you take me somewhere to stay? Do Miss Tee still have rooms? Get in the car with me. I'll take you somewhere to stay while you here. I think you like where I'm taking you, well tell me what you been doing? Are you still living in Little Rock? Yes. Pete where we going? You out by my old place, oh just sit back and ride you can stay with me. When we drove up I couldn't believe it Pete took me home what the hell is this? My mama house was still standing the chicken house was still there. The grass was cut, the house was painted, the yard was clean I just stood there I couldn't move. I was waiting for my mama to run out that house.

Pete is someone living here? Go in and I'll get your stuff. I went inside and my entire mama's stuff was still inside the house it was clean as if she still lived there. I couldn't believe it, I turned around and looked at Pete what the hell is going on? Who would take care of my mama's little shack and why? After you left I, been coming out here taking care of your mother's home. Why Pete? Well it's a long story. I been paying the bills and keeping, up the place I knew you would come home one day and you need a place to stay. Leroy, do you remember they told you about your mother leaving the bar that night? Yes I remember. Well she was with me. You why you?

75

I didn't know Al Jenkins was waiting for her that night I wouldn't have let her go in that house alone.

Your mother and I had been seeing each other for a long time I was married she miss John and just wanted someone to talk to. And I would drive over here from Stillwater at night so no one would see us. No one here knew me we didn't do nothing but talk; I liked her because she was a good woman only needed someone to talk to. One night she was telling me how much she loved John and he was always gone and how scared she was of James. She was crying so I just put my arms around her just to comfort her and we start kissing each other and we just started seeing each other. No one came out this way much at night, she made me wait until you was good and sleep before I came. She didn't want my wife to know I fell in love with her. She met Al Jenkins so people would think he was her man.

She loved me. I had to take my wife to Tulsa to the doctor she was real sick. Her family lived there and my family lived there so we had to stay there for three days to take her back and forth to the doctor. When I heard your mother was dead I was so hurt I knew Al Jenkins had to be the one who had killed her he was crazy about her she didn't want him. He tried to buy her things to make her go with him I told her to stop working at the bar.

I would taken care of her. That night she made up her mind she would stop working at the bar and left with me. I went to kill him but he had left town, when I heard he was back in town I went over to kill him. I saw Mary's car parked down the street I knew you had been driving her car. I turned out my lights I was coming to tell you to let me do it. You came running out of the house down the street to get in Mary's car to drive off. You left the door open I went in and saw Al lying on the floor dead.

I went in and I took his wallet and a few things to make it look like a robbery. I closed the front door and I saw two foot prints in his blood so I went in the kitchen stopped the sinks up, turned on the water in the kitchen so it would flood his house. I went out the back door and locked it when I left no one saw me. I knew you had on gloved but I made sure you left no prints.

Pete you knew all these years and you said nothing. No son, I haven't told no one that is our little secret I love you. I wanting to tell you all these years how much I loved your mother she didn't want me to tell you. Tears started running down Pete's face I went over and put my arms around him and I started to cry and said thank you Pete thank you. I asked God to let me find someone I could talk to and I could trust. I can't sleep at night without drinking I couldn't tell anyone Pete. Leroy, I need to tell you something but it can wait you go and get some rest and I'll be back tomorrow. I keep food out here so when I'm working out here I stay sometimes. What does your wife say? My wife died a few weeks after your mother. Do you have any kids or someone at home? No one home but me I've always liked you Leroy. I always wanted a son I told your mother to tell everyone that you was my son. So people wouldn't talk saying you was James son but she told me she didn't want to hurt my wife.

Me and your mother always talked she told me about James. I wish you was my son cause I really loved your mother. I didn't start sleeping with your mother until you left we were just friends, after you left we fell in love. I'll like to get to be your friend Leroy. I think your mother would like that I feel close to her when I come out here after my wife died.

I bought me a house here and moved here. I'll go and let you rest I will see you tomorrow. Pete, will you stay here with me while I'm here? Yes son. We were up all night talking I told him about my life in Little Rock, about Terry and JJ and the others. And why I came back. I'm here for you Leroy anything you need I am here. It was almost daytime and I fell asleep it been years since I fell asleep without a drink I felt so relaxed. Mama I'm home I felt a warm feeling all over me I just wanted to lay here in my own bed. I went back to sleep after a while I could smell coffee, and food cooking then I could hear my mama calling Leroy get up baby time to eat. Wash your hands.

I woke but she wasn't there it was Pete in the kitchen. Pete you home? Yes son it's after five.

You mean I been sleep all day. You must have been really tired, you need the rest so I didn't wake you are you hungry? Yes, I'm starving. Do you like pork chops, mash potatoes, and peas, biscuit and gravy?

Pete my mama use to cook that for me. Yes I know she told me that when you was gone. Boy you and my mama sure were close. Yes we were. We sat down and ate the good food. I was so happy to be back in Derry.

We went on the porch I always like sitting on the porch. I told him about the big porch Johnnie Mae had on her house and I would love to sit and watch the people going by working in their yards, cars driving by and the kids in the street. I told him about Hattie, Sam, Sally Cross, Old George Cross, Lucille, Johnnie Mae, Jimmy and others. I told him about Linda and Ice Man, The Paradise Club and the shop.

Pete love hearing about everything, he act happy I was back. Peter and I laugh together and we did some crying together while we sat on the porch.

Son I'm glad you back you just made an old man happy. He put his arms around me. You make me happy to Pete I just found a real friend that I need in my life. You know what Pete the place looks real nice but one thing missing. What's that son? Chickens, there is no chickens mama always had chickens. We both laughed. We'll go to town and get some. Good I said. Peter do you know if someone stole my mama car? No it's still out in the barn. I uncovered it and it still looked the same, I kept it up too it still runs. I drive it sometimes I hope you don't mind. Oh no Pete come on let's drive to town. We drove to town and everything was closed at 5:00 p m. The joint where James killed Andy Brown was still open we went in they was dancing and having fun the place was full. We found us a table. Pete said they only had beer, I told him I don't drink beer. I'll be back Pete said, he went to the bar I saw him talking to the bartender.

The bartender left and came back I saw him give Pete a jar Pete gave him some money and he came back with a jar of water. Here drink this, it's all they had. I looked at Pete and said man you mean you paid him for a jar of water.

Pete started laughing just drink it slow, I opened up the jar drunk it and damn it was good. What kind of water is this? It's corn whisky pure corn. This is some good shit Pete. Easy son it will slip up on you. Next thing I knew I was out there on the dance floor dancing and the people started to clap their hands and a young lady started to dance with me I was having some fun.

I started laughing and feeling good I was having so much fun I wasn't thinking about no damn body. I could see Pete smiling, a man walked over to me and said are you James Chester's son?

I gave him a dirty look if he fuck with me his ass will be laying next to James. Oh, I didn't mean nothing son I just thought that you was his son. Have you moved back here? Pete walked over and said let's go.

I want another drink Pete. Come on I got some to take with us. We got outside and Pete said he would drive. We were driving and this song came on the radio and I started singing baby shake it shake baby. Pete was laughing at me I think I was real drunk Pete helped me in the bed.

When I woke up the next day my head felt like John Chester ran over me with that damn train he rode on. My head was hurting so bad I heard someone say you sorry bastard I'll fix you.

You ain't going to ride this train. I looked and I saw this man standing in my door way. Leroy, drink this. Who the hell are you? There's, two of you bastard, think you can whoop my ass come on. I cut your damn throat before your ass hit the floor pussy ass mother fucker. I passed out when I did wake up it was 2:00 pm that afternoon. I saw Pete standing in the door just looking at me, shit this mother fucker gone kill me oh shit. When his old ass, get close to me I'll knock him down run to the kitchen and get me a knife.

Leroy, are you okay man? I don't think you need any more of that corn whisky drink this it will make you feel better. What is it? Just drink! I took the glass out of his hand and drunk a little. Drink all of it he said. Take a cold shower it will help you. He was smiling at me I knew he wouldn't kill me. After I took that cold shower I felt so much better. Son I don't think you can handle that corn. You know Pete I don't think I can but it sure was good going down. I thought I could drink I would drink every day in Little Rock. But that shit. Pete laughs at me. What was that you gave me to drink?

It was only a raw egg, tomato juice and a little hot sauce. Oh was that it well I know next time.

No you won't I got you out of the joint last night a man walked up to you and asked if you was James son. The look you gave him, I knew it was time to take you out of there. I'm sorry Pete. Son you have to stop drinking you may one day say too much and get hurt. I wish I didn't buy you that corn you can't handle it.

I sure hope I didn't embarrass you Pete. No you didn't. I'm off today you want to go back to town with me? Before the store closes

I need to get a few things and go by my house to check on it. Yes, let me get dress. Why don't you put on these jean and, shirt people around here don't dress in fancy clothes like that. Okay Pete. We went into town. Pete have been nice to me since I been here. I don't want to make him mad at me he know I killed Al Jenkins.

When we got to town Pete went to the grocery store. Pete I need to go to the bank. You need something out of here Leroy? No, what ever you think we need. I walked over to the bank. I walk in and the lady said may I help you? Yes I want to see if my money is still here. What's your name? Leroy Chester Do you have your ID and your account number? Yes, may I see it? Yes, Mr. Chester your money is still in here. We sent statements out to you and they all came back we didn't know how to find you. We didn't know if you forgot. What it's been over three years now. Do you come to take your money out? No I want to put more in. Well I'm Brenda let's sit over here at this desk.

Mr. Chester your money has grown you have 518 dollars now. How much do you want to put in? 2,000.00 cash she looked at me as if I had stole the money out of her bank. I have to call Mr. Flowers. I waited then she, come with Mr Flowers. I here you want to put money in the bank? Yes, if it's too much I'll take it to another bank. Oh no, I see you haven't been here in over 3 years to take any out. Where did you go? Before she said anything else, no I ain't been to prison and I ain't robbed a bank. I'm a part owner of a business in Little Rock, if you have a problem call Mr. Sheets at the train station. I use to work for him in Little Rock I saved my money. Oh no, Mr. Chester no problem, let me give you a receipt.

I want to put Peter Marshal name on my account I want to give him what ever he need when ever he come in. When the account get low I'll put more in. Okay Mr. Chester, I'll take care of everything for you. Where can we get in touch with you if we need to reach you? Just get in touch with Peter Marshall he will know where I am at all times. He work at the train station. Okay we thank you Mr. Chester nice doing business with you have a good day.

Damn people always want to know your business. Pete was coming out of the store when I walked up Leroy is everything alright? Yes, everything is fine. You were in the bank a long time. Did you get what need? Yes son. You ready to go by my house? Pete you have a nice a nice place.

You know Leroy, I didn't have kids but I have a brother and his family is in Tulsa.

They never come down see me unless they want something. Sometimes I go over there for Thanksgiving and they always need money to help buy the food so I stop going so much. I know if something happen to me he will be here to take my house and every thing else. Pete, do you want stay home?

I'll be alright out there. Well son I'm enjoying you but if you tired of me I'll stay home. Oh no Pete I'm enjoying you too. Well come on I have one more stop to make, I'm going by Anna Bell's house. Do you remember her? Yes she's the one with all those kids about 7. No she has 9 now. Man (I said). What you need to go by there for? You'll see. We pulled up in the yard and kids come from everywhere up to the car look like 15 of them. I'll stay in the car.

Pete said what you scared of the kids he laugh and laugh. Some of them came to the car who you master? What's your name? What you come here for? To see my mama we ain't got no daddy Mama said when he looked at all of us he took off running and he ain't coming back.

Pete came back with a big box in his hand. Open the car door I got something for you. Put the food in the trunk I need to put the box in the back.

Damn Pete it stink. It's chicken, for you. Pete you didn't have to do that. What am I going to do with chickens I was only teasing you. I don't know if I'm going to stay in Derry. Well you can have them while you're here. As we was driving home I looked at Pete and it was like I had me a real father glad to see me back home. He asked me to help him take the chicken and put them in the fence. They ran in the chicken house and I stood there looking at the spot where I buried the clothes and knife I killed Al and John. I saw where I found my mama I kept standing there with tears running down my face.

Pete called my name. Leroy what are you thinking about? I looked at him and he said you thinking about your mother or the clothes and knives you buried. How did you know?

I was out here one day and it started raining so hard the water got up a little high and flooded the chicken house. When the water went down a few days later I went in there and I saw clothes and two knives lying on the ground. You didn't burry them deep enough, I put two and two together and I figured one set was yours because I saw you running with nothing on. I knew they had to be in that bag. I don't know who the other clothes were because Al still had his clothes on. Did you kill someone else Leroy?

I wouldn't say anything I just kept standing there looking at him. Then he said I burned the clothes. The knife I took them to my house and bury them behind my shed case the finger prints maybe on them. I stood there looking at this man for a long time and then I burst into tears crying. It's the first time I cried so hard not because of Al or John but because of this man standing in front of me.

Son why you crying so hard is it because of what you did? I walked over to him and hugged him I'm crying because you love me and you really don't know me. Sure I do I watched you grow up me and your mother been friends a long time. I loved her and you are a part of her I can see a lot of her in you. Thank you Pete thank you. Pete I want you to take this money for helping taking care of my mama's home. Here is eight hundred dollars. No son! You don't owe me I did it because I wanted too.

Son where you get all that money? In little Rock Johnnie Mae Left me a lot of money, if you need more I'll go back to Little Rock and bring it back to you. Son I don't need the money, I'm an old man I may not be here long my wife died and I got her insurance money. It will last me for a while I still work at the train station.

Please Pete, take this money and use it. I also put some money in the bank today and I fixed it where you can go and get what ever you need. Oh son you didn't need to do that. Well if I need it I'll go get it if it makes you happy. You know son I don't know why you buried that second knife. Did you kill someone else? Who did you kill son? I remember that day when you got off the train and I asked you where you been. You told me Arkansas. Before your mother died she told me you went looking for John Chester did you find him son? I couldn't speak I just stood there looking right at him in his eyes. Your mother told me you hate him for never coming back to her. Your mother and I told each other everything she loved you more than her own life. She would tell me how proud of you she was. She didn't care how people talked around here about her. You was hers and she loved you she told me how James raped her whenever he wanted to. She couldn't leave because she had nowhere to go and she was scare of him. She hated him because he was so mean when he was drinking.

One night James had raped her she was crying so hard she was tired of him I was going over to kill him but she begged me not to. She thought if John came home he would put a stop to it that was the night James killed Andy Brown. He had raped her and left and went to the joint and got in a fight with Andy. John came home a few hours later. James came back and told John to help him to get out of Derry. John helped him and neither one of them came back. I saw John one day coming through here on the train and I asked him where was James he told me somewhere in Dallas Texas. I went to Texas to find him I didn't want him to hurt Mary anymore. I thought since he had killed Andy no one would care about him.

I was gone for three weeks it took me that long to find him. He was walking down the street in south Dallas I followed him I saw him go in this alley to a small house. He was opening the door he turned around and I was standing there. What the hell you want he said, I pushed him inside and shot him in the heart. I never went inside I only pushed him inside and I pulled the door shut as fast as I could so blood wouldn't get all over me. I picked up the shell case and I ran hoping no one saw me.

No one came for me. I did it for your mother I didn't want him to hurt her anymore.

I stood there looking at Pete wondering what should, I say to this man. This is the man that loved the same woman I did. What do I say to this man that killed James Chester for hurting my mama. All I could do was put my arms around him and just hug him and held on to him and cry. I turn and went in my room I didn't know what to say and I closed the door and I cried and cried I stayed in my room I wouldn't come back out that night. When I came out the next morning Pete was gone the eight hundred dollars was left on the table.

Two days had gone by and Pete, haven't been back to the house I thought he wanted to be alone. I went by his house his car was in the driveway I got out knocked on the door. He didn't come to the door. I called out Pete's name and he still didn't answer, Pete, Pete are you in there? Lord please let him be alright I tried to open the door and it was lock. Pete can you open the door? He still didn't come to the door, should I call the police to break in to see if he was alright. I started to go around the back of the house and here he comes. Hey Leroy, what you doing here?

I ran to him and gave him a hug oh Pete I didn't know what happen to you. I thought you were inside sick or something was wrong and you didn't come to the door. I haven't seen you in two days I didn't know if I said anything to make you mad at me. Leroy I just wanted to give you time to get over the shock I kind of felt bad telling you I killed your father.

I didn't know what you thought of me when you went to your room and closed the door. I felt you needed to be along. Oh Pete I really don't know James that much he died when I was so young. The things I remember about him I didn't like I love my mama more than I ever cared about him. I didn't care what happened to him I was so surprised what you told me that you loved my mama so much that you would kill for her. James never spent a lot of time with me I want you in my life forever Pete. Thank you son I want you too.

What are you doing back here? Come on I'll show you. You and I are going fishing. I, never been fishing. Well you, going now. I'll leave my car here and ride back with you. You know there is a big pond on your land. Yes. Have you been all over you land? You have over ten acres out there son real good land. I knew we had a lot of land, I didn't really care. Mama made me stay close to the house she didn't want the people always teasing me about James. When I went to Blaine school I kind of stayed to myself as much as I could I had a few friends. I really didn't want to be around a lot of people telling me James was my daddy. Pete I'm glad I came back home to find you. We went back to my house we walked round back to the pond. Pete showed me how to fish and we caught six they were some nice ones.

We took them back to the house and Pete cleaned them and said we would eat them for dinner. I went inside and took a bath while Pete cleaned the fish.

Sure was good. I'm happy to be with Peter I was happy being home. I haven't had to drink myself to sleep at night I really haven't had a drink every day since I drank that corn whiskey. It has been good here with Pete. It's been over four weeks now since I been here. I walked out on the porch I sat down and I could see the train go by. Pete spent all of his time with me while I was here.

The Man on the Train

    I saw a car coming up the road the car came closer and closer. We didn't have no one coming to the house since I been here I was wondering who it was. They stop the car and sat in it for a second they didn't get out. What the hell I thought (Pete, Peter I called out.) Pete ran to the door. Who is this? I don't know, Pete got the gun came back to the door. I got up to go in the house the car door opened I saw this big back man step out. Oh my God what the hell Ice Man doing here?

    It's okay Pete it's Ice Man. I started walking to him. Ice Man where the hell you going? When you get that new car? How did you find me? Ice Man opened the back door and out come Linda I was really shocked. Linda where you going what you doing here? How did you find me? We hugged each other I'm glad to see you guys come meet Pete.

    Pete this is Linda and Ice Man I been telling you about. Leroy it's been over a month since you been gone I came to get you and take you home with me. You had a long enough rest, How did you find me? That is one of Ice Man jobs to find out what I need. It wasn't hard after talking to a lady name Hattie. Damn Hattie still putting her nose in other people business. I'm glad to see you both come in my house is not like your but you're welcome Pete was getting ready to cook dinner you guys going to stay for a while? Well we are a little tired. Linda said. Leroy, are you alright? Yes I'm fine Pete been taking good care of me I don't know if I'll ever leave again. I saw Pete looking at me I knew he wanted me to stay.

    All the people, asking about you at the shop Lilly said she really need you and I need you too that is why I came here to take you back with me. Get your things and let's go. Can you stay the night?

    Well we are tire. Pete asked them if they would stay and have dinner. Ice Man said let's eat.

    Linda looked at the food. I told Pete Linda don't eat home cooked food she have chefs cooking for her. Pete is a real good cook Linda try it this is how we live in Oklahoma she smiled.

    It's late will you stay the night?

    Do you have somewhere here I can shop? Yes we have stores maybe not the things you use to I'll take you in the morning. Leroy I guess I'll go home so you can visit with your friends. No you won't you stay right here I don't want you to leave. We have room we make room if I have to sleep on the porch you know how much I love the porch. Man this is what you call country it's so damn dark out here you ain't scared. No man you get use to it. Round here no one bother you. Ice man you can take the bedroom at the end of the hall, Miss Linda can take Leroy room and Leroy you take my room. I'll sleep on the couch no Pete you take your own room I'll sleep on the couch.

Thank you Pete for the good dinner I think I can take you back with me and you can cook at my Club. You welcome Miss Linda. Ice Man said he was going to bed. Pete said he was tired and went to his room Linda and I went out on the porch to talk the moon was shining. The night was so nice you could hear nothing but quietness. Leroy, I really miss you and I want you to come back. Who is Pete he your uncle or something? No he is like a father to me and I love him more than anything. He use to be in love with my mama I became real close to him since I been here I want him in my life forever. I could tell you love him by the way you were looking at him when he told you he was going home.

He loves you too. We have learned a lot about each other since I been here I don't think I'll go back to Little Rock. I may come and get my stuff and move back here I have a bad feeling going back.

Are you still in love with that Terry woman? No but I like her a lot I thought I was in love with her but I have put her out of my life after all the things that happened. I don't want to see her it had been eight months before I saw her, after what she did to me I don't want to ever see her.

Linda and I fell asleep talking most of the night the next morning we was in each other's arms. I woke up to the smell of coffee and breakfast cooking it smell so good. Ice man came running to eat. Pete said Miss Linda if you stay one more day I'll take you to Tulsa they have more stores there.

There is a lot of colored stores there and some ladies make clothes out of their homes.

The next day we went to Tulsa, Linda and I shopped for things to take back to her shop. When we got back to Derry Linda said, "Well Leroy you ready to go back with me" I really need you to run my shop.

I just have a feeling I shouldn't go back. Oh Leroy nothing is going to go wrong please come back with me. Leroy what are you

The Man on the Train

going to do? Stay or go back with us, I could see the hurt in Pete's eyes he wanted me to stay with him. I wanted to stay home because I was happy while I was here. After telling Pete what was on my mind I really didn't want to leave him after all the things he did for me. Come on Leroy we have to go? Pete, will you go with me? No son, I have a job and a home here I can't go. Quit your job. I have enough money to take care of you. Let me take care of you?

No son. I have some money you go on just don't forget me. Oh Pete I can never forget you I will always keep in touch. I love you. Will you promise me you will go to the bank and take money out for taking care of my place? Yes, if I need it. Pete I will let you know where I am at all times.

Pete eyes began to fill with water. I had to leave because I didn't want Linda and Ice Man to see me cry. We drove off and I went back to Little Rock with them, on our way back to Little Rock I kept feeling that I needed to stay in Derry. Being with Peter was the happiest time I ever had being back at home.

I wanted to tell them to turn the car around and take me back to Pete but I didn't want them to think I wasn't a man. After we got back to Little Rock we went to Linda's house changed, and took the things she bought to her shop.

Hi Lilly, Hi Leroy! Is everything okay Lilly? Yes fine Linda told Lilly she was going to the office to check on sales I helped Lilly put the new things on the shelf and make a few changes. Lilly was acting real quiet and kept looking back at the office. Lilly is everything alright? You acting a little funny you sick?

Oh I just need some rest Leroy. Well do you remember what you told me the first day I started to work? No what did I say? You said, "When a man look like I did that means he ain't had pussy in a week or he had something to hide so are you hiding something Lilly? Do you need a man? Oh Leroy, help me put this rack Up Linda came out of her office she walked over to Lilly and said, "I don't understand sales have went down since I left and started to work at the Club." I been watching for the past month since Leroy been gone I'm glad to have you back Leroy. Lilly need you here and I really need you. Lilly was so quiet. Leroy come on I want you to go home with me, I want to teach you how to help Lilly order supplies and teach you how to read sales.

I want you to learn to help Lilly take care of my money, she looked at Lilly and said, "I don't want to lose my shop Lilly." Linda gave Lilly a strange look and walk off. Linda what's wrong I said. Let's go. Lilly I'll be back later today. After we got home Linda said, her sales had went down real bad since I was gone and she thinks Lilly was stealing her money. Leroy my money is not adding up for all the clothes and all the other things that I'm buying for the shop. If she not stealing, she giving away my shit. Linda, are you sure? Hell yes I'm sure. This is why I'm teaching you to take over the shop the Club is a lot harder for you to work right now. I work to damn hard to get my shop and I'll be damn if I lose it. I need to spend more time at my Club I don't want to lose my Club either.

Okay Linda, but Lilly has been with you for a long time. If Lilly is stealing from me I'll kill her damn ass. You don't mean that Linda. The hell I don't no one take nothing from me. How the hell you think I got to where I am today I don't take shit from nobody.

Do you want me to go back to the shop? Yes, for a while to see what's going on. Linda you just talking about killing Lilly I don't believe you could ever do anything like that. She looked at me and walked away I went back to the shop and Lilly wasn't very busy. After I was back two weeks, sales went sky high people came in saying how good to see me back they were going elsewhere they love having me waiting on them. They loved my smile and my kindness to them and how I help them put their clothes together. I got most all women sales when they came in and Lilly would wait on the men. It felt so good to know people liked me. I really couldn't believe how much money we were making since I was back. Linda grabs me and started kissing me. Thank you Leroy I love you. She kisses me again, and I kissed her back and the next thing I know we were making love. I thought making love to Terry and Johnnie Mae was good but making love to this older woman was off the hook. She make love to me slow and easy she know what she was doing she was blowing my mind it was all good.

I think I'm falling in love with Linda after we made love Linda fixed us a drink. I remember this is the first drink I have had since the last time I had a drink was when Pete gave me that corn whiskey. After that Linda and I got closer and closer.

The Man on the Train

One night Linda asked me about our age difference I don't have a problem about it do you Miss Linda? She smiled and gave me another kiss. Girl if you keep kissing me and hugging, me we will never get out of bed.

We made love again I knew we would have to stop and get ready to go to work. Linda said the Club was doing so good she said I was her good luck charm. People were coming to her Club the music and food was so good. The Club was a nice place to come. Linda started to close up after lunch and reopen the Club for dinner so we could spend more time together.

I learn how to take care of both businesses every day Linda taught me how to do the books at both businesses. I asked her one day if she had a lawyer to help her with her business taking care of her taxes.

What do I need a lawyer for I take care of my own business. I been doing it all these years, Pete told me one day that when you make money and have property you need a lawyer.

It won't hurt to check Linda. I will one day. I went back to the shop and Lilly said we were Almost, out of things for the shop the last shipment just came in. The people we were getting shipment from said they were going out of business and would not sell anymore things. What are we going to do Lilly? Can you call someone else? I called Linda and told her she said, we need to go to New York they had real nice things. I been waiting to go for a long time do you have enough things for at least a week? Yes, we will go in a few days.

Linda called Ice Man over and she was talking to him and he looked mad. Linda is everything okay? I want him to make sure Lilly take my money to the bank every day. We will be gone for a few days I think Lilly is taking money from me I want Ice to make sure she's not. Linda you are not sure you do not have proof. I meant what I said, "I'll kill her ass nobody take from me and get away with it. If you think she stealing just let her go and find someone else.

We'll talk about her later come on let's get ready for New York. Are we flying or driving? No I don't want to fly I don't want to drive unless Ice Man drive we going to catch the train. Do you like the train Leroy?

It's okay I have a lot of memories on the train. All good or bad she said. No it's a part of my pass that I don't want to talk about. Well do you want to drive? No I'll catch the train with you. When we got to

New York we checked into a real nice hotel. It was the first time I ever been in a hotel. The man at the desk said Mr. and Mrs. He looked at me to tell him my name. Linda looked at me too so I sign Leroy and Linda Chester he gave us our key to room 310. We walked in and boy it was nice Linda this is nice. She could tell it was my first time in a hotel. I see this is your first time she said.

I felt like a fool for acting all excited, I went to take a shower and when I came out Linda had order us dinner and wine. I like this life. Money can make you happy and you can live a good life style. I told Linda how happy I was with her I put her in my arms and kissed her next thing we were in bed making love. The next morning we went shopping for things to put in her shop. We heard about these sisters who make clothes they told Linda that they would make sure they send her clothes every month and if she didn't like them she could sell them back to them.

They wanted Linda to send them a thousand dollars a month and they would make sure she got the best. Linda told them she would be in New York for a few days and if she decide, to do business with them she would be back. We went to a factory that made clothes shoes and jewelry they had real nice suites and dresses. They said they would ship as often as she needed them too.

So Linda made a deal with them to ship all the things she picked out. She picked out over ten thousand dollars worth of things the factory was owned by an Italian. The owner of the factory wanted to take us to lunch to his restaurant. The food was good Linda told him about her club and shop. His name was Levi Roman he gave Linda his personal phone number and address. Levi said, "He would ship all of her things back with us when we leave on the train.

He said to her that he like doing business with her and you too Leroy. We thanked him and left. The next day we got on the train back to Little Rock. Ice man picks us up and we had to wait until they got all the stuff off the train. We took everything to the shop when we got there Lilly was real busy. The shelf was almost empty I started to help her Ice Man and Linda went to the back. After awhile Linda and Ice Man came back it was time to close the shop I waited on the last customer.

Linda walked over to Lilly and said to her how much money you been taking every day? Don't you lie to me you know that I told you

The Man on the Train

what will happen if you take my money. I haven't been taking money girl you know I wouldn't take your money. Well what the hell you taking my damn clothes and selling them on the side?

Girl no. Ice Man giving, you a ride home today. Leroy and I will lock up. Linda I don't need Ice Man to take me home I have my own car. What's wrong with you Linda? I work hard for you I have been here over six years? I want to know why you think I'm stealing your money. Why in the hell the money not coming up right with the clothes I been ordering? Tell me bitch what you doing? Why did you think I left Ice Man with you? He saw you selling my clothes on the side and putting the damn money in your pocket. Linda I am sorry I need more money to pay bills and help my mother.

Why didn't you ask me Lilly you know I would given it to you? I just gave you a twenty five dollars raise when the business picked up. You took a lot of money from me I don't need you anymore your fired. I'm sorry Linda I won't do it anymore I know the hell you won't I promise that I would kill anyone that fuck me over. You should thought about that when you stole from me. Get the fuck out of here Lilly before I kill you right now. Lilly ran out of the shop got in her car and drove away. Linda, Lilly is nice she just made a mistake. You stay out of it! Leroy I can handle myself! You can't let people push you around because you're a woman.

The next day I went and opened the shop it was almost noon and no one had came in I put things on the rack and changed some of the things around. I like working at the shop meeting different people, business was slow today. I close early and went home. Two days have gone by and I worked at the shop alone. One of the ladies that came in a lot said I'm so sorry to hear about Lilly. What about Lilly? You mean you don't know she use to work here. Yes she quit a few days ago. Well ain't what I heard.

I heard she was caught stealing money and was fired. They found her dead this morning. What you say? You mean you didn't know what happened to her? They found a bottle of empty pills next to her bed she took too many and she had been drinking. They found the bottle of whisky on her table next to her bed. They checking into it making sure she did it.

Oh shit the woman looked at me and said you really didn't know she was dead. I'm sorry I need to close the shop and find out what happened.

I just told you what happen did you just hear me. Yes, yes I hurried the lady out the door locked the door and went to the Club to talk to Linda. Did you know Lilly was dead? Oh she is to damn bad. Linda you don't care? I don't give a damn no one take from me and think they gone get by. I had a feeling Linda had something to do with Lilly's death but how can I be sure. How come you here why you not at the shop? Business is slow I lock up when I heard about Lilly I couldn't work. She looked funny don't worry I'll open back up in the morning. I got me a drink.

I found me a table and Ice Man came over and sat with me. Ice did you know Lilly was dead? Yes, I know all about it. What do you mean? Did Linda have anything to do with her death? I ordered more drinks and Ice was drinking with me then he started telling me that Linda told him to take care of Lilly.

What you mean man? I went to Lilly's house late that night she let me in she was drinking I saw a bottle of pain pills on her night stand and I made her take them she left a few in the bottle. I told her to take the rest of them she fell asleep with them in her hand.

I never had to touch her I left and came back and told Linda what happen. Did someone see you leave her house? I don't know I got out of there as fast as I could it was real dark the other night. I made sure I left nothing I never even sat down. She knew Linda sent me she never said anything to me she just did as I said she never tried to get away or nothing. Ice I don't believe Linda told you to really do that. Poor Lilly I liked working with her I couldn't believe she was stealing she was a hard worker. Linda came over and said what you two guys talking about?

Nothing I said, I was telling Ice I need someone to help me at the shop maybe he can help me until I find someone. No! (She said) I need Ice at the Club he work for me I'll find someone to help you. She left and went back talking to her customers. Thank, you Leroy, for not saying anything about Lilly. Ice I don't want to get in the middle of nothing I have too much to deal with of my own. I just don't want to get into anymore than I have too.

Linda hired a girl to work with me her name is Lisa Smith.

The Man on the Train

Lisa is a real cute little black girl have a nice shape, shoulder length hair, and about size ten she worked out good she caught on fast.

Everyone thought Lilly died of suicide they never found out that Ice helped cause her death. I knew I should tell the police but how could I talk after all the wrong things that I did. I know I need to turn myself in for all my crimes. One day I will it hunts me all the time I haven't forgot what I did in my past. Some days it almost drives me crazy I get a drink and it calms me down some. I try to block it out of my mind as much as I can. I got to thinking about the day I was leaving Derry with Linda and Ice I had a feeling not to come back to Little Rock with them.

I been back only a few weeks I called Pete to see if he was alright. He wanted me to come back to Derry because he really miss me he didn't think Little Rock was a place for me anymore. Oh Pete I'll be alright I'll come see you in a few weeks if you need me before I get back just call me.

It's been another year and things are going fine I haven't seen JJ or Terry since she tried to kill me. I really don't want to see them any more.

Days and days have passed by. I knew everything about running the shop Linda let me take over the shop.

One day I looked up and in walk JJ, hello Leroy. Hi JJ what are you doing here? I heard you worked here and I came here to see if it was true. It's good to see you I heard you moved back to Oklahoma and I thought you were still there. I just went back long enough to get better after a few weeks I came back. I felt bad about what happened to you and Terry. How is Terry? She is doing okay she really feels bad what she did to you man. She wanted to tell you how sorry she was and to thank you for dropping the charge on her but she think you in Oklahoma.

Leroy I know you two will never be together again but I like you and I want you in my life I miss you man. I fell love for you for some reason I don't want you out of my life. I'm sorry for what Terry did to you but I had nothing to do with that it's between the two of you.

I told you a long time ago I felt like I knew you all my life remember you said you would like to be my brother. I looked at him and tears filled my eyes when I looked at him I saw John Chester's face and all I could say was JJ I am sorry I' m so sorry. What for man? One day I'll tell you everything I hugged him and he had a big smile on his face.

He looked around the shop and said, "So this is where you work, do you like it better than working at the train station? Yes I do I don't have to look at Old George Cross we both started laughing.

Look around JJ see something you like? This is Lisa, will you help him? He and Lisa started to talk and she was helping him to find something. Do you see anything that you want?

Man I can't afford nothing in here. Get what you want we have sales and I'll pay the balance. I will give you a real good sale.(he smile). Okay man I like these pants and this shirt. You need some shoes to go with them? Don't worry about it I got you man. Thank you Leroy I am glad I came by now that I know where you are I'll be back. We hug and he left.

Linda's Club was still doing good everyone started calling me Mr. Chester because I dress in fine clothes, shoes, and I drive a Cadillac I began to like it. After I closed I went to the Club Ice Man asked me if I wanted to play dice with him. I never played dice for money with anyone.

Ice do Linda know you doing this in her Club?

No she went home early we just having a little game tonight.

Ice said he would teach me. All you have to do is throw the dice.

I played and won four hundred and fifty dollar. They said it was beginner luck.

I remember hearing James kill Andy over a dice game. They wanted me to keep playing but I stop. It was getting late so I went home I was still living with Linda. I walked in and looked at this woman and wondered who was she? What was she really like? Was she that cold that she could have Ice kill Lilly over money. I kept looking at her she looked at me and said, "What the hell you looking at me like that"?

I looked like some kind of damn animal to you. I had to think fast I didn't want her to put Ice on me. No Linda I'm looking at you because you're a beautiful woman. She smile and said you're a very handsome man, Leroy I think you're the man I want in my life I like the way you handle yourself. I'm looking over my sales and there's more money at my shop than I have ever made. I think I put the right

The Man on the Train

one in charge here is some extra money for you. Thank you Linda she gave me a thousand dollars. Linda I need Ice Man to help me pick up some thing I ordered at the train station I'll need him early in the morning. Okay she said, I went to my room so I could relax.

After I got in bed I heard my door open Linda walked in with a light blue see through gown on and a tray of food. She said you like snacks? She walked over to the bed with the tray in her hand and sat on the bed. There was strawberry cheese, crackers, grapes, and whip cream and a bottle of wine. She, bend over and started to kiss me. She turned on music. She started to strip dance for me she was beautiful. Do you like what you see Mr. Leroy? Yes, yes I like what I see she came over and put her breast in my face and her nipples stood out I put my hands on her breast. We kissed and kissed next thing I was making love to her and she knew how to make a man cry. All I could do was keep making love to this woman and I loved it she made me feel like I was a real man and I pleased her. I showed her what I could do and I had her screaming Oh baby, oh baby please don't stop." I was fucking her so hard I couldn't stop. All the things, that was built up in me I tried to take it all out on her me being a young man I could go for a while and she loved it. She could take it because she was an older woman and she knew how to take it. She knew how to please me too she told me to give her what I got and I showed her what I had. She knew how to teach me a lot we fell asleep.

We never got to eat until the next morning. I got ready for work and called Ice Man to come and take me to the train station to pick up my shipment. When I got there I saw Sally Cross she came over to me and she act like she was so glad to see me. She told me how happy she was that I found another job and she was doing well. She hugged me and said she wish me well. I turned around and low behold there stood old George Cross. Boy get your damn hands off my wife this will be the last time you put your hands on her. I, been watching you and I know a lot about you now I am just waiting for the right time to turn your ass in. You, going to be behind bars for a long time. I looked at him and I was ready to cut his damn throat right then and there.

Sally said, Leroy don't let him get to you he just trying to make you mad.

He still acting a fool he ain't got nothing on you (she said) and walked away. Ice Man came with a box of things and we was leaving George said boy I see you got yourself a big black body guard his ass ain't gone help you when you take your ass to jail. Ice Man started walking to him and he started backing up scared as hell. Ice stood over him looked down at him and said old man you better watch yourself I don't take shit off no one. Not even old gray ass white men next time you see me I'll get in that ass and you better leave Leroy alone.

Keep your noisy ass out of people business. Come on Ice. Ice Man had George running in the office with Sally and he closed the door. Ice and I took the things to the shop I told Ice to pick me up after work.

I didn't want to go to the Club tonight I wanted to rest. I knew Linda would be at the club and I wanted to be sleep before she got home.

We had a good day at the shop Lisa was so good she and I became friends. I told her if she, need extra money to please tell me I didn't want her to take any money from Linda. I knew what would happen to her.

I count the money to get it ready to take to the bank the next morning.

I lock the money in the safe and got ready for Ice to pick me up he was late picking me up. I got in the car and we started to go home we had to go across Jasper Bridge to get home. We saw someone driving down the road on a tractor we got closer and closer and low behold it was George Cross. Ice said, I ought to run his old ass over. No leave him alone.

Ice drove up beside of him and said to him you old gray ass bastard you out here by yourself I should get out and kick your old ass. Old George eyes got so big I thought they would jump out of his head. Git, git the hell away from me you black bastard. Ice got mad at him and tried to run him off the road. I said Ice please leave the man alone he ain't worth it.

George tried to out run us we started laughing and laughing. After we cross the bridge we were still behind him he pulled over on the side of the road and we went by laughing. We drove on off laughing because we scared him. We said, "Bet he would leave us alone." I looked back and I didn't see him. Ice said, "Look like old Sally Cross will be washing George shitty drawer tonight. We laugh and though no more about it. Then I thought oh Ice what if George call the police on us you know how much he hate us. Ice what have we done let's go to the Club so we can say we were there all night then we will have a lot of witnesses.

He so glad to be home with Sally he ain't gone mess with us no more.

We stayed until the Club closed. Ice I'll ride home with Linda and talk to you tomorrow. Keep your mouth closed. Oh man we cool the next day we didn't hear anything that George told anyone. The next day we heard that he was missing they had it on the news he had been missing for twenty four hours.

If anyone knew where he was call the police or his wife Sally Cross. His wife said, he didn't come home all night and she had not seen him the next day. She said it was not like George not to come home she said he had a bad back and he may be hurt and couldn't get up. She said, the last time she saw him he had left the train station on his way home. She told the police he was talking to me and Ice Man the police came and asked me where was George Cross?

Have you seen him lately? Did, he said anything to you when you were at the station? What did you talk about? What are you asking me for I don't know where he is? You and your friend was the last one talking to him the other day. I saw him at the train station he was telling me how glad he is that I found me another job so I wouldn't be working with his wife we laughed and left. Boy you better not be lying to me if I find out you done anything to George you will never see the light of day. I tried to stay calm I didn't know what Ice Man would say. I had to go see him so we would tell the police the same story. After the police left I went to the Club to talk to Ice when I got up there they said Ice had left. Where in the hell did he go? I went back home and called back to the Club to see if Ice had made it back. They said, "The police came and picked him up and took him with them to ask him about some old white man name George.

Okay. I hung up I didn't know what Ice Man would say we only was just teasing him, and just having fun. The last time we saw him he had pulled on the side of the road. If that bastard get down there and tell them that we was teasing George no telling what they will think if something happened to George. I couldn't go down to the police station what the fuck can I do? I need me a drink I sat there for a minute. I thought about calling Donald Smith Johnnie Mae's lawyer. He had told me Johnnie Mae told him to help me. I knew I had to be careful what I said to him. I knew he loved black women and he would do what ever he could to help and I knew he was white too. I had to trust him so I called him and I took another drink. Donald this is Leroy Chester, "Oh yes Leroy what can I do for you?

I have a friend at the police station they picked him up to question him about a white man name George Cross They came by asking me about him being missing. We talked to George the other day at the train station. The police said that we were the last one's who talk to him. I want to know why they took him to the police station and if he needs a lawyer?

You know what happen to black people at the police station can you help him? I'll call you later when I find out what's going on. You can reach me at Linda's dress shop I'll get back to you Leroy.

What's his name? Jericho Young we call him Ice Man. I waited and waited it seem like for hours I couldn't keep my mind off Ice Man wondering what he was saying. Business was slow so I fixed me a drink I can think better after I had a drink. The phone rung, I grab it before it could ring again. Hello, Leroy this is Donald. They only questioning Mr. Young about George they said he didn't know where George was. I told them I was his lawyer and they can't talk to him until I came down. I talked to Jericho and told him you hired me to be his lawyer and for him not to say anything unless I was there. I told him to keep his mouth closed until he talked to me. The first thing in the morning I need you and Mr Young in my office at 9:00 a m. Thank you Donald.

Boy was I relieved a few minutes later Ice Man came in, thank you Leroy for getting me out of there. I kind of felt they thought I knew more about George. I told them I didn't know where he was, you know Leroy I been to the pen and I don't want to go back. We have nothing to hide there's nothing wrong with teasing anyone, George is probably home telling Sally he was over his girlfriend house. Ha, ha. Come on let's go to Linda's I'll call Marie and tell her to fix us something to eat.

We can sit by the pool and relaxed. Leroy I love you.

Lisa said she would lock up. We got ready and left when we got to Jasper Bridge there were a lot of red flashing lights. When we got close there were police cars every where the ambulance was there when we got closer the police was stopping cars. What happen I said? What's wrong? Keep moving the police man said, we kept moving when we got over on the other side of the bridge we asked what happened?

They said they found George Cross's body he been dead for a few hours. Oh my God, what happened? Why is he dead? Look like he pulled off the rode and his tractor, hit a hole flip over and he fell under the tractor. The ditch was deep and you couldn't see it from the rode. Some kids were playing under the bridge and found him.

A few days later I heard George had a heart attack and died at the scene they said it was a freak accident. They said they didn't find anything else showing any different. They only saw George tire tracks I felt so bad that we may have been the cause of his death we didn't know. I went back to the train station to see if Sally knew but someone had all ready told her and she was gone. A few days later they buried him I really felt bad.

Now I go to the train station I don't see him anymore. They said, they didn't know when Sally would be back.

I sat down and started to think about my life the secrets I have and can't tell anyone but Pete. I can trust him we talk over the phone a lot it had been a few months since I was in Oklahoma.

I fell it's time I go back to Derry to see Pete.

I need to feel safe I know I'm being punished for the things I've done. I know one day I will pray for my crimes. Ice came and said he was leaving and going back to New York for a few weeks. His mother was sick and, he wanted to go to be with her. I understand man I know how it feels to be near your mother. I really miss my mother, when I'm at my mother home I really feel safe. I feel her around me and I know I'm okay.

I think I'll go back home too Ice. Say man why don't you go to New York with me it will do us both some good. Let me show you around and you can find new things for the shop. They have new things there everyday Linda can help Lisa or hire someone to help her for a few days or do it herself. Oh man I don't know. I know Linda don't want me to leave for a few weeks. Leroy she ain't your mama I know but she been so nice to me. She, haven't been taking care of her taxes so I been paying them and reporting them to the IRS.

I tried to tell her about the Club and she got mad at me. She said she been taking care of it all these years she didn't need anyone telling her what to do, and keep my nose out of her shop she can run it anyway she want. She stop checking the sales since Lilly died long as money coming in she happy. I make sure she get her money I don't want you to take care of me like you did Lilly.

Oh Leroy I wouldn't do nothing to you. You like a brother. I really appreciate you getting that lawyer for me I know you called about me thank you man. Now will you go to New York with me? Let me see first I need to make sure Lisa have help at the shop and check with Linda. I told Linda I was going back to New York to get more things I wanted to put in the shop and I wanted to rest while I was there. She said she would take care of things and keep and eye on the shop. I told her Ice and I was going she had a lot of help at the club. The next day Ice and I drove to New York we arrived at his mother house and she was very sick when we got there. His sister was there and she said the doctor said she wouldn't get any better. His mother wanted to talk to Ice alone. He went in to her room and was in there for a long time. His sister was looking at me the whole time I felt so uneasy. She never said anything to me. Ice came out and asked his sister if she would fix us something to eat.

Who is this you bringing here she said? This is my friend Leroy. Well you and your friend find someone to cook for you because I damn show ain't. Cause I ain't nobody's damn maid. Ice looked at her and said Lola Mae you still a damn fool. Kiss my ass she said. Come on Leroy let's go. He took me to a place called mama Queens a soul food place we walked in and everyone came up to Ice Man saying where you been Ice? Good to see you when did you get out of the joint? I been out, I been living in Little Rock I came back to check on my mama. You, coming over to Faye Allen place tonight we still having parties over there and they having a big game tonight?

The pot is big tonight come on over and get you some of that money. I don't know maybe I well see you later. Ice showed me around I saw the Statue of Liberty and a few more things Ice said his mother told him she wanted him to stay with her until she died. She, really need him to take care of her. She, need him to make sure he take care of everything for her. She didn't trust Lola Mae, she said, Lola Mae would take every thing she had. Because she drank a lot and was on some kind of drugs we went back to Ice mothers house. Lola Mae was gone Ice went in his mothers room and a few minutes later he called me into her room. This is my mother Rita Young, Hello, Mrs. Young. How are you?

She smiled and nodded her head.

Ice, do you need to take her to the doctor?

She said it was nothing they could do for her they did everything they could for her. She said for her to keep taking her pain pills. That damn sister of mines, been stealing some of them. I have to stay and take care of her mama. Mama said she take them from her when they deliver them. She told Ice to give her some and she will sleep all night he tried to get her something to eat but she wouldn't eat. After, his mother went to sleep. Ice wanted to go to Faye Allen house to gamble. When we got to her house there were a lot of people there Ice got in the game and I watched. The money got higher and higher Ice was winning then he lost three hundred dollars. He got mad and said they were cheating.

Come on man lets leave come on I want to leave. Okay, ok man we got in the car and started to talk I told him about my dad killing a man over a dice game. Come on Ice lets go check on your mother she is alone and she needs you. When we got back to his mom's house his sister still wasn't home. His mother was screaming she was in so much pain. We put her in the car and took her to the hospital after she was there for a few hours they moved her to the basement with a lot of other women.

We went down there and Ice tried to talk to her but she never said a word to him. I looked at her and I started to cry, Ice looked at me as if to say what the hell is wrong with you?

We sat beside her bed and a hour later she was dead. I tried to comfort him it's real hard to loose your mother. We went back to the house and Ice found a letter from his mother she had written it before she died.

He read it to me she said.

Honey I hope you find this letter before your sister I been working all my life to save money to retire. After I got sick I knew I had to save money for you and your sister. Here is an insurance policy to bury me with, everything else is paid for. Take the money I have in the bank and help your sister. I want my funeral at Great Baptist Church Rev. E R Jones is the pastor I told him what I want him to do and all the songs I want to be sung at my funeral.

My body is to go to Scott Funeral Home my funeral is paid for. Two days later he buried his mother. Ice where is your sister she need to be here with you. I don't care Leroy I have you with me that means more to me than anything. I don't want her drunken ass here with me. I would have pushed her ass in there with mama. Oh Ice you don't mean that. The hell I don't. I don't know where to find her she somewhere so high, she don't care. I helped him with everything he needed to do because I had nobody to help me when my mother died.

I knew how he felt. I wonder how, could his sister not come to her mother funeral. After the funeral the people came back to Ice's house.

They brought food and were telling him what a good mother he had and how they would miss her. The house started to fill up and I couldn't take it so I went for a walk. I walked around a few blocks and found me a dress shop I went in and bought Linda a beautiful dress and some jewelry I bought myself a new suite. After I got back a lot of people had left and Lola Mae still wasn't home. I told Ice I was tired and needed to go back to Little Rock. He said he had to stay and take care of his mothers things and to see about his sister. Leroy, do you want me to find someone to drive back with you? No Ice you keep the car and bring it back later I'll catch the train. I called Linda and told her to pick me up at the train station the next day I left.

When I got to Little Rock the train pulled up and there were police everywhere. What the hell is going on? My heart was pumping so hard I thought I was having a heart attack. I thought they were looking for me to ask me about Al and John. I sat there I wasn't getting off the train but I looked out the window and I saw Linda waving at me. I got up slowly and when I got off the train the police showed me a picture of a man and wanted to know if I saw him on the train. I looked at the picture but I didn't know him. Linda ran to me and said hello baby and put her arms around me. Hi baby I miss you come on. She, grab me and I took off with her. Baby wait you okay? Yes let's go home I'm tired. You have to get your bags, Leroy what the hell is wrong with you? After I got home I had to have me a drink before I could calm down. What's wrong with you? "Nothing" Bullshit I know something is wrong you was so damn scared when you saw all them policeman. I thought you were getting ready to run that is why I came and grabbed you.

Linda I just don't like the police they always make me nervous. Come here I got something for you from New York. What did you bring me? Oh Leroy this dress is beautiful thank you and I love this jewelry oh baby thank you. Linda started kissing on me and hugging me Leroy I love you and I miss you so much while you was gone. She kept kissing on me so next thing I know we were making love. That was the first time she told me she loved me she wanted me to tell her I loved her. But I couldn't because I was still in love with Terry I knew I would never see her again.

Linda wanted me to keep making love to her but I couldn't I knew I had to be careful with this woman. I know she can be cold blooded when she had Ice kill Lilly. I don't think I can trust her anymore I couldn't get it back up after thinking what she had did to Lilly.

What's wrong with you? You been fucking some other woman I looked at her and I wanted to slap her but I just turned over I'm just tired. I need to rest from the long trip from New York, I'll make it up to you later Linda okay. I kissed her on her forehead and she jumped out of bed and she said fuck you and went out of the room. I just laid there for a while and thought about Terry I knew I hurt her. I thought about the baby we would have had. Lord my life is so screwed up I'm still a young man and I don't know how I screwed up my life. I feel like an old man every since I left home looking for John Chester and every since I lost my mother.

I just kept laying there I didn't want to get up and fix me a drink. I need to stop drinking so much the only time I stop drinking so much was when I was in Oklahoma with Pete. I got up the next day and went to work we had been real busy that day. I told Lisa I was going to work on the books and she could lock up I went in the office, a few minutes Lisa came in and said someone wanted to see me. I walked out to see who it was and I just stood there I couldn't believe my eyes. It was Terry and JJ. Hello Leroy. Hello Terry.

Leroy I'm so sorry for what happened can you forgive me? I can understand if you don't Leroy I been hurting so bad for what I did to you I miss you so much. I had to come tell you how sorry I was JJ told me you worked here. If you want me to leave I will, I forgive you Terry I should have explained to you about me leaving I was thinking about you last night. I miss you too I thought how much you must hate me for what I did to you causing you to lose the baby. Lisa and JJ had walked over to the other side of the room to talk and left me and Terry to talk. Terry I'm seeing someone else. I know Leroy I'm not here to start anything I just wanted to come to see you and ask you for forgiveness.

Terry my life is a little screwed up right now I don't want to hurt you anymore. Leroy if you ever need me you know where to find me. I still love you. Leroy, don't forget me. I won't Terry.

How is Hattie and the kids? Oh Hattie moved to Mississippi she met a guy there the year she left Sam. She told me he was the father of her last son so she went back to him. Well I'll be damn she went back to her secret. What you mean? Oh something she told me a long time ago it's good to see you Terry.

You to Leroy you look so handsome I like your new look thank you. Do you need anything Terry? How is David? He's still with his father, I don't need anything David's father is giving me money and I found me a job.

Lisa came over and took Terry by the arm and walked away with her to show her something. JJ came over for me to show him something he said, Lisa told him that my girlfriend had just drove up and she don't want trouble. JJ grabbed a shirt let me buy this shirt. I rung it up. I told him to bring it back and I would give him back his money. Linda walked up and said hi baby. JJ went over and took Terry by the arm as if she was his lady and they walked out. I wanted to go to both of them. I wanted to go to both of them and tell them don't leave me. I wanted to say to JJ I'm your uncle. I just stood there looking at them drive away. Lisa started talking to Linda so she wouldn't think anything was wrong with me.

I could tell Linda was looking at me so I started to mess with clothes on the rack. Leroy, are you alright? Yes I'm fine.

I just stopped by on my way home to pick up some things for the Club. I'll see you later. I was so glad to see her leave. Leroy are you alright?

Yes, thank you Lisa for what you did? I owe you one. Oh I just didn't want her coming in here starting no shit JJ told me you use to be in love with his sister. When I saw her drive up and she came in and saw you talking to her you know she may have acted a fool. Yes she would have I was glad to see Terry. It's been over a year between us you know Lisa I'm getting tired of so many things. Do you want to talk Leroy I'm a good listener?

Thank you Lisa, there is only one person in this whole world I can trust and tell anything to and that is my friend Pete. I think I'll call him now I need to talk to him. Thank you again Lisa.

Hello Pete, are you okay? Yes Leroy I'm fine the police was out to your house looking around but they couldn't find anything. They said, they think you had something to do with Al Jenkins death they said they just can't prove it. They couldn't find anything I made sure everything was clean around the place. I made sure the car was clean. Thank you Pete I love you. I love you too Leroy. Don't worry they can't find nothing it's been four years ago.

When are you coming home Leroy? I don't know real soon I know real soon Pete. Remember the girl Terry and her brother JJ, John's kids they came to see me today and I fell a little upset. What did they do? Oh they were real nice you know how sad I get sometimes. I'm getting soft Pete if old James Chester knew that he would kill me. You will be alright son do you want me to come to Little Rock? I would like to see you, when you coming? Well I have to call you back I need to get something's together. You take care of yourself son and I'll get back with you. I love you Pete. Love you too son bye. It feels so good to have someone you really trust in your life. I thought about Terry she looked so good to me I wanted her so bad.

God what's wrong with me she is my nephew's sister come on Leroy I said to myself. I need more in my life I just go to the Club, to the shop and back to Linda's house. What can I do to make my life happy? I think about the long talks to Pete and how I had gone fishing with him living back in Derry. Everything was so quiet and peaceful outside of town I miss Pete. I have money, I have a new car, and I live in a beautiful home. I drink the finest liquid I can go to New York when ever I want and eat at the finest restaurants. I can go every where I want to and I'm not happy. I fell alone the only friend I have is JJ. I talk to people that come into the shop or the Club.

I miss Johnnie Mae she was crazy but I miss her, I miss Hattie she got on my nerves sometimes she was okay just nosey she knew everything that happened on our street. I miss sitting on Johnnie Mae porch watching the people go by and the kid's playing on the street. I said I like the new life I live but something is missing in my life. God what do I need to do to make me happy? Do I need to go to the police station and tell them that I killed Al and John? Do I tell them that Ice and I was the cause of George having a heart attack? Should I just take a damn gun and shoot myself?

Lisa, come in the office. Leroy you been in here for an hour I'm ready to close JJ coming to take me to dinner. I looked at her and said you and JJ are seeing each other? No he just asked me for dinner the other day he was here. Well you go ahead and I'll lock the door and turn the sign around. I'll see you tomorrow.

I got out the books to write down the sales we made today I didn't want to hear Linda's ass crying about money she didn't make today. After I finished I fell asleep next thing I know Linda was shaking me. Leroy, Leroy get up. I jumped up and said all your money is here we did not take it. Leroy what's wrong with you? I know you wouldn't take my money. Why did you say that? Oh Linda I was having a nightmare come on let's go home you look tired. I got up to go home with her. What time is it?

It's, two thirty after I closed the Club I came by the shop and saw your car was still here. That is why I stop by to see if everything was okay. I fell asleep I did the book work. Leroy you look tired do you need a few days off? If you do I can help Lisa with the shop you want to go see Pete? I would like to go back to New York. I like New York let's go have some fun and relax go to dinner and shop. I miss Ice Man I'd like to see him. Oh Leroy I have so much to do here.

Please Linda go with me it will be good for both of us. Well let me get a few things and make sure everyone will come to work while I'm gone. A few days later we left for New York. Ice Man picked us up at the train station. He wanted us to stay at his house but I wanted to stay at the nicest hotel in New York I just wanted to spend money. I just wanted to see if I could leave my past life behind me for a few days. After we got settled in we got dressed for dinner I put on my finest suite and my alligator shoes. I looked in the mirror and I looked

The Man on the Train

good, Linda came out in a beautiful dress and jewelry and her shoes were real nice.

She was very pretty we called for a limousine to pick us up when we walked out to get in the limousine people thought we were singers.

They wanted to know our name we laughed and got in the car and drove away. We told the driver to take us to a fine dinner Club he took us to Roman's. When I walked in I thought Linda had a nice Club but this one was real nice. The waiter sit us down at the table they had a nice band the table had nice silver ware and glasses trim in gold. When the waiter came to take our order I look up and here come Tony Roman. Hello friends, I saw you coming in hello Mr Roman is this your place? Yes, what brings you back to New York? I'm not sending enough clothes. Oh we are just here for fun. Well everything is on me have fun. Thank you Mr. Roman. Call me Levi. He told the waiter give us what ever we want it's on the house. Miss Linda you look beautiful. Thank you she said. I have some new things I would like for you to see before you go back home. Linda was just smiling he was looking at her like he had something real nice to give her. Linda you can stop grinning he's gone. Oh Leroy you jealous? Let's dance. Linda and I danced, we drank, ate, all the food was so good. We were having so much fun I forgot everything for a while. I got so drunk I didn't remember anything when I woke up the next morning I was in bed at the hotel. Linda wasn't in bed with me I looked in the bathroom and Linda wasn't there. I wonder where was she I called down for breakfast for both of us I took me a shower and she still was not back. I waited, and waited for her?

Maybe she went shopping it was over four hours and Linda was still not back. I called Ice Man to come get me and maybe we would find her. Ice pick me up and we rode around the shops were we thought she would be. I was really worried about her Ice said he had to go back by his house for something. I thought about his sister Lola Mae. I asked him, if he and his sister were getting alone better?

Man my sister is dead what! What happened? Why didn't you call me to be here with you? Oh man we didn't get alone she been a fool all her life. I just buried her. I didn't have any money I took the money mama left her and I used it to put her away. Now she, don't, have to be a fool anymore. She was so drunk she walked out it the streets and was hit by a truck. She didn't have a lot of family or friends so I just buried her. I didn't have a funeral I have my mama's house up for sale I was going to surprise you and Miss Linda and come back to Little Rock. Ice I sure would like to have you back I miss you. Okay let's take you back to the hotel to find Miss Linda. We walked in the hotel there was Linda and Levi they were hugging each other. I walked up to them and said, what is this all about?

Oh Leroy you was sleep and I couldn't wake you so I went to Levi clothing factory and picked out some more things for him to send back home for me. He was just thanking me we had lunch together he's having a party tonight and we are invited. Yes, Leroy and bring your friend. Hello Miss Linda? Hello Ice is everything fine I was so sorry to hear about your mother? When are you coming back to Little Rock? Do you have everything taken care of? Almost Ice said.

I'll see you tonight Linda, okay Levi thank you for a nice day.

I wanted to grab her by her damn hair and drag her damn ass up to the third floor. What! What! Why are you looking like that she said. I thought we came here to spend all our time together and have fun. Listen Leroy, you are not my husband I told you I know how to take care of myself. I don't need, no man telling me what to do this is why I'm not married. I don't take shit off nobody and that mean you too. I'm a smart business woman and I know what I'm doing. If you don't like my friends I'm sorry. Find you some. Linda you didn't have to say all that. she went in the other room. That damn woman is crazy come Ice let's go to the bar I need a drink. We found a bar and we talked I saw a nice looking woman across the room looking at me. I told Ice I was going to introduce myself Ice said, man come on let's go get ready for that party tonight. I like eating all that good food. You go ahead Ice I don't want to party with Linda tonight.

I want to meet new friends and I see who I want to be with tonight and it damn sure ain't Linda. She can kiss my ass oh do you still work for her?

I don't, won't to be found dead in my room. Leroy, man you didn't have to say that you drunk. Fuck Levi damn party. And fuck Linda. Come on man. Ice caught me by the arm and took me to the room. I walked in and Linda was in the bathroom. Ice said he would

The Man on the Train

be back to pick us up. Miss Linda what time do you want me, to pick you up.

She yelled seven thirty I sit down and went to sleep. I didn't want to talk to her right now. I was still mad at her for leaving me and going off with Levi. She didn't say noting to me until time to go to Levi's party. Leroy wake up and get ready for the party, I just kept laying there she said well I came to New York to have fun with you so get ready. I'm going to this party with or without you it's up to you. I looked at that woman and I knew then that I really don't like her. I don't know this woman I thought about her having Lilly killed. I believe she would do me the same way I got up and took me a shower when I came out Linda was standing there dressed like a movie star she looked beautiful. She looked at me like I was shit I didn't understand I thought she loved me. I thought she was mad at me for the way I acted around Levi.

You look nice Linda is that a new dress? Yes Levi picked this dress out for me to wear tonight when I went to the factory. He, help me pick out a lot of things to send back to my shop. I do look good Levi knows how to make beautiful clothes. He said, I need to go up on my store prices a little. I could make more money when we get back home I'll go over things with you. Knock, knock, at the door I went to the door and there stood a man in a black suite and black hat. He said, I'm the driver for Levi he sent me to pick you up. We ready she said. Linda we have to wait on Ice he wants to go with us.

Oh shit Leroy he should have been here we need to go.

Linda can't you just wait for a few minutes for Ice? I'm ready to go! She told the driver let's go she told me to keep my ass here and left me standing there. I couldn't believe Linda I wonder what's wrong with her about five minutes later Ice came. You ready to go Leroy? Where is Miss Linda? She left without us, she what! Yes. I told her to wait until you came but she didn't want to she left with Levi's driver. You mean she couldn't wait five minutes on me Leroy you better watch that bitch she said she had to kiss a lot of ass to get where she is today.

I know a nice Club we can go, to you want to go? Yes, let's go we don't have to kiss her ass she can take her uptight ass to the rich man's house.

She think she is rich anyway she can kiss our ass. You right Leroy let's go. Ice and I went down to Harlem and boy did we have fun they were jumping. We went to another club. We danced and danced with all kinds of pretty girls. We were out all night long. I didn't give a damn about Linda I was having so much fun with Ice Man. I drunk so many different kinds of drinks I never tasted before. The food was the best in New York I think I'm going to stay here I love New York. I didn't want to go back to the hotel I went home with Ice. The next morning Ice took me back to change my clothes Linda was not there. I found a note she left it said I'll see you back in Little Rock.

I didn't know where you were I had to go. Man that bitch left me and went back to Little Rock. Leroy I been trying to tell you she is a cold blooded woman. Ice I'm staying the rest of the week with you.

I got all my stuff out the room Ice helped me carried my bags. When I went to the desk to check out they said everything was taken care of.

Ice and I was riding over the New York Bridge there was so much to see. The ocean was beautiful after my fourth day there I knew I had to go back to Little Rock. I knew Linda may have put my things out side I knew I would have to find me a place to stay when I got back. Ice will you take me to the train station? Sure man why don't you just stay here with me Leroy you cane find a good job here? No Ice I need to know what she up to. Okay, man if it don't work out come on back.

Ice was taking me to the train station. When we were was passing Levi's Club I be damn there stood Linda and Levi. He had his arms around her. Ice stop that bitch is still here with that damn Italian she been here for four days. Stop the damn car. Man what you going to do? Stop the damn car I said. I'm going back I want to see what she up too.

Leroy please don't go back, stay here with me man.

These Italians here don' t play. You don't want to mess with them. Ice I don't take shit either I been trying to keep my cool. There is a lot in my pass that I said I would never do again. I won't let no, one make an ass out of me. I know now what I need to do when I get back to Little Rock.

I was so damn mad at Linda I wanted to cut her damn throat I caught the train and went back home. I know how to hurt her and not put a hand on her. When I got off the train I heard someone call my name. Hello Leroy, I turned around and it was Sally Cross. Hello Sally, how are you? I'm doing okay Leroy. Sally I'm sorry about George.

Thank you, Leroy. I been out of town a lot Sally I just got back it's good to see you. You too Leroy, Here Sally I know it's not much but will you take this money to help out a little. It's all I have on me right now. Why this is seven hundred dollars I can't take all this money. Please Sally I want you to have it if you need more come to me and I'll help you. Thank you, Leroy I told George you were a good man. Sally you was good to me when I first moved here. I have a good job and money now I can help you if you need anything. Sally hugged me and kissed me on the cheek.

I caught a cab and went to Linda's house packed all my clothes and put them in my car. Leroy what's wrong with you and Miss Linda did you have a fight or something? Why didn't you come back together?

She called and said she would be back tomorrow. Why you moving? I just need a place of my own. Thank you Marie for all your kindness while I here I just need to move on. I went to the dress shop to take care of things before she came back. Pete told me I would have to always take care of myself in life I'm glad I listened to him. He said, there are some people in this world you just can't trust. After I saw what Linda did to me in New York and what she had Ice do to Lilly I knew I couldn't trust her. I kept two sets of books I was smarter than Lilly. At the end of the day I put money to the side for me. That was what I was doing when I worked late at night doing book work. Linda was so greedy for money all she wanted to know was what she made.

When she turned the shop over to me I ordered all the supplies I would order more than she did. I wrote all the checks to pay all the bills at the shop I wrote checks to Levi every month that is why I kept a set of books. One day she came in a hurry and I gave her papers to sign she didn't read them. They were papers giving me her dress shop if anything happened to her. I told her they were order slips she signed them and left never reading them. As long as she got money she was happy I got all the books and the paper work and put them in the trunk of my car.

Lisa was not there she had closed early.

Linda was spending a lot of time at the club she loved that club more after I started working at the shop. I got paid every week. She paid Lisa every week also it made her feel good to come in and give us what she wanted to and she would keep all the rest. I was sending money to Pete every month I knew one day I would have to stop working and I would have me some money. When, I move back to Oklahoma.

I need to find me somewhere to stay before she came back. I left the fake papers in her desk and the fake books. I was just ready to walkout when the phone rung I knew it was Linda. I started to not answer the phone.

It was Marie she said Linda called and said she would be back in a few more days. She said she would explain everything when, she come back. Leroy the police called here for you and said for you to get back to them it was important. They didn't say what it was. Thank, you Marie. Leroy where can I get in touch with you if we need you? What do you want me to tell Miss Linda when she get back? I'll call her later I don't know right now where I'll be. You take care of yourself Leroy I will miss you.

Marie thanks again for all of your kindness.

I wonder what the police want with me I didn't want to call but I called. Hello this is Leroy Chester I was told the police wanted me to call is anything wrong? What do you want with me?

Mr. Chester we got a call from South Carolina to tell you to come to South Carolina Bobby Parker died and they need you. Bobby is Johnnie Mae's cousin living in the house she left me. I called Pete and asked him if he would catch the train the next day to go with me I need him to go with me. I'm on my way son pick me up at the station tomorrow.

I called Lisa and told her that I would be off work for a while I had to go to South Carolina. I didn't know how long I would be gone she said she would be okay and she would tell Linda when she came back. I took some nice clothes for Pete because he only wore jeans. I already had real nice clothes for me I called JJ and asked him if I could come over and talk to him he told me I could.

I looked around in the shop and said good bye Linda I got in my car ad went to JJ's house. When I got there JJ was waiting for me with

The Man on the Train

a drink. Leroy you didn't sound good are you alright? You remember Johnnie Mae. Yes. Her cousin in South Carolina died and I have to go there to help take care of things. I never been to South Carolina and I don't know what to do when I get there. Johnnie Mae told her lawyer what to do if I need to know anything. May I use your phone? Sure. Donald this is Leroy Chester. Yes Leroy. Johnnie Mae cousin died this morning and I don't know what to do. Leroy you don't have to do nothing but go and take charge of your house and what's left in it. Johnnie Mae took care of everything but you do have to go as soon as you can, so your things won't be stolen. Johnnie Mae wanted you to be at her cousins funeral to be apart of his family because he didn't have no one left.

Do you have the address? Yes, she gave it to me before she died. Call me when you get there. Thank you Donald good bye. When are you leaving Leroy?

As, soon as my friend Pete gets here from Oklahoma. You know I never been to South Carolina mind if I go? Do you mind if I spend the night with you? Sure man I would love for you to go with me. Man what about your girlfriend? Think she mind? I don't think so I don't think I want her as my friend anymore. What happened? I don't think she like me anymore I don't have enough money for her. Oh man for real. Yes.

I think this trip to South Carolina may do me good. I don't know how long I'll be there do you still want to go? Yes, what about your job? I don't care I need to get away I need to call Terry and let her know I'm going. He called Terry and told her. Leroy she want to know how we going? Tell her I'm driving my car, we can get there faster. You and Pete can help me drive and we will be there in no time.

We will have a car to get around when we get there. We picked Pete up at the train station we hugged each other I was so glad to see him. I asked him if he was tired and needed to rest before we go he said no. This is JJ the one I told you about, nice to meet you JJ. You too Pete hope we enjoy the ride together Leroy always talk about you he really loves you.

We had a nice drive there, Pete and JJ got alone fine we got there before it was dark. We asked for directions and found the house. Oh my God, I wasn't looking for a house so nice Pete said, are you sure this is the right house? This is the address she gave me we pulled in the driveway and a lady came out of the house. Hello, are you Leroy Chester? Yes, well get out and come on in.

We all looked at each other and got out and went in. And oh my God the inside was just as nice as the outside I loved it. Pete this is ours. The lady who told us to come in said her name was Sarah. She said she lived here and took care of Bobby, I was told after Bobby died you would be here to take care of everything. Johnnie Mae didn't know if you would want me to stay here or not. I been taking care of Bobby since Johnnie Mae and her mother died. Let me show you your room Leroy. I walked through and thought I had died and went to heaven. Linda's bed room was nothing like this room it was beautiful the bed was a king size with a blue and gold bed spread with drapes the same color. It had a bathroom in the bedroom everything in that room was light blue gold and white. The furniture was cherry wood there was a big couch and end tables in the bed room and it had beautiful lamps. I couldn't believe all this belong to me. She showed Pete his room and JJ his as well everyone room was beautiful. Johnnie Mae's mother had the house decorated. She owned one of the finest restaurants in South Carolina. In the den there was a bar with all kinds of liquor in it there was a kitchen with a lot of food. She had a double car garage and a big front porch. Pete what, do you and JJ think of this?

We went in the back yard and there were beautiful trees and flowers the yard was so beautiful. There was a patio with tables and chairs everything was nice. Sarah said Johnnie Mae packed a lot of stuff and put it in the garage. She was coming back to get it but she died before she could come back. I know you're tired if you like to rest I'll cook you all something to eat I know you must be hungry make yourselves at home. As long as you're here Leroy I will take care of you. Thank, you Sarah.

We got our things out of the car and we each went to our rooms. I just stood in my room and just looked at all the nice things in there. I was so lucky to have met Johnnie Mae I felt bad the way I treated her. Thank you, thank you Johnnie Mae I don't think I will ever go back to Little Rock. I'm going to live here forever except to get my money out of the bank. I think my pass is behind me.

The food Sarah cooked was so good. The second day we were there Sarah took us to Bobby's funeral. The three of us dressed like we were the riches men in town when we walked in I could hear them whispering that is Bobby's family from Arkansas. I never saw Bobby or ever talked to him I didn't know him. I been going to so many funeral and I'm only twenty eight years old. After the funeral here come people with food telling me how sorry they were to hear about my cousin Bobby. He was a nice young man we sure put him away good. I didn't know what to say. Pete said yes he sure was and we sure will miss him.

I looked at Pete he said they don't need to know that we don't know him just go alone with them. Pete stood right by my side and when any one said anything Pete did all the talking. After the people left I asked Pete why did, he tell them that we were Bobby cousin. Man you had them thinking we really knew Bobby, JJ and I laughed. Pete I like you he said. Leroy you lucky to have a friend like Pete. Yes I know each day I love Pete more and more. Sarah drove us around to see the town and it was nice I liked what I saw. Pete and JJ liked South Carolina also I told Pete I was going to stay and I want him to stay also. JJ said he was sad that I wasn't coming back to Little Rock. Pete said he had to go back to Oklahoma all his things were there and he had to look after his things. Three days later Pete and JJ left to go back home.

I felt like a king in this big house I told JJ I have nowhere to live in Little Rock. Linda don't want me she found her someone else. Sarah still lives with me taking care of me she have her own room off from the kitchen it was just as beautiful as the other rooms. She had her own bathroom in her bedroom. The other two bedrooms had to use the bath room down the hall.

Sarah how much you charging me to stay here? Leroy you don't pay me nothing, Johnnie Mae had her lawyer to send me money every two weeks to take care of Bobby. I called him and told him Bobby was dead and what did he want me to do?

He said, he will send money to you to take care of me and you for one year and then you will have to find a job to take care of me and the house. Well Sarah that is fine with me in a year Sarah you and I will have enough money to last us a long time because I'm going to open me a business here. If you like Sarah you can help me and I will take care of you. I love Sarah we talked a lot and I told her a lot about my life in Little Rock. We talked about Johnnie Mae, Lucille, Terry and Linda. She laughed and laughed about Johnnie Mae and Lucille. She knew Johnnie didn't take a lot of shit off nobody but she was a good girl. Sarah started to treat me like I was her son some times she remind me of my mother. Sarah was a brown skin lady with a little gray in her hair she had a big smile on her face when she looked at you. She weighed about 145 pounds and was 5'5 boy she was a good cook.

For the first two months I did nothing. I would drive around town to find my way around Sarah told me where not to go. One day I went to this bar and was gone along time when I got home Sarah said, she was so worried about me. Don't worry Sarah I can take care of myself. You haven't been here too long to find out where you can go and not go. Have you had anything to eat? Where have you been so long? Oh Sarah I was just riding around. After we had dinner we sat on the porch. People would come by and say hi Miss Sarah is that your son? I told Sarah about the porch Johnnie Mae had on her house, I loved to sit on the porch. Leroy, tell me about your family? I don't like talking about them Sarah.

Well Leroy I had bad folks too but I still love them I try to get alone with some of them. Sarah they are all dead.

You know Sarah I want to open a big restaurant I want to have dancing, and want everyone having fun. I want to serve real good food like yours. My boy you got big dreams. It's no dream Sarah I'm going to do it and I want you to help me. Will you help me? What do you want me to do? I want you to help me to cook your food and you will be the boss of the kitchen, whatever you say will go. I want the help in the kitchen dress like a chef in white shirts and black slacks and black shoes. I want my club to be so beautiful the people will feel welcome ad leave with smiles on their faces. I want to call it Mr Chester's Club and have the sign in a lot of bright lights. You know Sarah I bet Johnnie Mae knew if I came here I would never leave.

Leroy she had plans to move back here after she retired. That is one reason she sold her mother's restaurant to have a lot of money and she got a lot for it. She never wanted the restaurant because it was too much work and she never like being around a lot of people. Her mama tried to get her to move back and help with the place. Johnnie Mae helped her mama buy the place and when her mama made money she would send it back to Johnnie to repay her for helping

The Man on the Train

her buy the place. You know Sarah she was kind to me she told me she loved me but I didn't know she loved me this much to leave me everything she owned. I feel so bad now about the way I treated her.

Mae told me about you when she was here Mae was always jealous of things she loved. She always thought she wasn't good enough for any man until you came in her life. Well Sarah I'm happy I came into her life, Sarah I have to go back to Little Rock on business and to take care of something's I don't know how long I will be gone. When are you leaving? As soon as I pack a few things maybe tomorrow I need to get there as soon as I can. I need you to take care of things here for me are you driving? Yes, I need a car to get around, I may go to Oklahoma to go see Pete he didn't look happy when he left. When I got to Little Rock I went to the bank to get all my money out. When I got to the bank they told me I didn't need to carry so much money with me they could have it transfer to South Carolina bank for me. They said it would only take a couple of days. I needed a drink I didn't drink every day I was in South Carolina. I had a bar full of liquor and didn't need too but I need one now. I went to the bar on State street hoping to see JJ when I got there they told me he was not there he only worked at night. I went to Linda's dress shop to see Lisa JJ was there.

When they saw me they both gave me a hug and said how glad they were to see me. What you doing here man come to get your job back? No. I'm only here for business, good to see you Leroy. You too Lisa Is Linda treating you good? Oh you know Linda, long as the money coming in she is happy. She ain't changed she hired JJ to take your place. Get out of here. I hope you don't mind Leroy. No, no I ain't ever coming back here to work I'm going to open me a shop in South Carolina. How long you going to be here man?

Just a few days I need to find me a place to stay while I'm here. No you're not you're staying with me and I ain't taking no for an answer. Thank you JJ. We getting ready to close wait a few minute.

I started to look around and, everything was the same as I left it. I loved working here, meeting all different people and dressing nice every day. I didn't really know Linda I didn't trust her after what she did to Lilly. JJ I'll meet you at home I have somewhere to go. Okay Leroy.

Before I, could walk out the door in walk Linda and Levi.

She looked at me and dropped her head, hello Linda.

Hi Leroy, what you doing here? I came by to see Lisa. Leroy I'm sorry Levi told me how much he loved me and how he could show me how to make more money at my Club and shop. He showed me how much he made at his Club he came back with me to help me and when I got back you were gone. The way you treated me in New York and the way you act around Levi, Linda we went to New York to have fun just the two of us. You only spent one night with me you were with him. I spent the night over to Ice's house he brought me back to the room and I found your note. I thought you went back to Little Rock without me I didn't know what I had done to you for you to leave me like that. I stayed the next four days with Ice when he was taking me to the train station I saw you out side of Levi's Club and you was kissing him. I wanted to stop and beat you and his ass but Ice wouldn't stop. I knew then that I didn't want you I could never trust you. You lied to me I came back and packed my clothes and left. I'm so sorry Leroy I still love you. If you love me so damn much why are you still with him? You know what Linda I feel sorry for you. You use to tell me how smart you were well what happen? I guess Levi is a little smarter than you. Kiss my ass nigger.

No I don't kiss ass to get what I want all I have to do is be nice to people.

I didn't have to work hard to get what I have. What the fuck you got nothing and you, will never have nothing. Well Miss Linda, I have a beautiful home in South Carolina I have money in the bank and one day I'm going to own this shop. Over my dead body you bastard get the hell out of here and don't you ever come back here or I will have your ass.

What you going to kill me like you had poor Lilly.

Yes, I know all about what you did. I ain't done anything.

Well you try me Miss Linda you fuck with me and your ass will be away for a long time.

Get out of here right not you son of a bitch get out!

She started screaming for Levi to put me out. Levi, make him leave! Get out. I stood there Levi came running over to me when he got close to me. I looked him straight in the eye and said, you fat belly mother fucker put your hand on me and you will never make it back to New York. I ain't scared of nobody touch me mother fucker

The Man on the Train

he backed off and said Linda call the police. JJ and Lisa told me to leave it ain't worth it. JJ put his arms around me and walked me to the car. I'll see you at home. JJ I need to go somewhere. I drove off and went to Donald office and told him what I needed to do about Linda shop. I told him she had signed the papers giving me the shop. Do you have the papers? Yes. I have them in my brief case I gave him the papers. He looked at the papers and said, "I can help you I have to keep the papers for a few days how long will you be here?

I don't know, after I get everything in order I'll mail them to you. I promise Johnnie Mae I would help take care of you. Thank you, Donald. I'll send your bill in the mail. I talk to Sarah and she sure likes you, I like her too How you like South Carolina? I love it I don't ever want to move back here. I'll see you Donald. I went to JJ's house he and Lisa had dinner ready. Guys I'm sorry for the way I act Linda made me so mad.

Here man, have a drink you look like you need one. I looked at JJ standing there he was so nice to me I just wanted to tell him how sorry I was for killing my brother who was his father. Oh man how can, I tell him I feel so guilty. Are you alright Leroy? Linda upset you that much? No JJ one day you and I will have a long talk I have something I need to tell you but not tonight. I was so mad at the way she did me she didn't have the decency to tell me when we were in New York.

She never tried to call me or get in touch with me she didn't waste time replacing me. Come on man Lisa cooked all this good food let's forget Linda.

Leroy I was telling Lisa about the beautiful home you have in South Carolina. Leroy what did you mean about Lilly and what did you mean about you going to own Linda dress shop? You look like you really own it. Oh JJ I was just mad at her, when I get mad I say a lot of things. I want to go to bed early I'm getting up early and going to Derry to see Pete.

I been worried about him for some reason, last time we talked he didn't sound good you know he getting old. You want me to go with you? No not this time JJ I need to take care of him I love him so much I don't know what I would do if he ever leave me. Don't talk like that, that man is a strong old bird he will be here for a long time. I sure hope so JJ.

You and Lisa living together may I ask? Yes, we are we getting married and I want you to be my best man. Will you please and don't say no? I feel you are apart of my family I love you man. You really want me to be your best man? Hell yea we like brothers. My eyes filled with water I still have night mares about my brother and Al Jenkins. Some days it's real bad and some days I can block them out of my mind. I know one day I'll wake up and my pass will come for me. Leroy I see that look on your face a few times like you need to talk to me. What is it man you can talk to me maybe I can help you?

I'm fine good night, talk to you in the morning. I woke up smelling breakfast. We ate together and I told them I would see them in a few days. I left for Oklahoma when I got there I went to Pete's house and he was not home so I knew he was out to the shack. I should have called and let him know I was coming when I drove up his car was there. I blew the horn and he didn't come out I got out and went to the door and it was open I walked in. Pete where are you? I went through the house and he wasn't in there I had a real funny feeling. I didn't want to go behind the chicken house I was scare something had happened to him.

I got up the nerve and went back there and he wasn't there thank God I said.

Where could he be? God please don't let, nothing happen to him like my mother. I kept having this strange feeling I began to cry Pete, Pete where are you? Pete, where in the hell are you? I went to the barn to see if he drove my old car when I got there he was on the ground. Oh no, no. Please God don't let him be dead too Pete, Pete! Please get up what are you doing out here? There was blood all over him not again, not again God! Pete wake up please are you dead? I picked him up and took him in the house I laid him on the bed and got a cold towel and put it on him. He moved a little oh thank you God thank you.

Leroy is that you? Yes, Pete it's me. What the hell you doing here? I came to see about you I'm taking you to the hospital do you know what happened to you? I found you in the barn why were you out there?

Come on you can tell me later I took him to the hospital in Derry. The doctor asked him what happened he said, oh my head, my head! The doctor said he was hit real hard he had a brain concussion. They would keep him in the hospital for a few days. The doctor called the police and they came and asked me what happened. I told them I didn't know I found him in the barn and he didn't tell me I brought him to the hospital. I remember we came out to your place a few years ago and found your mama we still haven't found out who killed her.

Yes I know. Maybe the killer is still around here we going around to check we will be back to talk to Pete when he wakes up. I stayed at the hospital all night Pete woke up the next day. Leroy what are you doing here? Are you alright Pete? Yes, I feel okay now. Can you remember what happened to you? I heard someone out there trying to steal your mama's car I got my gun and went out there to see who it was. When I walked in someone hit me on my head that's all I remember.

The doctor, call the police and told them Pete was awake. Pete told them what happened. I told the police I didn't see the gun I guess they took it. After Pete got out of the hospital I took him home. I told him I didn't want him out there anymore. I told him I was going back out to the shack and I would be back to stay with him.

When I got out there police were everywhere. Whoever it was came back to the house. It's was in a mess. The police said they didn't find the gun and would find out who did it. Yes like you found out who killed Al Jenkins and my mother. I didn't know if they would come back so I spent the night out there they never came back. The next morning I put a lot of things that belong to my mama in the car to take Pete's house with me. I let all the chickens out of the pen and let them go free.

I boarded up the house. I drove my mama's car to Pete's house. Pete I don't want you to go back out to the shack any more.

I'm going back out there and get rid of the things I buried in the chicken house. Don't worry son I won't let nobody hurt you trust me. The police still think you had something to do with Al Jenkins death. They come out to the shack every now and then so I moved them off the place. Pete what am I going to do with you? You just saved my life and I will never forget that son I owe you. One day I will pay you back Leroy. If you had not came home and found me I would have laid out there and died.

Pete you don't owe me anything. I love you I'm just glad I got here when I did.

I went back out to the shack and check around and no one was there. I don't think they will be back I told Pete what I had did to the house and I don't want him out there anymore. I don't want anything to ever happen to him out there by his self. I stayed with Pete for four weeks he was doing better. I took care of everything for him while I was there.

Pete I want you to call your brother and tell him you moving to South Carolina with me. I'm not leaving you alone I want you to put your house up for sale and we will sell all the things you don't want and we will take what you want. I will have the other things you want shipped to South Carolina. I'm taking care of you. Leroy I think I'm going to love South Carolina before I call my brother I want to pack all my things and take them with me. Pete I don't have a lot of room in the car. I'm going to the bank here, and have them send my money to South Carolina. Well if I go with you I want mines sent too. Pete told Mr Flowers to put his house up for sale. How much money do you want for it Pete? I would like to have twenty thousa Mr Flowers because I not coming back. Pete have your lawyer draw up the papers for you and I and have it sent to the bank or you can pick it up. Thank you Mr Flowers I will have my lawyer get in touch with you.

Pete I'll have Donald take care of everything for you I trust him. Okay Leroy what ever you say. After we got everything out of the house that Pete wanted Pete called his brother. He told him he was moving to South Carolina and if he wanted his car he could come get it because he would be leaving the next day the keys would be under the seat. We went and got the car put it in his brother's name we took care of everything. We sold everything we could and what we couldn't sale we left it in the house for Pete's brother. I pulled my mama's car back with me and we were driving off when Pete's brother drove up.

Pete what the hell, you doing? Who, in the hell is this you going to South Carolina with? This is my son and I'm going with him. What you talking about you don't have a son? What have you done to my brother? Pete you get out of that car! I'm calling the police you ain't taking my brother nowhere! Pete you come on and go to Tulsa with me. Damn you Dan I 'm grown you don't tell me what to do you hear me? I don't hear from you until you want something I was in the hospital five days you never came and checked on me. Leroy came all the way from South Carolina to take care of me why didn't you call me?

If you love me or care about me you would have been here for me. So damn you leave me alone if you want my car you can have it and the things left in the house, I sold my house. When I get where I'm going I'll call you Leroy is my son I been, knowing him every since he was a young boy. You didn't come to see me enough to find out nothing about me let's go son. Dan stood there looking at Pete and said nothing more and we drove away. I went back to Little Rock we spent the night with JJ and the next morning we left. Pete told me how happy he was to be with me and going back to South Carolina with me. I was so happy because he told his brother I was his son I never loved my father he was mean to my mother. Pete is the man I want for my father, he is the father I want in my life I love him so much.

After I got back to South Carolina Sarah was surprised to see me back so soon. She said JJ called and wanted me to call him when I got home, I'll call him later I need to get Pete settled down. Some man name Ice Man called while you was gone he said he needs to talk to you. Pete I know you tired you need to go rest, do you need me to take you to the doctor? No son I'll be all right. Sarah would you fix Pete something to eat for me please?

Sarah Pete will be living here with us I'm not letting him go back to live in Oklahoma. I told Sarah what happened to him and she said she didn't mind she liked Pete. Pete looked so much older and so tired I made him go to his room and rest. After Sarah cooked I made him a plate and took it to his room. It makes him so happy to have me wait on him. The next day was Sunday, Sarah asked Pete and I to go to church with her she said we would love her church. I told Sarah that I went to church when my mama and Johnnie Mae died and their funeral was so sad but Sam had a happy funeral. Pete and I got dressed and went to church with Sarah.

I remember going to her church to Bobby funeral. It was a small church we walked in the people was looking at me smiling it was the same church they had Bobby funeral. I started to turn around she knew I was about to leave. We sat down and people started to sing and I began to like it. I looked at Pete and he was just smiling the preacher came up and started to preach. He said, "You have to ask

God to forgive you for your sins." God will forgive anything if you ask him.

When you left your husband for that other man it's a sin and you will have to pay for it one day. It looked like he was looking at Pete and me he said you know that man you killed you going to pay for it. I thought he did know about Pete and me oh my God, he must have told that preacher that. He kept looking at me he started to say something about Cain killing his brother Able God forgave him. I don't know what in the world was happening to me. I started crying saying "I'm sorry, I'm so sorry."

I didn't mean to do it, please forgive me God. I'm so sorry for what I have done I jumped up and ran to the preacher and he put his arms around me. He told me to say God is my saver and I believe he died on the cross for my sins and he will forgive me for my sins. I was going to tell the preacher what I did and I was crying so hard. Pete and Sarah came up and got me and took me out to the car.

Pete put his arms around me and said son it will be alright. Just cry, cry all you want to get it out he kept hugging me. When we got home Sarah was looking at me so strange, Sarah I'm sorry for what happened to me. She said, God came into your heart and God loves you and you have to confess your sins. How do I confess Sarah? You get on your knees and pray say whatever is in your heart and ask God to forgive you for your sins. How do I know he hears me? Believe me you will know he comes in your dreams he sends people to talk to you. He always finds a way for you to know he hears what's in your heart.

He forgive you he give you different signs and you have to choose that right ones. Sarah I don't understand. Oh Leroy you will know when God talks to you like when you was in church. He knew you had something on your heart that you needed to tell. Oh Sarah, I don't think I'm going back to that church Pete started to laugh at me son you will be alright. When Sarah left the room I had to fix me a drink Pete started to laugh at me again. Pete did I act a fool? Well you sure had a lot of eyes looking at you. Oh shit I ain't going back there no more.

Sarah came back in the room and said JJ and Ice Man said for you to call them it's important. I wonder what they want I'll call Ice first. Hey Ice you been trying to reach me? What's going on? I been down

The Man on the Train

in Oklahoma I brought Pete back with me I'm keeping him with me. How you doing man? Did you know I moved to South Carolina? I was going to tell you I been trying to get things together. Leroy man will you shut up and let me talk I heard from Linda and she want me to come back to Little Rock. She, want to talk to me about getting rid of you she want me to take care of you. Take care of me what the hell you talking about?

She, want you dead! Well Ice what did you tell her?

Man she offered me a lot of money I told you that you couldn't trust her. I called JJ and he told me that you moved to South Carolina.

Are you on your way to South Carolina to take care of me? Leroy you know I will never do anything to hurt you I love you man. You always been there for me don't worry Leroy that is why I called you to let you know what she wanted me to do. What happened man why in South Carolina? I told him about Linda and Levi and why I was in South Carolina. Ice you have to come see me sometime you will love it here, I have a big house it's really nice.

Man the food here is just as good as it is in New York you really have to come see me Ice. I will soon just watch out for Linda she real upset with you thank you Ice. I'll be okay I'm not scared of her I can take care of myself she better watch out for me I'm just as bad as she is. Ice I'll call you soon Pete asked me if everything was okay. I told him what Ice told me about Linda Leroy I'm here for you I won't let nobody hurt you. I called JJ to see what he wanted I hope it will be better news. When I called Lisa answered the phone Lisa, JJ home? Yes just a minute.

Hello Leroy, man Linda is mad at you Levi told her to sell her shop so she can spend more time with him in New York. When she put it up for sale she couldn't sell it because your lawyer did something and said you own the shop. She closed the shop and said she was on her way to kill you. I'll be okay she have to come to South Carolina to get me and I'll be waiting her.

Man you be careful. I will JJ I'll wait until she cools down and I'll come back and open up the shop. I told you that one day you and Lisa will own the shop be a little patient with me.

I told JJ and Lisa to reopen the shop until I come back; Lisa knew what to do and knew how to order the things for the shop. I told him

I would send ten thousand dollars to reopen. I told Pete what JJ said she really going to kill me I knew she would be mad at me I didn't let it worry me.

The next morning Pete and I rode around town to find me a nice place to open me a club. I wasn't scared of Linda, Pete told me I need to find me a small place and then let it grow to see if it worked out. It may not work out the way I think I found me a place on Canal Street. It was a very nice building on the corner it had a lot of parking space it use to be a bank. I checked into it and talked to the owner he said he would let me have it for twenty six thousand because it needed a lot of work that is why they moved. I called Donald and told him what I wanted to do and if he would draw up the paper and take care of the legal work.

I thanked him for the paper work on Linda's shop I'm sure glad Donald was my lawyer he is real good. Three weeks later I started to have some one come out and get my club ready, after four months my club was ready. I made it a nice jazz club everything was going so well. Sarah took care of everything in the kitchen I took care of the front. Pete wanted to help Sarah in the kitchen he didn't want to be out front.

I hired the girls I wanted to work in the front and I hired the bar tenders. I found a local group to play in the club they sure were happy to play every night. I was so happy the people started coming in and they said they loved it. The first week we opened I made over a thousand dollars, people came because it was a new club and they wanted to see what it was like. Pete loved being with me we got closer and closer there was a lot of beautiful women coming in asking me for dates they said I sure was a good looking man.

I had been so busy I didn't have time to find me a date I sure like looking at the women coming in I talked to them. After I closed at night I was too tired to date I opened every night except Sundays. Sarah said we had to close on Sunday because it was God's day we would sleep late at home she said it was her day too. So Pete and I would go out to eat or get something to bring home I wasn't drinking so much I had to get a license to sell beer and liquor. I thought about the corn whiskey I had in Oklahoma I asked Pete if he could call Red the man he bought the whiskey from if I could come to Oklahoma and buy cases for my club. Pete said Red makes it and if I was caught with it I would go to jail it was against the law to bring corn whiskey to another state.

Pete called Red and he told Pete he would bring cases of whiskey to South Carolina for me he would bring six cases. A week later Red brought the whiskey he told me that Pete said he could trust me. For bringing the whisky Red charged me eight hundred dollars so I gave him an extra hundred. Leroy you call me whenever you want more I like doing business with you. Pete said Red was a black man he was so light skinned everyone called him Red.

Red told me to only sell it in shot glasses it would last longer and I can make more money if I sold it like that. He didn't want to make too many trips to South Carolina. Red said they had a lot of corn whiskey here in South Carolina. I just have to find where they were. He said he would ask around, if they find out he was bringing it from Oklahoma he may end up dead. Oh no, Red I don't won't that I wanted some to start out with because I really liked it.

Just bring it whenever you come here I won't tell no one. Pete, Sarah, and I were so happy everything was going fine my club was making more money. Sarah told me and Pete we really need to go back to church and thank God for our blessings.

Oh Sarah can I just thank God from home? Yes, you can but it will mean more to him if you go to church. Just come back with me one more time. Okay, okay I'll do it for you. When I walked in the people was nice to me they came to me and welcomed me back. No one said anything about my last visit I felt better. The preacher told us about Jesus dying on the cross for our sins, after he preached he asked everyone to come up for prayer. I went up there I asked God to forgive me for my sins, I felt so much better when we got home I didn't want a drink. Pete also looked happy as if he had asked God to forgive him too. Sarah was so happy for us she fixed us Sunday dinner, while we were eating the phone rang.

Sarah got up and answered it she gave me the phone and I said hello. Leroy this is Ice Man I sold my home I want to come to South Carolina can you find me a place to live? Sure Ice come on. I'll be there in a few days.

I started to wonder about Linda she never came to kill me. I did wonder about her and that fat belly ass boy friend of hers. I hope she happy with him I guess I scared his ass the last time I saw him. I was happy, shit on Linda and Levi they both can kiss my black ass the way she did me in New York. A few days later Ice Man came to see me I told him he could stay with me until he found him a place. I hired him to help me out in the club. I called JJ, and he said the shop was doing good and Linda haven't been back she was in New York with Levi. He said he saw Linda at her club one night and she look so unhappy.

Levi was spending a lot of time with her. Man I don't see why she is with him he is so much older than she is. Levi, weigh over two hundred pounds I don't understand why she gave me up JJ for him. JJ I'll send you more money soon.

I called Donald to put insurance on the building and change the name to Leroy's. I will take care of everything you will get my bill in the mail. Okay Donald. I work hard at the club I go home every night because I'm so tired. I still love Terry, JJ said she really miss Hattie and Lucille she misses Hattie gossiping. It's been a few weeks since I talked to JJ he said the shop was still making money and he and Lisa was putting my money in the bank Donald was still giving them their checks every week.

I came home from work one day and Pete was in his room when I went in he said he wasn't feeling too good and he would stay home from work that day. Pete do you need me to take you to the doctor?

No Leroy I just have a headache, I'm taking you to the doctor! I ain't going to no doctor I just have a headache I'll be alright. Sarah told him she would fix him some hot tea and for him to drink it she said it has herbs in it.

Pete said he felt better after he drank the tea the next morning I checked on Pete and he was still asleep. Sarah and I left to get some things for the club before we opened up. When we got back I went straight to Pete's room he was real sick I put him in the car and took him to the hospital Ice came with me. I wonder what in the hell was in that hot tea Sarah gave him we waited for almost an hour the doctor came out and said Pete wanted to talk to me.

What is wrong with him? He wanted to talk to you before I said anything to you. Damn you tell me what's wrong! Your father is real sick we got his fever down and we are running more tests.

I ran in Pete's room they had tubes running all over him Pete, Pete! He had his eyes closed Pete are you okay? Please wake up I started to cry. He caught me by the hand and said don't cry I love you too. Son you brought me so much happiness since I been in your life. I was a lonely old man until God sent you in my life. I'm glad you brought me to live with you here in South Carolina I'm proud of you son. You the son I always wanted. Oh Pete you know how much you mean to me. I'm going to take care of you the rest of my life. When you come home we going fishing I know how much you love it. I been so busy with my club, well you come first from now on. You get well and hurry out of here. Leroy you remember when we went to church with Sarah?

I asked God to forgive me for all the wrong I did in my life. When I went to bed last night Leroy I felt a warm feeling in my body and then I saw your mama and she said she was happy I was in your life and taking care of her baby. She said to tell you she, always love you she is right by your side. She said you can feel her in your heart and you will be alright.

Leroy I think I'm going to be with your mama. Pete please don't talk like that I need you I'm not ready for you to leave me. There is so much we have to do together. Pete, please get well and come home with me. Son you know every since they hit me in the head in Oklahoma that day that you found me in the barn. I haven't been feeling good I didn't want to tell you because I didn't want you to worry about me. Leroy if I don't get better I left all my money to you and everything else.

Donald know what to do I told him everything. Pete I don't give a damn about your money I rather have you. I done gave my brother all I wanted to and don't give him nothing else. He was never close to me like you and me. I broke down and cried and cried to sit here and listen to Pete talk like he was leaving me. I never cared about my father or my brother like I do Pete. It hurt so much when it's someone you love. I looked up and Ice was standing in the door with tears running down his face. Leroy, man what's wrong? Is Pete going to be alright? I'm here for you please don't cry Pete's going t be alright.

The doctor came in and checked Pete. I told the doctor I would give him all the money I have and my home if he didn't let Pete die. Please take care of him I love him. Pete is very sick the only one who can save him is God. He has a big blood clot in the back of his head. It looks like he was hit real hard with something. It looks as if someone or something was trying to kill him. You have to pray son I'll do what I can I'll be back in a few minutes.

I sat back down beside Pete's bed I took him by the hand. Daddy Pete can you hear me? He opened his eyes and smiled and said yes, I can hear you. Pete the doctor said they need to operate can I let them? If you think they can save me Leroy let them. the doctor came back in and they took him away. After everyone left I got down on my knee and told God I didn't know how to pray I don't even know if he hear my pray. Sarah believes in you and Sarah said all I have to do is ask you to hear my prayer and you would hear me.

God I don't care about myself I'm here to pray for Pete he said he asked you to forgive him and he think you have. Please don't take him from me I love him I know I done so much wrong in my life you take me and leave Pete. I heard a voice and I looked up and it was Ice Man on his knees praying out crying out so loud. This big man on his knees crying I helped him up and we hugged each other. He said man if God is not here for you I am. Thank you Ice. I'll always be here for you Leroy no telling where I would be if it wasn't for you.

Sarah came in and asked about Pete he was still in surgery. Leroy, do you want to open the club tonight or close? Sarah I'm not leaving here until Pete is well, I like to open I don't want to start closing so soon. Ice said he and Sarah can do it they had enough help Sarah said she would get her cousin to help also until I came back. Thank you guys I'll take care of you don't worry. Just take care of yourself and Pete. After we closed I'll be back. It seemed like Pete was in surgery for days but it was only a couple of hours. The doctor come back in the room and said Leroy. The way he looked at me my heart stop and tears started running down my face. I was waiting for him to tell me bad news he said your father is in recovery and will be there for a couple more hours. He is still in a lot of pain but after a few more days he will be doing better he will have to have a lot of care because of his age it will take a long time for recovery. Thank you God I was so happy to know Pete was still alive. Can I see him? Yes, he won't know you and he won't hear you we have him sedated so he can't move. Someone was really praying for him if we had waited three more hours he would have never made it. I didn't walk down the hall I ran I went into the room they had him in and he had more tubes on him than he had at first. Pete can you hear me? I am here. They said he couldn't hear me. I stayed at the hospital everyday I didn't go home Ice would bring me clean clothes and Sarah would bring me food and take my dirty clothes home wash them and send them back with Ice. Three days later I was still sitting beside Pete's bed and he still couldn't hear me.

The doctor said he was recovering I put my head down to say another prayer when I heard a voice Leroy, Leroy you okay?

When I looked up it was JJ. I just got up and put my arms around him and broke down and cried. Pete will be okay man. JJ I'm so glad to see you. When Ice call me I came as fast as I could. Lisa sends her prayers and if you need her she will be here. Terry said if she can do anything for you please call her.

JJ I'm so worried about Pete he still can't hear me. Give him some time I'll be here with you until he is better and at home. Thank you JJ I don't know what to say. Nothing I love you like family to me. I looked at him and I wanted to say yes, yes, oh you are my family you're my nephew.

All I could do was cry JJ, please forgive me? Leroy you keep saying that what am I suppose to forgive you for? Whatever it is I forgive you, you have been nothing but good to me, the shop is doing good Pete will be okay stop worrying.

Levi took Linda back to New York and he, have some of his family running her club. Leroy do you need a drink? No I don't want nothing to eat or drink come on let's go get something. No JJ I don't want to leave call Ice and tell him to bring us something. Sarah had cooked a nice meal and sent it by Ice it was good to have all of them here for me and Pete. The doctor came in and said Pete was doing better and I could go home and get some rest but I wanted to stay at the hospital. I wanted to be there when Pete woke up JJ said he would stay with me. Ice said the bar tender quit at the club and I need to come see what was going on.

I ain't leaving you and Sarah do whatever you need to do Leroy, I'll go and bar tender for you while I'm here. Thank you JJ because I don't want to leave Peter I'm lucky to have all of you in my life.

We love you Leroy you're a good man I see when you good to people they will be good too you. I was tired and I did need a good night sleep it's been days since Pete had his surgery and he was still sleep. So I went home and went to my room and got a good night sleep Sarah cooked a nice big breakfast and we all ate and I went back to the hospital. After I was there for four hours Pete started to come around when he opened his eyes I was so happy. Pete it's me Leroy he just looked at me and smiled and closed his eyes. He looked so old he was only seventy eight. So much has happened to me in my young life.

A week later they let Pete come home with me he was so happy to be with all of us. It felt good to me to have Pete and Sarah with me I felt like I had a father and a mother with me and they treated me as if I was there son. JJ left and went back to Little Rock because he misses Lisa.

Pete started getting better and better.

He was walking real slow and he stayed in the bed a lot and I spent as much time as I could with him. My club was doing so well and I loved it.

I wondered about Linda I couldn't understand what happened to her she was a strong black woman. She must really love Levi to let him control her. Levi's family was running her club and she was away. She said she worked too hard for what she had and she would kill anybody who would take it away from her.

Boy she must really loved that fat ass Levi.

JJ called me upset what's wrong JJ calm down he told me Linda was back in town. She came to the shop and said she sent Ice to kill me and she haven't heard from him. She was mad because he wouldn't tell her nothing about you she wanted to know where you were. I didn't tell her nothing after Lisa and I closed. Hour later your shop burned down we know Linda did it. What do you want us to do Leroy? You lost everything man. I did take all, the money home with me because I was going to put it in the bank the next morning. I also took all the paper work out because it was time for me to go over the books. I wanted to do it at home Lisa could help me better when we bring it home with us every night.

JJ I know that bitch did it I was just wondering what she was up too.

I'll call you back tomorrow. Okay man. I told Ice and Pete what she did Ice said man I knew she was mad I knew she wouldn't let you get by. Are you going back? I don't want to leave Pete He will be okay me and Sarah will take good take good care of him for you. Or do you want me to go with you man? I'll protect you from her. I don't need help Ice I can take care of myself I don't need help. I know I need to go see what's going on but I'll called Donald.

When I called Donald I told him what happened he said to stay in South Carolina and he will take care of everything and send me the bill.

He wanted to know if I wanted to rebuild. I told him yes so Lisa and JJ could have their jobs back I know how much they loved the shop. I told Donald about Pete being in the hospital. Pete was doing fine. He told me to stay home not to come to Little Rock he would take care of everything.

I know that bitch burned down my shop I would like to kill her ass but I guess it's my pay back for taking her shop from her.

Donald called me back in a few days and said they was cleaning up the mess and they would have shop rebuilt in about five months they couldn't prove Linda did it.

Pete was getting better and better I spent as much time as I could with him we went fishing took long walks, and sit on the porch and talk for hours. After six months Pete was able to go back to work at my club. My club was busy and I was still making lot's, of money. Sarah food was good and the people loved it. I see how Linda felt about making money. Ice found him a lady and he moved out of my house with her he still worked for me. I called JJ to see how things were going with the shop to see if it was almost ready or how long it would be. He said it would be a few more weeks they said they would need new things to buy at the store and he wanted nice things like the one's I ordered to put in the shop. I told him that I would be there in a week I didn't feel like driving and I need Ice to stay with Pete and Sarah to help them and be there for Pete, because I had planned to stay for a few days. I caught the train and went to Little Rock JJ was there to pick me up.

Sally Cross was still there she looked so old. I didn't know her she had changed I was walking by her and she said, "Leroy is that you"? You look real good. Sally Cross how are you doing? She hugged me and said how happy she was to see me all of a sudden I could hear Old George Cross say git, git, your damn ass away from my wife boy I'm still watching you. Sally and JJ was asking me was I alright. I thought I heard George telling me to get my hands off you. She laughed and laughed Leroy he always said that to you when he saw you around me. You haven't forgotten that yet she walked away laughing.

I looked at her and thought her ass was going crazy let's go JJ. Leroy you looked like Old George Cross was telling you off did you really hear him? JJ started laughing fuck you man take me to your house. Then I started to laugh did I look that scared? You did I'm sorry man I didn't know if George was coming after me. JJ don't drive across Jasper Bridge he started laughing at me again you don't think you will see George on that bridge do you? Hell No! Okay, okay I'll go the other way. Is the bar open today on State Street?

Let's stop by I need a drink some of the people I knew was still coming in JJ walked off to people he knew and I found me a table.

I looked up and my heart stop beating I was looking at the most beautiful woman that just walked in. I wanted to go over to her and put my arms around her but I couldn't move. I just stayed there looking at her and she didn't see me sitting there. She had on a real low cut tight dress and red pump heels. Oh shit she could always turn me on she gained a few pounds but in the right places I just kept sitting and looking at her. I saw her go over to JJ and give him a hug and I saw him pointing to me.

She came over to me Hi Terry, Hi Leroy what you doing in here? I can ask you the same I see you can't stay away. I guess not I'm here on business. I heard about your shop I'm sorry. Do you mind if I sit down? No. Leroy you look good just a little bit older. JJ told me about your friend Pete I hope he is better. Yes, he is doing better can I buy you a drink Terry? She looked so good to me I just wanted to take her in my arms and make love to her. This is the same woman who tried to kill me I had to cool my ass I didn't know what she thought. She started smiling at me like she used to I ordered our drinks and she wanted to dance with me it was a slow dance. They started playing a song stand by me. It felt good having her in my arms she pressed her body against mines and I knew she knew what she was doing to me. Next thing she kissed me she knew she had me I started to break out in a sweat. It's been a long time since I made love to a woman I was so busy trying to get my club and shop making money and taking care of Pete. Lets sit down I said I had me another drink and Terry asked me if I would go home with her just to talk. I'll bring you back to JJ's house when you want to leave he said you was staying a few days with him. I told JJ I would see him later he was smiling and said okay. After I got to Terry house I got out and we went in I looked around and she made a big change it looked real nice.

Make yourself home Leroy I need to get out of these heels.

I sat there looking at her like a black panther ready to pounce on her. But I knew I had to keep my cool because I really didn't know what she wanted. It's been a long time since I talked to her or seen her if her baby had lived it would have been four years old. I think that I'm still in love with her. You have that look in your eyes when you wanted to make love to me do you? Yes I do, she walked over to me and I got up and took her in my arms and started to kiss her and we both wanted each other she still loved me.

I started to back off from her but she pulled me back close to her and kept kissing me. My thoughts lefts my mind and all I could think was how to please this beautiful woman in my arms. I didn't care all I wanted to do was take her in the bed room and fuck her brains out. She smelled so good and her arms around me felt so good like that was where they belong. I tried to let go of her but I couldn't next thing I know she pulled her clothes off and stood there with nothing on and I lost my damn mind. I just started kissing her and next thing she helped me pull off my clothes and we were in bed making love and it felt so good to be back with Terry. It felt like she was made for me I really needed her and she acts the same way. Leroy I still love you so much and this time I'm not letting you go. Terry if you know all about me and my pass what I did you would hate me. Baby I don't care what you did I love you and I just want to be with you. When I saw you over to Hattie's house that day I was so jealous you looked so good and I was pregnant I thought you left me and went back to Oklahoma. No baby I left because I loved you and didn't want to hurt you with my messed up life. I didn't want you in the middle of things. Terry there is a lot of things in my past I haven't told you and you will never forgive me if you knew. If I tell you, you will never speak to me or want to see me.

Leroy what in the world you talking about did you kill somebody?

Why would you say something like that? Do I look like a killer? Well I don't know of anything that is so bad that you can't tell me. I grabbed her and I was holding her so tight she started to cry. She started to kiss me again we made more love when I woke up the next morning I starred at her lying there I wished that I could wake up every morning with her in my bed. Wake up sleepy head she turned over and smiled at me. Hi honey, you want breakfast?

Let's take a shower together and we can cook breakfast she kissed me again. If you keep that up I will keep you in bed all day we laughed and got in the shower and she said she like what she see all the way down from my head to my toes.

Oh girl I love you we kissed and we got out of the shower before we start making love again. Terry I left all my clothes in JJ's car I don't want to put the same things on I need to call him to bring them to me. I still have some of your things here I never got rid of them. Terry I don't deserve you. Sure you do we smiled and ate breakfast I got dressed and went to see if my shop was open. I wanted to see if there were any customers in there Lisa and JJ had everything looking real good. I like the way they had set up everything I told Terry that I was going it to the office and see if I could call my buyers to send me more things from New York.

Everyone I called said they couldn't help me they wouldn't tell me why. I called all the companies that I had brought from when I was with Linda I don't understand why. I found out from the last company I called that Levi and Linda told them not to sell to me. Levi was a big man in New York and they didn't want to mess with him. He could make it real bad for their company Levi owned the biggest factory in New York. I be damned they was trying to pay me back for what I did to Linda. I called JJ in the office and told him what Linda and Levi did. What are we going to do Leroy? Do you know somewhere else we can buy from?

I will go to New York and see if I can find someone who will help me. I need to call home to make sure Pete and Sarah is okay before I go. Maybe I can go with you Terry can help Lisa until we come back.

Sure you can go with me I would like for you to go and it will help you to run the shop and see how to order the best.

I called Pete and he said Sarah was fine and Ice was at my club everything was fine. I told him what happened and that I would have to go to New York, Pete said he was glad Linda was out of my life because she was crazy. I told him that I would be in New York a few days and I would call him when I got there. Leroy you be careful I don't want, nothing to happen to you up there. Don't worry Pete I can take care of myself.

You just help Sarah and I take care of my club, I love you Pete. I love you too son.

I look up and here comes Terry and Lisa. Where the hell you two going?

We going to, New York with you guy's.

The shop will be okay until we come back. We don't have a lot of things there anyway Lisa. Said she called Donald and he said he would have someone go by and check on the shop until we come back. Oh let them come on they can help us pick out things please Leroy we never been to New York please. Oh well come on it maybe fun we got on the train to go to New York I was glad Terry was with me.

When we got there we got us a hotel Terry and Lisa was like little girls happy they was in New York JJ was happy too they had never been there. I felt like a big man because I had been there before and I knew where to go. The next day we got ready to go looking around we had a hard time trying to get a cab they kept passing us by. I called Ice Man and he called one of his friends to take us where ever we wanted to go. I was happy because his friend was nice to us his name was Larry and he act like he like doing it for us. I had Larry to take me to the three black sisters that made clothes.

When I got there their shop was bigger and they had more people helping them. They had a lot of things to sell and I bought enough to send back to Little Rock and they know what I like and I made a deal with them. They will make things and send them to me whenever I place an order. They told me about another shop that makes and sell jewelry and shoes. Larry took us there and I made a deal to take my orders and send them to me on the train as often as I need them.

We had lunch and Larry took us back to the hotel I told him to come back and pick us up because we wanted to go out and have some fun while we was there. Later that night we got ready and Larry came back for us. I told him we wanted to go to a nice club that serve dinner. JJ, Lisa and Terry was having so much fun this is the first time they had been to real nice dinner clubs. They were eating like never before they said the food was so good. JJ said he loved New York and wanted to stay we was laughing and having so much fun.

It wasn't like the last time I was in New York with Linda Terry kissed me and told me how happy she was to be with me. The first night we were there she was all over me and I liked it. Larry took us around showing the guys all the nice spots. Our last night there they wanted to go to one more nice club Larry said he would take us to where all the rich black people go. The guys were so excited. He said some times stars would be there. The name of the club was Casino, we were drinking and dancing Jimmy Walter were there singing Shot Gun. Terry and JJ were very good dancer. They love music.

After we was ready to walk out Linda and Levi walked in. Well, well, if it ain't the damn shop thief I heard your shop burn down well shop thief pay back is a mother ain't it. She started laughing what you got here your watch dogs?

If I knew you like I know you now I would have never trusted your black ass you dirty bastard. JJ caught me by the arm and said come on Leroy let's go I don't know what got in to me, I caught Linda by her arm as if I was about to kill her. I told her if she, ever come near my shop again she will lose everything she love the most do you hear me bitch?

I'll kill your fucking ass. Levi reached for me and I wasn't scared of him. You fat belly moth back eating motherfucker you put your hand on me and I will cut your fat belly wide open. So you back away from me I don't play. Linda's eyes got so big and she didn't look so tough anymore. Levi said you not worth me getting my hand dirty come on Linda we will take care of this later. Linda and I will stay away from you and you stay away from us. I looked at Linda and Terry pulled me by my arm to leave. Baby, baby let's go please. I don't like to see you this mad. I kept starring at Linda she was so scared she couldn't move. I told you Leroy no one take from me and get by with it I work too damn hard you can have the damn shop. She looked at me and said now we even and walked away.

I kept standing there looking at her as she walked away.

Baby you scaring me please come on.

When I looked at Terry tears was running down her face I'm so sorry Terry you had to see me like this. You okay man? Yes, JJ come on Larry took us back to the hotel. He said he would be back to take us to the train station. After I got back to the hotel I felt like a fool that Terry had to see me act like that. I told them how sorry I was they all said they knew she had made me mad. We know you a nice man. JJ said he would have said the same thing we glad you told her ass off.

Now Lisa and I don't have to worry about her coming in the shop anymore.

All of a sudden JJ started laughing he couldn't stop we looked at him as if he was crazy. Terry, said JJ are you okay? What are you laughing about? He stop long enough to say did you hear what Leroy called Levi? Then Terry and Lisa started to laugh they all was laughing so hard I felt a little bad I didn't remember what all I said I was half drunk. I know I was mad as hell at Linda and; Levi what was so funny? Tell me! You don't remember? You called Levi a fat belly moth back eating motherfucker. Levi turned red as a damn cherry and Linda dropped her head man where did that come from?

I started to laugh I was so mad I don't know what all I said to him.

Well maybe they will leave me alone.

Terry and I went to bed when we were in bed she said she saw a side of me she had never seen before. She didn't know I could get that mad. Terry I am so sorry I tried to keep my cool. Leroy do you still love her? Was you mad because she left you for Levi you and her was together for two years? I'm sorry Terry I was going through a lot of things back then I was so mixed up and I was doing a lot of drinking.

No I never loved her it's always been you I love you and I will always love you. I just didn't want you to get mixed up with me back then I had to think and try to get myself together.

The things that happen to Johnnie Mae, Lucille, Sam. And other things wrong in my life. When Pete came into my life I found someone I could tell everything to that had been bottled up inside of me. I had to tell someone and I felt I could trust Pete that is why I love him so much I can trust him.

Leroy you could have trust me you knew how much I loved you. I'm still so sorry for what I did to you and for losing the baby all you had to do was tell me we could have work things out. When you left me and said nothing. and I hear you were still in town that is why I got so mad. I'm sorry Terry I did it the wrong way I don't want you out of my life anymore I love you too much to let you go. Leroy I would have listened to you I would have been there for you there is nothing in your life that you couldn't tell me. I would have understood I could have helped you all you had to do was trust me.

We could have been together and we would have had a family by now when I saw you at Hattie's that day I was so jealous you looked so good and I was pregnant I thought you had left me and wasn't coming back. No baby I left because I loved you so much and I didn't, want you in the middle of my mess up life. Terry there is a lot in my pass that I did and you would never forgive me. If I tell you, you will leave me and never want to see me or speak to me. Why would you say something like that?

I was holding her so tight she started to cry Oh Terry I'm sorry I love you so much. I never knew how to love a woman like this you make me very happy. I love JJ and I don't deserve to have the two of you in my life.

I'm so sorry for what I have done I was so young when I was eighteen back in Oklahoma. I found my mother dead she had been beaten to death and I just flipped out I couldn't think right and that is when I started drinking. I didn't care about no one until Pete you and JJ came into my life. I never loved Johnnie Mae or Linda they was something new in my life and they was kind to me. They taught me a lot of things that I didn't know Linda was okay until she met Levi.

After I moved to South Carolina I felt safe I didn't know anyone and I am happy there. When I went back to Oklahoma I was very happy after Pete came in my life, where do you really want to live? I love my home in South Carolina I gave up everything in Oklahoma I have my house up for sale in Oklahoma. I own a lot of land there are you selling all your land? No. Well don't sell your home or land maybe someday you may want to go back there.

No Terry I don't think I'll go back. Pete sold his home to come, stay and live with me I don't want to leave him. He is a real nice man and I love him. I kissed Terry and we just stood there holding each other. It felt so good having her back in my life and this time I don't ever want her to leave me again. Terry Johnson please, please, what ever you hear about me will you still love me?

She looked at me and said I promise you I will always love you forever. The next day Larry came back and took us to the train station after I was on the train for a while I closed my eyes I heard the man on the train telling me to stay away from Terry and JJ. I heard him

The Man on the Train

say I'll be back to get you stay away it was my brother John Chester. It was so real I started to shake and cried out I'm sorry, I'm sorry I started to cry. Terry, was shaking me Leroy, wake up. I woke up and she started to kiss me baby you alright you having a night mere. Are you okay? Yes Terry. What were you dreaming about? Oh I don't remember, Leroy I know you remember you had to remember for you to look that scared. I'll be back I have to go to the restroom.

When I got there I looked in the mirror and it was John's face I ran out of the room and asked the conductor if I could have a drink? Yes sir I'll bring you one you sit down you look like you seen a ghost. Could I go to the bar? Yes sir, right this way. I didn't know I was gone so long JJ came and found me at the bar. Leroy man I knew I would find you here. Terry is worried about you man you can talk to me what's wrong? Talk to me Leroy everything will be alright I'm here for you man. Thank you JJ maybe someday I'll tell you I promise we will talk when the time is right but not now.

Let's go back to the girls before they come looking for us. When I got back to my seat I could tell how worried Terry was. I'm okay Terry I feel better. Terry after I get back to Little Rock I'll stay a few days and help JJ and Lisa at the shop. After, we got back to Little Rock JJ help me pick up the things the things from the train station to the shop.

I didn't say too much. He knew I wasn't going to tell him what was wrong with me. I just wanted to hurry and get back to South Carolina. After a few days helping JJ at the shop I told him to put the money in the bank every day and keep out what he need to run the shop and Donald would still send him and Lisa their checks.

After I pay for reopening my shop I would let him and Lisa have it.

If you need anything JJ just let me know or Donald I'll take care of you and Lisa just ask if you need more. JJ I know you love me I love you but right now it's business make sure you put the money in the bank. Don't worry Leroy you know you can trust me and Lisa. JJ I don't want to lose you as a friend I love you. I love you too man it will be okay, Leroy I keep my word we hugged each other. Every since I know you Leroy you been good to me, JJ you will always be family to me. I don't have anyone but you we both had tears running down our face. Leroy all the time we know each other I never took you to meet my mother I need go by before I take you back to Terry.

No drop me off at Terry's I'll meet her next time I need to talk to Terry before I leave. I have to go check on things back home we went to Terry's house and she wasn't home so we went to the shop and she was there with Lisa planning how they was going to set up the shop. Well, well are you going to work in the shop too? Are you here to make extra money we all laughed then I asked Terry to come in the office I needed talk to her. What's wrong Leroy? I grab her and started to kiss her. Leroy let's go to my house not here. Not that Terry I want to make love to you but I just want to talk to you. Oh okay, I'm getting ready to go back to South Carolina and I want you to please come with me. Leroy I can't my mother is sick and I can't leave JJ to take care of her. I will come see you as often as I can you not ever getting out of my life again. I love you too much but right now am not the right time, I will be in South Carolina so much you will think I live there I promise you. Leroy I will have to get rid of my home and I just can't go back with you now I promise I will call you every day until I can come. I don't want to leave you Terry but I have to go back and check on Pete, Sarah and my business.

Baby, will you spend the night with me and I'll take you to the train station tomorrow. I spent the night with Terry and I still couldn't tell her about John and Al. I had nothing to do with Lilly, Johnnie Mae, or Lucille's death but I still feel real bad about what happened to them. I can't bring any of them back God I'm so sorry. I know one day I will have to pay for my crimes.

The next day I went back to South Carolina Pete and Sarah picked me up at the train station I was happy to see Pete. After I got home I told Pete everything that happened on my trip to New York. I told him about Terry and how much I loved her and I wanted him to tell me what to do. Son do you think you can live with her everyday and be around JJ all the time, knowing that you killed his daddy can you son? I don't know but I know I love both of them and I don't want them out of my life.

I guess I will have to tell both of them and just see what happens I guess I will have to pay the price. I know they will hate me and never want anything to do with me they will send me to jail for the rest of my life. Son wait for a while God always have a way of working things out. Pete, Sarah's preacher said you can't take a life it's wrong at the time I did what I did I just wasn't thinking. I was so mad at them I know now no matter who it is you don't have the right to kill nobody. I wish now Pete I wasn't so hot headed back then I was so young, I think I have changed now that I am older. Yes son, you are changing since you are older and that's a good thing.

Terry and I talked everyday on the phone and I still miss her. She said she was coming to South Carolina in a few days and staying a while.

Lisa said she would help JJ with her mother she told David that she was going to South Carolina for a while and he said he was glad he would have somewhere to come in the summer when school was out. I told Pete I would wait and see what happened. A few weeks later Terry came to South Carolina boy I was happy to see her, she was more beautiful than the last time I saw her. Pete and Sarah were happy she came, she and Pete hit it off. Sarah liked her too, I took her to see my club and she really like it she even started to help us out while she was there. Sarah said she liked having her helping out they got alone fine.

Terry was good for my club she asked me if she could make some changes. She wanted to make it a little classier she said.

She said she wanted it to look like one of the clubs we saw in New York. I told her she could and she had a big chandelier put in, she made the lights a little softer. The tables were elegant with white linen on each one with gold dinner ware. The people's dinner was served in white plates trimmed in black, the chairs was white with black seats.

She had my club painted white out side a sign with my name in bright lights. She put beautiful plants all over the place my club looked real nice the people that came in loved it. My Jazz club business picked up we was very busy every night. Terry would help sit the people to their seats she dressed real nice the men that came in fell in love with her. She knew how to treat them and they spent a lot of money, she would smile and take them to their tables. The waiter also dressed in black shirts, white pants, and black shoes.

They all fell in love with her at the club she treated people real nice and they worked to please her. Sarah and Pete was glad she came I couldn't believe how she had changed my club in the two months she was there. She made it classic Leroy I think that I have fell in love with South Carolina. I love you but I have to go back to Little Rock. No Terry I won't let you leave! Terry let's get married please don't go

I love you baby. I love you too is that what you really want to do? I know I want you in my life and I'm not letting you go I put my arms around her and we kissed.

I could feel her relax in my arms and I knew she wanted to marry me. Leroy I love you and I will marry you I just need to call JJ and my mother. I need to go back and take care of my home there is so much I need to do. I need to tell David. When are you going back to Little Rock?

Let me talk to JJ and then I'll know what to do.

I told Pete that I asked her to marry me. Leroy after talking to her I feel you can trust her. I believe she will stand by you and help you all she can. Pete I believe, JJ will stand by me because, he believe love is better than hate, but I will have to wait and pick the right time to tell them what I had done. I know I will tell them my life story.

Terry called JJ and told him I asked her to marry her he was so happy. She said he said I was a very nice man and he would love to have me as his brother. Terry stayed another month to help me with my club and we were making more money my business was doing so good.

That night the police came in and I saw Ice running out the back door and he didn't come back. I didn't know what to think the police walked up to me and said are you Leroy Chester?

Yes. We here to check out your club. What do you mean?

We heard you been selling corn whisky here. Do you have a license?

Yes I have a license there haven't been nothing wrong here. We heard you been selling corn whisky here it's against the law to sell it in a club. We need to check out this place if we find corn whiskey you going to jail. They was looking around they went to the back and that was where I kept my whisky.

Terry was so scarred what's wrong Leroy? I put my arms around her and told her it will be okay someone had called and told them that I was selling the corn whiskey and I had it stocked in the back room. While they was looking around I told Terry to go home and tell Pete to come and get me out of jail the next morning and tell him to bring Ice Man with him. I asked the police if Terry could go home she was scared they looked at me then her. I said go on home baby I'll be alright she left and they kept looking all in the back. I asked them who told you that I was selling corn whisky.

I run a nice place here and I have good people working here we don't bother nobody. The police came out and said, we didn't find anything if we come back and if we catch you your ass is going to jail you lucky tonight. We got a tip from someone. You have a nice place here I'd like to bring my wife here for dinner one night. Sorry we bothered you, We have to check out tips. That's okay officer.

I locked up and went home Terry was glad to see me. Pete said Ice Man just left. What the hell did he come here for. I saw his ass run out the back door when the police came in. What did he say Pete is he the one that call the cops.

Leroy be quiet and let me talk Ice said he heard the police was coming to raid your club and he knew you had that corn whisky he didn't have time to tell you so him and the fellows help put it all in his car and he brought it all here put in down in the basement. Said he would talk to you tomorrow. Pete I didn't know what he had done. Man Ice still got my back. Yes he do son you lucky you have so many friends that love and care about you. Yes Pete I am lucky I owe Ice a raise and an apology.

It was so nice to have everything going fine a few days later Terry left to go get her things together so she could come back. It has been two weeks and I miss her so much. If she wasn't back in another week I had planned to go get her. Leroy, yes Pete. Terry is on the phone she need to talk to you she sound upset. Slow down son don't break your neck. You got it bad.

What you talking about? You must have pussy idol. Oh Pete.

Hi Terry how are you baby, you ready to come back. No Leroy I called you to tell you I can't come back right now. Terry what's wrong why are you crying is JJ okay? Yes he is right here on the phone. Hello Leroy what's wrong man Terry found our mother dead mother has been sick a long time she just died in her sleep. I'm sorry I'll be there as soon as I can okay Leroy. Let me talk to Terry. Baby I'm on my way. No Leroy wait a few days and I'll call you back and let you know everything. Okay baby I love you if you need money let me know. I will, I love you to Leroy. Is Terry alright? No she found her mother dead. What you want to do son? I need to go be with her I know how it feels to find you mother dead. Okay when do we leave. I want to be with the kid's I love them too.

We driving or catching the train? You stay here I don't want you to take that long ride. I'm going and you can't stop me. I love those kids they have been good to me. I called Ice Man and told him about Terry mother and Pete and I were going to Little Rock. I'll see you in the morning. Sarah and her cousin can run the club they know what to do and I have enough people to help till we get back. We left the next day the three of us. When we got to Little Rock we went to Terry house.

When we got to Terry's house she was not home. Ice said they maybe at her mother's house he knew where her mother lived. I didn't want to go there Pete said son it will be okay I'm here with you. Terry and JJ car was there when we drove up we got out and knocked at the door Lisa came to the door.

She was glad to see us come on in she said You guys sure got here quick. Terry ran to me and hugged me and JJ came they was happy to see Pete and Ice. Terry started to cry and I held her in my arms it will be okay baby I'm here for you. They were getting ready to go to make arrangements for their mother they asked if we would go with them. We came back and I went in the house and looked around I saw pictures of my brother John around the house and it looked like they were all looking at me.

Pete could tell I was getting sick I was about to flip out. Pete just put his arms around me and said for me to try to calm down that is a part of your past you have to calm down son you don't want them to think you're crazy. Here have this drink and let's go outside Pete and I went outside and I felt better. Terry came outside Leroy you and Pete okay? Yes baby, I just need to get outside for a while. I know how you feel you thinking about your mother. Yes Terry I don't like being around things like this I'm tired from the trip.

Here you and Pete take my keys and go to my house and rest I want to stay here for a while. What about Ice Man?

I'll see if he wants to go with you. Leroy you take my bedroom Pete can have the other one and Ice you can have my son's room. Ice came out and said he wanted to stay because they had a lot of food and he wanted to eat. Pete and I left we rode around before we went to Terry's house. I drove by the house Johnnie Mae left me and the people that lived there had let the house run down. Hattie's house look the same. I showed Pete where Linda lived and drove by her club and it still look the same. I didn't want to go by Jasper Bridge so I drove the other way to Terry house when we walked in Pete said he liked her house he felt welcomed there. He was tired and wanted to go to bed early I tried to wait for Terry but I went to bed early also. I don't know when she came home she didn't wake me. When I woke up the next morning she was lying next to me I wanted to make love to her I didn't want to act like a jack ass. Her mother just died and I know she wasn't in the mood for making love with me so I just laid there and just looked at her.

She was so beautiful to me. I got up and let her sleep I went in her kitchen and cook breakfast for her Pete smelled the food and came into the kitchen he said Ice said he would be back later he had somewhere to go. I want to have breakfast in the room with Terry. Go ahead son I will be fine. When I went in Terry was still asleep I kissed her on her cheek and she woke up.

Leroy baby how long you been up? Oh you cooked me breakfast she had a big smile on her face. Leroy I'm glad you're here with me. Terry do you mind if Pete, come in here with us he's at the table by himself.

No, I don't. I went and told Pete to bring his food in with us.

Terry I hope you don't mind. I love you I want you here with me. I want to thank all you guys for being here with me.

It means a lot to me and JJ.

After their mothers funeral we planned to stay one more day. Terry said she will be back to South Carolina in a week JJ and Lisa was moving in their mothers home and she was going to rent out her home.

Pete told Ice to take him to say good bye to JJ so Terry and I could be alone before we leave. So we spent some time together.

Terry got dress and said she would take me to the shop so I could say bye to JJ and Lisa. As we were turning to go by the shop we saw a lot of smoke. It was a big fire I wonder what's going on drive by Terry and let's see what's on fire. Terry said she think it was the Paradise Club. What! (I said) I hope not Linda will go crazy if it's her club. I don't want to go by there now Linda will think I did it. I don't feel like talking to her or dealing with her or Levi I got enough of them when we were in New York.

We went on to the shop. After we got in I was looking at some things Lisa had ordered when I heard someone coming in crying and screaming when I turned around it was Linda. "Leroy, Leroy" I saw you going in here help me please. I stood there looking at her and she ran in my arms screaming. Linda what's wrong? Leroy I didn't mean it I didn't mean it. You have to help me please! Linda is that your club on fire? Yes! What happened calm down? I set it on fire, why Linda? Leroy I was a damn fool I'm sorry for what I did to you.

You were the only man in my life that treated me good I was a damn fool for letting you go for Levi. He only used me after he came and saw my club and how well it was doing he liked it. He told me how much he was in love with me, he was so kind to me and he spent lot's of money on me. He was helping me with the club and was giving me drugs all the time he was taking over my club. He started to beat me and I was scared of him, he made me stay in New York with him and he sent his family here to run my club.

When I came to myself he had already taken over my club and I shot that fat bastard. I killed him and set the club on fire and burn his fat ass up I threw the gun at him and I got in my car and drove off. I came by here and saw you going in you have to help me please Leroy.

Please forgive me for what I did to you. What do you want me to do I don't know what to do?

Can I come back to South Carolina with you? I looked at Terry and I could see the worried look on her face. I'm sorry Linda you can't go with me you have to turn yourself in. Terry walked up beside me and put her arm around me and said help her Leroy. I don't know what to do Levi belong to a mob they will be coming after her. I'm sorry Linda you killed the wrong man. Leroy you told Levi you would kill him," Yes if he hurts me." Well I killed him because he hurt me. Pete and Ice walked in they saw Linda what's going on? Linda your club is on fire, what you doing here girl?

Are you messing with Leroy and Terry? Ice help me please Leroy won't help me! What you talking about woman? Be quite Ice she know she set it on fire, What girl you done gone crazy. Yes, yes, damn you Ice I'm crazy. Linda started walking back and forth and crying. Leroy I need you to get me out of town fast the only thing I can think

The Man on the Train

of is your place in Oklahoma in the country. Oh Leroy, I'll go there until I can think what to do please take me there. No one will find me there I looked at Pete and he didn't say anything Pete what do you think? I think you should stay out of this mess. Pete Linda was nice to me until she met Levi I have to help her. Ice here is some money take, Linda to Derry this is enough money to last you until you think what to do. Leroy I have a lot of money in the bank I'm scared to go by there I'm going to write a will giving, you control of my accounts whenever you need to.

Take care of all my affairs if anything happened to me and take it to your lawyer.

I dated it three months ago I signed everything over to you if I get caught I won't need it where I'm going. Take it to your lawyer before you go back to South Carolina I'll get in touch with you when I get to Derry. I'll call Mr. Flowers at the bank and have him to turn everything on for you by the time you get there. Ice you call me after you get there you know how to find the place.

Yes, come on Linda thank you Leroy I'm sorry for the way I treated you please forgive me. It's okay Linda they left. Pete I hope I haven't made a mistake helping her. Terry put her arms around me and said it would be alright. I took the will to Donald's office and told him she left everything to me if anything happened to her. Don't worry Leroy I can take care of everything for you if anything happened to her I'll have everything legal. Thank you Donald I'm so glad Johnnie asked you to take care of me.

Well I like you Leroy, how's your business doing in South Carolina?

Fine whenever you get a chance come down and spend some time with me everything is on me. I may take you up on that, we left and went back to Terry's house.

Terry called JJ and Lisa and told them what happened to Linda. JJ said Linda have gone crazy he felt sorry for her. Man I can't believe Linda had everything. A beautiful home a nice businesses all that money and now she is on the run and may lose everything she worked so hard now she have to hide out in a little shack outside of town in Derry, Oklahoma. The police came by Terry's house looking for her and we didn't want to tell them it's their job to find her. I heard she and Levi had got into a fight because she found out he was taking her club from her that is why she shot him in his fat belly three times and one time in the neck. She dropped the gun and ran out and got in her car and drove away.

The next day the police came to take me to the police station for questioning. I told Pete to call Donald to meet me there after I got there they started asking me questions about Linda. They found out I use to live with Linda and I owned the shop. They wanted to know where she was I told them that Linda left me two years ago for a man named Levi Roman I wasn't in her life anymore I lived in South Carolina and I was only in town for my girl friends mother's funeral.

I'm getting ready to go back to South Carolina. Donald walked in and they was mad. Donald we need to keep him here for questions.

Is he charged with anything? No. Well I want him out of here now.

They act like they were scared of him. I know Donald's family was one of the riches families in Little Rock they had a lot of pull. One of the officers said, "Boy don't you leave town." Donald turned around and said he don't live here and he have to go back home I know where he live if I need to get in touch with him. He had nothing to do with whatever Linda Edward did you find Linda and leave Leroy alone.

Well he better not have anything to do with it. Donald take me back to Terry house I plan to leave tomorrow to go back home. I need you to stay a few more days I need you to come in the office and talk to me I'll be in the office all day. Okay man see you tomorrow, I went in Terry house. Terry, and Pete ran to me you okay? Yes, I'm fine what happened Terry said, I was so worried she hugged me. I'm fine I told them what I wanted to I just hope and prayed they don't find out I helped her.

Linda and Ice should have made it by now I don't know why Ice haven't called me I hope nothing is wrong. Pete, Donald wants me to stay a few more days I need to go to his office tomorrow. You know Pete I have the same feeling I had when Linda and Ice pick me up in Oklahoma.

I told Pete and Terry I was going to bed it was too much for me I was tired. The next morning I was waked up to the door bell ringing I looked at the clock it was 7:00AM. Terry and I got out of bed and went to the door and there was the police. I thought oh shit what

The Man on the Train

they want this early in the morning I was scared they found Linda and Ice in my shack.

Mr. Chester? We got a call from the police in Derry, Oklahoma they found Linda Edward and a Jericho Young body outside of town. Body what do you mean body? They both are dead. What oh shit did the police kill them? No if you want to come down town we need t talk to you.

Mr. Chester we already called Donald and told him we need to talk to you he will be at the station when we get there. Pete came to the door what's wrong Leroy where they taking you what happened? They said, Ice and Linda is dead. What happened? I don't know Pete I'll talk to you when I get back. When we got to the station Donald was there. Leroy they need to ask you questions because they was murdered. Murdered! Yes, do you know anyone that would do this to them?

I was so shocked they told me to sit down and they gave me a drink of water. The police asked me questions about Linda that could just give them something to go on. They asked me if I knew Levi Roman ad why was he shot in Linda club. I told them that I think Linda shot him for taking her club. I told them that Levi belong to the mob in New York they asked me a few more questions and told me what happened to Linda and Ice.

They said a man saw a car drove up beside them and started shooting it was three men. He saw Linda get out of the car and started running, two of the men got out of the car and followed her and shot her. They got in the car and drove away. They said he was so scared he hid.

He called the police after they left. Young was shot in the head lost control of the car and ran into a ditch. That is when Linda got out and ran they shot her five times. Whoever killed them wanted to make sure they were dead. She was shot at close range. We came to you because we knew you use to live with her and could tell us who may have wanted to kill them. Your name and the name of the dress shop was found in Young's pocket and they both have Arkansas license that is how Derry officers knew to call us. They need their family to come and claim their bodies. They don't have family, I'll go to Derry and take care of everything. Donald took me back to Terry's house I told her and Pete what happened. They made it to Derry I wonder who knew they were going there beside us. I'm was going to Linda's house to tell Marie what happened to Linda. I rang the door bell and Marie came to the door.

Hi Mr. Leroy you came to see Ms. Linda? She and Ice Man gone to Oklahoma. Marie how did you know they went to Oklahoma? They came by here before they left Ms. Linda was in a hurry she said she need to get some things and told me you would be by to take care of everything until she got back and for me to do whatever you wanted. Marie did you tell anyone where she was going? Yes, Mr. Levi's son and his brother came by looking for her they said Mr. Levi was in the hospital and they came to tell Ms. Linda. I told them she just left she was going to a small town called Derry, Oklahoma. They said okay and left. After they left I heard the club burnt down and they took Mr. Levi to the hospital. What's going on?

Marie, Linda and Ice Man was killed in Derry. Oh no! What happened who killed them and why? Ms. Linda was a good woman who would do that to her and Ice? Marie, do you want to stay here until I find out what to do? I have to go to Derry and take care of everything. No Mr. Leroy I have a home of my own and I just want to go home I just stay with Ms. Linda she didn't like living alone after you moved to South Carolina.

Mr. Levi would stay when he was in town you know she started acting strange after she got with Mr. Levi. I told her to stay away from them people and she wouldn't oh my God.

Marie since you won't stay I need to. Well I will leave today and I will take only my things.

I went back to Terry house got Pete and we boarded up the house because Linda had expensive things in there. I'll broad the door and the windows. Pete and I went to Derry and had Linda and Ice's body sent back to Little Rock on the train. I gave them a grave side funeral.

I was really going to miss Ice Man. I cried out God Please help me I can't take it anymore I need to get out of here. I was so tired I just wanted to go back to South Carolina and never come back to Little Rock. They couldn't prove that Levi's son had killed them they never found out who killed them. Peter and I went back to South Carolina I started back to drinking every day I didn't feel like doing nothing. I didn't even go to my club for weeks Sarah was doing a good job. I saw the box of corn whiskey that Ice had bought to the house before we left for Little Rock. Ice always had my back I don't think I can make it without him. Pete was telling me I need to get my stuff together I can't bring Ice back by drinking every day. I can't live like that I didn't even talk to Terry or JJ I just wanted to be left alone. Pete called Terry and told her what was going on with me he told her to come to South Carolina he need her. He really love Terry. Terry sold most of her things she didn't want and put the other things in her mother's garage and she moved to South Carolina. I was so happy to see her she said Leroy you take as long as you like to grieve over Ice.

As long as it is more than a week then get yourself together you are putting too much work on Sarah she is nice to help you out. Sarah is too old to work hard we can do what we need together.

Terry was helping Pete and Sarah at the club. It took me a few days to try to get myself together I miss Ice Man we went through a lot together. I felt if I had not told him to take Linda to Derry he would still be alive. I wished I had listened to Pete when he told me to stay out of Linda's mess. Sarah was praying for me every day she kept telling me everyday bout God.

One day I stopped drinking I said to myself Leroy get off your lazy ass and stop feeling sorry for yourself you can't bring Ice back he would want you to live your life. I put on one of my fine suites and dress shoes fixed myself up and went to the club. I walked in the club I could see all the people working for me to help because they loved and cared for me. I saw the biggest smile on Pete's face. Terry came over and hugged and kissed me I love you baby. Sarah said thank you God I realize they hurt too but they knew they that had to go on. They gave me time to find myself. I looked around the club and I thought "I heard Ice say you can make it you can go on you can do it we all have to pay for the wrong we do to people." Leroy, are you alright? Yes, Pete I'm okay I walked over to Terry and I saw the smile on the woman I loved and knew everything would be alright. Two weeks later Terry and I were married the I was the happiest man in the world. We got married in Sarah's church JJ and Lisa came to the wedding JJ was my best man and Pete gave Terry away. Terry wanted to go to Mexico on our honey moon we had so much fun. After a few days she was ready to come back to South Carolina.

Every Sunday Sarah said we had to go to church together. Pete loved our family he said he was so proud of me. He and Terry was always together and that made me feel good. He was like a father to her after six months Donald called me and told me that all of Linda's things belonged to me. All her money in the bank and her home and everything in it (He said), Leroy Chester you are one of the richest black man in South Carolina. She had jewelry in the bank worth over fifty thousand she had hundred thousand in a saving account and her house is worth over hundred thousand. I don't know how much everything in her home is worth you will have to come down and take what you want to have appraiser. Plus you have that money Johnnie Mae left to you, you have the dress shop and it's making money in it each week.

The money you making in South Carolina at your club, you are worth over 20 million dollars. You only have to pay tax on the money you make everything else was a gift. You have to pay my bill and you have to start taking care of Sarah.

Thank you Donald I don't know what to say. After I send you my bill call me and tell me what you have to say good luck Leroy. I'll be hearing from you soon by Donald. After I hung up the phone with Donald I sat down and started to cry. God I don't know how to pray I don't know why you bless me like this I know I been through a lot in my young life and I'm still going through things. What can I do for you for watching over me all these years? God oh God what can I say but thank you. I was crying so hard Terry came in the room. Leroy what's wrong baby what happened now? Mrs. Leroy Chester I'm crying because God love me because you love me because Pete and Sarah love me and JJ and Lisa love me and I don't deserve it.

Yes, you do baby because you are a good man you are kind to others you are always helping others. This is one of the reasons I fell in love with you I came in to tell you something but I think I will wait later. Tell me now well Mr. Leroy, I think we should make our club a little bigger. Pete said the time is right we getting more business and there is not enough room. What do you think? Well look like you and Pete have already decided it. Leroy I would like to have town nights of soul music Friday and Saturday nights. Some people don't like jazz they like to have fun. What else you and Pete want to do with my club? Honey, I'm sorry I didn't come to you first Pete and I was talking are you mad at me Leroy? I got up from behind my desk and looked at this beautiful woman God gave me. I put my arms around her and kissed her. No baby I'm not mad at you do whatever you and Pete want to do with the club. Oh honey thank you.

Terry when it comes to you and Pete and JJ you are my whole world. She started screaming Leroy, Leroy I love you. She was so loud Pete came running in the room to see what was wrong. What the hell is going on in here? He thought I was hurting Terry she ran to Pete and said Pete we can do what we want. Do what? Change the club like we want, I was coming in here to beat Leroy ass. Whip my ass old man I think I'm a little too big for that. We all laughed. Pete I will never hurt Terry I love her too much. Pete when can we start? Whenever you want how about today? Terry, would you go on a trip with me?

I need to get away honey. I know you haven't gotten over Ice but if you can help me and Pete get the club together I'll go where you want and if Pete want to come he can. Terry and Pete went into the other room and I could see them talking. I wanted to know why they were talking and not telling me everything I was a little jealous of Pete and Terry always talking behind my back. I love them and I was glad they love each other. I fixed me a drink and I couldn't stop thinking about Ice, Al, John, and Linda. Pete come back into the room and said Leroy I need you to go to the club with me. What for?

You need to get out of the house you been in here too long. You been drinking everyday and it's not good you can't bring Ice back none of the people in your past you need to get your life back if you don't you going to lose all the good things in your life. Sarah said, God have been good to you and it's for a reason. If you don't know what to do God will tell you what to do and if you turn your back on him he will take it all away from you. Pete I don't want to hear all this shit today when I get ready to listen to the shit you and Sarah talking about I'll listen but not today. Leave me the hell alone I walked away and got another drink. Pete walked over to me and slap my face.

What the fuck is wrong with you old man? Do you know who the hell I am? Put your fucking hands on me again and I'll beat your ass. Pete slap me again and said you know me and I don't play I can fuck you up too I ain't too old to kick your ass. When I tell you to do something damn it I mean it you hear what the fuck I say! I say get your ass in there take a shower and get dress and come with me now and I mean now get a move on your black ass.

For the first time in my life I backed down I saw a look on Pete's face I had never seen before. He was ready for me he was ready to beat my ass If he needed to. I couldn't whoop this old man I love him I looked over to the door and Terry was standing there with tears running down her face and she never said a word. I felt like a damn dog that went crazy and ready for someone to shoot me. I just ran out of the room took a shower and got dressed. When I came out I knew I had to hold my head up because when I came out that door I knew Pete and Terry would be looking at me. I wanted them to see the man they loved.

When I walked out they was smiling at me I went to Terry and said I was sorry and she kissed me if there will be no tomorrow.

I don't want to act that way or say the thing you said to me.

Son you are a man and I want you to be a strong man there are times we have to let go of people we can't help. Son we can't worry about things we cannot change. Sarah said you pray and God can change things and make things better for you and take your worries away you just have to ask him and have faith.

I didn't want my wife to see me break down and cry I kissed her on her cheek and went outside and went to the club. I understand what this old man was talking about after we got in the club Pete put his arms around my shoulder and said you my son and I love you. I just want you to be the man you can be. I knew in my heart what it was like to have a father. I mean a real father who love and care, I never loved my real father and I know he would never be the man Pete was. I went in the office and close the door and cried Pete came in son cry get it all out. Its okay I'm here for you I'll always be here for you if God let me.

If I can come back for you I will. I tried to stop drinking to make my wife proud of me each day was getting better after a few months I didn't think about Ice and Linda. A year has passed and I bought me another club a blues club I left the other one Jazz I named my new club Jericho's after Ice. I knew Ice would have liked it. I need someone to help me run my club someone like Jericho to have my back, and not scared.

That could stand behind me and trust. I know I could never have no one like Ice. Terry and I worked hard at the clubs we didn't see each other a lot only at home at night and at breakfast. I ran the Jazz club.

Sarah was getting tired of cooking everyday and helping Pete.

So Sarah quit and Pete was getting too old he was tired also so I told him and Sarah to stay home and I hired extra help at both clubs.

I made sure Terry had a lot of help so she wouldn't have to do much.

Pete was getting around slow and was almost eighty years old. I had stopped drinking I came home one night so tired I really wanted to make me a drink so I could go to bed and sleep all night.

I looked up and it was 3:00 and Terry was not home shit I better go to the Blues Club and see what's wrong just as I got to the door she drove up I opened the door. Baby you okay? Why you so late? I was coming to get you. You alright? No I feel sick I think I'm coming down with the flu or something. Terry you working too hard I want you to stay home and I'll help run the club and I'll check on each of them. Leroy I'll be okay I just tired tonight I'll go to bed and I'll feel better in the morning.

Can I get you something? No I just want to go to bed.

I called JJ and asked him if he could come to South Carolina a few days and check on my clubs. He Sarah and Pete could just close up at night for me and put the money in the bank. I was taking Terry back to Mexico for a few days rest she liked it when we were there the last time. Terry was ready to go she said she need to rest.

JJ came and Terry was so happy to see her brother. JJ I really love your sister and I want her to take off to rest and have her all to myself. I want her in my life for the rest of my life I started kissing her. Okay, Okay I get the picture I may have to go back tomorrow I miss Lisa. Leroy when you come back you, need to do something with Linda's house.

Donald is having a hard time selling it and you need to get that stuff out of there before it gets broken in you can tell someone been trying to get in there. Good thing I had it boarded from the inside to. Yes, I will go back with you when we get back. Terry and I flew to Mexico for a few days we had a good time she didn't get sick at all while we were there. We got back JJ was ready to go back home Terry wanted to go back with JJ. Leroy you need the help getting rid of a lot her things you don't have room to bring it back here. Can we go with

JJ tomorrow? Terry I have to check on the clubs and make sure I can trust people. Okay Terry you and I will go later I'll show Victory and Betty what to do and I can get Sarah and Pete to go take the money.

When I came down I'll see what I want to sell I want to keep.

The next day I left I went to Little Rock when I got there Donald asked me if his family could come first and buy some of the things. He told me to get an appraiser to be there to tell me how much things were worth while I was selling them. I was so happy that Donald and his family bought most of Linda's stuff they paid sixty thousand dollars for her things. I kept some of her jewelry for Terry we had a garage sale and sold most of her other things and we made 3 thousand dollars. I didn't know Linda's things were so expensive. Some of her clothes, shoes, hats, and scarf's. Terry took them to the shop to sell there I had Donald to go by the bank with me to put the money in the bank. Mr. Jackson knew me but with that much money I wanted Donald to be with me. Donald is the only man I can trust with money.

I gave JJ thirty thousand and Lisa twenty. They both were so happy JJ said man I love you, you a good friend. I wanted to say and I'm your uncle I wanted to so bad but I couldn't I just hug him and said love you too. God if he only knew what would he think of me? The next day JJ asked Terry and I if we would go to the court house with them. Terry wanted to know for what? JJ told her he and Lisa was getting married. Oh no I want you to have a big wedding and I will help you. No Terry we don't want a big wedding right now maybe later we just want to get married today. We went with them and they was married we went out danced and had fun. I didn't drink it's almost been a week since I had a drink.

Pete and Terry was so proud of me and my body felt good, Terry and I left and went back to South Carolina when we got back Pete said he wasn't feeling too good and Terry said she was sick too. What the hell is wrong with you two? I'm taking you both to the doctor.

Leroy wait until tomorrow and see how we both feel by morning.

The next morning Terry told me to take Pete and she would go along she didn't mind. She said she felt better. I took Pete to the doctor and he said Pete was old he maybe still having problems from the surgery he had a few years ago. Pete said he was in a lot of pain with his head the doctor gave him some medicine and told him he needed to rest more and take it easy. When we got home Terry left and went to Club Jericho Sarah said. She said she would be home later.

I need to go to the club will you be okay Pete? Yes, I just need to go rest Sarah will be here if I need anything. Sarah I'll call you later if you need me call, Okay Leroy. After the club closed I came home Terry was already there Pete and Sarah had gone to bed. I went in my room there were candles soft music, the room smelled like roses my wife had a small tray of food and wine on the side of the bed. What is all this?

She was lying on the bed with a low cut gown on with a lot of beautiful lace on it. I didn't know what to think Terry you okay?

What have I done to deserve to come home to all this?

She got up and came to me and said Mr. Chester this is for the both of us we have been too busy for each other since we came back from Mexico.

I need you tonight we kissed and pulled off each other's clothes off and I made love to her as if it was the first time I made love to her only it was better. The she let me fuck her as if she was leaving me and wanted to give me something to remember her by.

I let her enjoy me from head to toe we kiss each other until we both were tired. We got up and ate the food and got back in the bed and she got so close to me I put my arms around her and we both fell asleep in each other's arms. Terry you didn't tell me what the doctor said to you yesterday. Oh you took care of that problem last night and this morning she kissed me and said all I need was the love of a man.

Girl what did the doctor say and are you okay? I'm fine and it wasn't anything I just need real good honey from my husband to relax and show him how much I'm in love with him. Well Ms. Lady if you need some more I'm here to give you what you need. She came over and kissed me.

This woman is my world she makes me feels good about myself. She is what I need in my life I don't think about my past much.

I tried to block it out of my head and mind I have enough money for a life time I'm on top of the world. The two clubs are doing so good I had help working at both clubs. I wanted to spend a little more time at home with Pete he was getting around very slow and it was too much on Sarah to help with him. Terry spent a lot of time with him in his room she would take care of him. He was like a father to her she said Pete was a wise man he treat her like his daughter if he had one.

Weeks and weeks have gone by and Pete looked real sick and I had to put him in the hospital. He stayed in the hospital a week and when he came home he had to have someone with him. Sarah said she wanted to help take care of him she liked him too. I hired a lady to come in and help Sarah I told Sarah to let her do all the work and give her orders.

Sarah said God told her to stay out the clubs he didn't want her to be around that kind of life any more.

Sarah loved going to worship God. I had made a lot of money and I was tire of the Jazz club I knew I should be home with Pete as much as I could he was felling fast. I sold my Jazz club to a rich man that moved to South Carolina from Florida. He wanted a nice club I sold it for ninety five thousand dollars with everything in it. He wanted to keep the name Mr. Chester's he liked the name. It was fine with me.

Terry wanted to move out of the house Johnnie Mae left me she wanted a home of her own. I wanted to stay a little longer it was paid for and I liked it.

Terry got sick again she looked like she was gaining weight, I didn't say too much because I know she loved the food at the club. Terry I'm taking you back to the doctor you don't look good and don't tell me you need me to make love to you. Come on we, going now. Leroy I know what is wrong with me come on into the bedroom and I'll tell you. We sat on the bed and she took my hand and put it on her stomach she kissed me and said Leroy Chester I love you more today. I smiled and when I was looking at her she had changed her face was fatter then it use to be. Terry what's wrong with you? Just rub my stomach Leroy you going to be a daddy I'm pregnant. You what! I'm going to have a baby. I was just shocked I never thought she could have another baby after she lost our baby.

Leroy, say something. I took her in my arms and just hugged her for a few minutes. Oh baby, you okay? Are you happy? Yes, yes baby I am having a baby I, mean we having a baby.

We told Sarah and Pete smile he was so happy for us. Pete you going to be a grandpa what do you think about that? I think I like that Leroy I hope I live to see him. Oh Pete don't talk like that you will. Terry said Pete you going to make a good grandpa he hug Terry and said thank you young lady. We were all happy. I wanted Terry to stop working at the club and stay home. Everything was going so well for us.

Seven months later Terry had a little boy and he was beautiful he look just like me. She named him Peter Leroy Chester, Pete was so happy she gave him his name I liked it also. He brought so much joy in our house Terry was a good mother her son David came down and stayed the summer he liked his little brother he was so much older than him.

He and I had started to get alone so much better I asked him if he would move in with us and go to school. H wanted to stay with his dad because he didn't want to leave all his friends. Terry really wanted him to stay.

JJ and Lisa came to see the baby for a few days. JJ and I spent a lot of time together while the girls stayed home. JJ would go to the club with me at night. JJ couldn't see how I could work at the club and not drink every day. I had promised Pete and Terry that I would stop.

My son was born May 12, 1970 when he was three months old Pete called me into his room. Leroy I'm 81 years old and I'm glad I lived to see your son and I think everything is going to be fine. I want you to take good care of Terry and your son you have a good family. Always take care of them. Okay Pete I will. I wish I could live long enough to see him grow up. Pete you going to live a long time don't talk like this I don't want to hear this do you need anything? Leroy listen to me I left a letter with Donald telling him what to do if anything ever come up with James death. Al and John you don't have to worry if you keep your mouth shut Pete what have you done? Nothing for you to worry about I will, never let anything happen to you Leroy. Pete, oh Pete stop talking why would you do this? I don't want to talk about this anymore have you gone crazy?

I started to walk out the room and Pete called me back. Leroy! What!

Son always remember I love you son I did it because you need to be with your family. You have made me a happy old man you all I have.

Thank you for my grandson always tell him about me. Pete please stop talking like this. Will you listen to me nigger? I love you Pete it hurts me to hear you talking as if you're going to die.

Do you know how I feel about you old man? I walked over and hugged him and we both started to cry he closed his eyes and had a smile on his face. Pete, no, no, Sarah, come here quick. what are you yelling about? Terry Pete won't wake up. I was crying so hard Terry walked over to him and then she started to cry. Leroy he is dead! No he is not he would never leave me no, no! God why you do this to me not Pete?

You said you forgive me for my sins! Damn this world and everybody in it I ran out of the room and fell to my knees I couldn't move and I couldn't speak. I passed out when I woke up I was in the hospital they said I was in shock.

They kept me in the hospital over night. When I came home I saw the corn whiskey I went in the kitchen put me some ice in a glass and some water I wanted Terry to think I was drinking water when she wasn't looking I poured out the water and filled my glass with corn whiskey. What in the hell I'm going to do without Pete? Pete died August 10, 1970. They said it was time for him to go. Terry called JJ and Pete's brother in Tulsa, Oklahoma and told them Pete had died. His brother told Terry to do whatever she wanted he didn't have any money to help out. Terry told him she will send money for him to come to his funeral and let him know when it was. JJ and Lisa came out to help I didn't feel like doing nothing I just couldn't get myself together. I was drinking everyday and I didn't care if Terry knew. Terry sent Pete's brother three hundred dollars to come to the funeral and he never showed up or sent the money back and he never called. We had Pete's funeral at Sarah church I don't remember what the preacher talked about I do remember when I went to view the body I cried so hard it felt like my heart jumped out of my body.

JJ took me out of the church and put me in the family car.

I remember Terry, Lisa, Sarah, and the baby coming in with us. We drove away to the grave yard and I saw them putting this body in the ground but I didn't remember if it was Pete. I remember it was my mother and I cried and cried. I remember going back home getting me a drink and looking at all the people in my house eating and drinking through my house. I wanted them all to get out people from the club was there I didn't want to eat or talk.

People kept coming up to me and I could see their mouth but I didn't remember what they was saying. Terry came over to me and said baby it will be alright JJ came and took me to the club to be away from everyone. He drank with me and we talked he loved Pete as much as I did. When we got back home all the people was gone I went to my room and passed out. I got up the next morning and I fixed me a drink Terry started telling me what to do and it was time to get my ass together. I couldn't stand to be there without Pete. I started staying away from home a lot when I came home Terry was always mad.

I didn't remember when JJ and Lisa went back home I couldn't understand what was happening to me. I started staying at the club and drinking every day I didn't know what was going on at my club half of the time. I woke up one morning and I was in the bed with some woman I didn't know. I didn't remember who she was I think I met her in the club. I started to spend money on other women and there were a lot of women around me I stayed away from home for days. I didn't know if Terry and the baby were alright she had plenty of money to take care of her.

I was drinking and having fun she wouldn't come to the club looking for me. So I thought she didn't give a damn what I did I didn't remember how many days I was gone. I went home and Terry and Sarah was there. When I walked in Terry said where have you been Leroy you need to stop this shit do you hear me? Do you think Pete would like what you doing? Terry don't start with me. Sarah said Leroy let me fix you something to eat. When the last time you ate? You look so bad you have lost a lot of weight. Leroy you need to go back to church with me God can help you, you need to pray. Sarah I didn't come back home to listen to no shit about God and your prayers. Your God took my mother and Pete from me I took two people away so we even. What you mean you took two people? Just as I said I took two people away that didn't mean a damn thing to me. I cut their fucking throat and I didn't give a damn and I don't give a fuck now. Both of them sorry motherfuckers can still kiss my ass they both are in a place you call hell. So I'll be running into their asses soon.

I walked out and went into the bedroom and went to sleep.

I woke up the next morning and I could smell food cooking I took a shower I haven't had a bath in days. I got dressed I felt so bad and shame when I came out. Sarah said, Leroy come on food is ready Terry was standing there with the baby in her arms. Terry I'm so sorry for hurting you. Sarah, please forgive me for what I said to you last night. I'm going to do better I took my son out of Terry's arm and kissed him. Little man I love you I'm going to be a good father to you. Terry took him back and said eat Leroy. I sat down and man the breakfast was so good I ate like it's been two weeks. Sarah did you take Pete something to eat?

Can he get out of bed? I'll take him something. Terry (said,) Leroy sit down.

Why you looking at me like that? They both dropped their heads what, what. Leroy you forgot. Forgot what? Terry gave the baby to Sarah I ran into his room and there was no Pete where is he did he go back to Oklahoma? Yes. Why did he go back. Leroy Pete is dead you remember. Before the funeral home covered him up I asked them if I could change my mind and have his body sent back to Derry. It costs you a lot of money to do it but you got money you can do anything.

I took some of your money and bought a plot in Derry next to your mother. You was so drunk every day I tried to tell you.

You left and you didn't come back I thought you would like that. I bought one for you the way you was drinking I didn't know what would happen to you. You acted like you had given up Leroy your money was coming out of the bank so fast almost every day large amounts was coming out.

I sat there looking at this woman in front of me and I kept looking at her. She was over forty in such a short time. Terry was only 31 Leroy say something and stop looking at me like that. I didn't say a word I just kept sitting there trying to think where in the hell I was when all this shit was happening. Was I at Pete's funeral? Yes, you were so drunk.

You been, drunk for four months. I didn't try to find you I just wanted to leave you alone so you could find yourself. I knew you would come back when you wanted to. I was drunk for four months where was I?

You mean I was out of my son's life for four months.

Sarah brought me the baby. I looked at my son smiling at me and the last time I saw him he was three months old. Terry just walked out of the room and I was wondering where was I for four months.

I looked at Pete's bed and I swore I saw him looking at me and saying Nigger I told you that you couldn't handle that damn corn whiskey.

Oh Pete, you're not dead.

I told you I will never leave you. I got out of the chair to go to him but he wasn't there. I ran out of the room with the baby still in my arms. I gave Terry the baby and went to fix me a drink and all the liquor was gone. Leroy you don't need any more to drink I got rid of it. Bitch you did what! Do you know how much I paid for that shit? Sarah said, you shouldn't talk to her like that she been going through hell too and you're not making it easy. You need to stop drinking you need to get help.

Come on and go to church with me. Sarah you need to get your ass out of here you been here for six years, you leave me the fuck alone and take your ass to church and keep praying to your God. Leave me the fuck, alone get out of here.

Sarah left crying and I didn't give a damn I went and sat on the porch because Terry kept looking at me as if I was crazy. It's been a long time since I sat on my porch I watched the people go by and I watched Sarah walk out get into her car and drive off. I never said good bye and she never looked back. I kept sitting there because I know Terry will have something to say and maybe put me out of my own damn house. So I kept sitting there after a while I went in the house and Terry was in the bedroom. I guess she didn't want to talk to me. I went in the kitchen to fix me something to eat. I couldn't so I went down in the basement and there was all my whiskey. She and Sarah put it down there I saw four more cases of corn whiskey in the corner that was all I needed. I took some of jars out and hid them up stairs so she wouldn't see me going down there. I drank some and it was so good. I left and didn't wake Terry I had to go check on my club just before I drove up in the parking lot here come the police. They said I was driving across the lines and I had ran a red light. They took me to jail for the first time I was ever locked up.

I panicked called my wife and tell her to come get me.

Sorry buddy you're staying here until tomorrow they finger printed me and took my picture. Now I have a record I don't want to be locked up ever again. I couldn't sleep all night I just laid there and did a lot of thinking about what I had done to Terry and Sarah and I felt like a damn jack ass.

How will they ever forgive me. I felt like a big black bear behind bars. The next day Terry cam and got me when I looked in her face I could see so much hurt on her face and I was so shame. She had to take me to go get my car out of the impound she didn't say too much. Baby I'm sorry this time I'm going to stop. Leroy you need help and I can't help you, you will have to it yourself. I'm getting tired and I don't know how much I can take. She drop me off at the impound place and drove off after I got in my car I went home and went to bed. I woke up that afternoon and there was a lady sitting in my living room. Who are you? I'm Jean the baby sitter where is Terry? She gone to work, work what work? She said the Jericho club, someone didn't show up.

I got dressed and went down to the club Terry was surprised to see me. We worked together like old times when we first opened up everyone was glad to see me. I went in the back to check on my books and the food to see what we all need. The people I had working for me was real good they kept everything running smooth for me. My books were in order and everything was accounted for my money came out right. Terry said she hired an accountant to keep up with everything. Donald told her who to get and she could trust.

That was my job but I wasn't there for Terry. Terry said, the money I was spending she replaced with the money we made from the club. I thanked Terry and told her I would take it a day at a time to stop drinking. Leroy if you don't stop I'm taking the baby and you won't see us anymore do you hear me? Yes baby. I hugged her and said I don't want you to leave. You will have to prove thing to me Leroy. I will Baby.

A lady I was messing with when I was so drunk after Pete died came in the club asking where have I been and how much she miss me.

Terry was looking at me talking to her. I could see her starring so hard I knew she was coming over to see why I was talking so long to seat her. She came over. I said this is my wife Terry baby the lady is

The Man on the Train

telling me how nice the club is and how she like coming here. Terry said thank you. Leroy we have to leave so the baby sitter can leave.

The lady looked at me in shocked and walked away. I left with Terry.

I didn't want to talk to the lady.

Terry still looked tired and old I just realized that it's been months since I really took the time to spend with her and really show her how much I loved her. I didn't know if she wanted to make love to her anymore.

I think I will wait until she can have respect for me again.

She came in the living room after she got out of the shower I could smell her perfume as she walked in I wanted her so bad. Terry I'm sorry for the way I acted I couldn't take it when Pete died. You're a good woman and I don't deserve you I don't know why you put up with me?

Will you give me another chance? I'll get help I love you baby I want you to stay in my life I want my son.

Leroy stop crying I can't stand it when you cry. I love you to baby I just want things back the way they were. I took her in my arms and held her so tight I won't let you go Terry. I started kissing her and she wanted me as bad as I wanted her. I made love to her like I was never going to see her again. We couldn't let go of each other after we stop I saw this big smile on her face I knew I had made her happy because she always smiled when I please her. She got out of bed where are you going? I'm going to check on the baby, bring him back with you and we both can keep an eye on him. When she came back with my son they looked so beautiful together. How could I have been so stupid to leave them?

She gave him to me and I looked at him and he was still sleep with no care in the world. I laid him down between the two of us and I felt like a man that got his life back. I was beginning to feel like I had my head back on straight. I found out where Sarah was I went to her and I knocked on the door and she came to the door. Sarah I'm so sorry for what I said to you will you forgive me? You mean a lot to me we been through.

You know Leroy God said we have to forgive each other like he forgave us. I know there are some people you don't want to be around you don't have to. God will still love you anyway. Sarah, will you come back with me?

No son I bought me this home and I love it this is mines and I want to stay here and I can let whoever I want in here. You and your wife need to be alone together I been with you long enough you need to be with your family because God is going to put you through hell and you will need help when you come out you will be a better man. What do you mean Sarah?

Oh you will see. Oh Sarah I kissed her on the cheek and started out the door. Leroy, I'll see you and your family at church Sunday. By, Sarah.

I went home and told Terry what Sarah said and Sunday morning we went to church. Sarah was so glad to see us there. I heard every word the preacher was saying he was talking about how to be the man of your family. I thought I was a good husband to my wife.

Sarah started coming back to my house and she been telling me a lot about God and I sure started loving hearing about him. Terry stop fussing at me. My son was growing up so fast and weeks was going by so fast.

I wasn't drinking anymore. JJ called me and said the shop was doing well and he just wanted to tell me he gave him and Lisa a raise. It's alright with me JJ we both laughed. are still good friends. I still wanted to tell him I was his uncle but I now I had to pick the right time. I feel he will hate me and I wasn't ready I know I have to one day confess my sins.

I know that one day I couldn't keep lying to myself and people. I started going to church every Sunday I learned when you do wrong to people you suffer when you take from others that don't belong to you, you suffer. It's been a year since Terry and I made up we decided to go to Little Rock to spend some time with JJ and Lisa. We drove my new car I bought a new 1972 Cadillac and Terry wanted a small car a 1972 Chevy. I still had my mama's old care I plan not to ever sell it. I was still in very good condition we spent a few days JJ was so happy he loved little Pete. He said he was ready for a baby in his house. We all stared teasing Lisa telling her she better hurry she was getting old. JJ was just grinning. Okay JJ what's with you I know that grin.

Lisa is going to have a baby. Terry you're going to be Aunt Terry in seven months. I'm going to be a uncle again. What you mean again?

The Man on the Train

Terry was looking at me so funny. Oh I'm so excited for you guys I said it wrong, I mean I'm going to be a uncle and I'm happy for you guys. Terry said she was going over to her ex-husbands to tell David good bye you want me to go with you?

Leroy stay here with me. Lisa can go with her come on man let's play some pool. Terry said she was taking David shopping before she leave JJ and I was happy together he wanted me to go to the shop with him. Lisa had changed the shop and it looked real good how do you like it Leroy?

I like it you guys have done a good job. Well when are you going to give it to me since we having a baby we need to make more money and I want to own something of my own. You said you would give it to me one day how much do you want for it? I, been saving a little money.

I'll call Donald and tell him to get the paper work together for you.

I like to give it to Lisa as soon as I can for her birthday. I want to put the papers in her hand and say happy birthday it's all yours.

Sure JJ I owe you that much you don't have to pay me nothing I'm glad I can do this for you.

Thank you man you just made me happy, Leroy you are a good man and I'm happy you and Terry is doing so well. Thank you for making my sister happy she looks happy just gaining a little weight. I think you need to keep her out of that club eating all the good food. I love her the way she is I don't care how fat she gets. Thank you man I love you. I love you too JJ come one man let's ride around for a bit before we go back home to the girls. I went back to the neighborhood where Johnnie Mae use to live Johnnie Mae's house was gone they said it burnt down Hattie's house still look the same. We went by Linda's house the people that bought it had it looking really good they had a lot of beautiful flowers around the house and it had been painted. I asked JJ to stop I wanted to go in for some reason he said he would stay in the car. I knocked on the door and a man came to the door, hello my name is Leroy Chester, I use to own this house I just wanted to meet the people that live here.

Oh come on in my name is John Henry I'm a lawyer and this is my wife Willow she is an accountant honey this is the man that use to own this house. Come on and look around. I looked around they had made a lot of changes as I walking out the door Willow said Mr. Chester you left a box of things here in the closet. I was going to call Donald Smith to tell him to come by and pick it up. Do you want it? Well what is it? Just a few things you may want to keep thank you very much.

Oh your welcome I 'm glad you came by. She gave me the box of junk and I took it. It was nice meeting you. I got to the car JJ, asked me what did I have in the box? Just some junk I left in there and they saved it they were going to call Donald to pick it up.

We drove by Linda empty lot where her, club use to be.

I never want to come back to Little Rock to live to many bad memories for me. JJ wanted to stop by the bar on State Street. No I don't drink anymore! Well you can drink some pop or water when I walked in everybody was happy to see me the same people were still coming in there.

They wanted to buy me a drink I really tried to say no but I had one drink and the next thing I had another one JJ and I was having fun we was dancing with the girls. When we got back to the house Lisa and Terry was so mad at the both of us. We didn't want to listen to them so we went to bed. The next morning Terry was ready to go back to South Carolina. We left and she was mad all the way back after she got home she took the baby to the bedroom and locked the door. I tried so hard not to drink. I went in the basement and got me another jar of corn whiskey. I was getting bored and wanted to go to the club I went on to bed in the other bed room. I got up early the next morning and as I was driving out of the drive way I could see her peeping out of the window.

I was gone for over two hours looking for me a good place to open me a dress shop since I was giving JJ and Lisa the one in Little Rock. I knew Terry was going to start on me as soon as I walked in that door.

I sat in the car for a few minutes soon as I walked in she said you just coming in from being out all night. Terry why do you keep nagging me you know I have not been out all night. You just want to start something are you tired of me do you want to move out.

Well that maybe a good idea then I won't have to look at your drunk ass all the time. If I knew you turn out this way I would have never married your damn drunk ass I would have stayed in Little

Rock I wouldn't have sold my nice home. This ain't my home this is one of your damn women home. You put me in your woman house you been fucking I tried to look over it because I loved you I stayed here because of you.

My dumb ass was so much in love with you I wanted to make you happy. I hate this damn house I thought I could look over it I let Pete talk me into staying here because he loved you and this damn house.

I loved that old man and I wanted to make him happy too it hurt me when he died you was so damn busy thinking about yourself.

What about my pain I had the baby cause I wanted to make you happy. I thought you would be so happy you would stop drinking and help me with the baby.

So you can get the fuck out and go back to a drinking and chase all the damn women you want you think I'm stupid. Terry was crying the whole time she was talking to me I just stood there and listened to her. All the years we been together I never have heard her talk like that and she made me feel like the dirt on the floor I was standing on and I could feel it deep down. I didn't know what to say I know I really need a drink after listening to all that but I just stood there. She got on the phone and called JJ and told him she was moving back to Little Rock. I looked at her and she had gained so much weight I know it was because she was under so much stress and she was eating a lot. Terry I'm sorry. Leroy if you tell me you sorry one more damn time I will come over there and slap the shit out of you. Stop saying you're sorry to me and you keep doing the same shit. I tried to put my arms around her and she told me to leave her alone and get the fuck away from her.

So I just left I stayed away for three days when I came home Terry was on the phone. She dropped the phone and was screaming so hard and crying. Terry what's wrong baby what's wrong? She fell to the floor. Baby what the fuck is wrong with you? She pushed me away I picked up the phone hello, hello who is this? Leroy this is Lisa. Lisa why are you crying what's wrong where is JJ? Put him on the phone. Leroy JJ is dead.

What! No, no what happened?

He was on his way home from the bar on State Street and he was drunk lost control of his car and hit a tree he was going too fast.

He died before they could get him to the hospital. I couldn't move I had the phone still at my ear and Lisa was saying Leroy.

I couldn't say nothing I hung up the phone bent down and picked Terry up and took her in the bedroom. I put her on the bed and just held her baby I'm sorry.

Leroy why did God take my brother he is all I had. Why did God take him when I needed him more than ever? Now I have no one in my family. Terry you have me and Little Pete come on we will catch the train I can't drive in the state I'm in I'll call Sarah and see if she can keep Little Pete oh Terry I'm so sorry I 'm here for you. I was crying to because I love him I was going to one day tell him who I was. Now I can never tell him about me and John I really need me a drink. Oh God why you always take the good people?

God JJ was good and you wouldn't even let him live to see his child born you should have taken me. Terry, was so hurt she look like she was going to die. They were so close. I know how you feel Terry I lost people I love Pete said cry all you want. She looked at me with tears in her eyes.

After Sarah came to stay we caught the late night train to ride to Little Rock. It seemed like the longest train ride I ever rode. I close my eyes and I saw the man on the train. He was coming toward me with so much hate in his eyes. I could hear him telling me "You black bastard I told you to stay away from my son." He had a big black butcher knife in his hand I started screaming John I'm sorry please forgive, me.

No I will never forgive you! You took me from my son. I opened my eyes and Terry was shaking me Leroy, Leroy why do you keep having these night mares? Did you really kill two people? I looked at her and she said one night you was drunk after Pete died you said you cut two men's throat who did you kill? Are they coming after you? I didn't say anything I just wanted to get off this train. When the train stop I hurried off Lisa was there to pick us up I ran to Lisa and told her how sorry I was. Terry let's go to a hotel I don't think I can take it there. Come on Leroy I wasn't you and Terry to stay with me. I'm sorry Lisa, Terry can stay I just want to be alone tonight.

Lisa and Terry dropped me off at the hotel they thought that I was missing JJ and I was so shaken up. When I got in my room I ordered me a drink I stayed in the room all night thinking. I didn't

The Man on the Train

think I could deal with it anymore. The next morning Lisa and Terry came to pick me up and I couldn't move. Leroy, Leroy get up I know JJ would want you by my side he don't want you drunk at his funeral like you was at Pete's and Ice Man's. If you drunk you can't help us get up and get dressed.

I just lost my husband and Terry lost her brother and you lost a man who loved you like a brother. Come on man. Terry I'm. Shut up Leroy.

IF you tell me you sorry one more time I'm going to kick your ass I don't want to hear another I'm sorry anymore.

They walked out while I got dressed I tried hard not to drink while they was taking care of everything. I followed them to everything they need to do for JJ I was there I didn't do nothing. Terry had cried and cried until she looked real bad and she, look like she was getting bigger.

I didn't want to say nothing because she looked so unhappy all the time. JJ was buried January 15, 1972 He was only twenty eight years old.

Lisa wanted JJ funeral to be a happy funeral he didn't want anyone singing sad songs. Everyone acted happy accept Terry and Lisa and I we were the only one's crying at the church. I was wondering what would he have said if I told him I was his uncle how would he felt then about me? What would he have said if I told him I was the one who killed his daddy? After the funeral we went to Lisa's house there was pictures of John, JJ and his mother.

Lisa put them out because they were not there the last time we were in Little Rock. I didn't want to stay inside looking at those pictures I knew I should be by my wife's side. I sat on the porch the house was full of people. I didn't feel like talking to people telling me how sorry they were. I had been to, to many funerals in my short life. Terry came on the porch Leroy you alright? You want something to eat? Come on in. Terry I'm okay. It's cold out here. I'm fine she went back in the house I know some of the people may think I'm crazy for sitting out in the cold. This man came out the door and said man come on and sits with me in the car. I got in with him he said he was Hank one of Lisa's cousin.

Want a drink? No I don't think so I need to keep my head for my wife. Well this is some good corn whiskey man it goes down like water. This is some good shit you sure you don't want some its cold out here. Yea, I'll take one drink. Hank pull out a cigarette do you smoke?

No.

Damn your old lady won't let you do nothing. Take a hit off of this you will like it. Makes you relax I drank the whisky and took a hit off his cigarette next thing we were drinking more and smoking it made me cough. Hank was laughing at me and I started laughing we drank up the corn whisky and smoked up the cigarette then I started to cry.

Hank, said get your ass out of here. I made him mad and told him that I would cut his fucking throat if he messes with me. I started calling him a crazy mother fucker I told him when I get back on that train John come after me trying to kill me. I'll kill his fucking ass again. Hank jumped out of the car and called Lisa to come out.

I was going crazy. They call the police. I saw a man coming toward me and he look like Al Jenkins. I grab my knife out of my pocket and I started swinging at him. Calm down man it's going to be alright he kept coming toward me and I tried to stab him and he jumped back. You two motherfuckers stay away from me. Terry came out Leroy what is wrong with you have you gone crazy?

Stop acting a fool she was walking toward me. Give me that knife!

You come close to me bitch and I'll kill you. You ain't getting by this time come on if you want to. Someone grab me from behind and was holding on to me. The police came up and put me in the car and took me to jail.

I was tired and didn't give a damn anymore I told the police I killed Al Jenkins and John Chester. I need to be punished for my crimes.

The police thought I was drunk and was just talking.

The police asked me when I killed these people. I said in 1957 and 1961 or something and I passed out. The next day I felt like shit. I told the police to call my wife to come get me. Leroy we want to know about the two you said you killed. I ain't killed nobody we believe you did I want my call. They let me Use the phone and I called Lisa house. Lisa let me speak to Terry. she's not here. Where is she? I said she's not here Leroy.

Well come get me I'm in jail. Yes, I know I can't come because I'm busy. What the fuck you say? Come and get me now bitch she hung up on me I waited and waited and she, never showed up. I was wondering where in the hell was Terry. I called Donald and they said he was out of town three days later they bought me before the Judge and asked me if I had my lawyer there?

No. Mr. Chester you are here for disturbing the peace and for threaten to kill someone with a dangerous weapon. Mr. Chester, can you afford a lawyer? If not we will appoint one for you. Yes, I can't contact my lawyer. Lock him back up until he talks to his lawyer. I called Donald office and they said he was still out of town. Well you find him and tell him I said I need him to get me out of jail this is Leroy Chester. I kept calling Lisa and she wouldn't answer the phone I called the shop and they said she was not working today. A week later Terry came to see me I was so happy to see her baby where you been you here to come get me out today? "No" Terry you are crazy. Hell no I think you are. I came here to tell you black son of a bitch I never want to see you again. I want you to stay away from me and my son. How could you lie to me and my brother all these years? How could you smile in our face and tell us how much you loved us?

How could you lie beside me and make love to me with your lying ass? How could you? How could I fall in love with a man like you?

Terry listen to me baby listen to me. No you black bastard you listen to me you said you killed two people and the police said you told them you killed somebody. My brother died loving you like a brother he thought the world of you.

Terry you don't understand you mad right gets me out of here and I'll tell you everything but not here. The police just found out today that JJ daddy name is John Chester he was from Derry, Oklahoma. When he moved to Texas he changed his man to Jerry Johnson. Do you know him Leroy? Is he some kin to you? Terry, please. You kiss my ass and your ass can rot in here for all I care. You didn't love me or trust me enough to tell me about your family. You said you just killed two people how do I know someday you won't kill me?

Terry I would never hurt you. You stupid bastard what the hell you think you're doing to me. Look at me motherfucker this is the last time you will see my black ass. Terry, Terry please, listens to me. I love you Terry. Fuck you Leroy. I watched Terry walk away from me forever all I could do was sit there and cry. The love of my life is gone I have no one now I understand what Sarah was saying you going to reap what you so.

I lay there thinking about all of them.

I remember Lilly saying Leroy one day all your secrets will one day come out. I was in jail for four months and they kept questioning me about John. They said they think I killed him and they were going to charge me for murder. They also think I killed Al Jenkins they said they, was going to charge me for his murder because I had reason to kill Al. They came and got me to go to court. When I walked in there stood Donald I knew there was nothing he could do to save me this time. He come over to me and said hello Leroy. Hi man where you been? I been in this jail over four months Terry left me in here she never tried to get me out. I didn't know if you would come help me I thought you had turned your back to.

No I have been out of the country I just got back a few days ago.

Lisa called me and told me you may get life for killing somebody.

Did you confess? Not really I got drunk and I told the police I killed someone I think they ran a check on me from Derry Oklahoma and they told the police here they had bought me in for questioning of Al Jenkins death. They found out I was kin to John Chester How was you kin to him? He was my brother did you kill him? Yes Donald I did and I can't live with the guilt anymore. Leroy I been up all night trying to figure out how to save your ass. I remember Pete left me a letter saying if you ever got in trouble open it. Your ass is lucky.

Judge I'm here to represent Leroy Chester he's being charged with the death of a Jerry Johnson and Al Jenkins. Judge there is no proof he killed these people and my client plead not guilty. I have proof that my client is not guilty we don't want a jury trial.

Judge if you let me tell you of my proof today maybe we can end the trail today. Go ahead let me hear what you have to say. When Leroy said he killed two people he was drunk and out of his head. He didn't mean it that way he have lost a lot of people in his life he feels like he killed them because he had love for them.

What proof do you have? This is not what I want to hear. Judge I have a sworn confession about the men that Leroy is being charged with.

Go ahead.

When Leroy said he killed two people he was referring about his two best friends JJ and Peter Marshall. I have a notary confession from Peter Marshall it was signed and sealed by Peter Marshall before his death. May I read the court his confession? Go ahead I Peter Marshall confession to the murder of Al Jenkins because he killed my girl friend I went to his house and cut his throat I wore gloves so I wouldn't leave finger prints I left the water on in his kitchen sink so his house would flood and wash away anything that I may have left.

I found James Chester in Dallas Texas and I shot him in the heart and left his ass in the door of his house in the alley. I also confess to the murder of John Chester I didn't like James or John because they treated my girl friend like shit she was a nice girl. Kind, loving, and caring, I didn't understand why they didn't treat her good.

Leroy Chester did not know about this because he is such a good boy I love him because he is like his mother. I never told him what I did to his family and he never knew I stayed around him because I knew I took his family's life. I wanted to easy my mind if I could help him in any way I could. I did all the crimes alone because I didn't want anyone to know. What I'm saying is the truth and nothing but the truth so help me God. Sign Peter Marshall.

Judge Peter Marshall did the crime alone Judge this is a confession from Peter Marshall. He died August 10, 1970 judge we would like to ask the court if all charges will be drop on Leroy Chester. Judge Leroy never knew Mr. Marshall killed his family Marshall kept it all to himself.

The Judge said case against Leroy Chester dismissed Mr. Chester you are free to go. Oh no Donald what have Pete done? He just saved your ass you had a real good friend and a man that loved you so much he rather go to hell to save you. Oh Pete, oh Pete thanks to you. Donald can you drop me off at Lisa's house. I don't know if Terry is still here or gone back to South Carolina. I have to stay and finish paper work and it will take me a while. Can I have some money from you to catch a cab?

Thank you Donald I'll pay you back. You will be getting my bill in the mail. I called a cab to take me to Lisa's house to see if Terry was there.

She never came back to see while I was in jail I guess she meant it when she said it was over. When I got to Lisa's house no one was home I didn't know where to go all my friends was gone from Little Rock except Lisa. So I sat on the porch waiting and waiting. I knew she and Terry would be back soon after sitting there for almost an hour I was hungry and needed to take a bath and have clean clothes. I just realized I was sitting on John Chester's porch waiting for his daughter in law and his step daughter to come home.

I started feeling sick thinking that JJ will never see his son. What kind of man am I? I got off the porch and went and sat on the curb then Lisa drove up. I was so happy to see her I jumped and ran to the car. She got out of the car Lisa where is Terry? Did she go back to South Carolina?

I don't know what you mean you don't know? Leroy you need to leave her alone and go get you some help? You need to give her some time alone. You been lying all these years why don't you stay away from here? Tell me where she is and I promise you I'll get help please Lisa.

She went back to South Carolina. Thank, you Lisa.

Lisa, can you take me to the train station? Yes, Leroy can I come and take a bath and I have something to eat? Come in. Lisa gave me some of JJ's clothes to put on after I was ready she took me to the train station.

I caught the train back to South Carolina. When I got there I called for Terry to come and get me. The operator said the number was no longer in service I didn't understand all the money we have and she haven't paid the phone bill. I called the club and the phone was no longer in service. What the hell is going on? I called Sarah to come pick me up and she came. Sarah I'm so glad to see you thank you for coming to get me.

I been trying to call Terry but they said the phone is off do you know what's wrong with her. Did she change the number? Leroy, I don't want to get in your business you need to talk to Terry. Well take me home Sarah dropped me off and drove off I ran to the door and it was locked. Terry, Terry she never came to the door. I went around to the back door and it was locked I kicked the door in and everything was gone.

Terry what have you done to me? Where are you with my son?

The Man on the Train

You can't do this to me? I love you where are you? I'm so sorry I didn't mean to hurt you oh God where are they?

I walked into each room and everything was gone even the drapes. I went down in the basement and all that was left was a case of corn whiskey. My car and my mother car were gone too. I called a cab and went to the bank to get me some money and when I got there they told me Mr. Chester we sorry your account has been closed. What the hell you mean close? I didn't close my account your wife closed the account her name was on it and there was nothing we could do but let her have it.

We didn't know how to reach you she said you was on your way to prison for life.

You wouldn't need the money where you was going, You sitting here telling me you gave that bitch all my fucking money?

We sorry Mr. Chester Do you know how many million dollars I had in this damn bank and you gave all my fucking money away to her. There was nothing we could do Mr. Chester we sorry. Did you give her cash or did you put it in another account? It was put into another account.

Well give me my money? We sorry sir you name is not on the account the money is not in our bank. Well where the hell is it? It was transferred to another bank out of town. We sorry Mr. Chester our hands are tied there is nothing we can do good luck to you. I left and went to the club everything was gone that bitch took everything. I own all I had was the clothes on my back I only had fifty dollars in my pocket and nowhere to go. I went back to the house I couldn't believe Terry would do me like this. I went in the basement and bought the case of whisky up stairs and sat out on the porch I sat on the steps she even took my favorite chair.

I started drinking I was in jail only four months and she did all this to me I went in the house sat on the floor and drunk until I passed out. I woke up early the next day I was hungry I went next door and asked if I could use their phone. I was so busy with my clubs I never took the time to visit the people next door. I knew their name is Melvin and his wife Ruby.

I ask Melvin if I could use his phone. I call Sarah and told her what Terry did I told her I was hungry and I had no money. Sarah, will you come get me. Melvin said Honey, Leroy is hungry can you find us something to eat. I'm sorry I never took the time to come over here to get to know you Melvin. Terry would come over all the time and talk to us she was so sad when she was moving. She said she didn't know where she was going but she wanted to get far away from you.

Terry really loved you and your fine son. Ruby and I would say what a fine couple you two ere. We thought you two would never leave each other what happened to you son? I got put in jail for something that happened over twenty years ago and now Melvin I lost everything that means so much to me. Well when does she have her baby I hope everything will be alright for her? Terry is a good mother. What you mean have her baby she don't have Little Pete with her?

You didn't know she's having another baby?

Oh my God that is why she was gaining so much weight I didn't know God what have I done to her. Leroy would you like to spend the night or stay here till you get yourself together?

Thank, you do you mind if I take a bath? I don't even have changing clothes Terry took everything. Well you about my son's size go on end there and take a bath. Thank you so much Melvin. After I bathed and put on some clean clothes I felt a little better. Ruby had cooked food I sat down to eat with them. Ruby the food was so good thank you very much, Melvin I'm so sorry I didn't take the time to come over and visit you.

We heard a car horn Melvin looked out the window and he said it was Sarah. We know Sarah for many years she is a good woman you go with her and she take good care of you. I went out to the car, wait Sarah! I went back in and thanked Ruby and Melvin or their kindness. I got in the car with Sarah and she took me back to her home we talked most of the night. She didn't tell me where Terry was but she did say Terry was going to have the baby in two months. Sarah where could she be? You know she took everything and all the money I had. Sarah why did God do this to me? You did it to yourself God gives you a choice in life and you choose what you want. When we choose wrong then we are the one that suffers that is why. God is there for you to help if you really believe him. Sarah you really do believe in God? Yes, I do I can't live without him in my life he always make a way for you. All you have to do Leroy is get down on your knees and ask for forgiveness. Will he forgive Terry what she did to me? Yes he will if she, ask him. Sarah I didn't think Terry would do me this way? She never told me she was going to have a baby.

I may never see them again I hurt her really bad for her to take everything from me and didn't even care.

She could have left me some of my money to live off of. Leroy you have to go on with your life and try to make the best of it. Maybe one day if God see's that you deserve it you will get to see your family. You know Sarah I don't know if I ever want to see Terry she tried to kill me once. All I would like to do is see my kids Sarah I miss Pete so much if he was here he would know what to do. You know Leroy God do strange things and he do things for a reason.

When he put a man a woman together he want them to stay together for better or worse. Thank you Sarah can I stay here with you until I find a job and think what to do. I wish she had left me enough money to open my club back up. Sometimes Leroy we have to let some things go in our past to find something better. Maybe things will work out you.

Sarah do you think that I will see Terry and my kid's someday? Because if I see her I don't know what I will do to her it may not be nice. Leroy if God wants you to see them then he will make a way. You know she is still you wife you took those vowels before God and you promised before God you would stay together. I didn't leave her she left me, If God feels you deserve your family back he will bring them back to you. I don't want Terry only my kid's Sarah. Leroy God will work everything out of you just be patient. The next day I got up and Sarah had breakfast ready we ate and talked. I told Sarah I wanted to go to see if I could find me a job. Leroy do you need me to take you or do you want to drive my car? No, Sarah I think I'll walk maybe I can find something close. I walked a few blocks from Sarah house and a car drove up. Leroy, Leroy is that you? Yes, who are you? I'm Rita remember me we use to get high together we use to have a lot of fun. You use to make love to me and you don't remember me. I stayed drunk everyday for four months. You lived with me before you went back to your wife. I left town and just got back where you going dressed like that? I ain't ever seen you dressed in blue jeans and a pull over like that, I almost didn't know you.

What happened to all your fancy suites I'm homeless my wife took everything I had. Oh shit you got to be kidding me you didn't get none of that money? Damn you really must have fucked up she caught your ass with another woman. Come on get in the car. I'm going to look for a job. Get the hell in the car nigger.

I got in the car with Rita and she took her to her house, After I got in the house she said to make myself at home. When I was down you help me so now I can help you back. That is a damn shame that wife of your stole all your money what in the hell did you do to that woman? Nothing.

Shit now you know I don't believe that. How much money did I give to you? Shit you gave me enough to last me alone time it's been two years and now I have very little. Now I had to get off my ass and find me a job because the money is running out. So that pretty as wife of yours left you if you stayed with me we would still be together and you will still have everything.

I don't know how you dumb ass men don't learn them pretty ass cows only marry you for your money and what they can get out of you. That's not always true Rita there's a lot of women that love their men for them. But one day they all suffer for what they do to us men. I must have been really drunk when I met Rita, Rita is a short black woman with a big ass, short hair, she is cute and has a pretty smile but she is crazy as hell.

Why did I live with her for four months when I was drinking? When Pete died I don't know what the hell I was thinking about maybe it was her pretty smile? Want a drink Leroy? I don't know, what the hell you mean you don't know you do or you don't? I took it and it was some cheap ass Gin but I drank it Rita and I got so drunk we both looked good to each other. I haven't had sex in four months and I made love to her and I know why I was with her those four months. She was good and I liked it.

The next day I told her to take me home so I could get some whisky.

I went back and got the last of corn whisky. Rita got out of the car and came in with me. She looked all around the house, damn Leroy all she left your ass was a bunch of empty rooms. This is a nice house. I went in Pete's room and I could hear him telling me to stay off that damn corn whisky or you will be sorry you need to find your wife and kid.

Come on Rita let's get out of here. Rita and I left. Leroy do you still own that house? Yes I own it. Your wife just moved out and left it?

Well let's move in it, it's bigger than this place of mines and we will have enough room. I can move all my things in there until we can buy more things.

You can reopen your club that wife of yours ain't never coming back she took everything. You ain't going to see her ass again she is a rich woman and she, don't need you anymore I'm here for you. I won't ever do you like that let's move in today and I won't have to pay rent. I can take the money and have all your bills back on I'll help you get back on your feet. I have a friend with a truck that can move us in today. Come on let's start packing you can have your life with me. Let's go and have the gas water, and lights turned on I got the money. By the end of the day we will be in there Rita I don't know. I need money to do the things I need to do.

I just told you I got the money don't worry. Rita and I went to have all the bills turned on. When we got to the light office we told them we wanted the lights on they check the address and said the lights was turned on an hour ago.

What I don't understand do you know who had them turned on. Yes, a lady came in. We went to the others and they said the same thing. Well shit Leroy look like your wife is coming back what we going to do? We went to my house and there was people moving in what's going on here this is my house? Not anymore we bought this house two weeks ago from a Terry Chester she can't sell my house without me. I didn't sign any papers well sir you have to talk to your wife and her lawyer Donald Smith in Little Rock Arkansas. I don't believe this Donald is my lawyer and my friend. I'm so sorry to say sir but me must be your wife's friend now because he is the one who helped her sell this house to us and a club called Jericho. Oh no Terry, why, why you do this to me. When I find her ass she is going to be sorry she ever met me. I fell on my knees and just cried. Sir, are you okay? Hell no, I just lost everything can you tell me how much you paid for my house and the club? Yes, we paid $275,000 for the house and $55,000 for the club. I'm sorry sir what in the world did you do to your wife that she would do you like this?

What caught you with another woman? I was crying so hard Rita helped me up and took me back to her house. I was so mad I told

Rita I was going to go find her and cut her fucking throat. I'll show her black ass how John Chester felt when I cut him. I started flipping out and knocking over Rita's stuff in her house and breaking things. Rita told me to get out of her house before she called the police. Leroy you need to calm down. Don't tell me what to do no fucking woman will ever tell me what to do.

I just lost my mind I was drinking every day I didn't give a damn about myself and nobody else. Rita told me she was tired of looking at me drunk, everyday and I just need to get out.

She put me out and I just walked the streets I was begging for food. One day this lady said are you Leroy Chester the man that owned the Jericho club? Yes that's him he, use to be riding high look at his ass now out here begging.

Girl I wonder what happened. Oh he lost it to gambling. Yes, that must be what happened. Well he ain't shit now. I ran in the alley and just cried and cried. God where do I go from here? Where are you? Why you let all this happen to me? Sarah said you always here for me if I just call your name where in the hell are you now? I'm calling your name where in the hell are you? God I don't have a friend and I don't have money. When you don't have money you need a friend I can't find one so I'm calling on you to be my friend. Where are you God? I called Sarah, hello Sarah this is Leroy. Yes, Leroy did you find a job you been gone for three weeks and I haven't heard from you. I was so worried about you, Sarah I'm so sorry. Can you come get me I'm tired and hungry? I have been walking the streets for days please Sarah come get me I promise I'll do right. Terry sold my house and my club I don't have nothing and nowhere to go. Please Sarah, don't do me the same way. Leroy I'm sorry I can't help you anymore you have to call on God. I have Sarah and he won't answer me he turns his back on me to. Keep calling on him one day he will hear you, good by Leroy. Sarah, Sarah, don't hang up on me I was good to you please Sarah I need you. I went back to the street I walked the streets drinking after whoever would give me a drink. That cheap whisky tasted just as good to me I didn't give a damn. God didn't come to help me I was a good looking man and women still thought I looked good.

For days I didn't know where I was or who I was with I met a lady named Sandy on the streets. She took me home with her and cleaned me up and told me to find a job and I could stay with her she would charge me 35 dollars a week. One day I went to my club to see if I could get a job there.

They changed the name to Sugar Brown Blues Club. I met a young lady named Sally Jo and she said you a damn good looking man, seem like a good man. I'm going to hire you I need a dish washer can you wash dishes? I told Sandy I had a job and she was happy for me, she let me stay with her. I told her it would be two weeks before I got paid and I will give her some money.

She let me eat with her and she was nice to me. I tried not to drink and it was so hard for me. Sandy said I couldn't drink in her house I worked at the club for a few days and it was killing me knowing I use to own this club and all that money I made here. Now I'm washing dishes after I got my first check I was on my way to Sandy's house and I passed this liquor store. I thought I would just have one drink by the time I got to Sandy's house I didn't give her all my money. I told her that I only made ten dollars and she took my ten and told me to get my drunk ass out.

I didn't even care I was back on the streets again I was so drunk I sat down in this door way and I started falling asleep when I heard this voice say Leroy, Leroy, I forgive you for killing me. What I did to your mama was wrong I can see you are in hell now and I need you to come out and take care of my grandson Terry and the kids. I 'm so sorry will you forgive me? Then I heard Al Jenkins, Leroy will you forgive me for killing your mother. One day you will come out of hell, I started screaming and yelling I wanted to die I wanted to drink myself to death. The next thing I remember I was being put into an ambulance. It was four days they said I had a nervous breakdown and I was in the hospital for the insane. I gave up I didn't want to get well I didn't even try. The doctors kept giving me pills and I didn't even try to stop them I thought one day they will give me too many and I would die. One day I kept hearing voices and I kept hearing Sarah saying you have to suffer for the wrong you do in life. I tried to tell the doctor I that I could hear all these dead people talking to me telling me I need to get out of hell. I know I'm in a mental hospital and I need to try to get myself together. I looked all around and I'm in this hospital with all these crazy people. Even the staff is crazy, the damn doctors are crazy.

There was this old man that said to me I hate you niggers get out of my house git, git, and I thought about Old George Cross. I told him I'm sorry George I didn't mean for you to die we was just making fun with you. We didn't know you would have a heart attack I'm sorry. That old man got up and hit me I told you George I was sorry. He pushes me and I fell down. I tried to be nice to him but I came off that floor and I tried to beat the shit out of him.

One of the stupid ass nurses came over and I tried to tell them he started it but they didn't listen to me. They slammed me on the floor and put a straight jacket on me and put me in a padded cell for three days. I cried and cried I told George Cross I was sorry they asked me if I could keep my hands off people. If not they would put me back in there for two weeks. They gave me shot and I don't know how long I was sleep.

Some days I didn't know what day it was when I walked in the game room I saw the old man I beat up. He looked at me and ran to the other side of the room. He never said nothing else to me I guess he wasn't crazy as he thought. He had sense enough to stay away from me.

There was a new doctor that came in to work at the hospital he would talk to me every day. I would tell him about my life, about how much I loved my wife and the way she did me that is what hurt me the most. Because I loved her the most I would have to tell him how I felt every day. I been in this place for a year now and they said I wasn't ready to leave. I told the doctor I wanted to get out of here, I told them that all of them were the one crazy and I didn't need to be in here. One day this nurse gave me a card. Your mother told me to give this to you.

My mother is dead. Yea right (she said) The, card said I still love you, I can't help you now but you have to help yourself. Who gave this to me? I knew my mother was dead. I knew and she was crazy saying my mother sent this card. I started to sleep all day and take pills some day's I couldn't remember. I felt I needed a drink and no one would give me one. After a few weeks the same nurse came with another card and said it's h from your mother. You stupid ass woman I told you that my mother is dead.

Sarah how come you won't come in and see me. Why don't you bring the card inside to me are you still mad at me. Once a month at 1200 p m those card come and I knew then that it was someone

The Man on the Train

out there who still loved me. But why she won't sign her name to the card. I knew it wasn't Terry because she told me it was the last time I see her when I was in jail.

She knows she better stay hidden from me because when I find her she is a dead bitch.

Crazy bitch taking everything I own the doctor told me I have to let go of Terry before I can heal I can't get it back. She will never come back to me. He said she was apart of my past. I need to forgive and move on with a new life I looked at him thought to myself doctor you are the one who is crazy she didn't do it to you. So how in the hell can you tell me what to do, how do, you forget losing everything you own.

Time has gone by so fast it has been another year and I'm still in this damn nut house. No one has came to see me not even Sarah. How can they all forget me even Lisa? The only one who still cares about me is the person who still sends me the card and I don't even know who it is. I started crying again I had my head down on the table when someone touch my arm Leroy. I looked up and there stood the nurse with that card in her hand. This time the card said Leroy you still have your ass in that nut house. It's time you start working on getting the hell of there you want to live in hell the rest of your life. What do it take for you to stop feeling sorry for yourself you need to learn to fight. You can never make it out of hell when you give up. Can you remember all the promises you made to people. Have you forgotten what a nice man you are and how kind so many people have been to you. You will stay in hell until you start pulling up and that is yourself I love you.

I sat there reading the card over and over for hours I read that card. What do they mean? The next day I picked up that card and I read it again I sat there I closed my eyes and tried to think. Then I saw Pete, Son it's time for you to go so get the hell out of there. God, haven't forgotten you. You have one more chance in life.

I could hear my mother saying Baby it's time for you to go back home. Go home baby. I cried out Mama, Mama help me I saw my mother and Pete together. Then I knew what the person sending me those cards and meant. I have to get out of this place this is my hell and only I can make it out of here. But how.

Oh God how do I get out of here I sat there and I tried to think how to act. I know if I'm crazy I will never get out of here. God what do I do? I been here two years tell me what to do I picked up that Bible that was on the table. I started to read it I took it to my room and I read and read the more I read the more I liked it. I got down on my knees and said God I am a sinner I have did a lot of bad things in my life and I made a lot of mistakes. I don't know how to pray to you that you want to hear me say but I know I ask you to forgive me God for my sins. Guide me in the way you want me to be and do. I want to thank you for all my blessings you have giving me. it was my fault that I lost everything I had. God I just want to get out of here, God I want to move back to my little shack in Oklahoma. Help me get out of this place I don't want to be here anymore. You know God when I lived in Derry Oklahoma with my mother I was happy. When she left and I went back and met Pete I was happy I had nothing but that was the happiest time in my life. The other time in my life was when I found Terry now God they are all gone. God I just need a little peace back in my life. I want to give my heart to you an invite you into my life. Thank you for forgiving me I love you God. After three months I was feeling better and my whole attitude had changed. The man I beat up in here I went to him and I looked in his face and I could see how scared he was he thought I was coming to beat him up again. When I got closer to him tears started running down his cheeks. I put my arms around him and told him I was sorry and forgive me.

He gave me a big smile (and said). Well, well young man you found God in your life. Thank you and I walked away I went in the doctor's office and said to him I 'm ready to leave and go home. What do I have to do to get out of this place?

I feel like I been here too long. All you have to do Leroy is sign yourself out and you can leave when you're ready. You are free to walk out that door whenever you want. Just sign these papers saying you left on your own. Good luck Leroy. I took off running to my room changed into my clothes I came in with. Got my box of cards and ran down that long hall way as fast as I could. I got to that door I stood there praying it would open I touched it. I pushed it and the door came open and I walked out that door with no money in my pocket and nowhere to go.

I was walking down the side walk.

The Man on the Train

I saw that nurse standing beside a car and I saw someone give her a card she always brought to me. Now I know who it was I walked up to the car and said hello Rita. This time I remembered her name.

Leroy what are you doing out here? I'm free to go wherever I please.

Rita can I have a ride? Get in. Nurse thank you for bringing me those cards. I gave her a hug and got in the car with Rita and we drove off. Thank you Rita one day I will do something good for you. I will be back on my feet. There no words I can say to you but thank you and I appreciate what you did for me. Why did you not sign your name on the cards?

After I put you out I felt bad and I went looking for you and I saw the police putting you in their car you was screaming. I asked them where were they taking you? They said Redland Hospital. I felt so bad if I had let you stay with me you wouldn't have gone there.

I knew then that you needed the help so I thought if I didn't sign my name you would fight to come out to see who it was. I knew then you would really fight to get out. But damn I didn't know it would take your ass two years. I saw what drinking did to you I went and joined church. I'm a Christian now I don't drink anymore I go to church every Sunday.

I gave up all my habits you see Leroy I still love you.

After we got to Rita's house I said to her Rita I believe God sent you today to pick me up. If I can do anything for you I will you was right I wanted to see who cared enough about me thank you.

I hugged her and kissed her on the cheek. I sat back and looked at this short black woman with a sweet smile I could see the kindness in her.

I bet you like something to eat? After we ate we talked for a long time and Rita asked me if I was ready to go to bed. I know you ain't had no good loving in two years.

You want some now come on. I looked at her and realized I wasn't drunk, all the time I was with her I never remember if I had ever made love to her. I was always drunk I took a good look at her and I wasn't ready. I still love Terry all that, she had done to me and I still loved her.

Rita I'm sorry I haven't made love in two years and I don't think I can. Rita I do appreciate what you have done for me. Well what do you want to do with your life? I want to find me a job I can run clubs or work in a department store. I know that I will never go back and get all the things I lost. I had a lot of time to think when I was in the hospital. Leroy how did you let yourself stay in there so long without paying? It's the best nut house here and it's very expensive someone had to pay for you to stay there because it's a private place. Who paid for you? I don't know I guess the state paid like they do when you go to prison. No Leroy that place is for people that have money to pay to stay there. Well I didn't pay and I don't have money to pay them. Maybe you will find out one day. I just need to find me a job can I use your car tomorrow to go look?

Yes take me to work. Thank you Rita. You can sleep in my son's room tonight I know you tired and want a good night sleep. My son won't be back for a few months he is out of town. I didn't know you had a son Rita you never told me. Well he stays with his daddy and come here when school is out and doing the summer.

I went to bed and just laid there hoping and praying she wouldn't come in the room. I just didn't feel like fucking no woman right now.

I would sure like to have me a drink. But I know it would put me back in Redland Hospital. The next morning I took Rita to work and I drove around looking for a job. I couldn't find one so I started to go back to Rita's house but for some reason I wanted to go by and see Sarah.

I didn't know if she ever wanted to see me again. I knocked on the door I could hear her in there but she didn't come to the door. Then I had this really funny feeling that something was wrong.

I started to walk away but turned back and knocked again I heard a voice saying help, help, please help me. I pushed the door open and I called out Sarah, Sarah you home. Help me I ran to the room I heard the voice. Sarah what are you doing on the floor? I picked her up and put her on the bed. Sarah let me take you to the doctor or I'll call an ambulance.

Leroy, thank you God he sent you here to help me. Sarah, can you tell me why you were on the floor? Leroy I been down there all day I couldn't get up I told God to send someone to help me and he sent you.

I'm so happy to see you. I'm happy to see you to Sarah. I'm taking you to the hospital. No I need a bath first, I need something to eat I ain't ate all day. I helped Sarah in the bath tub and went and fixed her something to eat. I helped her out and put her in bed and brought food to her.

Sarah tell me what happened? I just got out of bed and my legs gave out and I fell and just couldn't get up on them. Every time I tried they just gave out on me and hurt to bad to try to stand on them I just kept falling down. Leroy what are you doing here? I came to see you I been in the hospital for two years that is why I never came back.

Yes, I know you were there. Why didn't you ever come to see or write to me? Why you never came to help me? Son I did help you I'm the one who came out and told them to put you in there. I went looking for you and I saw the police putting you in the police car and I told them to take you there because I knew you were having a nervous breakdown. I follow the police to the hospital and I told the doctor I wanted him to let you go when you felt you were ready to leave. I didn't think it would take you that long to make up your mind to leave. I'm the one who paid two hundred dollars a month to keep you in there. I knew if I came to see you I wouldn't be able to leave you there and I know it would have broken my heart to see you every time I would have to leave without you so I thought I was doing you a favor to leave you there.

Look in that box, go ahead look. I went over and got the box and looked in it and there were a lot of receipts what is this Sarah?

Those are the receipts. Sarah why did you do that?

Because I love you and because you're a nice man you helped me make money when I worked for you at the club. Johnnie Mae left me money for taking care of Bobby. Sarah someday I will pay you back. Well when you take the right path God leads you it will be worth it all. I hugged her and kissed her on her forehead thank you Sarah I have to go and take a friend of mines car back.

I'll come back tomorrow make sure you stay in bed until I come back to help you out of bed. Lock my door on your way out. Look over there on the table and get my keys so you can let yourself in. What time you coming back? Around 9:00 a m. If my friend let me use her car. I left and picked up Rita from work, when she got in the car she said did you find a job? Did you go looking, where did you go? No! I didn't say nothing else to her if she kept that up I'm gone. When we got home she started again well Leroy what happened?

Nothing Rita I'll find a job I been out of the hospital one day damn give me time. Can I use your car tomorrow? Yes, and you better be looking I went to my room and laid across the bed thinking if she keep that shit up with me I'm gone.

I don't want no woman telling me what I can do or can't do.

I'm a man I can think for myself if I make a mistake it's on me.

I didn't want to listen to her shit. I don't know why some women want to treat you like a child. I know Rita want me to make love to her I could see her standing at the door I pretended like I was sleep. It's not that I didn't like Rita I don't want to make love to her I appreciate what she did for me. When she was down I helped her I feel she only paying me back.

I want to change my life I feel like a stronger man I haven't had a drink in years and I feel good. I just need to think what to do with my life and where to go from here.

How can I get my life back together? The next morning I went back over to Sarah's to check on her, when I got there I walked on the porch and I could smell food cooking. I opened the door and Sarah was up cooking breakfast, Sarah what in the world you doing up out of bed?

Leroy I asked my God to help me out of that bed this morning and he answered my prayers. Well why he didn't answer you yesterday when I found you on the floor I'm the one who helped you. Son he did answer my prayers when I called out to him he sent you didn't he.

Sarah you really believe in your God. Yes Leroy and he is your God too he been here for you all your life but you haven't seen him yet.

One day you will and it's sooner than you think. Sometimes it takes some of us longer to open up our heart and let him in.

He is waiting Leroy, for you to let him in.

I ate breakfast with Sarah and helped her clean the kitchen.

Sarah do you need to lay down? No I ain't sick get your coffee and let's sit on the porch you ain't sat on the porch in a long time. Sarah and I sat on the porch watching people go by some of them would say hi Miss Sarah, God bless you Miss Sarah. One lady came by and said hello Miss Sarah is that your son? He's like a son to me.

You need to stay home boy and take care of your mama she all you got. Yes mum I will always take care of her because I love her. Sarah smiled so big I could see all her front teeth. We talked for hours about God and I was beginning to like hearing about him. I'm suppose to be looking for a job where I'm staying if I don't find one the lady will put me out. I have her car and I have to pick her up from work I'll have to see you later Sarah. Leroy do you love this lady? No not the way you think I only stay there because I didn't have anywhere to stay she picked me up when I got out of the hospital. Are you happy there? No because she want me to sleep with her and I'm not ready so I pretend I'm sleep or let her think I lost everything when I was in the hospital. Well son you can always stay here with me you won't have to pretend you're asleep I won't ask you to sleep with me. We both laughed see you later Sarah, I went to pick up Rita soon as she got in the car well did you find a job or did you go look? Hell Rita how was your day? Don't change the subject where was you today all day?

Don't lie one of my friends said they see my car for two days over on Roosevelt street you got some damn woman over there? Yes, I was over a friend of mines I went by there yesterday and found her on the floor I went back to check on her we got to talking and time flew by so fast. I met her when I first moved to South Carolina she lived with me and my friend Pete she took care of us. When I married my wife she still stayed with me and I love her. What kind of shit is that? All you stay in the same house? Yes Rita we all lived in the same house.

I was drinking a lot after my friend Pete died and she and my wife left me that is why I ended up in the hospital her name is Sarah and she have always been there for me. I'm the one that fucked up I will not turn my back on her and if you have a problem with it I'll get out. Maybe you should go let her take care of your ass. I don't take care of no man that don't like to work. You know Rita I'm sorry you feel like this I never wanted to hurt you. I'll leave because I love Sarah more than I do you. Sarah have always been like a mother to me.

What you mean a mother? Come on get back in the car. Where are we going? On Roosevelt Street I took Rita to Sarah's house I knocked o the door and Sarah came to the door. Leroy you back so soon. Yes Sarah I want you to meet someone Rita this is Sarah I was telling you about. Hello Rita he been telling you how mean I am. No he said you was like a mother to him and how much he loves you. I wanted to know who you were. Yes Leroy is like a son to me and he is a good man. We stayed for a little while and Rita said she was ready to go I kissed Sarah on the forehead and told her I would see her and if she need me call me. If I'm not there tell Rita. I will son nice to meet you Rita. you too Miss Sarah. Leroy, I'm sorry I didn't know she was an old lady. You just jump to conclusions that I was cheating on you. I'm so sorry Leroy, you been home for two days and you haven't tried to make love to me what would you think if it was you? What's wrong with me? Nothing Rita I told you why. Leroy I'm off tomorrow what would you like to do? Tomorrow is Sunday I would like to go to church. Church are you kidding? I looked at her and then went to my room and closed the door I laid across the bed and closed my eyes all I could think about was Terry. I wonder where she was and what did she have?

My son should be four years old and the baby she had is three years old and I don't know if it's a girl or boy.

Where are you Terry? Why did you do me like this. You know how much I loved you and my son did you hate me much? I wonder if she was right when she said I saw the last of her black ass. I got up and went in the living room to use the phone to call Lisa. Rita maybe sleep now.

Hello, Lisa this is Leroy how are you? I'm fine Leroy I know you had your baby what did you have? I had a little boy I named him Jerry Jay Johnson after his daddy. He is two years old now do you still have the shop open? Yes, and it's still doing very well I'm happy to hear that.

Lisa do you know where Terry is? Yes, I do where is she? I want to see my kids what did she have? Leroy you should have thought about all that shit when you was lying to everyone and keeping secrets. Didn't you know that one day that it would catch up to you? I'm sorry Lisa I just didn't want to hurt anyone. Well you did and you lost everything you had for that. I'm not telling you where Terry and the kids are I promised her I wouldn't if you asked me.

If she want to tell you maybe she will. Lisa I been in the hospital for two years and I just got out. I don't have any money and no job where are you? I'm still in South Carolina, well Leroy you really need to go back home to Oklahoma. Because you always said how happy you were at your mother's house you and Pete. How can I with no money? You need to find a way I hope you take my advice, Lisa I been good to you and you doing me like this. Leroy you fought to get out

The Man on the Train

of hell now you fight to get home maybe you will find your life back good luck and good bye. Lisa what in the world you talking about you're not making sense? That bitch hung up on me good as I was to her she got all my damn money to. Who is Lisa? another lady? I heard you talking on my phone; you know what Rita thank you for letting me stay her with you. I don't think I can live with you right now. I feel like I need a drink I'm trying to keep my cool and if I stay here with you I will be drinking every day. Where you going Leroy? If you walk out that door you can't bring your black ass back. Bye Rita and thank you. I took out walking I just walked until I came to this bar I was about to go in when I heard Pete's voice say to me Leroy don't go in there don't go back to hell son. I ran away I ran and ran until I came to Sarah's house it was 1:30 am I didn't want to wake Sarah up.

So I just sat on her porch I fell asleep I woke up to Sarah saying Leroy, baby you been here all night? I started to cry. Baby what in the world is wrong with you?

Sarah my heart is so heavy it hurts so bad. I told Sarah about me talking to Lisa and what she said. I told her what Rita said I told her about hearing Peter telling me to go home. What do they mean? I don't want to go back to Derry Oklahoma, I want to live here. Sarah what's wrong with me? Come on and have some breakfast with me it always make you feel better. After you eat go take a bath and relax Sarah I don't even have clean clothes. I'll be back I'll run down here at Spartans and pick up something for you. Thank you Sarah I love you. Sarah came back with three pairs of pants, three shirts, socks, underwear and a pair, of shoes. Thank, you Sarah. Go get ready we going to church I got dressed and went to Sarah's church with her.

When I walked in I felt good I wasn't scared I listened to what the preacher said and I didn't run out I wanted to hear every word he was saying. He talked about heaven and hell believe me hell is like what he said. I don't think I want to go because the hell I been through. I felt so good in church I felt like I belong there. After Sarah and I went back home we talked for hours and after dinner we talked more about God the more she talked the more I wanted to hear. Doing the day she would read the Bible to me and then I would read to her. I like going to church with her my mind and heart began to feel so at ease I felt like I was a new man. The old Leroy Chester had died and went to hell the preacher always ask if you want to accept Christ as your savor I guess I was ready. The next time we went to church and he asked if anyone wants to give their hearts to God come up. I went up there and I was a little scared the preacher touched my hand and started to pray for me and I just cried and I felt that the whole world had lifted off my shoulders. I could feel all the evil things that I had ever done was forgiven. My body felt so tired I fell to the floor and I cried out God please forgive me I will do whatever you tell me and I will do what you want.

Then I heard all these people clapping their hands, the music, and they were singing and some was dancing. I looked up and I could see my mother and Pete smiling at me telling me it was time for me to go home. I still don't understand why they keep telling me to go back to that little shack in Derry Oklahoma. There is nothing there my legs got weak and I fell to the floor someone picked me up and said now you are a child of God. I never experienced anything like that Sarah said I been saved from the devil. I been out of the hospital two months and I still live with Sarah. Sarah told me to wait and just stay home with her for a while to help her repair things around her house.

She said that God told her to help and take care of me until it was time for me to leave. Sarah I can't live off you. You didn't say that all those years I lived with you. So let me pay you back. You have paid me back for all the money you spent on me paying the hospital. Son I'm just happy having you here with me. I 'm getting old and I need someone here with me. When time for you to move on you will know. And follow your heart and do what God tells you to do. Sarah how will I know? Oh believe me son you will know. Sarah, keep teaching me about the bible the more we read the more I wanted to go to church.

The, ladies in church was smiling at me and some of them would talk and invite me to dinner. Sarah would say come on I can cook you dinner. I told Sarah I was ready to live my life I know Terry have gone with her life. I met one girl that looked a little like Terry I walked over to her and started talking to her. I asked her if she would go out with me sometime and before she could say anything Sarah came up and said I'm ready to go. I'm tired and you a married man she walked off and I felt like a fool. I just followed Sarah out the door I was so mad at Sarah. I wouldn't say nothing to her all the way home. She knew I was so mad at her so she just sat in the car humming. When I got

The Man on the Train

inside the house I said to her Sarah you know I don't know if Terry is still married to me. Terry may have married someone else and have another baby with him by now. She ain't got no mo kids how do you know?

Terry is a good girl. Good girls don't steal everything form the man she love. All she wanted from me was what she stole from me. Leroy you have to let all of that go how are you going to get on with your life thinking about what Terry did. You have to forgive her and let God take care of her. Sarah would fuss at me like she was my mother and I was getting a little tired of it. Sarah had me cutting her yard, fixing things around the house, she was keeping me busy. I believe she was trying to keep me busy so I wouldn't think so much about Terry. I don't know what I'll do to her if I every see her again.

I knew Sarah needed me here with her. She will never put me out until I'm ready she loves me. A few weeks later Rita came by. Leroy I'm sorry for I what said to you I miss you and want you to come back.

I thank you but I don't want to move in with you I hope we can still be friends I'm very happy here.

Rita stood there looking at me not saying a word; Sarah opened the door and said come on Leroy it's time to go. Rita was still standing there looking at me real strange as if she could kill me. Sarah locked her door and got me by the arm and said let's go I didn't know what got into Sarah. She was looking so scared. So I followed her to the car I told Rita I was so sorry and I would see her later. So it's over with us Leroy?

She put her hand in her purse and come out with a gun. Oh shit Rita, put that gun down I know you don't want to do this. Sarah get in the car Rita what's wrong with you?

You are the one who told me to leave and don't come back. I'm sorry if you think I hurt you I can't do what you want me to do. I can't make love to you I started to back up slow and got in the car with Sarah. Hurry an get in the car Leroy. Rita you don't want to kill me if you do you will end up in hell like I did. Believe me it's not a nice place to be. I made it to the car and got in she aimed the gun at me and said you black ass bastard. You ain't worth me killing you. You keep your black ass away from me do you hear me? Sarah took off as fast as she could pull around the corner and stopped the car.

Sarah was shaking I put my arms around her to calm her down. Sarah I didn't know she would come to your house like this. She must be crazy Sarah she wanted to kill me I could tell by the look in her eyes. Leroy what did you do to that woman? I didn't do nothing that is why she is acting crazy. I'm glad you was ready to leave I had a feeling she was up to no good. Sarah is the devil ever going to let go of me? No he won't. You have to have God in your heart and God will always be there for you. If she come back I'm calling the police on her Sarah and I went back home and she was gone. But she left a note on the door, Leroy I'm sorry I wasn't going to shoot you I just wanted to scare you to come back home with me because I love you and I miss you.

Tell Miss Sarah I'm sorry Rita. Leroy you stay away from that girl she is crazy. Yes she is.

I love being around Sarah she still teaching me about God. I still go to church every Sunday. My heart was happy and my mind was at ease when I go to church and see the lady that look like Terry my eyes fill with water. Sometimes I look at Sarah and I know she know where Terry is with my kids. She, never want to talk about Terry she said it always makes me so unhappy. So I don't ask her anything about her I know in my heart Sarah knows because she and Terry had become very good friends. I really wanted to know what the baby was that she had or did she have the baby? Sometimes I hear Sarah whispering on the phone and when I, come in she hurry and get off.

Sarah who are you talking to? Do I ask who you who talking to when you are on the phone? Sarah do you know where Terry and my kid's?.

Why would you keep anything about Terry? You know she left here two years ago. Son if you want to know where your family, is all you have to do is ask God not me. So what you trying to tell me I ain't man enough to find my family? What do you think son?

Oh Sarah I walked outside and sat on the porch I was watching the people moving in next door to Sarah. The little boy came over and said, "Hello mister, will you play ball with me?" What's your name? Leroy.

Do you have any kids I can play with? He looked the same age as Little Pete so I got off the porch and said what's your name?

The Man on the Train

T Ray. Yes I'll play with you and yes I have kids. Can they come out and play with me? No they don't live here. where do they live? I don't know is they lost? Yes, well can you go find them? No I don't know where to look.

My mama said if she lost me she would call the police you need to call the police they will find your kids so I can play with them. I'll do that T' Ray I played ball with him for a little while. His mother came to the door and told him to come eat I remember my mother use to call me in to eat. Leroy, will you play with me tomorrow?

Yes, I will. Okay (he said) and ran in the house I went inside I broke down and cried. What's wrong with you son? Sarah I miss Terry and Little Pete I want them back if God give them back to me I'll be a good father and husband and a good man forever. Where can they be? Sarah I had a friend in Little Rock named Hattie she left her husband and found her another man but Sam had the police to find her and his kids and he went and brought them back to Little Rock. Do you think they can find my family? Son I hate to see you in so much pain.

God don't like to see you in so much pain but some times he let us go through pain to see how he suffered and died for our sins. His father was in pain when they took his only son so we have to suffer too. That is why he tells us to call on him he will help you with your pain. When you suffer you can feel the pain his son went through on the cross. When God take away your pain you will come out of it a strong man, a caring loving forgiving man.

Your time is almost here and you will know when God brings you out of your pain. He will give you back what the devil stole from you.

Only thing son you have to have faith in him, believe in him and be good to one another and love one another. You know son there are people you may not like and you don't want in your life. You don't have to be around them, they may be fools but you still have to love them.

Leroy you going to make it because all those people you may have hurt in your past will someday forgive you. So you can go on with your life the way God want you to and you almost there.

Sarah you keep saying that and I don't understand. Oh your see come on let's go to church Sarah I don't feel like going to church tonight. What if God said he didn't like answering your prayers tonight? What if God said he didn't feel like helping you find your family? Sarah they left me two years ago and he ain't found them yet. Oh yes he have he know where they are all the time. He just want you to find them so come on let's go.

I got dressed and went to church with her sometimes I wish I had found me some where to stay Sarah would have me in church twenty four hours a day if she could. After we came home from church I was still thinking about Terry and Little Pete.

I sure felt like having me a drink. If I had a drink I could think better.

I was thinking about that corn whisky. It's been six months since I live with Sarah and I haven't had a drink. Just one drink is all I needed I ask Sarah if I could borrow her car. No you ain't getting my car tonight and you show don't need a drink tonight. I know that look on your face when you need a drink. You in my house and I don't like drunks in my house I think you tired son here drink this it will make you feel better. What is it? Oh it's just herb tea. Is that the same tea you gave to Pete and he got sick the next day.

It wasn't that tea that made him sick just drinks it. It will make you see life better. Sarah I know my life I'm the one who lived it. Sarah you always coming up with something If I didn't love you so much I would be gone; I need to find me a job I'm getting tired of sitting around here every day. I took the tea and went to my room I drank the tea and as soon as I got in the bed and laid my head down and closed my eyes I went to sleep. I heard a voice say to me Leroy, "I'm going to give you back what was taken from you and even more. I have to take two more things first to see if you are ready to do what I want you to do. I already know but I want you to see and know on your own".

I could see two friends of mines but I didn't know who they were.

All I could see was that I was at their funeral. Who are they oh God who are they? What are you doing to me I don't understand?

"You will always remember son I am always with you". I got up the next morning and I didn't smell Sarah cooking breakfast. Sarah maybe still sleep I went in the kitchen and started to cook breakfast for us. I knocked on the door and Sarah was just lying there trying to speak. Sarah what's wrong? She pointed to her mouth you can't talk. She shook her head no and pointed to the, envelope on the night stand it said Leroy put this up until after my death.

Sarah what's wrong I'm calling the ambulance I could see her lips moving she said she loved me. God please don't take Sarah away from me too.

I looked on her night stand and I saw all these bottles of pills what has Sarah done why are all these pills here?

The ambulance came they said she was having a stroke. They put her in the ambulance and took all her pills with her.

I lived in the house with Sarah and I didn't know she was taking all those pills. She kept them in her night stand and would take them out when she went to her room. Sarah was a strong woman never complaining about being sick. I followed the ambulance to the hospital. I waited and waited for someone to come and tell me what was going on.

I couldn't think of whom to call but one of her cousin. I called him and he came to the hospital. I called Lisa.

Lisa this is Leroy how are you doing? Not so well I been sick the past few weeks I been having a lot of problems with my feet and legs. I found out I have diabetes and problems with my kidneys. I'm so sorry to hear that Lisa how is, Little Jerry?

He is fine what you call for Leroy? To see if you would call Terry and tell her that Sarah is real sick she is in the hospital they haven't came out to tell me what's wrong. I think she had a stroke I know how much she loved her.

If I hear from her I will tell her. Do you want Sarah number? No I have it. I went in her room and like Pete she had all those tubes all over her. Sarah this is Leroy I'm here with you she opened her eyes and smile.

She grab my hand and look up to the ceiling and smiled Sarah what are you trying to say to me? Why didn't you tell me you were sick? She kept looking at me and holding my hand. You want me to pray for you? A big smile comes on her face.

"Lord, Jesus Christ I am a sinner I have done some bad things in my life and I don't even deserve to call your name Lord I'm not here for me I'm praying for Sarah God, I know you know Sarah is a good woman she always helping others. She helped me God when I was down God Sarah is the one who been teaching me about you. God Sarah loves you I don't know what you want me to do with her. I just want to ask you if it's your will take care of Sarah I love her to God.

Show Sarah how much you love her give her hope. God I need Sarah in my life God will you take me and let Sarah live. I will die for her please, please God take me. I love you God let your will be done in the name of Jesus amen."

Sarah kept holding my hand and she was smiling. She closed her eyes and let go of my hand. Oh God I cried out the nurse ran in the room Sir what's wrong? Sarah is dead. No sir she not dead we gave her pain pills to make her sleep. Oh Thank God, her cousin ran in the room Leroy everything all right did Sarah leave a will? Or tell you what she want done to her and who she leave her stuff too?

She's not dead. Well I heard you in here crying I thought she died.

Since you out here I'll leave and come back later do you want me to go by her house and get anything? No I don't need you to even go by her house. If you go near her house I'll call the police on you. Man you crazy she's my cousin not yours. I'll be back out later to see Sarah.

When Rev Jones came I gave him the keys to Sarah's house and told him to go by and check on her house every day for me because I'm staying until she got better.

Rev Jones bought me clothes to change in. I set beside Sarah for three weeks the doctor said she was doing better and they was sending her home but she would need a lot of care.

I had my head down be side her bed praying and she touched me.

Sarah how do you feel? I been so worried about you, (she smile) and said ell. Each day Sarah was getting better and better. I went home to check on everything Rev. Jones had been going by every day. After three days they let Sarah come home from the hospital. Sarah voice had came back but she talk slow. Leroy thank you for taking, care of me. If you were not here I don't know what I would have done. Remember you said you always had someone to help you have you forgotten?

No God is always beside me. The ladies at Sarah church came over and bought food and they would help take care of her. They did whatever she wanted them to they said they love Sister Sarah. Some of the ladies were still asking me out this one lady came over and I knew she really came to see me. Hello, I came to see Sister Sarah I brought her a sweet potato pie she was looking at me just smiling. Come on in I was smiling at her because I wanted to get to know her. After she

The Man on the Train

came in I took the pie and said I would put it in the kitchen. I heard her say Sister Sarah I came to help you out what can I do for you? I spoke up and said oh you don't have to do anything. Just have a seat I know Sarah just like to visit with you. When I looked at Sarah she was looking at me as if to say Leroy sat your ass down.

Leroy I didn't get to introduce myself before you had to leave the last time I was at church I been away for a while but I'm back now.

My name is Lorie, I'm Leroy. Yes I know. I think I'm falling in love I knew she was liking, me. Sarah kept looking at me I knew she didn't like me looking at Lorie the way I was. Sarah said thank you Lori for the pie I'm not feeling well. I need Leroy to help me to bed. Sister Sarah I'll help you No! Leroy will help me thank you for coming by.

Leroy will you walk Lorie to the door. I'll see you later. Okay Leroy if you need me call me. Bye Sister Sarah. After Lorie left I told Sarah to come on I'll help her to bed. I change my mind I don't want to go to bed.

You don't like Lorie do you? Leroy, Lorie is looking for a husband I keep telling you that you can't date no one caused you a married man.

Sarah I been telling you it's been two years and nine months do you think Terry is still married to me I don't think so?

Leroy do you remember you told me about John Chester left your mother and found a new family and how you felt when you found out. Have you for got you have a son? What are you going to do when your son come looking for you and you have another family?

How do you know he won't feel the same way you did? All he gone care about is you wasn't there for him in his life. I'll tell him Terry walked out on me and left me I didn't leave him or his mother. What you going to say when he find you with Miss hot pants. Sarah I keep telling you I'm not married. Lorie and I haven't even got to know each other yet. Well if she got anything to do with you she will have you in her bed the first night and have you married the next day.

Oh Sarah, how many pills have you took today? Sarah you need Jesus in your life. I got God you the one who need him, if you think Miss hot pants going to let you off easy. I want to get to know her I need a woman in my bed. Well if you need a woman so bad how come you run from, Rita.

She was willing to give it up to you she wanted it so bad she came after you with a gun, and I show didn't see you running to her to get you in her bed. I looked at Sarah and all I could do was laugh you know Sarah you always right. Boy that chick is crazy. I think she need to go to that hell house I was in. Then I could take her a piece of sweet potato pie every month we both laughed. Sarah I may lose it for a while I don't know how long I can do it. I really need me a woman in my life. Leroy you got that letter I told you to put up for me what did you do with it? I put it under my mattress I forgot about it Sarah. You want it back? Yes go get it.

I went to my room and got the letter. Sarah it got my mane on it that's my letter. Not now because I ain't dead and I want it back. Can I see what is in it? Go ahead and open it, Oh my God Sarah how much money you got in here? It's just five thousand dollars. I left it to you so you could go back home where you started from.

Sarah if I go back I will be all alone. I don't want to hear anymore about going back I'm not going so forget it. You know what Leroy you won't be alone because I'm going with you. No Sarah. You listen to me you need to forget it. Why don't you want me to go to home? Because it's your mothers place and you need to go see if it's still there, I don't care.

Pete told me how happy you was there, how you and him would go to Tulsa. You would go fishing and sit for hours on that porch Pete made it sound so good. I'd like to go and go fishing with you and go to Tulsa to shop, I never been to a small town.

Pete said it was a nice quiet town. Boy Pete told all of you guys about my little shack. Sarah no one has kept the place up, the house may not be there the grass have grown so high. We can't see the house from the road Pete is not there to take care of it for me anymore. I never been to Oklahoma I'd like to go just to see what it looks like. Sarah there is no furniture or lights nothing I don't know if the house is still standing it's only a little shack outside of town there in nothing but darkness.

Well you and Pete, was happy there come on son let's just ride down there and see.

I got the money we can have the lights turn back on, Okay, okay Sarah I'll go but I am not staying. Go pack your things and I'll go pack mines I have to make a phone call. It won't take me but five

The Man on the Train

minutes I don't have that much. Get on out of here boy. I went in my room and put my things in a brown paper bag. As I was walking out I heard Sarah say we will see you Wednesday. Sarah who are you talking to? I need someone to take care of my house while I'm gone. Rev Jones is going to check it every day for me till I get back. Till you get back? Yes till I get back, Sarah I ain't staying out there by myself I'm coming back to. Sarah did Pete tell you I found my mother dead there? Pete was almost killed there I can never live there anymore Sarah. I will end up back in the hell hole I was in. I'll start back drinking being out there by myself. Son you need to go back to see if you want to leave. Sarah you still not making sense. Okay Leroy if you don't want to stay we will come back together and I will never say nothing about your home again I promise. You have to promise me if you don't want to stay you will live with me and find a job and move on your own.

And if you come back with me I promise I won't say anything about, Miss Hot pants. You live your life the way you want to and do whatever you want. Because I know I would have done what God wanted me to do for you. Son God want you to remember he is always there for you.

Sarah was talking crazy again. Leroy God will help you make a new life for you if you just have faith in him. When you have faith son God will do miracles for you look what happened to me. Yes Sarah I see what God have done for you. You see son God wanted you to stay here long enough to help and teach you about him. He has forgiven you son he need you to pay him back. How can I pay him back? I don't have anything to pay him back. What do he want from me?

You will have to ask him and believe me he will tell you and show you just open up your heart to him. Sarah I'll go back for you I need to see about my land if I still have it. Leroy I want to catch a train I ain't never rode on a train I'll get Rev Jones to come and take us to the station. Sarah something bad always happened to me when I ride the train. Oh nothing going to happen you still trying to get out of going home. Okay, okay Sarah I'll ride with you I sudden had a feeling Sarah was up to something but I didn't know what. I said to myself Old lady I know you up to something but I'm going with you just to see. Pete sure did a lot of talking before he died I wonder what else he told her. Sarah when we get to Derry we have to stay in a hotel down by the track. I'll see if I can get a room as close to me as I can. No, you ain't putting me in no room by myself. I'm staying in the room with you I don't believe you, try nothing funny with me will you? You don't want me to show you what I can do because my gun is bigger than Rita's. Ha, ah, ha, Oh Sarah I don't think you gone ever let me hear the last of that. No. Pete, told me you wasn't scared of nothing but when I saw your face when Rita pulled that gun out you show looked scared to me. Ha, ha, a. I hope I never meet another crazy ass woman again in my life. It was kind of funny after it was all over and she had the nerve to leave me a note.

Sarah and I got on the train I look out the window I all the beautiful things God had made. I saw horses, cows, and wild animals. All the times I rode he train I never took the time to look at all the beautiful things God had made. I never felt so much at peace on this train ride. I didn't feel the hate of the man on the train. I felt I could close my eyes and go to sleep. I closed my eyes and I could feel I was in a deep sleep. I did see the man on the train John Chester he had no hate in his eyes. He had a smile on his face and I could hear him saying Leroy take care of my grandson. I'm sorry for not loving you and the way I did your mother can you forgive me? Oh my God John I'm so sorry will you forgive me?

Sarah was shaking me son, son, wake up why are you crying?

Sarah they are tears of joy and relief that have been inside of me for years. Sarah I believe I can go on with my life.

Sure you can when you find God. I love you Sarah I hugged her.

John Chester has forgiven me thank you God. Where do I go from here? What do I do now God? Tell me what I need to do for you. As the train pulled into the station I started to have a funny feeling I just sat there wondering if I should get off the train.

When the train stopped people started getting off and I kept sitting there. Come on Leroy let's get off this train Sarah I don't know. Sure you do son you at home back where you came from. Sometimes Sarah coming home is not always a happy place to come to. Well you don't know till you see. Sarah was just smiling. I can't wait to get to your house.

Sarah we have to find us a room first I have to find away to get out there. I can walk but it's too far for you to walk, we may have to buy a cheap car to get around. You will see and I want to see your face see I brought me a camera to take pictures of you while I' m here. So get your butt off this train. We got off and I got our bags, Sarah let me use one of her bags I wasn't going nowhere with her carrying a brown paper bag. While we were standing there here come this beautiful black Cadillac, boy what a pretty car. I wonder what rich man around here own that car the driver got out and said Mr. Leroy Chester. Yes. I came to pick you up.

Who sent you? Whose car is this? Who are you? Sarah what is this?

Leroy God always send the best to pick up his King. Well it show ain't me cause I ain't no King. She laughed and took a picture of me. Sarah did you spend your money on this car?

I sure didn't well you going to get in that car? Sarah I don't know what this is all about. Sir who sent you here to pick us up? Nobody knew I was coming, sir. I was asked to pick you up. Before I get in this car tell me where you taking me. I was told to bring you home. Oh Leroy, get in this car because I'm tired. Sarah do you think Pete left money for me at the bank and Mr. Flowers did all this?

Pete told me he left some money in the bank, for, you. He knew you would maybe come back home one day. Look like somebody loves you to send a big black skinny car to pick you up. Yes Sarah Pete really did love me. The driver drove us down the road to my little shack outside of town. I didn't know what to expect I thought that Pete told Mr. Flowers, to keep the place for me. We came down the drive way and the shack was still the same and there was chickens there. Before I got out of the car I sat there waiting for Pete to come to the door. But he didn't I was getting ready to get out when the driver started to drive off.

No Mr. Chester not here. I need to take you a few steps down the way.

I looked up and there stood this big beautiful house just like the one Johnnie Mae left me in South Carolina. Sarah am I dreaming someone moved my house here. No son this is a new house. Sarah what have you done? I ain't done, nothing. I told you God take care of his Kings.

When the car stopped I got out and I couldn't believe it my favorite chair was on the porch. God what have you done? I don't deserve this I started to cry and I looked up and saw the door open and this beautiful Angel walked out in a white suite with a red blouse on with her arms opened wide. Welcome home Leroy what took you so long?

Beside her there stood two little angels. I just fell to my knees and cried. God, God thank you, you did find them for me I couldn't move. Leroy baby we here for you, come on baby. Terry got on her knees and started kissing me and I kiss her I wouldn't let go of her.

Terry oh Terry I held on so tight she was so happy to see me. I felt something pulling on me and there stood this beautiful little girl. Who are you? Are you my daddy? Yes baby I am your daddy where you been? Baby I been to hell but I will never go back. My son said you my daddy to. Yes, Little Pete and I missed you so much. You have grown so much I hugged him so tight he said you have to let me go your holding me to tight. I didn't want to let go of him.

Terry said come on Leroy let's go in the house. Terry hugged Sarah and she was happy to see her. Little Pete looked like me and my daughter looked like my mother.

She said my name is Mary Louise Chester, I know your name your Leroy Chester. Oh baby yes I am. Terry you named her after my mother.

My name is Peter Chester this is my mother her name is Terry Chester. Terry named the kids after people I loved the most, they saw Sarah hello grandma Sarah. They know you Sarah? Yes Leroy Terry and the kids been to see me we been in touch with each other every day. Terry would call to see about you. Terry why didn't you come to see me I thought you hated me for what I done to you. Leroy I had to find myself I had to get my life together. I had to stay away from you so you could get our life together. I wanted you to do it on your own I knew I would be waiting for you when you was ready. Pete and I talked a lot before he died and he told me to make a home for you.

I knew how much you love the home in South Carolina that is why I had this one built. I had to take all the money out of the bank and sell the business because God told me to because you had to suffer for the things you had done. Sarah and I knew if we came to see you it would be hard on you and us to leave you there and we knew you needed the help.

The Man on the Train

That is why we left you there to see if you would fight to come home or put your life together. It was so hard for me when I would come to see Sarah and not be able to see you.

I love you so much I felt I had to stay away from you to make you strong. When Sarah was in the hospital I called every day the nurse would put the phone to Sarah ear so I could talk to her because you were always there. Leroy Chester I will never let you out of my life again. When Sarah called and told me you were out and living with her I wanted to get you then. But Sarah said it was not the right time and when the time was right she would bring you home to me and the kids.

Sarah was standing there smiling. Sarah all those times I heard you whispering on the phone you were taking to Terry Yes, Leroy.

Sarah what am I going to do with you?

How can I ever thank you for what you have done for me?

Just stay with your family and always keep God in your life and in your heart that's all the pay I need. Thank, you Sarah.

Sarah and Terry went in the kitchen with my kids and we talked and I just hugged and hugged them. Mary asked me daddy why are you crying so much? You cry like Peter he cry all the time too. Oh baby I'm happy I found you Pete and your mother. We ain't been lost you been lost.

Yes, baby I been lost but now I found you. Did the police find you?

No baby God found me and he showed me how to find you.

I ain't never been lost I told you. Oh Mary I love you.

Do you love Peter to? Yes, I love Peter to. You love grandma Sarah too? Yes and your mother. I stood there looking at my beautiful wife and she kept smiling at me. Terry I am so. Leroy don't you say you're sorry I don't want to ever hear you said that again. You ain't changed. Yes I have I have grown up a lot I have found God in my life. I had to leave you Leroy because I was so hurt about everything I didn't think I could forgive you for the things we were going through. I went through hell to trying to make since of all the mess we were in the women the drinking.

You coming, home late at night, losing Pete and the way you flip out after JJ death. I knew I needed to be by your side but I need you beside me to.

I didn't know who to turn to so I went back to South Carolina. Sarah and I talked she took me to church with her and I found God and he told me what to do. I called Donald and explained everything to him and he helped me to sell everything.

He had his friends to buy the clubs and the house. I knew how you and Pete would talk about Oklahoma, all the time and I could see the joy and happiness you to had, in your faces. I made up my mind I would come here and build a home for you and the kids. I knew how much you loved the house in South Carolina. Donald found the company that built the house in South Carolina so he sent them to built, this house like that one. I knew if you love me and your kids you would want to find us after you found yourself. Terry I'm so. No, Leroy. Terry, forgive me.

I couldn't understand why you left me in jail all those months and didn't try to help me.

When I went back to South Carolina looking for you and I couldn't find you and all my money, my club and my home was gone. I started back to drinking. I thought you was through with me. I did it Leroy to save your life. I knew where you were all the time I wanted to send money to pay your hospital and doctor bill. But Sarah said, she would take care of everything and for me to just make a home for you when the time for you to come home and for me to just take care of the kids. She knew I had a lot of work to do to get the house ready for you when you come home.

I beg Sarah to promise me not to tell you where I was and what I was doing. I knew you would go to Sarah when you found out I was gone. Sarah called me the day you come to her house and the day you moved in with her. What else she tell? What do you mean? Nothing, I made Lisa promise not to tell you because I knew she would be next. Lisa wanted to tell you everything when you called her but she had made me a promise. She said she told you in so many ways but you didn't catch on. So she hung up the phone up on you to keep from telling you.

She love you. Sarah helped me so much for two years, Terry I haven't had a drink but when I came out of the hospital and found out what you did to me it hurt me so bad and broke my heart. I thought you hated me so much you took everything and moved on with your life. I thought you had stolen everything from me. I started back to drinking because I knew I had lost it all. I went to Sarah and she told me I couldn't live with her drinking. I had nowhere else to go so I stopped I started to go to church with her and I found peace. Sara was so much help to me I haven't had a drink in months.

Sarah wanted me to come here and I couldn't understand why she wanted me to come here. Now I know to you find you and the kids.

I don't want to ever loose what I just found. Terry, forgive me for what I put you through. Thank you for what you done for me.

Terry took me in her arms and we started kissing and we were holding each other in our arms when I heard giggling. Mary Louise was giggling seeing her mom and me kissing.

Sarah said Leroy take Terry go for a walk I'm here with the kids.

Sarah thank you. Terry and I started to walk down to the shack.

You know Terry I love Sarah so much when she was sick I thought she had died it broke my heart so bad. God gave Sarah a miracle she got her voice back and she is doing well. God took me and changed me into a man, I have a long ways to go but I will always keep God in my life.

Terry and I walked down to my little shack. When we walked in I looked at Terry and she said Pete told her how this house looked and where everything was. I couldn't find all of your mother's things, some of the ladies from church helped me find things as close as I could. I fixed it up so when you want to be alone from me and the kids you could come down here.

I couldn't help it I just fell to my knees and cried God what are you doing to me? Leroy God told me he want you to work for him. That is why he wanted me to stay with you he want me to be a help to you. To stand by your side for the rest of our lives. Terry this is where I came from and this is where God wanted me to return to but why? Terry smiled and said for me. We kissed and kept kissing. Terry I haven't made love to you in so long. I looked in my wife's face and I saw so much love and peace she was smiling at me. I haven't seen her smile like that in so long. I remember the last time I saw her there was so much sadness in her eyes. Leroy are you alright? Yes, yes, I took my wife by the hand and told her how much I loved her, how much I missed her, how much I wanted to make love to her, and how much I needed her, I took her in my old bed room I sat her down on the bed and I started to run my hands down her back I kept looking in her eyes and I could tell she wanted me so much to. I ran my hands down her arms and kissed her. I could feel her melt in my arms I need you baby. We made love and it was so good all I could say was thank you God. Thank you God you do love me, I pleased her. Leroy you still crazy. You still make me feel good. Boy I was ready for a drink she got up and came back with two glasses in her hand. Leroy I found some thing that really make you feel good. I saw the ice in the glass and it looked like corn whiskey. I looked at her and she said Pete told me about the first time you drank corn whiskey and you thought it was water. Terry are you crazy I don't want it. I don't drink any more please baby. Oh Leroy drink it you want to feel good. Terry no I can't go back where I came from just one drink will send me back. Oh Leroy come on one drink won't hurt you. I thought you didn't want me to drink anymore. She was shaking the glass and I could hear the ice in the glass. One drink Leroy and you can make love to me again and it will make you feel good. You can make love to me like you never have before. See I am drinking mines. And I feel like I want some more of your good loving. She sat the glass down and walked out of the room I looked at the glass of corn whiskey on the table side of the bed just as I was about to pick it up she walked back in with nothing on but those red pumps. I always like Terry girl please don't do this to me. She was standing there smiling at me and drinking her drink in front of me. I loved this woman and I just wanted to please her and make her happy. God sent you back you said I would find peace here. Devil stay away in my past I don't need you now. Terry I'm sorry I haven't had a drink in months and I don't need it now. I got off the bed and she came and pushed me back down on the bed and started making love to me again. She said this is my baby. Leroy you have changed your life. You really do love God you see baby I was just teasing you. I just wanted to see if you really love God and you passed my test. Here drink this it really will make you feel good it's Holy. I put the glass to my lips and took a little sip and it was good. Terry what am I going to do with you this is water. I told you, you would like it. We both laughed, we talked and talk for hours and held each other arms. We stayed all night in the shack, and just before day I swore I could see Pete smiling at me. But my mother wasn't with him. I kept lying there and my mother was smiling at me she said baby you gone to be alright. I felt so at peace we got up and walked

The Man on the Train

back to the house holding hands we was so happy. God brought us back together Sarah was up cooking breakfast the kids was up to waiting to eat. Little Pete said where you been mama? Me and your daddy went for a walk. The next day I got up a little earlier and I looked out the window and I saw Sarah going down by the pond. I was wondering why she was going down there by herself. I thought she wanted to go for a walk to be alone from the kids they was always all over her. I got dressed and sat on the porch with a cup of coffee. Terry and the kids was gone, I waited until Sarah came back Sarah you alright? Yes, Leroy I just like to walk early in the morning. Do you know where Terry and the kids? Yes she said she was going to church for something. She took the kids so you could sleep late. I was ready to find a job or open me a dress shop or something. Sarah said Leroy time sure have gone by so fast. What you mean Sarah? I think it's time for me to go back to South Carolina. Sarah it's only been two days I just wanted to bring you back to your family my work is done. I need to get back and see about my home. Sarah I don't want you to leave so soon I want to take you fishing and shopping in Tulsa. There is a whole street with black businesses you will like seeing them Sarah I'd like to open me a dress shop here. I want to open me a restaurant where everyone can come and I want to play gospel music all day. Will you like to help me? No Leroy, I'm too tired and I don't want to. I want you to be a part of it you see Sarah God is going to do good things for me. Please Sarah stay here just a few weeks I don't understand right now I have a feeling you need to stay here with me it's too dark for you out here. I'll put lights all over for you. Why you want to leave you was so happy to come up here with me? Son I need to take care of business. It can't wait will you stay a week? If I stay when you get ready I'll take you home. Okay, Leroy Okay, when I go back I want to ride the train I like the ride we laughed. That night Terry wanted us to go to church with her. She wanted us to meet her Pastor. We went to Mt Olive Church on Grove Street. The pastor name is Rev Jeffery Owens; Rev Owens is a tall slim man with black hard ream glasses about 165 pounds brown skin. He looked about 75 years old he had gray hair he act like he really love God, I like that church I felt Rev. Owens could teach me a lot There was only a few members about thirty. The church looked like it could hold about 100 people. Terry was a great worker in the church she was learning to be one of the Sunday school teachers. Rev Owens and I talked and I told him that I would be back. The next day we took Sarah to Tulsa to shop we had fun I bought me some new clothes. Terry saved all my old clothes. After we had lunch we came back to Derry. A week have passed and I was getting bored sitting around. I went out back and saw a little spot and started digging it up. My wife came out with a glass of water, drink it up its good for you. Terry Chester I love you. What are you doing out here? I'm making me a garden, I'm going to plant me some black peas, tomatoes, green beans, and greens. Well look like you sure going to have your hands full cause here come help. Hi Angel, Daddy my name is Mary Louise not Angel, well you my little Angle ad I can call you Angel can I? Daddy you funny, I grabbed her and I never wanted to let go of her she was so pretty. She giggled and giggled. It's been four weeks now since I been back with Terry and the kids I was so happy. Sarah was still there with me and I had my family back and we all together. Sarah like going to church with Terry and she like Rev Owens. She told him he has to come to South Carolina and meet Rev Jones and come to her church. Sarah was still going to the pond every morning I saw the kids following her one day. When they came back I asked them why they were following grandma Sarah. I didn't want them to go to the pond anymore. Pete said grandma Sarah is talking to herself when she go down there but we don't see nobody. Peter she talking to Jesus cause she said thank you for blessing me with my new family and she say it's time for her to go home. You kid's stop following her I knew then that Sarah was going down to the pond praying every morning she wanted to be alone with Jesus. When Sarah came back I could see she had been crying. Sarah are you worried about going home? Do you need to leave? I won't keep you if you ready. Yes Leroy, I need to go and get my things in order. Okay but I'm going back with you to make sure everything is alright. Leroy everything is fine I talked to Rev Jones it's time I leave you now that you home. You going to be fine son I don't want you to leave Sarah you know you are always welcome here. I want you to come and stay whenever you like. Oh son I'll be back, I got my things packed and I be leaving on the early morning train. Rev. Jones will pick me up when I get there. Sarah, Sarah, please don't go. I love you so much Sarah I love you to son. I'm tired I need to go to my room will you take me to the station in the morning? Yes, I will. Terry walked in Sarah what's wrong you okay? Yes baby I'm fine Sarah is leaving in the morning Sarah you don't have to leave. I know but I have to. Terry started crying Sarah you like a mother to me I don't have a mother and my kids love you like their grandmother. I want you to stay here so we can take care of you. I want to go to my own home I love South Carolina I been there all my life. The four of you can come see me whenever you can. I'll call you everyday so you won't miss me. I just need to check on my things. We hugged Sarah and we all cried. The next morning we took Sarah back to the train station. Sarah kissed the kids, bye grandma. When Sarah was getting on the train I could see she looked tired and walking very slow. When the train was pulling away I stood there looking at Sarah waving from the window with so much sadness in her eyes. I saw the man on the train John Chester. Please John take care of her while she's on your train. I took Terry in my arms and said to her that I had a very funny feeling something was wrong. I wonder if Sarah was telling me everything. Leroy she's going to be alright she just getting old. She know we here for her. Yes, you right. When we got home the phone was ringing, Hello, Leroy, Leroy this is Lisa. Hi Lisa how are you and Little Jay? Do you want to talk to Terry? Yes and I need you to come see me I need you? She started to cry Lisa what's wrong? Terry she said she can't talk on the phone. Leroy she been sick every since JJ died. Well let's get the kids ready and throw some things in the car. I can't pack the kids things that fast and I don't know how long we have to stay the kids may not need to be there. I'll go and you stay with them. I call Rev Owens and told him about Lisa and I need to go to Little Rock. He said he would call one of the ladies from the church to keep the kids and send one of the men to help out around the house I'm going with Terry. I told Rev Owens we were leaving real early in the morning. Rev Owens said he would call me back. Terry and I packed our clothes she had saved all my nice clothes and had them hanging up in the closet. The next morning one of the ladies come to keep the kids. I didn't want to leave my kid's but Terry said it would be best if they stayed. The kids were okay they told us bye they knew Mrs. Smith from the church and they liked her. I drove all the way as fast as I could. Terry was so worried and so was I. When we got there Lisa in bed. She saw me and said Leroy, I'm so happy to see you. How do you like your home in Oklahoma? I love it Lisa before I got sick I came and spent a week with Terry and the kids. Yea she was telling me on the way here. Lisa do I need to take you to the doctor? No Leroy I need to talk to you please listen to me. I already told Terry, I need to tell you I'm dying. Lisa no, Terry and I still have money we can find the best doctor to help you, get ready and we taking you back to Oklahoma with us. We will take care of you. I can't just listen to me your shop is still yours. I have someone there that I can trust I still been putting your money in the bank like you told me and JJ when he died. I just kept putting it in the bank. Lisa you didn't have to I told you that I was giving you the shop. I was so messed up after JJ died I wasn't thinking. I know you loved us. We loved you too we had to do what we had to do to help you. We wanted you to be strong and powerful the man you will be. We knew one day God would help you find yourself. Sure took you a long time Lisa please don't talk like that. I have to thank you for coming so fast. I want you to keep my son and raise him I know JJ would like that. Yes Lisa I will. Terry went through hell loosing you. She loved you so much that is why she moved to Oklahoma, to make sure you happy she had a hard time trying to do all the things she could for you and her kids. She had to sell everything to let you see how much she loved you. I see now Lisa, you know Leroy JJ wanted to be like you. He wanted the nice cars, home, and he wanted to dress like you, he loved you so much. I'm sorry he's not here I miss him so much. You see Leroy you have a chance to make your wife happy and to be with her so If you blow it this time I don't believe it will be a next time. Keep your head together and keep your family together. I will Leroy I put all my money I your account it would be easy for you to get to. All I want you for you to do for me is promise me you will be there for my son. I promise Lisa. Lisa had tears running down her face I could tell she was in a lot of pain. Teach my son about me and JJ. You just take care of Terry and those kids. Lisa I'm taking you to the doctor right now and I don't want to hear no more from you. Terry helped her put her clothes on. No Leroy, I can't make it Lisa pleas I started to cry please don't talk like that. I took Lisa in my arms and I said to her I love you Lisa and I promise I will take care of Little Jay. I kissed her on her forehead she smiled. Lisa died and I cried and cried. Terry called the ambulance when they got there I was still holding her. Terry took my arms from around her I felt so hurt and empty but this time I didn't feel like having a drink. This time I held Terry and told her it will be okay I'm here for you baby. We both held each other Lisa died from diabetes. Her kidneys had fell and she had died of a broken heart she didn't take care of herself after JJ died she missed him so. I knew Sarah had made it home so I called her. Hello Sarah? Hi Leroy, you know I made it home safe you know the strangest thing happened to me on the train. This young man came to me and said Miss Sarah my brother told me to take care of you while you was on this train. I'm here for you do you need anything and Leroy he just disappeared and I didn't see him anymore. You call to see if I made it? No Sarah I called to tell you Terry and I had to come to Little Rock Lisa just died. Oh no, no what happened? She been sick for a long time she never told me she was sick and I talked to her all the time. Terry never told me she was sick. I guess they didn't want you to worry Sarah. Are you and Terry alright? Do you need me to come back? What about the kids? They are fine we have someone taking care of them. I'm catching the next train I'll be there for you. No Sarah I need you to stay and take care of yourself I don't want nothing to happen to you. I wouldn't be able to take it if anything happened to you. You sure you okay son? Yes, Sarah I'm fine God is here with me you said he is always with me. You said he is always by my side and I know he will help me this time. I want to be her for JJ' s wife. You know Sarah I'm not scared being in this house right now I pray God will stay by my side. He will son you just keep the faith he brought you a long way and son you still have a long way to go. Call me back and let me know what's going on. I will Sarah. I picked up Little Jay and hugged him so hard I looked at him and I could see the big smile his daddy always gave me. I ask God if I could look at JJ son every day. Looking at him every day will remind me of what I did to his grandfather and not telling his father what I had done to his father. God please stay by my side because I know I will need you this is the first time I saw JJ little son and the first time he saw me. He said, Aunt Terry who is this man? That's your uncle Leroy your daddy friend. Oh let me down he said. The lady that was taking care of Lisa and Jay took him from me and said she would take him to the other room. We left and went to see Donald when we walked I told the lady behind the desk I came to see Donald. Do you have an appointment? No he will see us tell him Leroy and Terry Chester is here to see him. Donald came out Leroy, and Terry come on in sure good to see you Leroy. Leroy I'm sorry for what you had to go through I only helped Terry so she could help you and not lose everything you had. It's okay man Terry told me everything thank you man for helping Terry and the kids. I was mad at you when you never took my calls but now I know why. Are we still friends? Yes man. You here about Lisa? I'm so sorry to hear about her death last night. Leroy you know that shop is still yours Lisa worked there until she got sick. She have some good people working there and she asked me to make sure your money that was put in the bank each month. I made sure everything was taking care of you have sixty thousands in your account. She left a will to you and Terry. Sixteen thousand to help take care of her son she knew it was not enough to take care of him until he was eighteen. She left her son 25 thousand dollars for him when you feel he is ready for it. It was money from JJ's insurance. Lisa family will take care of her arrangement. She left them her insurance money to take care of everything. She wanted you and Terry to take care of her son because she knew that is what JJ would have wanted. Leroy what do you want to do about your shop? I won't be back to Little Rock so I plan to sell it whoever want it. Terry what do you want to do with your mother's home? I need to think about it Donald. Good to have you back Leroy. If you need anything you know how to find me will you get my bill in the mail? Do you have my new address? Yes, Terry gave it to me when she was having the house built. We left Donald's office and went back to Terry's mother's house where Lisa lived. I didn't know how I would feel spending the night there. I was so tired I just went to sleep. I wanted to be there for Terry and not make a fool of myself. I prayed and asked God to please don't let me act crazy. My wife came over to me and said Leroy everything will be alright this is my home and you are welcome. I love you and we held each other and I still felt a little sad. I knew I would never get over what I had done but with God's help I knew it would be okay after I got everything together. Terry put all of her mother's things in storage and gave all of Lisa and JJ to give to their son when he grew up. Before we were ready to leave I had two friends left in Little Rock I wanted to see. I went by the train station to see Sally Cross When Terry and I got there and went in I saw Sally at her desk. She looked so tired and old Sally, Sally she looked up at me what's wrong Sally? Leroy is that you? I'm so happy

The Man on the Train

to see you I heard you moved back to Okahoma. I put my arms around her. My heart went out to her, Sally what's wrong? Leory I don't have any one. What you mean? My two boys left town years ago and I don't hear from them a lot they said they didn't have money to come home. My oldest son moved to California and my other son is in Florida. Sally do you want to move in with them or go see them? No Leroy I'm their mother and if they love me enough they should come see me. Sally if don't have money they can't come. Leroy I fell like all I've done for them and gave them they at least they could come see me. I ain't really had no one to love me that's not true Sally I love you that is why I'm here. I came by to see you before leave. Sally why don't you come to Oklahoma and stay with me for a while. I looked at Terry to see what she would say and she was smiling at me. Leroy I have been here all my life and I want to stay here in my own house. I thank you for being so kind. Sally I want you to quit your job and stay home and take care of yourself. I want you to go to church and meet people God will give you a lot of friends. You can work in the church for God. Leroy I can't quit I don't have money saved up. Come over here with me Sally, I want to talk to you. Don't worry I'll take care of you I promise. Go in there and tell them your leaving this job now you been here almost thirty years time you quit. Do you want me to go in there with you? Trust me Sally please. Well I'm tired of this job and I 'm going to trust you son. Sally went in to tell them she was quitting. I talked to Terry and asked her if I could help Sally. I told Terry what I was going to do and she hugged me and tears ran down her face. Leroy you're a good man that is why I love you. Leroy Chester I'm happy I married you and I'm glad what I did for you. Whatever you feel like you need to do in your heart for Sally go ahead it's alright with me. We walked in the office and Sally was telling them she was quitting her job. Her boss said you need to give me two weeks notice so you can train some to take your place. Sally looked at me I said Sally is leaving today she is retiring. She's not quitting she been here for thirty years a she putting in for her retirement and she wants he check every month. Sally is tired and you going to pay her for the days she have already worked for today. We can't pay her today she have to wait two weeks for her check. No you going to pay her now. Who the hell you thing you are boy? Get the hell out of here I'll call the police on you. All of you get the hell out of here you too Sally. Terry you and Sally go pack her things now I closed the door her boss looked at me with a scared look on his face he knew I meant business. I said I don't give a damn about you calling the police and if you do believe me you will be sorry. I want you to give her money today if you have to take it out of your pocket and give it to her I don't play. Sally's boss looked in the desk draw and gave me 300 hundred dollars he asked me if Sally could come back in the office and sign for the money saying he paid her and he said this is what I owe you Sally. Sally was smiling so hard she almost fell to her knees. Leroy take me home I feel like the weight of the world just lifted off my shoulders. Sally was so happy all of a sudden I felt something near me it was Terry looking at me. What's wrong with you? I saw old George smiling at me. Sally said Leroy you see George? Yes, and he is smiling at me oh Leroy he has forgiving you. Oh thank God. Sally said everything is going to be alright. We ran out of the train station happy. We got in the car and I went to Donald's office, Sally said where are we going? Donald I want you to meet a friend of mines this is Sally Cross. When we walked the lady at the desk said, Oh I know your family go on in. We went to his office door and knocked, come in Leroy you back so soon. What happened now? Donald I want to meet a friend of mines this is Sally Cross. And I want her to be a friend of yours. I want you to take care of her I want you to take ten thousand out of my account that I have in Little Rock I want you to fix it where she can get a check every month until it's gone. Sally just retired and I would like you to help her receive her retirement every month from the train station. Sally how much you want to receive out of my account each month every month from the train station? Sally how much you want to receive out of my account each month every week or every two weeks. Leroy have you went crazy? Where you get all the money? Sally God been good to me and I want to share it with you. Oh son, I always told George you was a good man. I love you thank you. Donald take care of Sally. I will and you yes, yes, I know I will get your bill in the mail thank you Donald. Terry and I took Sally home. She thanked me Sally here is my address and phone number in Oklahoma if you need me you call me. Leroy I will and thank you Terry. Your welcome Mrs. Cross you have to come visit us one day. Oh I will I promise you, I have the money to come see you whenever I want to. We hugged Sally and told her bye, When

The Man on the Train

we drove off I looked back and I could see Sally waving good bye. We made it back to Oklahoma the kid's was so happy to see Little Jay and I was just as happy to see them I miss them so much it was so good to be back home. Things was going so well for me and my family I been two years and I'm still happy I went to school and studied the bible I took a lot of Bible classed I was working in the church Rev Owens was helping me so much. God have been working with me. Rev Owens hired me to work at the church I love my job. I still have a lot of money Terry put it up for me and we haven't had to use much of it living in Derry we don't have to use a lot of money. I feel good but sometimes I still think about the things that have happened to me in my life I don't think you ever forget you past but as the days go by you learn to try to live with it. May 14 1977 at 7:00AM I got a call from Sarah. Leroy this is Sarah I need you. Sarah was crying what's wrong Sarah? I'm very sick again I need you to come take care of me. I'll call the doctor and Rev Jones until I get there I'll catch the first plane. I called Rev Jones and told him to take care of her until I get there. I told him to take her to the doctor and call me back. I told Terry I didn't want to catch the train it was too slow. I called the airport and they said I could catch a plane at 12:00 that day. I threw something in the suite case Terry wanted to go we left the kids with a baby sitter from church. I called Rev Jones and asked him if he would pick us up from the airport He said Sarah didn't want to go the doctor until I came. In a few hours we was there. I ran in the house Sarah was in bed and she looked so old and had lost so much weight she look tired. I just had left Sarah two months ago and she looked okay. I had went and spent a few days with her. We talked on the phone every day and she never told me she was sick. She just got sick over night. I got on my knees and took her hand she had her eyes closed. Sarah I'm here she opened her eyes. Leroy I was waiting for you I knew you would come Terry is here. Hi Terry, Sarah how are you doing? We taking you to the hospital and you not going to stop us. Leroy God told me my job on this earth is done and it's time for me to come live with him. No Sarah, I 'm taking you with me I should have never let you come back here. Son South Carolina is my home I love it here. I want to be buried here. Where is Terry? I'm right here Sarah I need to talk to you. Sarah we need to get you to the hospital you can talk later. Let's go. No Terry I'm not in pain all my pain is over. Sarah have you had anything to eat? No, I just want you to stay with me. Sarah I'll stay here as long as you want. Leroy you a good son. If I had a son I would have wanted him to be like you are now. You're a strong man now. Terry you look over there on the table you see that brown box. Yes, Sarah. I want you to have it and I don't want you to open it until you go back to Oklahoma promise me you won't I promise you Sarah. Leroy look under my pillow and you will find a white envelope and don't you open it until you get back home put it in your suitcase right now. Leroy I told Rev Jones what to do cause you help with all the others. Sarah please don't talk like that your going to be fine like you did the other times you was sick. I'm telling you now I don't want you acting a fool at my funeral oh Sarah I won't. I 'm leaving my home to Rev Jones he always liked it and he liked my car and I gave it to him. It's okay Sarah I told him you and Terry to take everything you want in my home and what you don't want to be sold the money go to the church. You see Leroy God put you two back together because he has plans for you God need you Terry to stay by Leroy's side until he ready for you. No matter what will happen you stand by him. The time is coming soon. Leroy is going to be a very powerful man. You have to stay with him I want to thank the both of you for letting me be a part of your life. I want you to take good care of them kids Leroy. No Sarah we want to thank you. Terry started crying and she ran out of the room. Go to her Leroy she need you. Sarah I don't want to leave you she will be alright. You have always been like a mother to me., You have taught me so much since I known you. I will never forget you as long as I live. I don't know what I will do without you telling me about God. I don't know where I will be today. Son as long as you remember what I taught you God will be by your side and always treat people the way you want to be treated. You see son God has forgiven, you changed your life and don't throw it away. I won't Sarah I won't. Sarah closed her eyes Sarah please don't die on me. Open your eyes Sarah, please Sarah I love you I was crying so hard Terry came back in the room and Sarah opened her eyes. Leroy I ain't dead yet I was just resting my eyes. Leroy I do need you to do something for me. Yes, I will do anything for you. I need you to call the ambulance for me take me to the hospital, don't worry Leroy I just feel like I need to go I called the ambulance and Rev Jones, Terry and I waited and waited for the doctor to come by and tell us

The Man on the Train

something. I prayed and prayed I cried and cried. The doctor came out and said Leroy Chester Sarah wants to see you and you the only one who can go in to see her. After you talk to Sarah I need to talk to you. I went in Sarah's room hi baby. Hi Sarah, you okay? Yes, I'm fine I took Sarah by the hand I knew in my heart this time she might not make it. Because I remember when I was in the hospital God told me about Sarah but I put it out of my mind until now. Sarah when I was in the hospital after Terry stabbed me I could see my spirit leave my body I saw the most beautiful light I ever seen and I followed it. It lead me to this beautiful place I came to this gate that was so high and so wide. I never seen anything so beautiful not even Terry. I saw all these people with halo's over their heads and not a one would open the gate to let me in. The streets was the most beautiful gold I have ever seen. I never saw gold to bright. I tried to open the gate it would not open for me. I cried and cried and they still would not open the gate for me. I wanted to go through that gate so bad I could feel peace and joy in my heart as everything I did wrong was forgiven. I wanted with all my heart to go behind that gate but no one would let me in. Then I saw a man standing there with a beautiful smile on his face. His face was so strong but so kind he said my father said it's not your time you have to go back and pay for your sin. No, no please let me in, he said to listen to Sarah she need to help you so she can come through this gate. I feel my spirit coming back to my body I can hear a voice saying Leroy, Leroy can you hear me do you know where you are? Open your eyes man; I didn't understand what was going on. I thought it was only a dream I didn't want to wake up. Leroy, don't die I love you man please come back I need you please come back. God if it's your will please let Leroy come back. I could hear the voice crying so hard. I could feel the tears drop on my face. I opened my eyes and I saw JJ holding my hand I could see his face turn into a big smile. And then Sarah I really wanted to die because of what I did to his father. I tried to tell him but he told me to be quiet don't talk right now. Every time I tried to tell him what happened I felt God was telling me it was not the right time. And I couldn't talk to him about it. Only God know what he want us to do and when the time is right. Sarah I think the time is right for me to tell you what happened to me and what God said. Sarah smiled at me and I was still holding her hand she closed her eyes and this time I knew she would never open them again. My kind sweet Sarah was dead. I only had tears running down my face because I knew where Sarah was going and knew they would open that gate for her and she will never want to come back. I knew she was happy I don't want to let go of her hand but the nurse said I'm sorry Mr. Chester you have to let go of her hand. I walked out of the room and Terry ran into my arms. Leroy she said is Sarah gone? Yes, baby yes, you going to be going to be alright? Yes baby I'm going to be alright now. Sarah said God was by my side, The doctor came out and said Mr. Chester I have a message for you from Sarah. She said to tell you she loved you and she didn't want you to see her die because you had seen too many others and you couldn't take it. She wants you to all remember her and what she taught you about God. Mrs. Chester she said you promise her that you would always be by your husband's side and you won't be sorry. God will help you, Mr. Chester Sarah died of cancer she made me promise not to tell you or Mrs. Chester until after her death she didn't want you to feel sorry for her. She didn't you was strong enough to hear it the last time you brought her in here was when we found out. She was blessed that she never had a lot of pain. She always said God was with her because he needed her to help you. I took Terry by the hand and we walked out of the hospital together. Rev Jones took us back to Sarah's house. I wanted to go see Walter and Ruby to tell them Sarah had died. I told Terry and she wanted to stay she was tired. I went by and told them and thanked them for their kindness they showed and to tell them me and Terry was back together. I wanted them to know I haven't had a drink in four years. I told them I had found Christ in my life. They were so glad I found God my life I left and went by to see the nurse that was kind to me while I was there she was gone and they didn't know where she was. I also went by to see Rita she had moved. I went by the clubs I use to own they both was still open I didn't have a desire to go in I just drove by. I went back to Rev Jones house and Rev Jones had some of his church members there. I went outside and sat on the porch while I was sitting there I saw T'Ray coming up. I still see you playing foot ball. I'm going to be a foot ball star that is what Miss Sarah said. You know T' Ray Miss Sarah is always right you going to come see me? Yes, I sure will. My mom said Sarah died. Yes she did you gone live in her house? No I live in Oklahoma did you ever find your kids? Yes, did the police find them for you? No

The Man on the Train

God showed me where to find them. Was they glad to see you? Yes, and I will never lose them again I'm glad you found your kids, my mom said my daddy is lost. My mom said he left when I was three weeks he didn't love us. I'm sorry to hear that T'Ray do you still want to play football with me? Yes, I'd be glad to, I played with T' Ray for a while and Terry came to the door and told me to come in dinner was ready. I told T' Ray I would see him later. We packed everything, Terry wanted and we had them shipped back to Oklahoma on the train. Rev Jones and his wife took care of everything. I was very strong at Sarah's funeral I will miss her so much. After the funeral Terry and I flew back home. I was glad to see my kids when I'm gone away from them. They ran up to the car when Rev Owens drove up. I grabbed the both of them in my arms, hi Angel oh Daddy you need to learn my name. Hi Pete and hi Little Jay. I love all you kids Louise said what did you bring us? I brought you me I came back for you, oh daddy your funny I think about Sarah so much. She taught me so much about God. When we got back home I opened envelope Sarah gave to me. There was a note that said Leroy here is a check for ten thousand dollars I want you to put every penny on your new church you're going to build or get. In the box she gave Terry was a note Terry I want you to have all my good jewelry. I always liked wearing good jewelry all the jewelry in this box is worth twenty five thousand dollars you will look good in it. it was two rings, a bracelet, two necklaces, and a pair of earrings I love you signed Sarah. It's been four years since Sarah has been dead. I finished ministry school and all the things Sarah taught me. I felt like I was ready to start preaching, God told me he wanted me to be one of his servants. Rev Owens said he was getting too old and he wanted me to help him out more. He felt I was ready to start preaching he said he was there for me if I need him. Rev Owens I don't think I'm ready, when God calls on you Leroy your ready. Leroy I think you should try to get up there in two weeks. Give yourself time to study what you want to say. I went down to the shack away from the kids so I could study. I studied for two weeks for what I was going to say.

When that Sunday came I was ready to give my first sermon. I was in the back waiting to come out when I heard the choir singing and all of a sudden I heard the most beautiful voice singing. It sounded like an angel who in the world is that I thought? I had to come out to see who it was when I came out all I could say was Oh my God; oh my God I couldn't believe it. It was Hattie Hicks. When I looked at her I couldn't help but cry we hugged each other.

Hattie what are you doing here? Terry told me you was going to preach you first sermon and I had to come see this. Oh Hattie you sing like an angel. I didn't know you could sing. I found God too and I been singing for him ever since I left Little Rock. I couldn't make it back to JJ's funeral or Lisa but I wanted to make sure I come to see you. Terry and I still been keeping in touch with each other she told me everything. I hugged her again the church was so quiet and looking at the both of us. Hattie sat down when I was ready to preach. It seen a real good friend I haven't seen in years. You know it's good to have friends in your life that care about you and love you. I have met a lot of friends who really loved me and cared for me only because the grace of God. I looked in the back of the church a I saw my mother, JJ, Lisa, John and my Sarah they were all smiling at me.

I could hear Sarah saying you gone be alright now. I fell to my knees and cried. I had my head down I couldn't move all I could do was cry. God I thank you for help me God, I felt someone on each side of me holding me up. Terry had one arm and Hattie had the other one. Hattie started to sing I am weak I am tired. I turned to my beautiful wife tears was running down her face. I am here for you baby, I will always be here by your side she kept holding my hand. I told the church my name is Leroy Chester and I am a child of God, I am a sinner, I am a drunk, and I was a murderer. God has forgiving me for my past and my soul don't hurt so badly. I had been studying for two weeks to get up here to tell you everything. All I can say is God loves you; he gave his life for you and me. He is right by your side all you have to do is reaching out and touch him. God has come in my life he is in yours to. He have always been in my life but I wasn't smart enough to see it until God put a lady in my heart named Sarah who introduced me him. That is the most wonderful thing that has ever happened to me and my family. God gave me back my kids and my lovely wife. They were lost but he is the one to tell Sarah to lead me to them. I am so full of love and so much pressure has lifted off my heart. I just want to ask you to forgive me church. My Terry was standing by my side she put her arms around me and led me and sat down right beside me and Hattie. Rev Owens got up and said God is good all the time. God can come in our lives and change us to what he want us to be he can change everything when we don't know it. God bless you Minister Chester today we want the choir to sing. Terry and I got up and left we took Hattie and her husband with us. After we got back to the house Hattie told me she went back to Mississippi a year after Sam died and found her son's daddy. They were married and he is also a servant of God he was a minister. Her kids worked in the church Sam Jr. played the piano. We was so happy to see each other, we talked for hours and hours Hattie and her husband stayed for a few days and they had to go back home to be with their kids. As the years past I became a good minister there was over two hundred members in our church. I took every penny Sarah gave to me and added on to our church. Rev Owens put me in charge because he was so old he couldn't do it anymore. My church became bigger and bigger, people would come all around to hear me preach. They came from Stillwater, Tulsa, Enid and sometimes Oklahoma City. Everything was going so well for us. Rev Owens had a stroke and his wife had to put him in a nursing home he was 80 years old. The years went by so fast, Terry was still by my side and she was a hard worker in church. We opened a church in Tulsa on Greenwood Street. I have over a thousand members I still have my church in Derry on Grove Street. I have a young minister name Rev Miller helping me out he is a good man he sometimes remind me of myself. Terry and I drive back and forth to Tulsa to church. She doesn't want to give up our big home in Derry. I became a big powerful minister we did a lot of help for the young people and we did a lot of help for the homeless. I gave a lot of money to young people who wanted to go to college.

God has blessed me with so much money to help others. I wasn't tired of talking about how good he was to me. I felt so much better with my life. My kids are now teens Pete is going to college and Mary Louise is in high school. Little Jay is seventeen and he didn't want to live with us anymore. We were having a lot of problems with him skipping school. The more I tried to help him the more he was not listening to me or Terry. I prayed and prayed to God to help him I felt so bad I couldn't reach him I know John and JJ would have wanted me not to not give up on him. I told him that his mother and father was good people and it would break their hearts to see him act this way. I sent him to get help and he still wouldn't mind.

We found out he misses his mom and dad even though he never met his dad. He blamed his dad for drinking and killing himself and he blamed his mother for leaving him even though Terry and I was there for him. He felt he would be happy living in Little Rock with Lisa's people he didn't like my rules. So we let him go live with Lisa's family. God is still using me to serve him Terry and I are very happy together. I was going to different churches preaching Terry and I went all over the world traveling. We were on our way back from Africa, while we were on the plane Terry said Leroy I have a strange feeling. I can hear Sarah calling my name.

Yes, baby you must be tired and you just heard wrong. It was so good to be back home I was also so tired. I went right to bed after I fell asleep I thought I hear Sarah calling my name telling me I have to stay strong. I have to remember we don't always understand why God do the things he do but it's all for a reason. The next morning when I woke up Terry was not in bed. Terry, Terry I went through the house looking for her I found a note on the table. Leroy baby I went to the church in Tulsa to get things ready for Sunday morning. I love you Terry.

Three hours later I got a phone call from the police in Tulsa that my church had burned down and Terry was dead. She got out but there was too much smoke in her lungs. Sarah had come to warn us but we didn't understand. After Terry died I didn't feel like doing nothing I felt my whole world had fell apart. Nothing meant anything to me all the money the beautiful cars, expensive clothes, shoes, diamond jewelry, didn't mean a thing without my Terry I gave my kids a million dollars each I gave Little Jay a million dollars also. I gave to different churches. Mary Louise got married and moved to South Carolina, Pete became a doctor and moved to Oklahoma City and Little Jay took some of his money and became a famous Gospel singer.

Well I'm at peace I moved back in my little shack outside town and every morning I sit on the porch. I can still see The Man On The Train go by. Oh God, my God a wonderful change has come over me my heart is no longer sad. I can go on with life because I have you in my heart, my mind, and soul. Oh my God there is a change in me God I had it all clothes, cars, diamonds, family and friends. I had sad and happy times now God I have nothing but this old shack where I started from. I 'm lonely out here but when I look up I know you by my side. I know you love me because Sarah said you always would be by my side Because Sarah is always right.

The End

Made in the USA
Coppell, TX
03 December 2021